CHANGING WAX

By Jared Quan

12 Young person's themes suitable only for readers of twelve years and older

Big World Network

Utah

This book is dedicated to

my amazing *wife,*

and our five odd *imps...*

Changing Wax

Copyright © 2014 - Jared Quan
All rights reserved.

Without limiting the rights under copyright reserve above, no part of this publication may be reproduced, stored in or introduced into a retrieval system, or transmitted, in any form, or by any means (electronic, mechanical, photocopying, recording, or otherwise), without prior written permission of the publisher except in the case of brief passages embodied in critical reviews and articles.

This is a work of fiction. All names, characters, organizations, and events portrayed in this book are either products of the author's imagination or are used fictitiously. Any resemblance to actual persons, living or dead, business establishments, locales is entirely coincidental. The author holds exclusive rights to this work. Unauthorized duplication is prohibited.

The publisher does not have control over and does not assume any responsibility for author or third-party web sites.

Managing editor - Amanda Meuwissen
Associate Editor - Wendy Herman

Book layout/Cover design - Mario Hernandez

A **Big World Network** Book
Published by Big World Network
363 E. Woodlake Dr. | 232 | Salt Lake City | UT | 84107
www.bigworldnetwork.com

ISBN-13: 978-0692948118
ISBN-10: 0692948112

First U.S. Edition: August 2014
Printed in the United States of America

CHANGING WAX

By Jared Quan

TABLE OF CONTENTS

Episode 1....................................1
Episode 2.....................................9
Episode 3...................................15
Episode 4...................................22
Episode 5...................................30
Episode 6...................................36
Episode 7...................................44
Episode 8...................................49
Episode 9...................................56
Episode 10..................................63
Episode 11..................................70
Episode 12..................................76
Episode 13..................................82
Episode 14..................................89
Episode 15..................................95
Episode 16.................................101
Episode 17.................................106
Episode 18.................................112

Episode 19..............................118
Episode 20..............................124
Episode 21..............................130
Episode 22..............................135
Episode 23..............................141
Episode 24..............................148
Episode 25..............................154
Episode 26..............................159
Episode 27..............................165
Episode 28..............................171
Episode 29..............................177
Episode 30..............................182
Episode 31..............................188
Episode 32..............................194
Episode 33..............................200
Episode 34..............................206
Episode 35..............................212
Episode 36..............................218
Episode 37..............................224
Episode 38..............................230
Episode 39..............................236
Episode 40..............................242

Episode 41.............................248
Episode 42.............................254
Episode 43.............................260
Episode 44.............................266
Episode 45.............................271
Episode 46.............................277
Episode 47.............................284
Episode 48.............................291
Episode 49.............................297
Episode 50.............................303
Episode 51.............................308
Episode 52.............................314
Episode 53.............................320
Episode 54.............................325
Episode 55.............................330
Episode 56.............................337
Episode 57.............................343
Episode 58.............................349
Episode 59.............................355
Episode 60.............................361
Episode 61.............................366
Episode 62.............................372

EPISODE 1

If you were to walk outside right now and point towards the North Star, and then raise your finger a mere two millimeters above it, you would be pointing at the currently undiscovered solar system of Gray Asmith. It has a name because it will eventually be discovered by Trever R. Grey and Thomas D. Smith. The two men will be unable to agree on a name for the system and, due to a typo merging the names of the founders, it will be forever called Gray Asmith.

Of course, two millimeters does not seem like a great deal of distance, but when you have to travel nearly seven hundred sixty-two thousand, five hundred twenty-two million and five light years (give or take half a light year depending on Earth's rotation), then even a fraction of a millimeter can be the distance between landing an airplane at JFK International or somewhere in China. Though the math can be mistaken in light years, it would be hard to explain to the passengers on a flight to JFK, exactly why they were in China.

As it is commonly known, the starlight we see today is millions of years old, but what is rarely thought about is that each glimmer of starlight has its own story to tell. Tragically, most stories are pretty bland, just gasses or hot liquids stewing about. However, some offer the most brilliant insights into the universe, others offer the transcendence of good over evil, and some show how evil can devour whole worlds. The variety is as vast as all the cinema in the world multiplied by a few billion.

'Wax' would not be the first thing that would come to mind if you could sneak a peek at the Gray Asmith. However, for the last 14,000 years of record, 'Wax' is what the inhabitants of the sixth planet have called their world. Glimpsing the starlight of Wax, right now you would be witnessing the beginning of its fifteenth age. Someday we will have the technology to take the glimmer of starlight and download the history of whole civilizations, to then watch, like an interactive movie, as so many other worlds have done before, and embarrassingly, are doing this very moment to our own world.

As for Wax, at the beginning of the fifteenth age, it was home to some four billion inhabitants, who resided on four main continents and several hundred small islands. Roughly half the world is covered in darkness and the other half in light. At the center of the largest and oldest continent, Mazery, sat the grandest city in the whole world.

The magic in the world is dictated from the center of this city, the city of Ormolu, in the tallest spire in the world, from a book of rules, called the *Master Book of Magic*. The presence of the book literally made Ormolu the heart of the divide between light and dark.

The book started as a few dozen pages of very simple rules to guide the use of magic, keeping the magic within the book from consuming everything and destroying the world. However, the book had one flaw: the authors failed to take into account that the magic was alive.

Rule #1: This book is to always be the most powerful book in the world, and will be contained in the most powerful city in the world.

This rule was left open to interpretation, and the magic would take liberties to ensure these facts remained true. As books of all sorts were compiled, the *Master Book of Magic* grew in size, in height, width and depth. None had greater effect on the size of the book like the *Grand Master Herbalist Book of Flora and Fauna of the Southern Lands of Mazery, Second Edition, by Honest Thomas,* which included pressed samples of everything listed.

The book maintained its growth by breaking down rules, laws, and bylaws contained within it into the most drawn out and generic terms possible. Occasionally, while no one was looking, the magic would create a few new bylaws, which were of far less consequence, if only to add to its pages. This often created unnecessary events or traditions.

The city reacted in much the same way: as other cities grew larger, Ormolu grew in any dimension necessary to remain the most powerful.

Rule #2: The city will fairly represent the world's status, and no violence will be permitted within.

This rule seemed to cover every facet conceived by the imagination, thanks to its two hundred sub-clauses, and sixty-two by-laws.

Every night the city would change, mostly along the middle. It would shift houses and buildings to represent whether the world was controlled by the light or dark. On the positive side, the 'no violence' rule was strictly enforced at every level. Swords could not be drawn, harmful spells could not be completed, punches would not land, arrows would not fly, and…well, you get the point. Depending on the severity of the offense, the city would warn you by teleporting you a few feet backwards and, if you attempted the same action seven times, it would simply teleport you outside its borders to your respective side of choice. If you had been teleported outside the city seven times for separate infractions within a seven-month period, the city would simply reject your entrance for a day, then for a week the second time, then a month the third time, and so on.

The city, though always changing, did have some constants, as permitted in the book. Such as the main spire of the city always being half shrouded in darkness and half in light, only ever changing in size and grandeur in order to remain the centerpiece of the most powerful city in the world. The main spire of Ormolu was called the Candlestick, for the most obvious reason that it was always lit up and could be seen for a great distance in every direction.

The tower reached its current height of 2,718 feet during the aggressive tower building phase of the fifth age. Needless to say, none of the other towers or spires in the city survived more than a couple of years. The Dark Side towers suffered from poor craftsmanship, and the Light Side towers suffered from over craftsmanship.

Amidst the rules, the book outlined that on the Light Side of the city, a building clearly labeled, 'White Knight Tower,' would always remain as is, and in its place, even if the world were completely dominated by the dark, it would still be light. On the exact opposite side of the city, a building marked 'The Pessimists Edifice' would also remain as is even if the world were dominated by the light. These two buildings were the homes of the official newspapers for each side, established to let people know what was happening politically and the agenda of each ruler.

As tradition would have it, there was always a ruler for both the light and Dark Side. On the Dark Side, there was the Prince of Darkness or Dark Lord. Appointment of the Dark Lord position was carefully thought out to place the most intimidating leader in power, and was mostly acquired with an assassination of the previously appointed leader. With the average odds of twenty to one, the odds were not in favor of the challenger.

On the Light Side, there was the King, this divine and holy appointment normally addressed by a great quest to find three relics: a sword, a shield, and a crown, which was undertaken by the heir to the last King upon their death.

Wax was destined to always be at war, as was the nature of dark and light. Great battles would rage on both sides of the contested middle line. Occasionally the light would charge bravely into the dark lands, and sometimes the dark forces would swarm out into the light. However, as irony would have it, the two sides would also always be in eternal negotiations and trade.

In the center of the Candlestick, about half way to the top, was the Great Hall, where the Dark Prince and the Light Side King would meet on an annual basis to review their trade agreements and negotiate minor and insignificant details.

The Dark Lord at this time was Gordon B. Twiller. And, actually, Dark Lord Twiller had been in power longer than any recorded Dark Lord in history, having ruled for two hundred years, thanks to a bit of magic. The ruler of the Light Side was King Timothy K. Ragmon the seventeenth, from the longest ruling family thus far of the light.

In preparation for the annual meeting of rulers, special monks would study the *Master Book of Magic* and memorize it end to end. This would place them in a unique position to advise the two delegations as to both the formalities and where their ideas fell within the rules, laws, and bylaws. This also conveniently helped prevent anyone from spontaneously combusting in the middle of a negotiation. There were always three appointed monks to each delegation and a head monk to sit at the table as arbitrator.

With the well-established tradition of power, the largest armies in history, and the most magic manipulation Wax had ever seen, no one would suspect that a misfortunate monk, an unusual imp, and a teenager would be the ones to change everything.

As fate would have it, our story begins with the *Master Book of Magic*, chapter seventeen, section eight, subparagraph twelve, fourth sentence.

———

Gray hair topped the mostly bald head of the ninety-year-old monk. He barely made the five–foot-three-inch minimum requirement to use the various tools needed to read from the *Master Book of Magic*. His deep blue eyes strained to read the words through a large magnifying glass. He had only recently been given the responsibilities of head monk, as the previous one had decided to up and die at the age of one hundred and twenty-seven.

Head Monk Towe Frin tried to calculate the various mathematical variables necessary to see if one of the most obscure bylaws would apply to the annual review that was due to start in only ten hours.

"How could we have missed this?" he whispered to himself. His face was clearly filled with distraught over his most recent discovery. He quickly looked over the room to see which other monks were present. Out of the corner of his eye, he could see his most favored friend, the Honorable Monk Mussashi Gray.

With clear distinction, Towe cleared his throat loud enough to get the attention of everyone in the room. He quickly beckoned for Mussashi to join him.

"Yes Sir, what can I do for you?" Mussashi asked. The two men looked so very similar that one might mistake them for twins.

"Are you familiar with chapter seventeen, section eight, subparagraph twelve, fourth sentence?" Towe promptly asked in earnest.

"Oh yes, the review of death bylaw," Mussashi replied with a confused look. "Why?"

"Out of curiosity, would not this annual event qualify for this particular bylaw to be enacted?" Towe said with a bit of hesitation.

"Let me see, um…-'upon said year of which the Dark Lord empire shall pass the qualifying requirement of years as stated previous equals, and said light King's family reign qualifying in years to ser septum per equivocation, then the rite of review of death shall be provided at the annual review on the year of even equality between the two, by the designated witch of Ormolu. Sub note 'A' dash '1', please refer to reference sheet '2A' for calculations.' Or…-at least I think that's how it goes," Mussashi recanted while waving his fingers in the air as if reading it from the very page. "I do believe this is a qualifying year, Sir."

"I was afraid of that. How could this have been overlooked? We were so careful to prepare everything exactly, and to precise directions," Towe said, now intently staring at the ceiling. "I don't think we even have a witch designated for Ormolu anymore."

"Might I mention that on page two hundred seventy-two, third paragraph, it states that if no witch is currently designated as the official witch for Ormolu then one can be temporarily appointed by a high public official," Mussashi said in response. "I think of you as a high public official."

"Yes, exactly," Towe said in the high pitch of excitement. "I shall assign Monk Gorath Dale to beckon the nearest witch as soon as possible to my presence."

"Are you sure Gorath is up to this?" Mussashi asked with deep concern. "I only ask because he has had difficulties in the past accomplishing his tasks."

Head Monk Towe was painfully aware of the past Gorath Dale carried with him and, in fact, was counting on it. He was far more worried about one of his more competent monks being killed, or worse, being turned into some odd creature or slime for demanding something of a witch.

There were not many witches in the city, as they could not use any of their abilities, especially for devious acts. This meant that whoever took on this task would have to leave the safety of the city and wander into the dark lands. Towe had made up his mind to send Gorath.

"Here, Sir. You have need of me?" Gorath answered at his name being called out.

"Yes, I have a very important task for you to undertake, one of the utmost importance," Towe said with a solemn face.

"I am ready, Sir. What is my task?" Gorath replied in eagerness.

"Go into the Dark Side and bring a witch to me within an hour from now," Towe urgently instructed.

"Yes Sir, right away, Sir," Gorath replied. "And…what should I tell the witch as to why we require her presence?"

"I must speak with her immediately for an important job," Towe answered, holding out a piece of parchment. After a moment of thought, he added, "Also, take six of the underclassmen and two guards from the practice area with you."

"Very well, Sir," Gorath said, snatching the parchment away from Towe. With little notice, he ran off through the chamber toward the stairs. It was a good thing for Gorath that the parchment was magical and that the directions of his task had already scribed themselves onto the paper.

"Might I ask why so many resources?" Mussashi asked when Gorath was clearly out of earshot.

"I've barely given him anything, and with reason," Towe answered. "With Gorath distracting the Dark Side, I want you to go and get a witch. Take two of our best guards, and any other resources you need. We must have a witch as soon as possible."

Mussashi replied with a slight bow, "It is my honor, Sir."

EPISODE 2

Gorath hefted his usual leather pouch over his sixty-two-year-old shoulder. During his last assignment four years previous, he was captured by a rogue in cahoots with several other dark elements. He had failed to pack the proper items to defend against zombies, or vampires, and wanting to avoid a repeat of that last adventure, he had decided to carry an extra thirty pounds of gear.

Gorath opened the doors to the lower library, the location of the notorious underclassmen. Notorious because they were putting forth serious effort to move up in the order. The irony of the library was that it was so poorly lit, and everyone was studying so hard, it was difficult to actually find an underclassman.

As was tradition, Gorath laid out a paper on the large center table, and with a quick series of strokes, he wrote: 'Six to undertake extremely dangerous duty assigned by the head monk himself. All those who volunteer be presentable at the front door in five minutes.' Gorath then exited the lower library as slowly as he had entered, his next destination only two floors down.

A smile crossed his face as he heard the scurry of feet and several people whispering. These were typical events in a case like this. For underclassmen, it was required for them to not only be able to recite random pages from several hundred books, but they had to participate in no less than ten quests. Upon Gorath's graduation as the youngest to reach full monk status, the rules had been augmented. The first adjustment made it so that an underclassman could only choose to memorize no more than ten young adult books, as that made up ninety percent of Gorath's memorization. The second adjustment was that quests had to be handed down by the head monk and the head monk only. Gorath had been able to get away with counting common tasks as quests, like fetching water, and so on.

    He reached the ornate stairs and paused a moment to revel in its glory, as he always had. He admired the stairs themselves as they were made of a splendid white marble, and the railing was a dark stained oak, with gold and silver designs. Gorath felt that the most impressive part of the staircase was the walls. They consisted of a gigantic single painting, depicting major events in the world's history. The best part was that everything actually moved, with figures of good and evil charging into battle, treaties being signed, and great heroes and antiheroes. It was not recommended to stare at the walls if one was faint of heart, as it showed every gruesome and gory detail, alongside every wildly passionate moment. Gorath knew he had to be careful, as watching the walls could make a person easily lose track of time. He remembered when he had lost an entire day watching the walls. With that in mind, he shook his head and continued on his way.

    Gorath quickly reached the guards practice area. The guards here were less battle hardened veterans, and more fantastic situational thinkers. Of course this room was held to the restrictions of no weapons and no physical contact, so the guards would call out what move and counter move they were performing, and a third person would determine who won the encounter.

    "Who is in charge here?" Gorath asked.

"I am! What can I do for you, Gorath!?" A very short man called out.

"Aroon? When did they promote you?" Gorath replied in a mixture of surprise and horror.

Aroon was once a six-foot-two member of the Elite Eagles, which was made up of the best of the best soldiers from the light army. On one particular mission to rescue Gorath from a greedy cousin of the Dark Prince, something went terribly wrong. Gorath had prepped a shrinking spell to cast on his captors, and got Aroon instead. To make matters worse, none of the great mages could reverse the spell, and now he stood a modest three foot one. Needless to say, Aroon was removed from the Elite Eagles, and was demoted to Grunt First Class when he was transferred to guard duty at the tower.

"I don't think that is really important right now. Why are you here?" Aroon asked, his eyes wide with suspicion and a tone of clear irritation.

Gorath cleared his throat and, with an uncomfortable twinge, he replied, "I need two guards to go with me to the Dark Side to retrieve a witch, by the order of the head monk."

For a moment a tense silence filled the room, and then several guards began to step forward. This action was cut short by a loud cracking noise that resonated in the hall, made by the short staff held by Aroon.

"No one move!" he shouted. Aroon's eyes narrowed, and when I say narrowed, I mean to the point that people thought he had closed them. "Who here wants to die or be turned into some sort of hideous creature?"

Once again the room was filled with a thick silence. Gorath reached into his pouch and pulled out several small pieces of parchment, shuffling through them and mumbling to himself. "Homemade cookies, lemon drink, summon water, and—ah ha!" He held the paper up for everyone to see.

"By decree of the head monk, I command you surrender two of your men to this quest immediately." Gorath's voice was strained and, unlike the words dictated, the statement seemed more like a question.

"The five of you are coming with me to accompany this fool," Aroon commanded.

"Sir, why so many when they are only asking for two?" Corporal Stevens asked. Few men would ask a question like this to the height-challenged former Elite.

Everyone found themselves looking up at Stevens' towering seven-foot-six frame. It was hard for anyone not to notice the muscle girth of a dwarf, and facial features of a royal member of society. It was apparent to everyone that Gary Stevens was very different from most men. In fact, he was the result of the stewing pot effect created by the boarders changing hands. No one knew exactly what was in Stevens' genealogy. He had asked his mother on one occasion, whose only answer was a blank stare at the ceiling and an embarrassed smile.

Aroon knew that Stevens was exceptionally sharp when it came to war. Corporal Stevens had been a member of the Elite also, but defected with Aroon when he had been demoted. Gorath was in awe of the towering man's choice of weapons. Or should I say, he admired the fact that Stevens could not draw the two massive swords he held, because the ceiling wasn't tall enough. He was the sort of man for whom doorways and entrances had to be enlarged, and he never had to walk through a crowd, because everyone simply got out of the way.

"We need six of us so we can protect each other from him, not to mention whatever else we may face," Aroon said.

Gorath did not attempt to defend himself or even respond to the obvious verbal attack, and instead said, "Excellent, now that that is solved, let's be on our way."

Aroon held out his hand. "Let me see the orders."

Without serious argument, Gorath relinquished them with the shaking of his head and a little grunt under his breath. He started to walk to the entrance before the full thing could be read.

It took only seconds for Gorath to reach the front door where six underclassmen were waiting for him. Right behind him were the six guards, fully armed with weapons and wit, and ready for anything. Well...almost anything.

In the city, people noticed that whenever someone left the tower, they tended to be important. Curiosity filled the air, and soon a group began to follow Gorath's band as they slowly navigated toward the entrance to the dark lands on the Eastern side of the city. In no time, their followers had swelled into a large parade of people. The crowd began to ask questions like, "Who are you?" "Where are you going?" "Why are you going?"

Gorath had attracted more than just the average citizens. Those trained to notice things of this nature had also joined the gaggle. Without realizing it, he was being followed by nearly a dozen various groups, including the Assassin's Guild, the Thieves' Guild, spies from both major factions, and the City's Chief Police Inspector.

"Gorath, do you even know where to find a witch?" Aroon asked, his voice teeming with irritation.

Gorath, in his monkish wisdom, decided to reveal little about their quest and addressed the crowd. "I am sorry I cannot divulge the nature of my quest. However, I need some assistance. Would someone please be kind enough to point me in the direction of the nearest witch?"

"A witch? I know of a witch nearby. Look in the village of Stanzig," replied a goblin.

"Yeah, Orielia! She is definitely a witch!" laughed another goblin.

Gorath nodded and pointed toward the great gate. "Onward to Stanzig!"

After a few steps, he quickly pulled out his pocket guide to the dark lands, and found the village in question. With only five miles between him and completing a successful quest, it seemed inconceivable that anything could go wrong.

EPISODE 3

As Gorath stood just ten feet from the Eastern-most gates, he felt paralyzed as he always had before. He recalled that during his twelve years as a full monk, he had been assigned twenty different quests, and oddly enough, all of them were in the dark kingdom. It was obvious to him at this moment that the leadership trusted his abilities and judgment.

It was true irony that Gorath would use the word "obvious" in his thinking, as in his purview he was often oblivious of elements of danger. He was an optimist of the greatest sense. His ignorance of peril may have made him seem dim on intellect, but that is where Gorath shined the brightest. At one point in time, he had managed to cast a level thirty-two curse; tragically, the realm of magicians only went up to level thirty. This wasn't a problem, except for the poor soul on the receiving end of the curse.

Silence filled the air as everyone noticed that Gorath had been standing there for nearly two minutes now with a smile on his face. Aroon rolled his eyes and wished that Gorath was standing on the other side of the gate, at least then he could give him a nice sharp elbow to get him moving. As it was, he knew from experience that apparently the magic of the city felt that his elbows were dangerously sharp, having been teleported out of the city on more than one occasion.

"Come on Gorath, let's get moving," Aroon grumbled. His face started to represent his frustration as his comment seemed to be ignored. "GORATH!" Aroon shouted.

Gorath snapped out of his entranced state of reflection over his previous quests. He raised his arm and pointed into the dark lands. Everyone resumed moving about their business. Gorath began to walk forward then when he noticed a bag of money on the ground. As he bent down to pick it up, he felt a slight breeze. He stood and saw a couple of cloaked gentlemen standing several feet away, next to Aroon.

"What on Wax are you doing? As you already pointed out, we need to get moving," Gorath reprimanded.

He had missed the part where the two cloaked gentlemen had attempted to assassinate him, and Aroon's defensive response that thwarted said attempt. The two men now fell to the ground, lifeless, and Aroon quickly replaced his sword and dagger.

"Let's get moving," Aroon growled, stepping over the two assassins lying askance in the dirt, and glaring at them. He made sure he was well outside the boundaries of the gates before he turned and stared at the city for a minute.

Gorath rolled his eyes and held up the map. He traced his finger over the path he wanted to take and, as he did so, a faint glowing path lit up before them. A grin crossed Gorath's face, satisfied at the result of his spell. Everyone in the group seemed amazed at the incantation.

"Wow, that is pretty," Corporal Stevens remarked. "What is it?"

The underclassmen were clearly in awe of the lit path before them. They discussed the situation in their low mumbled whispers.

"It's called the Path of the Dead," one of the underclassmen replied.

"Out of curiosity, why is it called the Path of the *Dead?*" Aroon asked, suspecting that he would not care for the answer, but feeling that he needed to be prepared for the worst.

"It is said that anyone who follows the faint glow, is walking to their certain death," another underclassmen replied.

"Why do they say that?" Aroon asked.

"That's because no one has ever followed the path to its end and returned to talk about it," another underclassmen added.

"Don't listen to them, I have used this spell at least twenty times," Gorath quickly replied, with a hint of both annoyance and nervousness.

"Brilliant," Aroon said. He rubbed his head in anticipation of the severe headache that normally accompanied a mission involving Gorath.

The party faithfully followed the path for a mile before anyone noticed that they were all alone in a fog. Regardless of the weather condition, the blue light continued to lead them forward. Gorath noticed that the path had become increasingly tough to walk on, but he couldn't see through the fog to find out why. As they walked, he reached into his pocket and retrieved the *Handy Book of Convenient Spells – Travel Edition*. He thumbed through the pages for a moment before he found the Winds of the Sea spell.

"Hold on a second, everyone," Gorath said, slowing to a stop. Then he began to cast the spell.

Even with his warning, everyone had continued to walk until they ran into Gorath. The force knocked him to the ground. He discovered to his horror that he was face to face, or more accurately, face to nostril with a giant troll. Instantly, he realized that he had led the party over the resting grounds of the trolls, and for the last ten minutes, they had all been walking on the slumbering creatures.

Gorath decided not to cast the spell after all, or to reveal to the party his blunder and their most probable doom. Unfortunately, he had already started casting and the magic needed to be released, so he elected to improvise. In that moment, Gorath managed to twist the Winds of the Sea spell into the Sea Spray spell, and a massive tyrant of water began to pelt the party.

"What have you done?" Aroon asked, "Why would you cast *this* spell?!"

"Sssssshhhhhhhh!!!" Gorath attempted to calm the angry little man. "Keep your voice down and keep moving."

"I will not keep moving until you answer me!" Aroon knew better than to let Gorath's strange behavior go unanswered.

"Do you want to die!?" Gorath asked in a panicked frenzy. "Keep moving."

"Now this is where I draw the line!" Aroon said. He decided, and would forever regret, to draw his sword and make a line motion along the ground.

The loud and angry shrill of a wounded troll pierced everyone in the party down to the very core and invoked their deepest fears. Driven only by the primal urge to survive, the party raced forward with the greatest speed, every one of them certain of their impending doom.

"This IS the Path of the Dead!" Corporal Stevens shouted. Every moment new trolls were joining in the angry shrill.

"Fix this!" Aroon yelled.

"I'm working on it!" Gorath replied as he scanned his small spell book. He hated casting offensive spells, so he turned and cast Charmed Deep Sleep on the shrieking darkness behind him. Just as quickly as everything had begun, it was over.

Aroon jumped up and grabbed Gorath's robe, nearly pulling him to the ground to meet face to face. "Pull something like that again, and I will end you, understood?"

"Look, I saved us, and the party is intact, so let's keep moving," Gorath urged. He then glanced left and right very quickly. "Oh boy."

"What!?" Aroon asked, seeing the increasingly panicked look on Gorath's face. That's when he noticed that they were the only two standing in the clearing.

"Don't hurt me?" Gorath requested in fear. It was apparent that he had cast the Charmed Deep Sleep spell just a moment too soon, catching nearly his entire party in the radius. In fact, it was most probable that it was Aroon's height-challenged state that saved him from an ignorant slumber.

"What did you do this time? Where is everyone?" Aroon asked.

"They are somewhere back there…asleep," Gorath said. "We should go look for them, but I'm not sure I can wake them up."

Aroon let go of Gorath, but began to motion as if to strangle him with sheer force of thought. The fierce anger building in his eyes prompted Gorath to start looking for a spell to calm the other man down.

Gorath extended his hand and began to cast an Inner Peace spell. Aroon, in the meantime, had remembered his training and composed himself. He began to think about the task at hand, when suddenly the world around him began to change. His surroundings began to brighten up, and everything seemed warm and fuzzy. Without warning, a smile crossed his face and a giggle escaped his lips, all of which was beyond his control.

"What did you do?" Aroon asked in a bubbly, happy voice.

"I just gave you a little inner peace, equal to about ten of the herbal flower of Vikonis Trebidonis, or commonly known as the Valiumic Flower of Happiness," Gorath replied.

"You know when this ends, you will endure immense pain," Aroon answered with a laugh.

"Well, until then, let's go get a witch," Gorath said.

"Hold on a sec," Aroon said. He bent down and began to pet a large fluffy white rabbit standing at his feet. "What a cute little fella."

Gorath cringed at the action, as he knew in reality that Aroon was petting the slimy goop that makes up a Snot Toad. A shiver raced down his spine and he took a step back. He thought to himself that perhaps he had overdone it just a little.

"Alright there, Aroon, let's get moving," he said, taking another step back.

"I feel like singing...I hate singing..." Aroon said with happiness oozing from his words. "Doot, doot, dweed, dot, dot, dweed dow..."

"Okay, you should probably not do that," Gorath said.

Aroon stopped and stared at Gorath for a long time. "You know I just realized that I love you, man."

"Right..." Gorath said, "let's just keep walking."

Unexpectedly Aroon took Gorath by the hand like a child, and started skipping. The two started down the path again, leaving their slumbering party far behind. It wasn't long before they found themselves at the entrance to a small village. Gorath tried to pull out the map, but Aroon was refusing to let go of his hand. After several attempts, Gorath decided to just ask someone for assistance.

"Excuse me, can someone tell me what village this is?

"INVASION!!!!" a tiny goblin said, looking at the two men. Suddenly the air was filled with running and screaming.

"NO, I just wanted..." Gorath started to say. He was promptly interrupted by a large club smashing into the ground only inches from him. The shock caused him to forget to breathe for a moment.

The club began to rise again, and Gorath attempted to flee, but Aroon anchored him in place with his firm grip. Again the club smashed into the ground only inches away from Gorath's left foot.

"We have to move!" Gorath said in a frantic tone.

"Nope, I am not moving," Aroon said in a defiant voice. This response made it clear that Aroon was no longer under the Inner Peace spell. In fact he was now feeling the harsh depressing withdrawals that made the spell particularly unattractive.

Gorath cringed into a ball as he prepared to be smashed by the large club. Unexpectedly, Aroon let go of his hand and dashed towards the large ogre that was wielding the weapon. The motion caught the ogre off guard, and in one quick action, Aroon struck the ogre with an uppercut, knocking him out in one shot.

Gorath and everyone in the area stood in silence gaping at the result of the fight. No one seemed to know what to do.

"What town is this?" Aroon grumbled.

"Stanzig…and we surrender…" said an orc dressed in battle armor.

"Just brilliant," Aroon said under his breath, as he looked back at Gorath.

EPISODE 4

Gorath wasn't sure what the protocol was for un-capturing a village. He pulled out his *Nifty Guide to Traversing the Dark Side*, written by Honest Thomas. He panned down through the Table of Contents to find an answer.

"Chapter One: Dos and Don'ts of the Dark Side," Gorath mumbled aloud as his finger traced the page, "Section A: Don't go into the Dark Side if you can help it... Section B: Watch where you step..."

"Gorath, there can't possibly be anything in that book that could apply to this," Aroon said with a grumble. There were about seven heavily armored orcs, three goblins, and something resembling an old man, standing before them with their weapons on the ground and their appendages held high.

"Section H!" Gorath said as a giant smile crossed his face. "What to do if you have accidently captured a village!"

Gorath made it a point to hold the book where Aroon could see and tapped the page several times to emphasize his point. Aroon tried hard not to look at the book and thus give Gorath any sort of encouragement. However, his curiosity was too much to bear and he snuck a quick glance, and simply let out a sigh of defeat.

"'*If you have accidently captured a village, congratulations! And I'm sorry... As per the iconic Versaillic treaty, the capturing party (you) has to defend the territory for thirty minutes before the transfer of power is complete. Note that the moment you captured the village, all armies within a candlestick's view were notified via the giant marker that should be hovering over the village...'*"

"Great, let's grab the witch and get out of here!" Aroon said. "If we run now, we won't get slaughtered."

"'*...If you are thinking about running, don't. The treaty says the conquering party must remain inside the captured village until the thirty minutes is up, or suffer a penalty worse than death. Once again, congratulations, and good luck*'," Gorath finished with a big lump in his throat.

What Gorath had failed to do was read the very next section, "Section I: Penalty for fleeing combat," which would have told them that the penalty was "embarrassment and ridicule for running from a fight." The option the two men most likely would have preferred, given the circumstances.

"I should have known you would be the death of me," Aroon grumbled. "Well, let's get this over with."

"Let's find Orielia and send her back to Ormlu while we still can," Gorath said. Unexpectedly the mixed party of orcs, goblins, and possible human, broke out in a loud laugh.

"You captured Stanzig for Orielia?" one of the orcs said, doubled over in laughter.

"Not quite the reaction I would expect at the name of a witch," Aroon said with confusion.

"A witch?!" The group laughed louder, leaving several rolling on the ground. "Careful, or we will all feel the wrath of Orielia, the witch!"

"I don't get it," Gorath said. "Why are you laughing at this?"

"Because you think Orielia is a witch," a goblin chimed in from the ground.

"Is she not a witch?" Aroon asked with frustration building.

"Oh, no she is a witch of sorts," one of the orcs said.

"Okay," Gorath said in a confused tone. "Where can we find her?"

"In the small shack in the back of the village," the orc replied.

For a moment both Aroon and Gorath were thinking the exact same thought at the exact same time. This event would only happen twice in their lifetimes, now and later on just after they would fall off the roof of the Candlestick. Ironically, they would think the same thing both times, "Brilliant."

The two began to sprint in the direction indicated by the orc, carefully avoiding the sleeping ogre, believing that they were racing against their impending deaths. The villagers hid inside their homes, peering out to see the two run past. It didn't take long before they were standing at the doorway of a small shack. Gorath cleared his throat as he knocked on the door. It seemed like forever as the two could hear their hearts racing. Impatiently Aroon gave the door a good working over.

"She isn't going to answer," said a voice from behind them. "Plus, you don't want her anyway. She is not right in the head."

"Hello?" Gorath said loudly as he gave the door another rap. "Please answer the door, we need your help."

"You're wasting your time. I told you she isn't going to answer the door," the voice said.

"Is she out? Do you know where she is?" Aroon asked.

"Yeah, she is standing right where I am," Orielia said. "Now what do you want with her?"

Gorath looked down at Aroon with a giant smile on his face. It was clear that Aroon was not as excited to find Orielia as he was. Aroon looked her over and saw nothing but a crazy old woman.

It annoyed Aroon that her five-foot frame towered over him, and even her ratty farming hat mocked him.

"My name is Gorath, and we need you to come with us back to Ormlu. Head Monk Towe would like to talk with you about an important job," Gorath said.

"With Orielia? What kind of job?" Orielia asked. Her stormy grey eyes seemed to flicker with curiosity.

"A job for a witch," Gorath said.

"A real witch," added Aroon.

"I see, is there pay for this job?" Orielia asked. "Oh, never mind, she doesn't care about that. Let's get going."

"Oh yeah, there is one complication," Gorath said. He realized that he had nearly forgotten about the armies about to descend upon them.

"Yes?" Orielia asked. Just then she randomly bent down and put her finger to the ground.

"Ah…yes…we kind of captured the village, and several armies are on their way to wipe us out," Gorath said.

"Oh. So, did you want us to start walking towards the Candlestick?" Orielia asked.

"Um, no, I've got this," Gorath said. He reached into his pack and removed a small red pouch of blue dust.

"Oh no, I know what that is, and I want nothing to do with it," Aroon said, stepping back and waving his hands. The last time the blue dust had come out, he had lost his height and prestige in the same moment.

"Okay, I'm ready," Orielia said.

Gorath nodded his head and threw a small pinch of the dust into the air, and mumbled a chant that was inaudible to everyone. Then a mild thump sound filled the air, and all that remained of the witch was an outline of dust that was now drifting harmlessly to the ground.

"Are you happy? You blew her up..." Aroon commented. He waved his hand through the air where she had been standing previously.

"On the contrary, she is safely on her way to Ormlu. Just in time, might I add," Gorath said with a smirk.

Indeed Orielia was on her way to Ormlu. Of all the spells at Gorath's disposal, he had decided to use the Spell of Faster Running than a Bird of Prey. To top it all off, he had accidently mispronounced the last two words of the spell and sent her flying towards the city, faster than the fastest winds, which sometimes reached in upwards of one hundred miles per hour. So Orielia would reach Ormlu in just under three minutes.

At this point, it was easy to hear the hoard of dark creatures arriving at the edge of the village. The smile quickly dropped from Gorath's face. The first creatures to confront the pair were four vampires.

"So, you wouldn't happen to have anything anti-vampiric, would you?" Aroon asked as he watched the quartet slowly move forward.

"Um, can you give me a moment on that," Gorath said. He plopped his bag on the ground and began pulling out different items.

"Yeah, take your time on that," Aroon said. He began to move backwards when he tripped over the items Gorath had pulled from his bag thus far. Instantly one of the vampires lunged at him.

"Ah, ha," Gorath said as he put a wooden stake into Aroon's hand.

Aroon thrust the spike forward in desperation. Fortunately the vampire was already descending towards him and had no chance to move. As the spike pierced the vampire's chest, he turned to glittery dust. In the very next moment another vampire was diving for Aroon. His super human strength swatted Aroon's hand to the side.

Well, at least I put up a fight, and while defending a village I captured. Not too bad, Aroon thought to himself as he closed his eyes. Then, as the vampire looked posed to strike, he turned to dust. Aroon looked up to see Corporal Stevens looking down at him, as well as dust trails from the last two vampires.

"Just in time it seems," Stevens said as he extended his hand.

Aroon got to his feet in a state of disbelief. He glanced around to see the other guards and the underclassmen with him.

"How did you get here?" Aroon asked.

"Well, you see, we woke up, and that guy thought everyone was dead and that we should turn back..." Stevens began.

"Doesn't matter, prepare yourselves to fight," Aroon said.

"...and I said we need to follow the blue line, and he said it would lead us to our deaths..." Stevens continued.

Without warning the giant ten-foot ogre Aroon had knocked out came around the corner in a rage and charged at them. Without hesitation, everyone jumped out of the way, except for Stevens, who looked mildly irritated. Stevens used his metal bracer to deflect the ogre's left hand and gave the creature a wicked right-handed uppercut. The creature looked just as surprised as everyone in his party, and let out a whining noise before its eyes closed and it crumpled to the ground, unconscious for the second time that day.

"... anyhow, I said it was our duty to come and find you, and after a vote, here we are," Stevens finished.

"I'm glad you made it," Aroon said as he pointed to a new group of attackers. "Orcs."

"Zombies," Gorath said, pointing behind them. Gorath reached into his pocket and pulled out three large acorns, and one at a time, threw them at the slowly advancing undead. The zombies paused for a moment in confusion, before continuing their advance.

"What was that supposed to do?" Aroon asked. He glanced back in time to see Stevens use the flat side of his axe to knock a whole platoon of orcs down in a domino effect.

"Not sure, I was hoping it would turn them to stone," Gorath said. Gorath began to search his pockets for the *Offensive Spells for Defensive Magic Users Guide*. Just before the zombies were within an arm's reach of Gorath, large vines emerged from the ground where the acorns had landed, and firmly secured the advancing army of corpses.

Gorath looked around to see where he could help. Stevens was clearly dominating the small lane leading towards them against the orcs. Aroon was now leading his other guards against the right flank as goblins emerged from a nearby building. The underclassmen were taking turns using their magic to fend off advancing giant spiders and werewolves.

"Hum, kinda surprised a mage hasn't shown up…" Gorath said. Just as the thought completed, a large burst of energy threw him away from the main group. Gorath looked up to see a large mass of creatures racing toward him. He spotted his bag in the distance, and began to pat down his pockets in search of anything that could help him. Gorath climbed to his feet just in time for the lead horse of a light-side cavalry unit to knock him down.

Gorath let a little smile cross his face until he realized that he was in the path of a pack of charging war elephants. He knew that there was no escape from this and closed his eyes in preparation.

Mussashi was satisfied with his ability to track down and escort a witch back to the city as instructed. He looked over at the witch he had brought to the edge of the city.

"Just a few more steps and you will get half your gold, and the other half after the meeting," Mussashi said, looking over at the woman.

Then, without any warning, Orielia was suddenly standing right where the previous witch had been. "Well that was fun," she said.

"Who are you?" Mussashi asked.

"We are the witch of Stanzig! Gorath sent me," Orielia said.

"Okay, well…follow me," Mussashi said in suspicion. He glanced around quickly and verified that the witch he had brought was indeed nowhere in sight.

EPISODE
5

"Dallion Quimbie Haberdasher Nocks Drisbie Horlon Everton," A voice whispered.

The name would suggest a possible knight of the light realm, a thief, or even an assassin perhaps; however, it was the unusual name for an imp. Most every imp was named after a sound event, weather condition, or situation, typical examples would be like Gerr, Southwind, or Son of Eternally Grounded Daughter. Therefore, Dallion was most commonly known as Drip. He hailed from more than seventeen generations of personal servants to the most prestigious dark wizards, kings, and Dark Lords. Drip was reminded of this fact as he looked over a large library he was expected to clean consisting of strewn books, random discarded pieces of food, dishes, and various items scattered about.

"Dallion Quimbie…" the voice whispered again.

Ignoring the voice, Drip let his thoughts drift. *This torture has to be worse than being peeled and boiled.*

"I heard that, and I don't care for that tone of thought," the voice interrupted his thoughts.

Drip's head slumped and his shoulders dropped in defeat. As always, the voice grounded him, literally. The low-toned voice came from his bound friend, which happened to be a cursed talking boot. The curse of the boot was that it could never be taken off, not by him and not by anyone.

"Boot, for the ten millionth time, call me Drip," he said. Drip then began to pick up dirty dishes.

"Drip is not a name, it's a verb, and as you know, there isn't much we can do about this, so for the more accurate two hundred and twelfth time, let's try to come up with a common name," Boot remarked.

It clearly stated in the High Archives list of known enchanted and cursed items at number two hundred and thirty five, the Cursed Boot of Astankium was created in the early fifth age by a human cordwainer, a profession known more commonly as a shoe maker, who was secretly married to a most powerful witch. A pair of boots was made especially for the Prince of the small kingdom of Triks. The Prince enjoyed the boots so much that he called for another pair to be made. Unfortunately, the cordwainer was unable to fulfill the request due to a shortage of fine processed sheep skin, since the prince had earlier traded the kingdom's sheep for a fine cloth robe. The prince then killed the shoe maker, upon which the cordwainer's wife cursed the boots to never leave the foot of the wearer, and to talk to the wearer until that person was dead. The curse also made the boots indestructible. Drip came upon them on accident; he was technically born into one.

"As someone who was selected to be a servant by the Imp Trade School, I wonder if anyone else has figured out that all imps are selected to be servants?" Drip wondered aloud. He of course already knew the answer.

"Here we go again," Boot sighed. "The paper…"

Whatever it was that drove imps to want to serve was missing from Drip. All he wanted to do was write. During his two years of Imp Trade School, he had produced a school record two hundred various articles, essays, and short stories. As it turns out, the imp second to Drip had produced an astounding one paper, which in fact had been a random piece of paper that had been trampled in a mud puddle, and in the efforts of removing it from his shoe, the student had picked it up and set it on the teacher's desk. As another oddity, Drip could only produce works of a positive nature, which was often looked down upon in a dark empire. Despite this simple fact, Drip wanted to write for "The White Knight Tower" newspaper.

This particular wish teetered on the edge between ultra-rare astronomical occurrence, like a dying sun turning not into its natural progression of super nova to black hole, but instead turning into a dinner set of very fine china, and the simply absurd, example being a Politician actually telling the truth their entire life.

As fate would have it, Drip had a plan, and that involved getting on with *The Pessimists Edifice* newspaper. Even that was only written by powerful dark wizards, assassins, and dark royalty appointed by the Dark Lord himself. It was not that imps did not work there, on the contrary imps were the backbone of the press, but there was a nearly twenty-to-one ratio imp to non-imp. This was due to an overwhelming vote of confidence by the dark kingdom for imps to work at producing the paper rather than writing it. The vote had been a landslide of sorts; you see the only ones who voted happened to be the Dark Lord and his nephew, the editor of the newspaper. The two had agreed that the bad temper and unnecessary aggression of the orc, the poor intelligence of the goblins, and the destructive nature of the giants and trolls, simply ruled them out, so only imps *could* operate the paper, and if they were operating it, who would think to have any of them also write for it.

"As always I ask, what will writing for *The Pessimists Edifice* do for you?" Boot asked. If he had true eyes, they would be rolling with the sarcastic and rhetorical nature of the question.

"I've told you, if I gain respect as a writer with the dark newspaper, then it will help me transition into a role with the light newspaper," Drip answered.

Currently, Drip was employed by the seriously subpar, pseudo dark wizard, Dragin, not to be mistaken for the powerful, magical, and intimidating creature, the "dragon." Though his anger was near legendary, his power was not, and the former would possibly be the only thing he would be remembered for. Unfortunately, Drip had not been privy to that information, and was about to end up on the receiving end of Dragin's anger late on his second day on the job.

"Argon! Argon where are you?!" shouted Dragin. He stood in the middle of a modest entryway.

"Who are you calling for?" asked Tekan, master of the servants to Dragin.

"You know Argon, that lousy imp! I feel like kicking something!" Dragin replied.

"Sir, Argon has not been with us for a few months," Tekan said.

"I only employ ten imps; I think I can remember them," Dragin retorted.

"Well, Argon was killed by the fowl plant you created two months ago," Tekan said.

"Oh yeah, well then did we replace him?" he asked.

"Of course we did, with Spark," Tekan answered quickly.

"Ok then, where is Spark?" Dragin asked with annoyance.

"You killed Spark when you got angry and pushed him out the tower window," Tekan nervously answered.

"And we replaced him with...?" Dragin's eyes narrowed.

"With Stark, who died by food testing at your cousin's. He was replaced by Dangle, who was trampled by those random charging horses last week, who was replaced by Deet, who was conducting the rooftop signal flag test when that wind gust came along, and he was blown so far away, well, we assume he's dead, Sir. And he was replaced by Drip," Tekan stated.

"Which one had the really spiky hair?" asked Dragin.

"That would be Dangle, Sir," Tekan replied.

"I liked him, he was smart for an imp. He probably could have done your job even," Dragin said suspiciously.

"Yes, his death was most tragic," Tekan said.

"Well then, where is Drip?" Dragin asked.

Tekan walked over to a massive tapestry on the far wall with a floor plan of the castle on it. There were tiny portraits appearing and disappearing, marking the location of every living thing on the grounds. Gently he reached over and twisted a piece of parchment on the wall casting a simple retrieval spell. Then he placed his hand on the map and pressed on a particular set of footprints.

Drip had just finished picking up the majority of the mess that made up the library. He had started sorting the spells and books into alphabetical order and neatly placing them on the bookcases around the room, when he dropped a book. Unexpectedly a little fire nymph popped out of the magical pages and began to stretch. Drip had dealt with such creatures in the past, and knew that all he had to do was whisper a simple phrase. 'Dance back to where you came from or be doused with a bucket of very icky, cold green water'. He was, in fact, just about to let the first sound of the phrase exit his mouth, when he suddenly found himself teleported before the Master of the House, with the Master of Servants looking on.

"Drip, where have you been?" Dragin demanded.

Drip's mind raced with panicked fury as he could imagine the damage the very real fire nymph was now causing. Knowing that not answering would be bad, and giving the wrong answer would be worse, Drip announced, "I have been seeing to my fair and practical duties, Sir."

This answer left both Dragin and Tekan speechless. They, like many others, had no idea that an imp was even capable of answers such as this. As a matter of fact, they were used to the typical 'Um, I'm not quite sure what you mean' or 'I was just doing what I was doing'. By this time, smoke had begun to billow out of the tall tower above, and occasionally Drip could see a piece of falling fiery debris through the window behind the two men.

"Would you like to alter my directions, most powerful masters?" Drip asked quickly.

After yet another moment of confused silence, Dragin opened his mouth in anticipation of saying something, when the tallest tower simply ceased to exist with a very powerful explosion. Dragin leaned his head out of the window and looked up just in time to see a large section of the tower racing towards his head. With a panicked look, he ducked back inside. Anger erupted from his fingertips, as he fumed at Drip. He unleashed his power just as Drip decided that it was time to take his leave, but before he could move, the bolt raced past him and smacked a mirror, deflecting off and striking Tekan instead. This turned the man into a duck.

In frustration, Dragin let out another charge, as the fire nymph had decided to move to another section of the castle, and gracefully cause it to explode as well. The bolt struck Tekan again changing him into a half dog, half goat, and Dragin let out a primitive shout of rage.

Drip exited quickly, partly because he felt that his welcome had been worn out, and partly because he could see the fire nymph racing towards the next castle over, and it was not going to be pretty.

EPISODE
6

As was his routine, Drip walked home along the black lake of burning tar called 'Ste Tomerick' literally translated as 'the fire no one can seem to put out'. Like so many times before, he sat down at the edge of Tomerick and stared deep into the dark black plumbs of smoke. He would use his imagination and attempt to make objects or people appear within.

"No worries, pal, that guy wasn't worthy of your service anyways," Boot said.

For the first time in an hour, a tiny voice piped in, "Watching, winding, winding, willow, and wa…"

"Bean, I'm not sure where you are going with that," Drip said with a little smile.

He tapped on the bean hanging around his neck. Unlike Boot, Bean was not listed on the books as a registered enchanted item. Drip had discovered Bean when walking home one day. He saw it hopping along, advancing about three inches at a time. Picking up the charm seemed to please Bean. The only thing about Bean was that it only talked in rhymes, riddles, and never finished its statements.

"I appreciate your support guys, but something just is not right here," Drip said.

"I do not know about that, you just dodged Dragin's most powerful, or should I say *only* change spell. We could all be a part of some sort of creature or something," Boot replied. "Anyways, things will be different tomorrow."

"Right," Drip said with a deep sigh.

Drip carefully removed the small pad of paper he had been carrying around in his pocket and flipped past several written pages while mumbling various titles: "Dark," "More Dark," "That Dark Within," "The Clouds," "Ode to a Rabbit King," and "Odds and Ends."

Upon reaching a blank section of the note pad, he adjusted his sitting position and pulled out a small piece of graphite. In one very un-imp-like graceful stroke, he titled the page "Letter to the Editor of The Pessimist's Pestle." On the page he wrote an elegant letter of request to write for the paper in any capacity, and like so many times before, he listed his merit and offered several samples of his work. Then, as he completed the letter, a cold chill ran down his spine as it seemed a face of smoke was staring at him, and noting everything he was doing.

He shook the feeling and dusted off his clothes. Another sigh came out as he noticed a small runner heading his way.

"Drip!" the runner cried out.

"Yes?" he asked. He pretended to be ignorant of the coming news, though he knew exactly what it was.

"Here is a letter from the imp employment agency," said the runner. He handed the paper to Drip and quickly raced off to find the next imp on his list.

He opened the letter to find a very simple explanation of events that would occur, and a posting for a new job for him already. It read:

'Drip, you're fired. Going anywhere near Dragin's means death. Go to tower sixteen tomorrow. I.E.A. (Imp Employment Agency).'

His imagination did not have to stray far to figure out what the letter meant. His creative thinking offered a bit of embellishment to include words like painful, torture, agonizing, horrific, and dismemberment in regards to going near Dragin's again. He quickly decided to avoid the pseudo-dark wizard at all costs. With that thought, he happily strode off toward his residence.

Along the way he found an old copy of "The Pessimist's Pestle" lying on the road. Without any deliberation, he rescued it from the ground. He glanced over the paper to see if there was anything new. Most everything was terribly predictable: the Dark Lord was unhappy with production; overcrowding may lead to random executions, or pressed service into the army; the experimental half-orc and imp battalion was a failure; and last but not least, the Dark Lord, in all his wisdom, has chosen to now dump all garbage and bodies into the 'Ste Tomerick'.

"Oh now that is just fabulous, nothing like trash and dead bodies to enhance a two-thousand-year-old fire. I can only imagine the smell," said Boot.

"And what would you do with the trash and dead bodies?" asked Drip.

"I've seen things done with trash that you would never believe, like fling it at your enemies, or build structures out of it. Of course the most bazaar thing is that someone would put grass over the top of a giant pit of trash and knock around a little white ball with a metal pole," replied Boot.

"You don't even have a nose, or toes, or any…" added Bean.

"At least I can finish a sentence," Boot retorted.

"That is enough, we are almost home," Drip said.

The last leg of his journey was also the most dangerous. It was a place called 'Rohin's Rear,' where five major roads crossed each other. One of the roads included the only route open to the largest ogres, trolls, and other dark creatures. Another was a steady stream of different units moving from prep areas of the kingdom to the front lines of battle. Another was the information line, which was an endless line of riders carrying different messages to and fro, throughout the kingdom. Another was reserved for the Dark Lord himself, and no one traveled it without express permission. The last road went into the Candlestick itself.

At one point the Dark Lord had instituted a traffic control system at this very spot, after a family of trolls squashed half an elite battalion of orcs. The measure had indeed stopped the unnecessary loss of life at the juncture, but was removed when the Dark Lord had to wait for an hour to cross one day.

Drip stretched his neck and back until they popped just right. Then he placed his right foot against a large rock and leaned forward with his knuckles resting on the ground. Much as you would see at a typical track and field event just before a starting sound, he had arrived at Rohin's Rear and was prepared to cross at a moment's notice. He looked left to see two other imps, then looked right to find two more in the same position as him. He waited for the moment he could see a path in the chaos. Then, in that rare moment, an ogre tripped over a horse and cleared the middle for just a moment.

All five of them took off running for the other side. Drip could feel the ground trembling as the ogre climbed to his feet. Then, unexpectedly, he could not feel the ground below his feet for a moment. This was caused when three ogres traveling together all jumped up at the same moment and landed with a thunderous crack and boom. This was actually a typical event as this would normally clear the path for them to cross. For Drip and the other four imps, this spelled trouble. Each of them fell to the ground and slid a few feet. Knowing that there was no time to dust themselves off, they gathered their senses and ran.

The sound of everything racing towards him pushed Drip harder, but just like flash flood waters, he could see his exit closing off too fast. Horses began to race all around him, and goblins as well in their mad dash through the crossroads. He was able to grab a hold of the side of a catapult, and use it to make up an extra ten feet. As his feet touched the ground again, only ten more feet to go, he could feel the ground rumble harder.

"Watch out!" Boot yelled.

The warning came just in time for Drip to dive out of the path of a chariot, then a quick roll to the side past a dark elf platoon. He stood up on the right side of the road and dusted himself off.

"Another successful crossing, without a terrible tossing, costing a life, on the..." Bean said, once again not quite finishing his thought.

"I'll say," Drip replied.

"Wait a moment, what is that?" Boot asked.

Drip noticed that three of the other four imps had also crossed without being a fatality to be dumped into the tar pit. What Boot was pointing out was the fifth imp struggling with the last part of the road. A deep limp gave away a potentially serious injury. It did not take a dark wizard to see that the imp would be doomed without assistance.

Instinctively, Drip plunged himself back into the chaos, and was quickly by the imp's side. He was practically dragging the injured imp behind him, but fortune smiled upon the two as they crossed the last bit without trouble.

"Now that was exciting, wasn't it?" Boot asked.

"So unnecessary, a trip to get such a berry, and the..." Bean said.

"Are you okay?" Drip asked, ignoring the other two.

The other imp gave Drip a dark, angry look of contempt, and without hesitation, limped off mumbling. Drip shrugged and began again for his home. His eyes drifted to the horizon where the sun was setting behind a thick set of clouds. It made the sun look a lot like another moon. This bit of dark magic allowed the creatures of the Dark Side that otherwise only went out at night to move about all the time.

As his head dropped, Drip's eyes came to focus on the entrance of his house.

Drip lived in the outskirts of The Candlestick, as did all servant-style creatures. He lived in a small one room, cave-like shack in a honeycomb style housing structure. Most would find the room drab and depressing, which was the way the dark kingdom liked things.

As for you and I, we would think the place was…well, a literal hole in the ground, which of course it actually was. Drip, however, found it somewhat pleasant. The one thing that did bother him was the fact that he was a social outcast from his two-hundred-and-thirty-seven brothers and sisters, thanks to one simple additional decoration he chose to display in his living space.

In a corner sat a small yellow flower that had been pressed under glass for permanent preservation. The flower was not one that a human might pick out for display, it was a sad mostly dead version of a cross between a cinquefoil, or Potentilla of the Rosaceae family, and a hawkweed, or Hieracium of the Compositae family. If you were to cross such a flower in a field, you would probably go out of your way to put the poor thing out of its misery. To put it into prospective, Drip had to go out of his way to acquire such a rare plant; after all, most things tended to be dark in the dark kingdom.

In the world of Wax, it was generally known that imps were magically created, or duplicated…technically. Wizards of great power summon them into existence from a living imp for a life of service. What took the wizards of great power a while to figure out was that you have to summon two-hundred-and-sixty-seven in one shot. They had discovered that if they created less than two-hundred-and-sixty-seven, they ended up with imps with extra body parts, some with two heads or four arms, and such. It was even more amazing to learn that if they summoned more than two-hundred-and-sixty-seven, they'd have imps missing things: arms, legs, and yes, even heads sometimes.

This was all well and good when they finally got the number right, but two-hundred-and-sixty-seven imps in a batch caused several problems. For one, if you were short on imps, you would hesitate to create a batch, as you still have to feed and house the creatures. Wizards would sometimes create a batch, promptly sending half on an impossible errand to find some sort of rare ingredient, just to save themselves the headache of having to care for them all.

However, with this tactic you ended up with a hundred imps aimlessly wandering around never to complete their task, and this was bad because they would often end up looking for the 'item' they had been sent to find in a food supply and eat everything in sight when they didn't find it. On the other hand, the perk of sending them out was that, every once in a while, one would show up with the rare ingredient.

Some of the problem had been solved with the creation of the Imp Employment Agency, and imp trade school. Without the I.E.A., much as Drip didn't really care for the life of a servant, he would have nowhere to go tomorrow.

Drip curled up inside his small home with an eerie sense of misbelonging in a hill full of imps. He folded an old copy of the newspaper, and rested his head against it. A chill ran down his spine as he longed for this particular moment of the night, when the moonlight peeked through a hole in the ground and illuminated the dingy flower.

"Someday," Drip whispered, as his eyes gave way to sleepiness.

"I really wish that were true," Boot whispered.

Drips eyes were closed now and his breathing had begun to deepen, when something unusual happened. Bean began to light up and, for a moment, Drip's whole house was illuminated. This was interrupted by a thunderous noise and a terrible screeching sound. Then, just as suddenly, Bean ceased to illuminate, and Drip instantly woke up.

"What is happening?" Drip shouted as a loud shrill filled the air.

"There are a lot of noises, and that is pretty much all I know," Boot replied.

"Run, run, run, ton…" Bean added.

Drip pushed out through his door just in time to see an arrow racing towards him. He flinched away just enough that the arrow only grazed his arm, but at that moment, he understood what was going on. They were under attack!

EPISODE
7

Though always under the threat of attack, Drip had never actually been in the middle of a combat engagement. This made sense since his home was set ten miles inside the borders, and situated along the major artery of the dark empire. These facts gave Drip little comfort as he stared at the large arrow that had grazed him. His finger traced over the arrow, noting its amazing quality.

"Okay, didn't see that coming," Boot said.

The phrase caused Drip to take a moment and look down at the enchanted item. His forehead scrunched in confusion as he wriggled his toes, causing Boot to move.

"How is it that you see anything?" Drip asked.

"Is that really important right now, while a battle is raging on around you?" Boot replied.

"Fair enough," Drip said. Then, with the speed and agility he had demonstrated previously, he began to navigate the battleground. He visually plotted a course directly through the battle line, to a hill with a view of the situation.

"Are we really running into combat?" Boot asked.

"It is the best way to get to safety," Drip replied.

He slid under a dark Cavalryman and jumped over a couple of wounded soldiers. He paused for a moment to catch his breath.

"Duck!" Boot shouted. Drip lowered his head at the command; this was just as a sword took a swipe at his head.

"Thanks," Drip said as he started to move again.

"Thank me after we are through this madness," Boot said.

Reinvigorated at the near death experience, Drip began to run. His stature was a benefit as he dodged certain death time and again. Finally he found himself standing atop a hill overlooking the battle.

"Boy I am glad we are out of that," Drip said as he sat down.

"I think we should keep moving," Boot suggested.

"Pattern, concern, concentrating..." Bean added as he bounced excitedly.

"What's that you're going on about?" Boot asked.

"I see it too," Drip said.

"See what?" Boot demanded.

"There is a pattern to the battle, a purpose in every forward action," Drip said.

"Are you sure? I only see chaos," Boot said.

"Hold on, let me show you," Drip said.

He removed his paper and pencil, his eyes never drifting from the conflict raging on. Drip started by drawing out a map of the overall area, and then noting large units as a block. The larger the unit, the larger the block. In a matter of moments, he had captured the overall theme of the battle.

"See, here is where the light units are advancing, and here are where the dark units are trying to defend," Drip explained.

"I can kind of see what you are talking about, but why are the dark units losing so badly?" Boot asked.

"That is the brilliant part: they are emulating the movement of the ocean," Drip said as a smile crossed his face.

"How could you stop something like that?" Boot wondered aloud.

"There are a couple of ways that might work," Drip said.

Drip began to elaborate his counter attack on the paper in a series of diagrams. In that moment, Drip realized that amidst his odd talents he had an eye for strategy. This thought caused him to shudder uncomfortably for a moment. Then Bean began to bounce excitedly, but wasn't saying anything. Instead Bean began to start glowing again. Drip hadn't seen it happen before—though it had happened while he was trying to sleep—and he quickly placed his hand over Bean to keep it from turning into a beacon to the armies below. However, it was too late. A volley of arrows was already headed his way. He could see them approaching, but they seemed to slow as they got closer. Drip squeezed Bean harder, bracing for the impact, but it never came. The arrows sat frozen in the air just a foot away from him.

"Good show, Bean, I had no idea you could do that," Boot said.

Drip stood and touched one of the arrows. Another shiver raced down his spine. Then he noticed a different pattern forming in the lines of the advancing light army. Drip flipped his papers to a blank one and began to sketch out the new formation and advancing army.

What Drip did not know was that he was meticulously documenting the newest offense used by the light army, nicknamed the "Banner Smash" after its designer Captain Bruce. In the big picture, the dark armies would not be able to counter or even repel this attack if all went well.

Everything changed in an instant when time began to move forward again. The arrows missed their target as Drip was now standing several feet away from where he had last faced his mortality. An advanced scout for the dark army approached Drip from behind.

"You there! What are you doing?" the rider shouted.

Drip seemed oddly numb from the time shift. Unable to speak, he held up his hand with the paperwork of diagrams. The rider retrieved them and, after looking them over, his attention returned to Drip.

"Where did you get this!?" The rider shouted with much more urgency in his voice. After a moment of silence from Drip, the rider grew impatient and rode off.

"Are you okay?" Boot asked.

Then, without a word, Drip began to walk, as if in a trance of some sort. Drip was suffering from time dysplasia. This happens when someone shifts between two different speeds in time, and at least one part of the brain has not yet caught up with the current speed. Side effects of dysplasia are as follows: nausea, sleepiness, nervousness, change in vision (i.e. blindness, or change in colors), loss of taste, unreasonable fear of the color purple, constant smell of burnt tar, loss of short term memory, loss of muscle control, tendency to wander aimlessly, rambling, dyslexia, unusual alertness, unusual calmness, sharper vision, random loss of bodily functions, green spots, major déjà vu, and death.

Everything blurred for a time as Drip walked. During this time, Boot had offered threats like, "turn around this instant," and "where do you think you are going, I am talking to you." Nothing seemed to work, so Boot just went along for the ride, noting interesting things to keep himself occupied. After a while, he even gave up on that. Then, without explanation, Drip finally stopped.

"Where am I?" Drip asked.

"Great question, we have no idea," Boot replied.

"Giznats?" Drip said in confusion, as he stared at a sign beside the road.

"That doesn't sound right; that's an island off the Southern coast," Boot said. "Did you read that right?"

"I think so," Drip said. He looked around for the large tower that typically stood watch over a town like this.

"Hmm, that's odd," Boot said.

"That's what I'm thinking," Drip said with a puzzled look.

That was the moment they noticed a large burnt out building with several imps still throwing buckets of water at the smoldering ashes.

"Excuse me, Sir, what happened here?" Drip asked.

"Some nut job let a fire fairy out and it destroyed about a dozen towers in the area," an imp said.

"Nice," Boot said.

"Not now," Drip replied. "Please not now."

"I am eager to hear what the employment agency has to say this time," Boot said sarcastically.

Drip just glanced down at Boot with an irritated look. He decided to walk into town when, after only a few steps, he stumbled over a giant ogre. He looked around for answers and noticed a pile of weapons lying on the ground.

"Okay, I would like to see what you have for this one," Drip said.

"Yeah, I've got nothing for this," Boot said.

"What has happened here?" Drip asked a nearby goblin.

"Where have you been?" the goblin replied, "This village has been officially captured."

"What village is this again?" Boot asked.

"Did your boots just talk to me?" the goblin asked.

"Don't mind that, what village is this again?" Drip questioned.

"This is the village of Stanzig. At least for the moment it is," the goblin said. "Who knows what we'll be once those Light Side fools are done with us."

EPISODE 8

Drip carefully looked around at the village before him. Something wasn't adding up with the information he had been given. The giant ogre on the ground and the pile of weapons seemed to support the idea of the village being captured; however, the lack of Light Side troops preparing to defend the newly disputed territory did not sit well with him.

"Something is not right," Drip said.

"So I have some good news, and some bad news," Boot said.

"What's the good news?" Drip asked.

"I know exactly where we are, and it will not be very difficult to get home," Boot replied.

"That's great news," Drip said with a hint of excitement. "What's the bad news?"

"The burnt out tower back there is, or I should say was, Tower 16, the one I.E.A. told you to report to today," Boot said grimly.

"At least *that* wasn't my fault," Drip said.

"Duck, muck, stuck…" Bean added.

Without hesitation Drip ducked. At this point Drip was used to ducking anytime someone said the word duck. It was a good thing, too. A large bundle of newspapers just missed hitting him.

As the papers slid to a stop, a group of imps descended upon the pile to take the papers back to their employers. After the frenzy cleared, Drip picked up one of the remaining papers.

"Oh dear," Boot said.

"Eight Towers Destroyed by Fire Nymph, Released by Wanted Imp," Drip read aloud. "At least there isn't a picture."

"Turn to page two," Boot said.

Drip groaned as he flipped to the next page where a black and white drawing of him stared back from the paper, with his name printed clearly underneath.

Just then, a group of orcs looking over the paper turned to Drip.

"Are you Drip?" one of the orcs asked.

Drip took a cautious step back and looked at the ground so they couldn't see the terror in his eyes. "Um, I am Dallion Quimbie…" Drip started to say.

"… Haberdasher Nocks Drisbie Horlon Everton, aka, Drip?" the orc finished his sentence. The group of them started to move toward Drip.

"Ah, well you see, there has been sort of a mix up," Drip said as he backed away.

A goblin said, "Wait! Look at this picture."

Drip cringed at the comments as the orcs and goblins looked even closer at the drawing of him.

"Na, it can't be him, the imp in the picture is black and white," a goblin said.

"Well if you see this imp named Drip, let us know. There is a five hundred gold piece reward on his head," the orc said.

"Wow, five hundred gold pieces, huh?" Drip said nervously. With the average cost of a meal at ten bronze pieces, the cost of a dull sword at one silver, the royal treatment at the Dark Side river spa, which included three meals, time in the exclusive Karloki mud pit, and hand and foot service for one gold coin, and last but not least, a small castle with surrounding land for one hundred gold coins, it wasn't hard for Drip to figure out what kind of crowd would come looking for him with a bounty like that. Pretty much everyone.

Drip did not need a hint from Boot or Bean that it was time to leave this particular conversation. He promptly began to walk away. Drip made it about ten steps before the waterfall of trouble began.

"STOP THAT IMP! IT'S DRIP!" a familiar human voice shouted.

"Are you sure? He doesn't look like this picture?" a goblin asked.

Drip glanced back just in time to see the goblin turned into a pile of ash on the ground. His eyes drifted up to see none other than the pseudo-dark wizard, Dragin. Something seemed different, though, about his former employer. His rich red robe was coated in mud and ash. On top of that, he seemed a bit more angry than usual.

"You heard the man, kill the IMP!" an orc said, charging at Drip.

"Wow, I think you might not make it this time," Boot said.

With that, Drip made to run deeper into the village when he felt a snare wrap around his legs, causing him to fall. He managed to flip over and avoid the first sword swing.

"Thanks for the warning, Boot!" Drip said sarcastically.

Drip watched as the orc stabbed the sword downward in an attempt to impale him. However, Drip managed to scoot to the side just enough for the sword to sink into the ground right next to him. Unexpectedly, he watched the orc get thrown through the air in a bright flash.

"I said GET him, NOT KILL HIM!" Dragin yelled.

A confused look came across the faces of the assailants. In their years of combat experience, they had never been told to not kill someone. After a few awkward seconds, two goblins finally picked Drip up off the ground. Then, unexpectedly, the ground started to rumble. This fact seemed lost on Dragin who was slowly walking towards the captured imp, small bolts of electricity bouncing between his fingers.

"Dragin, I think this is just a big misunderstanding we will laugh over down the road," Drip said in an attempt to draw out the last few minutes of his life.

"Oh, I don't think so," Dragin said in an even darker tone than usual. "You have no idea what you have cost me. I am done as a dark wizard; I have been kicked out of the guild. My cousin, the Dark Prince, has officially disowned me. Your death will be slow and agonizing."

"You might want to look behind you," Boot said.

"I really can't at this point," Drip said, cringing at the massive lightning ball forming between the dark wizard's hands, who ironically seemed to have just upgraded from pseudo-dark wizard to an actual formidable magic user.

"I am talking to Dragin," Boot said.

Drip turned his head to the side and noticed the wave of orc platoons charging down the street towards them.

"Yeah, you might want to look behind you, Dragin," Drip said, clearing his throat.

"Do you take me for a fool?!" Dragin asked. It was clear that Dragin was preparing to unleash the built up power as he let his right foot step back and form a support.

The platoon of orcs did not care about the wizard or the spectacle he was creating. They were just after the Light Side forces that had captured the village.

"Charge!" the lead orc commander shouted.

The platoon crashed into Dragin just as he released the lightning ball. Drip watched as it seemed to drift harmlessly into the sky. He let a smile cross his face until he realized he was about to get trampled. The two goblins dropped Drip and ran for their lives, but Fortune smiled on Drip again as the orc sword still in the ground managed to cut the snare that had bound his feet.

"Well, I'll be," Boot said. "Run?"

"Escape, fate, hate…" Bean said.

"Right," Drip said. He climbed to his feet and began to run with the orcs, in an attempt to blend in. He looked back to see where Dragin was when he noticed that the orcs he had been running with were no longer standing around him, but were instead knocked out and scattered across the ground.

Drip looked up to see a large man wielding a massive axe. The large man looked him over with narrow eyes.

Instinctively Drip fell to the ground, and said, "Aaahhhh, I've been defeated."

"This is the dumbest thing I have ever seen you do, aside from burning down twelve towers," Boot said with a little chide.

"Hey," Drip said.

He let out a sigh of relief when the large man began to attack oncoming orcs. Drip began to move cautiously amongst the bodies of fallen Dark Side troops, and looked back again to see where Dragin could be.

"There he is! On top of the house on the left," Boot said.

The warning came too late as Dragin had already unleashed a large lightning bolt towards Drip, who managed to step out of the direct path of the ball of crackling energy, but not before it exploded, throwing him well away from the combat area.

"Holy snail snot," Boot said, "I think he has anger issues."

Drip prepared to respond to the statement but was interrupted by a unit of charging light cavalry. He dashed left and right as he dodged the horses, but dread overcame him as he looked up to see charging war elephants. That's when he noticed an elderly man standing next to him.

"Run?" Drip asked the old man.

With little time to respond, the old man simply shook his head. The two inched closer together and held onto each other for dear life.

What neither of them knew was that elephants, regardless of their war designation, were deeply afraid of only a few things, one of which was imps. So terrified of the imp in their path, the elephants gave the two a wide birth. After a moment, Drip and the old man each realized that the danger had passed and released their death grip on each other.

"Are you going to try and kill me now?" Drip asked.

"No," the old man answered. "My name is Gorath. I am a monk of Ormlu."

"I am Drip, of...well, the dark lands, I guess," Drip replied.

"Ahem..." Boot said. It was uncharacteristic for Boot to request an introduction, so this was new to Drip.

"Oh yeah, this is Boot and Bean," Drip said.

Gorath looked down at Boot closely before responding, "Ah ha, Boot! The Cursed Boot of Astankium to be precise! Brilliant!"

"That would be me," Boot said.

"You know about Boot?" Drip asked.

"Absolutely! Number two hundred and thirty-five of enchanted and cursed items," Gorath said.

"I am sorry to interrupt but we have pressing matters," Drip said. He pointed out the very powerful and very angry dark magic user.

Dragin decided not to use the ball of lightning this time. Rather, he wanted to ensure a death that the imp could not escape. He lifted his hands into the air and with it, pebbles, rocks, and boulders of every size rose into the air. In one swift motion, several tons of Wax was now flying toward the helpless human and imp.

EPISODE
9

Rain poured down on the skinny armored figure sitting atop an undersized and malnourished horse. The banner that adorned the flanks of the horse were unmistakable, the rider was a member of the Dark Scouts. Traditionally the scouts rode in pairs, and this time was no exception, save the fact that the companion to this particular scout was more than a mile ahead.

The Dark Scouts were by far the most prestigious unit fielded by the Dark Army, or they used to be. This was due in large part to the successful combination of highly rigorous testing and an unusually long life expectancy. Some of the requirements to be a member of the unit were: 20/15 eyesight, the ability to carry sixty-five pounds of equipment over twenty-five miles, a mastery of horses, the ability to understand and speak multiple languages and accents, and a mastery of weapons. However, due to the Great Scout Tragedy of Ameron Ridge, where the best half of the scouts were killed by lightning while posing for a canvas portrait, the scouts were now recruiting without testing. A brilliant decision was made to pair up existing scouts with raw recruits.

Thomas Twostead was not amused by the fact that her companion was nowhere in sight, and that the rain was making life cold and miserable. Nothing about Thomas or her upbringing was amusing. She was the youngest of twelve, and was named Thomas because of a prophetic wizard's bold prediction that her parents would have a twelfth child named Thomas who would accomplish great things. Even after she had been born a girl, the expectation of greatness, and therefore the name, stuck.

"Come on, Grendle, lets pick it up a little," Thomas said to the horse.

The horse promptly responded with a couple of quick steps and a neigh. Unimpressed by the very brief show of energy, Thomas reached into a sack hanging from the saddle and pulled out a sad looking apple. She leaned forward and ran her hand down the mane of the horse as she had done countless times before to the horses on the farm she grew up on.

"I will make you a deal," Thomas said, "I will give you this apple if you pick up the pace just a little."

Grendle responded by twisting her neck back enough for Thomas to give her the apple. Without hesitation the horse began to pick up speed. Thomas let out a sigh knowing that she had given away her lunch.

"The provisions seem to be a tad inadequate, or else I would offer you more," Thomas said.

Despite the fact that Grendle was underfed, she was still the product of two of the greatest war horses ever seen in combat, but was often dismissed due to her lack in size. It was interesting how horse and rider seemed to have so much in common. However, Grendle elected to hold her head high in response to the comment, and started to prance just a little in mocking of the other horses in the service of the Dark Scouts.

Unexpectedly, the pair finally stumbled upon their counterparts, albeit in a less than ideal state. Several arrows were protruding from the other scout. It was clear that the rider had just recently died. Thomas dismounted and searched the body for clues. She pulled an unusual paper from his messenger pouch. Instantly she recognized what she was holding, and had no idea how the scout could have come across the enemy's battle plan. As the rain stopped, the sounds of battle nearby reached her ears.

"Okay, this is our chance to prove ourselves," Thomas said. In one motion, she mounted the horse and flicked the reigns motioning for a full gallop.

Thoughts raced through her mind of how important the document would be to fending off the Light Side troops. It didn't take long for her to find the Field Commander's camp overlooking the battlefield. Understanding that her position as peon in the scouts would not grant her access to the commander himself, she stopped at the first set of guards.

"This is a vital document for the commander, from the field," Thomas reported.

"Who should I say is presenting these documents?" the guard asked.

Self-conscious of the fact that she was a young woman of barely twenty years, she decided to mask her voice. "Thomas. Thomas Twostead of the Dark Scouts."

The guard took the paper and raced back into the ranks of the camp. It didn't take long before a higher ranking Dark Scout emerged.

"Follow me. Given this new information, we need to attack the other side of that ridge," the man said to Thomas.

Once they arrived over the ridge with the new battle plans, it was only a matter of an hour or so before the complete surrender of the remains of the light army offensive force.

"I salute your attack on the support units! We could have pushed them back without you, but you saved us some time. How did you know where to strike them?" the Field Commander later asked the Captain of the Dark Scouts.

Captain Markus Lious was completely confused as he had thought that it was the Field Commander's plans that had given the direction. "Sir, what do you mean?"

"Do you not know?" the Field Commander wondered curiously, as he handed the paper to Markus.

It only took a moment to scan the combat report, and then Markus called out to the troops standing at attention nearby, and held the piece of paper up. "Who wrote this report!?"

Everyone looked confused at the request. All the educated leaders in the group looked around at each other. Unsure if it was a good thing or a bad thing, no one was willing to do the typical "take credit before anyone else does" move.

Ignoring her common sense, Thomas Twostead stepped forward and raised her hand.

The Captain of the Dark Scouts simply raised his eyebrow at the thought that this underling would have the gall to take credit for something clearly above her abilities. He responded by raising his hand and summoning Thomas forward. Quickly, murmurs of doubt spread throughout the group.

"You wrote this report?" Markus asked while he examined the gangly human soldier standing before him. As Thomas was attempting to gather her response, it was easy for the Captain to see that this was a poor recruit from the outer edge of the dark territories. Her long-outdated, oversized armor displayed a multitude of battle scars gained by her father long before her birth. In the corner of the breastplate it displayed a severely diminished symbol boasting a once-proud and powerful clan. What the Captain didn't see was the matching sword hanging at Thomas's side, which was covered by her overlong messy tunic hanging down over it.

"Yes, Sir," Thomas finally squeaked out. In instant response, the surrounding group erupted in laughter.

"May I see your sword?" asked the Captain.

"No, Sir," Thomas answered, now trembling a little in fear. She was not trying to be defiant or brave; she was merely stating a fact, one that she had no control over. Her sword could not be drawn unless her life was threatened. Powerful runes etched into the blade upon its birth, restricted the sword from any other use.

"What was that, scout!?" Markus replied. He offered up his most intimidating glare and slowly raised his right hand, a dark purple flame dancing on his palm.

Everyone in the circle took one collective step back from Thomas. This was the point at which they had seen many, many, many men, and creatures perish. It was unfortunate that no one had realized yet that Thomas was a woman. Without hesitation, the Captain released the powerful fireball.

Thomas had already been frozen in her tracks from the sight of the gathering magic. Few thoughts passed through her mind as the fireball seemed to glide in slow motion toward her head. She realized that her recent actions might have been more about proving herself to her family than any glory, and that was a really sad last thought to have before being horribly incinerated.

Then, prompted by sudden instinct, her right hand pulled the sword from its sheath and raised it in the path of the fireball, cutting it in two.

This action now had a captive audience, leaving everyone in silent awe. The Captain himself was even impressed, but this amusement needed to be put to an end, and he now wanted the sword for himself. He gave his ceremonial nod to the rest of the circle for them to attack.

As numerous bows simultaneously released their arrows directly at her, Thomas thought she was dead for sure, but this time her last thought was in wondering how she had cut the fireball in half in the first place.

I mean, it's just magic flying fire, there really shouldn't be anything to 'cut' in two, she was busy thinking when the sword flew into action again, but just as the Captain planned, one arrow got through the amazing sword's defense.

Confident that with an arrow sticking out of the center of the scout's chest, it was now safe to retrieve the sword, the Captain took one step towards Thomas when he noticed something even more interesting. The arrow that had stuck her continued to slowly move through her until it exited her chest, where it left no wound. Thomas was still very much alive. On that note, Markus took one step backwards very quickly, just in case this was a trick or an assassination attempt. Without a word, he continued to walk backwards until he was what he felt was a safe distance from the human, a good thirty feet or so, and then sharply turned and walked back towards his command tent with great haste. Following their Captain's lead, everyone else seemed to wander away in a similar manner.

Thomas was left alone with her thoughts. She carefully gathered herself from the ground and attempted to rethink everything that had ever happened to her, and as she had suspected, could not recall an instance like the one that had just passed.

"Twostead!" a scout shouted from a distance of fifteen feet or so.

"Here!" she replied.

"Is it okay to approach?" the scout asked.

"Yes," Thomas replied, recognizing that everything would be different for her from that moment on. The trouble was she could not figure out if it was good or bad.

"Congratulations, Twostead, you have been promoted to Senior Field Scout, and have been put in charge of a platoon of trolls to go track down any straggling Light Side units," the scout said, handing her a paper. "Yeah, good luck with that," he added sarcastically.

"Thanks?" she replied. It seemed more like a punishment than an actual promotion. It was at that moment that she decided things were going to be different for the worse.

EPISODE 10

Time seemed to blur since Thomas had first read the paper with her promotion. Everything about it seemed a little surrealistic, and quite frankly rushed. As she looked over the letter for what seemed like the hundredth time, she stopped and read the section where she was to meet her new command, and tried to comprehend what she was reading.

> By the Decree of both Field Commander Garret Trumble and Dark Scout Commander Markus Louis, Thomas Twostead of the border farmland of Reighland is hereby promoted to the rank of Senior Field Scout of the Dark Scouts. Under this newly promoted rank, we are appointing her with a field commendation of First Lieutenant in the regular army, and placing her in command of Fifth Platoon of Echo Company of the sixty-seventh division, currently based near Hobbs Hill. Thomas is then charged with utilizing the platoon of trolls to track down and eliminate Light Side forces, until completed or reassigned.

The decree, commission, and order took up less than a quarter of the page. Despite her mixed feelings of elation, terror, and shock, she had pulled it together to get to her destination. Thomas guided her horse, Grendle, through the mixed ranks until she arrived at the flag that designated her unit.

"Private, what is your name?" she asked the lone troll standing next to the flag. She looked him over and couldn't help but notice that he stood about fifteen feet tall. She nodded her head in satisfaction. Thomas knew that if the average height of the platoon was fifteen feet, then things would be looking up, both literally and figuratively.

"Sir, I am Private…um, Private…ah, I know this one," the troll said. "They told me this would happen."

"Don't worry about it. Who is in charge here?" Thomas asked. A feeling of dread started to creep into her thoughts.

"Yes Sir, that would be Sergeant…um, Sergeant…ah, I know this one for sure," the troll replied. "Come on now, think."

"Okay, how about this, *where* is your sergeant?" Thomas asked, hopeful that there was an actual answer.

"Yes, Sir! I know this one, Sir!" the troll blurted out in excitement. He danced as a child might on Christmas morning. This caused the ground to tremble quite a bit, but to her credit, Grendle remained calm. However, Thomas was slightly panicked as the force caused her to nearly slide off her saddle.

"And?" Thomas asked.

"And, Sir?" the troll asked.

"I want to see your sergeant at once," Thomas said with as much authority as she could muster in her frazzled state.

The troll gave a salute as sharp as he could, and raced off.

Thomas leaned forward and traced her hand down the side of Grendle's mane and gave her a quick pat. She reflected on the words of her father for comfort.

"No matter how good you are, what the situation is, or how many you have with you, you are always overmatched when dealing with trolls in any fashion. Despite this fact, trolls will always respect you if you screw your courage to the sticking place and never let them see fear in your eyes."

He would go on to talk about the best way to attack a troll, and the various weak spots that could give someone the advantage in a fight. Thomas quickly disregarded that part as the advice was actually being given to two of her brothers back when the farm sat on the Light Side of the world. It was ironic that she remembered his lessons, especially since not a single one was offered to her other than, "Don't screw this up," which were his departing words to her just before she left the family farm a few weeks before, the last living child in the Twostead line.

Thomas straightened in her saddle and turned Grendle to face the approaching troll. She was confident that she had used the time wisely to gather her confidence, but was a little deflated when she noticed that only one troll was approaching. Thomas started to rethink her prepared speech, when she noticed that there was a small creature riding on the shoulder of the troll.

"STOP!" a voice shouted. The troll stopped just a few feet from Thomas.

"Sir, this is Sergeant Armored Davis," the troll announced.

"At your request, Sir!" the small figure said while offering what looked like a salute.

"Sergeant, I am your new field commander, Thomas Twostead," she said in an official voice.

"Very good, Field Commander Twostead, what is your order?" Sergeant Armored Davis asked. Upon closer examination, Thomas could tell that the man, or creature, riding atop the troll stood about two–and-a-half feet tall, and as named, was covered head to toe in armor.

"Gather the platoon; we are to move out immediately!" Thomas said in a very commanding voice.

"Very good, Sir!" Davis said, then turned to the troll. "Alright then, let's get movin' to the rest of the boys!"

Thomas took a second for herself as she watched the troll run away from her, carrying the small being on his back. A shiver ran down her spine as she realized how comfortable she was giving orders. Then again, she had given plenty in the heat of combat.

As the clear sound and rumble of trolls approaching reached her ears, Thomas straightened, and once again she started to rethink her next phrase, when she noticed only three trolls advancing. Even Grendle seemed disappointed at the size of this platoon, and expressed it with a quick head shake.

"Davis, is this the whole platoon?" Thomas asked. She was thankful at this point that her face was obscured by the helmet's faceplate, as it would have given away her true emotions.

"Oh, sorry, Sir," Davis said. He turned and let out a loud and very distinct whistle. Then two dozen more trolls advanced to their position.

Once again, Thomas was glad that the faceplate obscured her expression; however, Grendle's expression was enough for both of them. The platoon of heavily armored trolls looked invincible, and their average height was about twenty-five feet tall. Thomas took a deep breath and walked Grendle out in front of them.

"Platoon, I am your new field commander, Twostead. We have been charged with marching toward the border and looking for any Light Side units that are retreating," Thomas said confidently. She turned to look them in the eyes and noticed that there was nothing more than confusion.

"Davis, do they understand?" she asked.

"Ah," Davis said as the trolls suddenly seemed agitated. "Sir, may we talk in private for a moment?"

"Very well," Thomas replied. She guided Grendle over to the short creature.

"Permission to speak freely?" Davis asked. It was interesting that he would make the request as few commanders tolerated their soldiers enough to listen to what they had to say, which of course had led to about a million deaths over the years. This particular instance was full of interesting ironies, as speaking in "private" required the troll that Davis was hitching a ride on to kneel down and look away.

"Go ahead," Thomas said.

"With all due respect, Field Commander Twostead, you might want to watch what you say in front of the troops," Davis said in a soft tone. "They don't seem to understand a lot of things, but they definitely understand when they are being insulted."

"I didn't mean to insult them. Can you translate for me?" Thomas asked.

"Absolutely, Sir, you can count on me, and I won't let them know that you are a woman," Davis said.

"What does that have to do with anything?" she quickly responded.

"No disrespect, but things get complicated with trolls when they think about gender issues," Davis replied.

"One last thing, Davis. What happened to the platoon's last field commander?" Thomas asked.

"Ah, yes, well you see, he was trampled to death during maneuvers, but in all fairness, it was miscommunication by the field commander. We didn't even realize he was gone for two days. But don't worry, it's only happened three times," Davis said. "Anything else, Sir?"

A lump formed in her throat before she replied, "Just relay my speech, and that will be all."

"Very good, Sir," Davis said. He tapped the troll on the shoulder, alerting him that it was time to stand up again.

As Armored Davis began to relay the information, Thomas started thinking of the best way not to get smashed by a giant troll foot. Interestingly enough, Grendle was thinking the same thing, as she took one good side step away from the trolls. Thomas waited only a moment longer before Davis finished the translation.

"Let's move out!" Thomas ordered. With that, the ground began to tremble as the platoon moved. Thomas was grateful for Grendle's ability to act as a shock absorber.

As they marched for the border, Thomas pulled a map from her satchel and began to figure out what path retreating forces might take. It was rare to actually catch the enemy running away, because almost all of the battles happened right at the border. After reviewing the different paths, she set her mind on an obscure road that ran past the insignificant village of Stanzig.

"Okay, now to show them what I can do in real combat. I only wish I had regular armor," Thomas said to Grendle.

In response, the horse let out a clear mocking laugh.

"And what is that supposed to mean?" Thomas retorted. "You don't think I could fight without this enchanted stuff?"

Grendle responded with a quick prance and a shake of the head. This caused Thomas to become irritated.

"Look, I didn't ask for this, alright? No one told me that when an elder sibling is killed or severely maimed, this armor seeks out the next oldest sibling," Thomas said. "I worked hard for everything I have, and to be honest, this armor has crushed everything I've tried to build of myself, and if I could take it off permanently, I would."

With that, Thomas let out a sigh, as talking about her circumstances tended to bring a little frustration. She tried to focus on the positive. After all, she had learned how to sword fight and figure out tactics with the help of her best friend, whom she could never see again because he was clearly on the Light Side now.

Well, that hadn't cheered her up at all.

"Enemy in sight!" shouted Davis, shaking Thomas from her train of thought.

Thomas pulled out her spyglass and figured out the distance of the retreating troops. It was as she had hoped. Their pace was slow after suffering a defeat, and at just under a mile away, they were within striking distance. Thomas wanted more than anything to show everyone that she was equal to the task at hand, and decided to order the attack.

"Platoon, ATTACK!" she commanded.

EPISODE
11

Without hesitation or translation, the trolls advanced, their long strides giving them impressive speed. Unable to draw her sword, Thomas grabbed the platoon standard, which sported a design she could not quite decipher, though it may have been a decapitated head, and charged forward. Grendle reached her full gallop and began to outpace the advancing trolls. Thomas rarely had the opportunity to enjoy a full gallop, with the wind rushing past her face plate and stroking her cheeks. Unbeknownst to Thomas, the wind rushing was also causing her long, dirty, blonde hair to flow out of the back of her helmet.

"Come on boys, keep going!" Davis could be heard shouting into the wind.

"Woohoo!" Thomas shouted. The excitement ran through her like lightning as she neared the end of the retreating Light Side units. Thomas was pleased that the light units were not organized enough to mount a proper defense on their rear. Just a handful of men had turned to face her and her platoon. However, as she neared the ragged defense, she noticed that something was missing. There was a definite lack of terror in their eyes at the advancing platoon. Regardless, her speed and distance determined that there was no turning back. She lowered the standard to be used as a spear. She chose that moment to glance back and reference her unit's position to avoid being crushed. That's when she noticed that her unit was no longer behind her. Thomas looked forward just in time to strike one soldier square in the upper chest, not enough to kill him, but causing him to fall back. She let Grendle's momentum plow through the small crowd of men, pushing them left and right.

Distraught at the fact that her platoon was not where she was, Thomas directed Grendle to retreat back the way she had come. Unscathed, Thomas and Grendle raced over the last little ridge back to her men. She shook her head at the sight of the whole platoon of trolls walking and panting.

"You can't even run a mile?" Thomas asked in an irritated tone.

"Kind of, Sir," Davis replied.

"Why didn't you say anything when I ordered the attack?" Thomas asked.

"I thought that the boys would be able to make it; it was pretty much all downhill, and all."

"Okay, they are just over that ridge. Do you think they can handle that?"

"Yes, Sir," Davis said.

"This time, try to keep up with the girls," Thomas said in a mumble. She raised the slightly dented standard and pointed it in the direction of the light forces. "Charge!" she shouted.

Grendle was displaying her heritage once more as she charged fearlessly at the enemy. Thomas lowered the standard again to use as a spear. This time, as she approached the enemy, fear could clearly be seen on the faces of the men before her. She lined up the standard for the first soldier's chest, when she realized that it was the exact same guy she had struck previously. The makeshift spear connected with the soldier for the second time;

however, this time it would catch him in the gut. Ironically, again not enough to kill him, but enough to knock the wind out of him.

As she had hoped, plunged into the thick of battle, her sword let itself be drawn this time around. Grendle had knocked six men to the ground. Instinctively, Thomas dismounted and engaged the soldiers. The fighting was getting fierce, but it didn't take long before she had cleared a circle. Then she paused a moment when she realized that again no trolls were participating in the battle. Thomas could see the trolls standing about a hundred feet from the fight.

"Armored Davis, get them in here now! That is an order!" Thomas shouted. It seemed an eternity before the trolls started to move. She glanced over at them in-between the sword play she was starting to enjoy.

The troll carrying Armored Davis was approaching first, but as it reached about fifteen feet from the fight, the troll tripped and began to tumble towards Thomas. It was at this moment that Thomas reflected on an important fact. Even though Thomas did not know how her brothers had died, she knew that it had been while wearing the enchanted armor and carrying the sword. She had imagined different ways that might not be protected under the enchantment, but being crushed by a tumbling troll was not on her original list. In this case, she figured that she would rather be safe than sorry, and penciled it in as a strong possibility.

Regardless of affiliation, friend and foe ran side by side away from certain doom. After about ten steps, Thomas realized that she was never going to outrun the sprawling troll, and had one possible exit come to mind. In full stride, Thomas sheathed the sword and dove to the side into a very shallow ditch. Instinctively she placed her hands over her head to protect it. It only took a moment before the rumbling came and went. Thomas took an extra moment getting to her feet as she was covered in a layer of dirt. It was clear that the troll had wiped out the entire retreating convoy with the one action.

"Are you alright, Ma'am?" Davis asked.

"I think so." Thomas began to dust herself off. "Huh, you called me 'Ma'am'. Aren't you worried about the trolls?"

"Not any more. According to my calculation, the retreating light forces are out of commission, and this concludes your field command over this platoon," Davis said. "It is impressive really; you are the first field commander to complete a mission with the trolls, and live."

"I will take it," Thomas said. "How did you know that my commission ended with the completion of this mission?"

"We all have our orders," Armored Davis said. "Good luck on your next mission."

"Thanks, I don't suppose you know where I am supposed to go next?" Thomas asked.

"No, Ma'am, Command did not think you would live through this one to bother with a follow-up mission. I'm glad you did though; there is something different about you."

"I appreciate that, I think," Thomas replied. "I'll see you around."

With that, Armored Davis started his long walk to the troll that had given him a ride. Thomas let out a unique whistle and, through the dust, Grendle appeared. Thomas was both surprised and elated that the horse had made it through the violent action. Grendle gave Thomas a nudge to get her moving. Thomas in return raced her hand down Grendle's neck and quickly remounted the horse.

"Well, we definitely earned our keep today," Thomas said to the horse.

Grendle just let out a long sigh.

"Let's get us some grub and go get cleaned up," Thomas said. Grendle nodded approvingly. With that, Thomas flicked the reigns and clicked her tongue a couple of times, indicating the deSire for a light trot.

It wasn't long before they were near the town of Stanzig, and Thomas noticed a bright burning symbol above the village indicating that it was in the process of being captured.

"Come on, let's get this over with," she said. Grendle responded with a quick trot.

As she approached, she noticed the burning tower that would normally overlook and defend the town. She concluded that there had to be a large force involved. As she reached the top of a nearby hill, she removed her spyglass to assess the situation.

"That's odd, the amount of damage does not seem proportionate to the number of troops; there is only a handful of them," Thomas said out loud. "One thing is certain, there is no use attacking from the front or the flanks, they have those locked down pretty good."

Grendle began to get jittery for combat. It didn't take long before the horse resorted to pacing back and forth to get Thomas to do something different.

"Alright, we need to attack from the rear, right now," Thomas said. She flipped the reigns and shouted, "Heeya!"

Grendle took off racing, leaving whole units in a cloud of dust. Thomas began to panic a little as this was the first time she realized that she did not have her sword available yet, despite nearing combat. As she approached the rear, she could see a very powerful man casting some sort of spell against two harmless looking creatures.

"It looks like we have to do this the hard way." Thomas said.

As Thomas watched, the wizard motioned upward, causing big and small chunks of Wax to begin to levitate. Thomas decided to do the sensible thing and attack the wizard. It was only a moment before her boot met the back of the wizard's head. Satisfied that the wizard no longer posed an immediate threat, she walked over to the two defenders.

"I am Field Commander Thomas Twostead. Who are you and what are you doing out here?" Thomas asked.

"I am Gorath, and this is Drip and Boot," Gorath said.

At that very moment, the whole planet seemed to shudder. Unbeknownst to the trio, the planet shuddered because even it knew that nothing would be the same after this moment.

EPISODE
12

A wave of nausea passed over Orielia as she crossed the threshold into Ormlu. Unexpectedly, she felt herself being pushed back, like someone was physically resisting her entry. After a moment, Orielia slid backwards until she was again outside the city limit.

"What's wrong?" Mussashi asked. He was letting his frustration begin to show, as he had only thirty minutes to get the witch to the middle of the Candlestick.

"I'm not sure," Orielia said. Then as if the clouds in her brain parted for just a moment, she looked the monk straight in the eyes, and asked, "Do you have the authority to declare me the Witch of Ormlu?"

"What? Right now?" Mussashi asked. He was clearly confused at the question.

"Yes, I will not enter the city until I have been declared as much," Orielia said. Even she did not know why she was demanding this right at this moment, but she was certain that this was the right thing to do.

"Very well," Mussashi said, "by the power and right of the Monk Order, and by the commission given by the High Monk, I declare you the Witch of Ormlu."

To this very day, Mussashi would be unable to fully explain what happened right after his declaration. Everything in a large fifty-yard radius, including him, was knocked down by a gust of wind, and lightning began to strike the ground around Orielia. Then she was levitated off the ground and a beam of sunlight focused on her so bright that Mussashi couldn't look directly at her. A moment later, he found himself upright and everything seemed to be as it was before he had said anything. Except that Orielia seemed a little taller, her skin glowed, and her hair had become soft curls instead of the matted mess it had been.

"Alright, I am ready," Orielia said, and even her voice seemed softer.

"Right this way," Mussashi said.

This time as she entered the city, loud thunder could be heard for several miles. Mussashi ignored this fact as his time table seemed to be more pressing than sound effects. What he was also ignoring or seemed to be ignorant of was the fact that everyone stopped and watched as they walked past, heading for the Candlestick.

After about fifteen minutes of fast pace walking and ten minutes of expedited transports up the tower, the two emerged next to the grand staircase with the moving walls.

"Wait here a moment, I need to talk with the head monk," Mussashi said. He rushed through the large doors leading to the library.

Orielia walked over to the ornate stairs and began to watch the moving walls. As things played out, images flashed before her eyes. Instinctively, she reached out and touched the wall. This action seemed to send a bolt of electricity through her.

"Our sister has returned," a ghostly apparition said.

"How has she returned?" another apparition asked.

"No matter. Let us rejoice," the first apparition replied.

"Let us see if she is strong enough to earn this," the second said with irritation in her voice.

Firmly, the first said, "Not yet."

"Master Head Monk Towe," Mussashi said upon entering the library.

"Ah, Mussashi, what a sight for sore eyes, tell me you have good news," Towe said.

"Yes Sir, I have the Witch of Ormlu just outside. Are you ready to proceed?" Mussashi asked.

"Yes everyone is in the Great Hall. Let us go forth," Towe said.

As the two men exited the room, an unusual chilling breeze passed by them. Once back out by the grand staircase, Mussashi held out his hand to identify the Witch of Ormlu.

"Ma'am, we are ready for you," Towe said.

Orielia nodded her head gracefully. She glanced around the chamber before moving, looking for the two apparitions that had been standing there just a moment before. She cautiously followed the two men into the Great Hall.

"May I present the Witch of Ormlu," Towe announced to the room.

The roughly eighty representatives all paused at the announcement, all sitting around a very long rectangular table, each affiliation clearly marked by one half in pure black obsidian, and the other in pure white marble. The lesser influential and classed were furthest from the center of the table. The King and Dark Prince were easy for Orielia to make out with their elaborate outfits, and extra lavish attendants. At the very center of the table, hovering about six feet in the air was an orb, half that looked like a burning sun, and the other half a cold dark moon.

"What is the meaning of this?" King Timothy Ragmon asked.

"Why have we never heard of a Witch of Ormlu?" Dark Lord Gordon B. Twiller chimed in.

"Your highnesses, I beg your forgiveness and the late notice of this addition to our agenda, but this is called for by the *Master Book of Magic*, so if you would please indulge us," Towe said.

The two leaders quickly retook their seats as a couple advisors started whispering amongst themselves. A moment later, several monks were summoned over to the table to help the advisors understand what was about to happen.

"The Witch of Ormlu will now grant unto each leader the opportunity to see how their rule will come to an end," Towe said.

Orielia was uncertain on how she was to accomplish the new and surprising task at hand, but before she had a chance to ask, something came over her. The room became dark and cold, and a wind began to circle around the table of aristocrats. Orielia found herself floating into the middle of the group. Lightning streaked through the room until it created a portal on the wall.

"Everyone's lives are intertwined and interconnected, and yours are no different. You will both die in battle against the same foe; the party will consist of a scholar, a heroine, and a poet," Orielia said. As she spoke, three silhouettes appeared in the portal. "You will be defeated on the field of fallen champions, by the champions risen from a new kingdom."

She paused a moment as the scene changed to a picture of a battlefield, where the two leaders lay lifeless. Thunder rumbled through the room.

"There will be four chances and only four chances for you to delay your deaths by twenty years, by killing the three. However, be warned, each chance you take and fail to kill the three, you will speed up your demise by one year. One last thing before I show you the three. If you attempt to kill or disband the three outside the four chances given, you will die within one day," Orielia said.

"How will we know when the four chances are?!" shouted King Timothy.

"Silence!" Orielia called back.

"Oh great Witch of Ormlu, how might we know when the four chances happen?" the Dark Lord Twiller asked more cautiously, very careful on his wording after seeing the reaction to his Light Side counterpart.

"You will know because the sky above the Candlestick will be blood red during each chance, and it will remain red for one week," Orielia proclaimed. "And now here are the three."

The portal switched back to the three silhouettes, which it now illuminated to reveal their faces. At that moment, the whole of Wax shook with the decree.

―

The combat had been so fast that by the time the three wandered back into Stanzig it was a ghost town littered with dead and wounded from both sides. As the three walked down the main road through town, Gorath had hoped to spot someone from his group but failed to recognize anyone. As they approached the front gate, a lone orc stood.

"You have captured this town and defended it, for what kingdom do you fight?" the Orc said to Gorath.

"Wait, you are the one who captured this town?" Thomas asked suspiciously. "I am sworn to defend the Dark Side from the light."

"Wait a second, this is all a misunderstanding. I don't represent the Light Side, I am neutral," Gorath said. "I need to get back to Ormlu."

"Well good luck with that," Thomas said.

Gorath nodded and took a couple of steps in the direction of Ormlu when the familiar grumbling sound of trolls in the distance startled him. He stopped and turned back to the other two.

"I don't suppose either of you are headed to Ormlu?" Gorath said with a chuckle. "I can pay."

"I am actually headed that way," Drip replied.

"I guess it is safer in the city than out here where everyone wants you dead," Boot added.

"High command isn't far from there. We can escort you as far as Ormlu, if you are talking twenty-five silver," Thomas added. The price was now being dictated by her stomach, and her knowledge of how Grendle was doing.

"Alright, fair enough, twenty-five silver to both of you," Gorath promised. He knew that the price was extremely steep, but the city would have to honor the price an official monk had agreed upon.

As the three began to walk, they all shared an odd feeling that people were watching them, lots of people. What none of them knew was that the *Master Book of Magic* was busy with recent events, and it would take some time before anyone would read the ten new pages of laws and bylaws that would pave the way for things to come. The most important was the very last line on the tenth page which clearly stated, "... the completion of these things will result in the destruction of the *Master Book of Magic*, all its rules, and all things bound by the magic written within."

EPISODE
13

The large body of assembled delegates could clearly see Thomas, Gorath, and Drip walking together in the large portal. The news of the leaders' deaths delighted some delegates and horrified others. Those closest to the royal seats did a great job of showing no emotion whatsoever. Everyone was in a flurry of discussion, even across the table from each other; never had the two sides been so socially agreeably. Speculations flew through the room like a soft spring breeze scattering leafs.

No one noticed that Orielia had slowly drifted back to the ground. She was confounded by everything that she had said and done, and felt physically weak from the event. A headache rushed over her, and she quietly excused herself back out into the hallway. She let her eyes stay shut to mitigate the pain as she rested her aching body in a large chair.

"She is weak," a ghostly voice returned.

"Yes, but she has fulfilled the prophecy. The three will assemble in the city," the second ghostly voice replied.

"The fools in there need to send them on quests or they will flounder," the first voice said.

"And what quest should they attend to?" the second voice chimed in.

"Argentauth," the word slipped out between Orielia's lips.

"Of course! Its brilliant!" the second ghostly voice agreed.

———

Head Monk Towe stood speechless next to his friend Monk Mussashi, who also had no idea what to say. In the clamor of the room, they stepped back into a corner.

"No one in the monk order has ever taken sides. This jeopardizes everything," Mussashi said to Towe.

"Not necessarily. In the vision both leaders are slain, so he does not take a side," Towe replied. "We must get in the graces of the two leaders and consolidate our position to gain leverage."

"What do you mean?" Mussashi asked in a confused tone.

"Hold on a second, you will see," Towe said with an eerie grin on his face. He summoned the two leaders' monk assistants over to him.

"Yes, Head Monk?" the two asked in unison.

"I need you to inform both leaders that the monks stand ready to assist them in this matter, and can offer special assistance since one of the three assassins is in fact a monk," Towe said. "However, special cooperation will require special compensation. Now go."

The two monk assistants quickly wandered back over to their delegates and delivered the head monk's message. In no time at all, the assistants returned to inform the head monk that he had the ear of the two leaders.

Thomas was pleased knowing that she had made a deal that would ensure food for her and Grendle. However, the thought was making her stomach rumble, and she could feel the horse's stomach growling along with hers. She looked down at her two temporary companions and was, for the most part, ignoring the rambling conversation taking place.

"Don't worry, Grendle, soon we will have plenty of food," Thomas said.

"What was that?" Drip asked.

"Nothing, just looking forward to food," Thomas replied.

"Oh, okay," Drip said. His eyes drifted back to the dim horizon and he let himself get lost in his thoughts, as he too was ignoring the rambling conversation taking place.

"That's fascinating," Gorath said. "Then what happened?"

"Well, Deson was essentially stuck in the mud, and unable to get his foot free or slip his foot out of the boots. He was trapped, and it wasn't long before a large war wagon came through and ran him over on accident," Boot said. "After a few centuries, Drip here was brought into existence in the right place and time, and here we are."

"I don't know that I would call it the right place, after narrowly escaping certain death, no thanks to you," Drip added.

"I see, still bitter at the whole 'I don't think you're going to make it' comment, eh?" Boot asked.

"It didn't help that you literally didn't help, thank you very much," Drip answered.

"So what has it been like being attached to an imp like Drip?" Gorath asked in fascination.

"It has been as pleasant as you can imagine," Boot said.

"That is a fine looking horse," Drip said to Thomas, in hopes of avoiding Gorath and Boot's conversation once more. But, since he was still rather annoyed, upon seeing a rather large rock along the path, Drip promptly kicked it.

"Ouch!" Boot shouted.

"Oops, that was an accident," Drip said.

"You can feel pain?" Gorath asked.

"It's complicated," Boot replied.

Thomas looked over at the two again, and shook her head. It was at that moment that the large fog they had been following parted and they found themselves just a short distance from the Candlestick.

"Okay, this is as far as I go. Where is my twenty-five silver?" Thomas asked.

"Ah about that," Gorath started.

"You better not have lied," Thomas quickly added.

"Oh, no, no, it's just that you have to come with me to the Candlestick, that is where the money is," Gorath said.

Drip let out a sigh but pointed ahead. "Lead on."

―

"They are entering the city," a voice in the back of the room said.

"Then we have come to a conclusion?" King Ragmon asked.

"Yes, we must send them on a quest to keep them together," Dark Lord Twiller replied. "Are the legal documents and treaties ready?"

"Yes, right here," Towe said, placing the papers before the two men.

"Now, what should their first quest be?" asked Ragmon, immediately after signing the pages.

"Perhaps something impossible, like put out the fire on the 'Ste Tomerick', or tame the giants of the Southern Plains?" Twiller suggested.

"I don't know that we want impossible. Maybe start with something long and drawn out, like seeding a thousand fields, or restoring one of the median checkpoints," Ragmon replied.

"Argentauth," Orielia's voice carried through the room with her sudden reappearance. "Naturally, the first thing that should be done is to slay that nasty dragon in the North that plagues both the light and the dark."

"Yes!" Ragmon said in unison with Twiller.

"I will draw up the paperwork, and have them questing first thing in the morning," Towe said.

An advisor to the two leaders set before them a large diagram of the massive dragon. It was by far the best picture of the beast, as no one who had ever been close to it lived to describe it. It stood fifty yards in height, by an outstretch reach of seventy-five yards wide, and from tip of the head to tail was seventy-five yards long. Besides the defining screech that could be heard for miles, it could breathe an impressive stream of fire.

Ragmon put his thumb on the table next to the picture and imagined it being the height of the group on average. He nodded his head, recognizing that they would surely be slain. Since they could only be killed at very specific times or risk both leaders dying within a day, the trick in them surviving would be in getting the timing down.

Gorath entered the city with his two party members in tow. No one in the city seemed to pay them any special attention. However, when they reached the Candlestick, the guards held them at the entrance of the main spire.

"Gorath, remain here until further notice," the guard chimed.

"I don't understand, I am permitted to enter the tower as I am a monk," Gorath said nervously. He could feel the glare that Thomas was giving him.

"Yes, you would be, under normal circumstances," Towe said, suddenly appearing in the doorway. "However, this occasion is anything but normal."

"Head Monk, what is going on?" Gorath asked.

"I will let King Ragmon and Dark Lord Twiller explain," Towe said, and turned to go back inside the spire to retrieve the two leaders.

This announcement gathered a large crowd, and the full attention of the three. By the time the leaders of light and dark had returned to the base of the Candlestick with Towe, the crowd had grown into a massive gathering.

"Gorath, it is my pleasure to announce that you have risen to the newly created rank of High Standard of the Watch," King Ragmon announced to the crowd. "This means that you will be assigned tasks that must be carried out using your experience and wit."

"Twostead and Imp, you are being assigned by myself to assist Gorath in all his duties until further notice," Dark Lord Twiller added.

The three stood in shock of what was happening, unable to speak. The crowd cheered the announcements.

"For your first quest, you are to make preparations and head to the North first thing in the morning to make sure that Argentauth bothers these lands no more!" Towe said.

Gorath could imagine the humongous dragon swallowing them in one bite, then he imagined that instead the dragon burned them to a crisp, and then he imagined that the dragon simply dropped him from an insurmountable height.

Then, to everyone's surprise, he passed out.

EPISODE 14

Thomas looked down at Gorath's passed out body. After nudging him with her right foot, she realized exactly why he had passed out. Her eyes narrowed as she looked up at the three leaders still standing at the entrance of the Candlestick.

"How does that work since I am an officer of the Dark Scouts?" Thomas asked.

"Good point, Twostead. Given your current commission, I am promoting you to Special Envoy, which will supersede your military duties," Dark Lord Twiller said.

Thomas was outraged at the reply. The position was obviously made up. However, since it was the Dark Lord himself giving the decree, it seemed un-Dark-Side-like to not take advantage of the system.

"Special Envoy. That pays one gold per week, right?" Thomas asked.

The Dark Lord smirked at the fiendish audacity of this peon, and recognized how unpopular it would be not to accept the request. Also, he figured that she wouldn't live long enough to get paid anyway.

"Of course. One gold per week," Twiller said. Instantly the crowd cheered.

"And, access to all arms and equipment needed for my quests," Thomas said with a smirk of her own.

"And access to all arms and equipment needed for your quests," the Dark Lord said with a little less of a smile. Again the crowd cheered at the approval.

"And..." Thomas began.

"And, you shouldn't press your luck," the Dark Lord finished.

"Oh boy, that's too bad. Without access to the royal food supplies, I don't know that I can accept the position," Thomas said.

"There is absolutely no way..." the Dark Lord started.

"Dark Lord Twiller, if she does not agree to stay with the group, then you will be cutting things short," Head Monk Towe said.

"Yeah, Twillie, I don't think we want things to end here, do we?" King Ragmon said pointedly.

"Very well, access to the royal food supplies, but that is all, and only as long as King Ragmon makes the same things available to the group," Dark Lord Twiller said, nudging King Ragmon.

As expected, King Ragmon shot the Dark Lord an angry glare. Then Towe gave the King an elbow in the back.

"Of course, let it be so," King Ragmon said.

"Very well then, take the party to the Master Field Inn, until morning when they will depart for their first quest," Head Monk Towe proclaimed.

Amidst the constant cheering, the three newly appointed heroes were picked up and carried to the Master Field Inn. Thomas and Drip were impressed that Gorath was able to sleep through the jostling of the crowd carrying him. They had been placed just inside the lobby, but not by choice.

Very few common people had ever stepped inside the Master Field Inn as only the most distinguished and renowned could get the special pass given exclusively by the King and Dark Lord. The exception to the rule, of course, was for those who provided the service for the Inn. However, even the lowest servants went through a rigorous interview process to be employed there. Without the coveted pass or position, the magic rules that pertained to the Inn would quickly eject any trespasser.

Thomas and Drip stood in awe of the amazing sight of the lobby. The grand marble floor was adorned with massive elaborate carpets, accented with extremely well-crafted furniture. The gold and silver was so abundant in the lobby that if anyone found a mine with the same amount they would be set for about ten generations of heavy spenders.

"May I show you to your rooms?" asked a very short man. The man was very well dressed and it was apparent from his facial expression that he disapproved of their presence—clearly the manager.

Thomas looked down at the very still, passed out Gorath and gave him a strategic kick. She gave a puzzled look to Drip, who simply shrugged. Satisfied that there was very little that could be done to wake him, she turned back to the manager.

"Yes Sir," she replied.

Drip silently followed the two, glancing back one last time to see if there was any change in Gorath's status.

"Interesting fact you are only the second recorded former Dark Scout to stay at the Inn, and I dare say we've never had an Imp as a guest before," the manager spouted as they walked down the hall. They stopped before a pair of doors and he promptly pulled a rope that rang a very distinct, high-pitched bell.

"First floor," the manager said into a gold funnel on the wall.

After a moment, and a very disturbing mixture of deep grunting and stone-on-stone grinding, the door opened. Thomas and Drip stared into the poorly lit box.

"Are we expected to stay in there?" Thomas asked.

"Hum," Drip said. His thoughts drifted back to his little hole in the ground that sadly no longer existed.

"No," the manager said, "as per policy, I must apologize. This magic lift hasn't been used regularly for about fifty years, but has been required to be used by visiting guests of the royal suites. Please enter the lift; I assure you it is completely safe."

The two cautiously entered the lift, and quickly realized that the short man was not joining them.

"Um, pardon me, but why are you not joining us?" Drip asked.

"Again, my apologies, I am not permitted in the lift," he said, "I will see you on the fifth floor shortly."

The doors snapped shut before anything else could be said. Then the deep grunting and loud stone-on-stone grinding began again.

"Remarkably a lot like home," Boot said.

"No doubt," Drip added. "How about you, Thomas?"

"Fine, I'm fine," she said with a very hesitant tone.

"Are you sure you are okay?" Drip asked.

"I am fine," she repeated. Then the lift began to shudder a little.

Drip felt compelled to reach over and take a hold of her hand. He could feel her hand trembling. For a moment she resisted, but then let out a sigh.

"Why are you not mean to me?" Drip asked.

"Drip, I have seen some terrible things in my life, but never anything terrible from an Imp," she said.

"Very nice," Drip replied.

As the lift stopped, both Drip and Thomas let go of each other's hands.

"You will never say anything about this or I will crush you," she whispered.

"So much for not being mean," Boot quietly added.

The doors slid open and sure enough the manager was waiting for them.

"This way please," he said.

They walked down the hall to the first set of very large doors.

"Madame, you are in this room, and Sir imp, you are in the next room, and should master monk ever wake up, his room is one more down," the man said. "Please feel free to utilize the hot water baths and change into something from the provided wardrobe. I will see you in the morning. Also should you need anything, please pull the green rope."

Thomas walked into her room, and looked up at the vaulted ceiling adorned with crystals, gold, and fine wood work. Drip walked into his room to find a similar view, except in the middle of the room sat a large pile of dirt with a small burrow in the middle. Without hesitation, they closed the doors to their respective rooms and retired.

Gorath's eyes slowly opened just a crack, as a headache strongly suggested that he not open his eyes the rest of the way. He sat up in disbelief of where he was. He had never imagined that he would be sitting on the floor of the great Master Field Inn.

"Sir, will you be joining your party for breakfast?" the short man asked, who happened to be hovering over him, as if he'd been standing there all night waiting for him to wake up.

"Is it breakfast already?" he asked.

"Yes Sir," the short man replied.

"Sorry, no time for breakfast," Thomas said, appearing next to the manager. "You slept all night and through breakfast. It is time for us to go."

"Just brilliant," Gorath said. He climbed to his feet and followed Thomas out the front door.

Drip was close behind them. He stopped at the door and turned back to the manager. "Out of curiosity, what is your name?"

"I must apologize, Sir, it has been so long since anyone has asked." The short man thought for a moment. "You can call me Carter."

"Great, see you later, Carter," Drip said, then exited the Inn.

"Where to first?" Gorath asked as they gathered outside.

"The royal armory," Thomas said with a grin on her face.

EPISODE 15

Gorath's head still throbbed from the night spent on a marble pillow. As he trailed behind Thomas, he noticed that people would move out of the way for them to walk past. Looking for answers, he turned to Drip.

"Okay, what exactly happened yesterday, after I lost consciousness?" Gorath asked.

"Drip, I think it would be prudent for me to explain this," Boot said.

"Okay," Drip replied.

"In a very unusual move, the leaders of both the light and dark kingdoms have appointed you to a newly created position and assigned both Drip and Thomas to aid you," Boot said.

"Aid me in what exactly?" Gorath asked.

"Quests, the first of which is to—" Boot began to say.

"I better cut you short on this one, Boot. I think we are going to have to ease him into certain pieces of information," Thomas interrupted.

"Wait, I am the leader of this party?" Gorath asked.

"Technically," Thomas said.

"Then I think I deserve to know what our first quest is!" Gorath demanded.

"Very well, I will tell you, but if you pass out, then we have your permission to transport you any way we see fit," Thomas said.

"Highly doubtful that I would pass out," Gorath stated.

"Do you remember why you passed out last time?" Boot asked. It was easy to hear the genuine curiosity from Boot.

"I don't recall, but it was a fluke," Gorath said.

"Then we have your permission?" Thomas asked again.

"Fine, what is our quest?" Gorath demanded.

"We are to kill Argentauth," Thomas said. She let a smile cross her face with the expectation that Gorath would drop like a stone.

"See, that wasn't so bad, was it?" Gorath said. "Onto the armory."

Thomas frowned at the reaction."Hum, unexpected," Drip said.

"No doubt," Thomas added.

"We will most definitely need some well-shined shields to deal with a troll like that," Gorath said.

"Troll?" Boot asked.

"Yeah, everyone knows that Argentau is a large troll in the Eastern hills," Gorath said.

A grin crossed Thomas's face. She walked up close to the monk. "My apologies, I must not have said that name very clearly," Thomas said.

"That's quite alright, the name can be tricky," Gorath said.

"Argentauth not Argentau," Thomas said making sure to say the names slowly.

"I'm sorry, what was that?" Gorath replied. "It sounded like you said Argentauth..."

Thomas acknowledged the comment with a head nod. It was at that moment that Gorath again crashed to the ground, completely passed out.

"Great, how are we going to move him?" Drip asked.

"We will come back for him," Thomas said. "He isn't going anywhere."

Drip shrugged at the comment, and continued to follow Thomas, careful to step over Gorath's body. It was especially humorous that the monk had passed out only a few dozen steps from the royal armory.

As they approached, the guards snapped to attention. Without hesitation, they moved aside and let them in. A well-groomed man met them just inside the doorway.

"I am the Master of Arms of this establishment, and I have been instructed to help you arm yourselves for your upcoming quest," he said.

"Very good," Thomas said. "As you can see, I am set as far as armor and sword goes; however, my friend here needs to be equipped."

"Excellent, we have a good selection of armors that will work for your friend," The man said. "Please follow me this way."

Drip was especially impressed that they might have some armor that would work for someone his size. He followed behind the Master of Arms down a long hallway and into a fairly large room filled with armor of every type and size. The Master of Arms reached up and pulled down a small set of armor. Thomas ran her hand down the front of the chest plate, and realized this was nothing more than standard issue plate.

"Um, yeah, that's not going to work," Thomas said. "Take us to your good stuff."

"I don't know what you mean," the man replied.

"Boots, you have been around for a while, do you think this is the finest in the Royal armory?" Thomas asked.

"I would say not. This is meant to distract the average," Boot said.

"Boot?!" the Master of Arms exclaimed. "Number two-hundred-and-thirty-five, of Enchanted and Cursed Items?"

"The one and only," Boot said. Then, mysteriously, a helmet fell on Boot.

"Ouch," both Boot and Drip said at the same time.

"You did that on purpose!" Boot said.

"Not I," said Drip.

"Okay, now onto the good stuff," Thomas said.

"Follow me," the Master of Arms grumbled with some reluctance. He started back down the long hallway, but paused in the middle to go down a set of stairs.

"That really hurt, you know," Boot added.

"It hurt me also," Drip said.

"Yes, but you were holding that helmet only a moment sooner," Boot said.

"That doesn't prove anything," Drip replied.

"Here we are," the Master of Arms said.

The two entered an area that looked like a museum. Weapons, armor, and miscellaneous items were carefully marked and positioned onto individual pedestals.

"Yes, this is more like it," Thomas said with an eager grin.

Drip paused at an empty pedestal with an engraved plate. He leaned forward and read the plaque carefully. "235th of the Enchanted and Cursed Items"

"Wow, both a tremendous honor and very deeply disturbing," Boot said.

"Is there something specific you are looking for?" the Master of Arms asked.

"A good set of armor for my size and a weapon of my caliber as well," Drip said.

For a moment, the man's forehead scrunched as he began to tap his chin. He would pause every few moments as if to say something, but then continued. Finally he had a look of exclamation.

"Got it! Just bear with me and put this on," the Master of Arms said as he retrieved a few items.

Drip did as the man said, and stood speechless as he looked into the long mirror before him.

"You look fantastic," Boot said.

"Change, challenge, choose..." Bean piped in after a long drought of silence.

"I look ridiculous," Drip said. The leather armor made his skin look a pale white, and the weapon resting in his hand looked like a child's toy.

"This leather armor was enchanted for Prince Dromma an age ago. It will increase your endurance, speed, and agility, it was named Dromma Escotta. The weapon you are wielding is the Feronis Akaham of Power, and though based on a child' toy, this is by far no plaything," the man said.

"I like the sound of that," Drip replied.

"It means 'Fear of Aka Power'. Anyone you hit with that weapon, whose will is equal to or less than your own will fear you so much they will run. It has no known recorded kills from a direct strike, but it is said that it has caused such great fear, it resulted in the death of its enemies anyway," Boot said.

"Spot on," the Master of Arms said.

"Perfect time to get out of this place, and start on our quest," Thomas said.

The Master of Arms looked around and noticed that several pedestals were now empty, but from the size of the items taken, it was impossible that any one person, or to be more precise, any one human and an imp could carry everything that was missing.

"I don't suppose you noticed anything disappear just now?" the man asked. He was completely baffled.

"Nope. Do you mind if we show ourselves out?" Thomas asked.

"Go ahead. I will talk with you another time," the man answered.

"Finally," Thomas said eagerly. "Time to get this thing started."

EPISODE 16

With literally hundreds of laws and bylaws that ran the great city of Ormlu, aside from the monks that studied the *Master Book of Magic*, only the Assassins' Guild knew every single one. By trade, the Assassins' Guild was severely restricted in Ormlu, but was not prevented from operating. Gorath was about to witness it first-hand as his eyes opened and he found himself being dragged into an attic space.

Gorath glanced around to get his bearings but could only surmise that he was indeed in an attic. He was unable to make out the faces of the two people who had transported him to his current location. Gorath felt it was odd that the magic in the city would let someone be tied up and dragged off into a corner. After fidgeting for a moment, he realized that his hands were bound with a sticky rope.

"Who are you?" Gorath asked.

"Do not worry about who we are, you should only worry about yourself," the first robed man said.

"Okay, what do you intend to do with me? You can't kill me," Gorath added with confidence. It wasn't necessarily misplaced confidence, but more like an ignorant confidence.

"That is true to an extent," the second hooded man said.

"We need you to pay attention, and understand that rules can be bent, even here," the first hooded man said. Then he raised his hand.

Gorath watched as the second man began to slowly spin in circles as if he were playing demon darts. Upon closer examination, he could see an unusually large dart in the man's right hand. Then, on the completion of the fourth turn, the man threw the dart. As typical, the dart tumbled through the air with seemingly no well-aimed destination. However, any silly thoughts vacated Gorath's mind when the dart grazed his left arm. He flinched from both pain and the shock as there seemed to be no punishment for the offender in this occasion.

"Wait, that doesn't make any sense," Gorath said. Then a second dart struck the floor next to Gorath's left leg.

"Get the point?" the first hooded man asked, holding up another large dart. The two men chuckled for a moment at their apparent joke.

"How are you doing this?" Gorath asked.

"It doesn't really matter," the second hooded man said.

"We need to give you a message, from a very powerful person. 'Beware the red sky over Ormlu; people will try to kill you'," the first hooded man said.

"You aren't going to kill me?" Gorath asked.

"If we wanted to kill you, you would already be dead," the first hooded man said.

"One more thing you should know about the men who are trying to kill you, and those who have hired us..." the second robed man said. He was promptly interrupted by a thunderous cracking noise. Within moments, splinters that used to make up the door were scattered across the room.

Gorath was both elated and terribly disappointed at the sight of Corporal Stevens. The two hooded men promptly threw down smoke pellets to prevent anyone from seeing their movement. Gorath could hear the scuffle of feet move around the room.

"Gorath, confound it, are you in here?" a familiar voice asked.

"I am here," Gorath said. Someone scuffled past, knocking him onto his side. Some of the smoke had begun to clear and he could see the two hooded men preparing to throw darts into the lingering smoke. Gorath scrambled to his feet, taking only moments since he had years of practice getting to his feet with his hands tied.

With no choice, Gorath began to charge at the first hooded man. He lowered his shoulder and prepared for impact when an arm out of the smoke attempted to stop him. It was too late, however; there was too much force and momentum. Gorath found himself standing outside, the arm still attached to him.

"Oh, this is nice," the familiar voice said into his ear.

Gorath turned to see that it was Aroon who had tried to prevent him from striking the hooded man.

"Aroon, you're alive!" Gorath said in excitement.

"For the moment," Aroon said. He made a gesture for Gorath to look down.

Gorath had always wondered what the view looked like from the very top of the Candlestick, and now he felt that his curiosity was more than satisfied. He could see a great distance in every direction. A light breeze brushed past the two men.

"So how do we get down from here?" Gorath asked.

"I hate you," Aroon said in a muddled tone.

"Well, that's not helping anything," Gorath said.

"I always knew you would be the death of me, and now you have done it," Aroon said.

"Look, maybe if we can secure ourselves to the weather vane, we can rappel down to the windows below," Gorath said.

"With what rope?" Aroon asked. He was keeping his balance very steady as not to disrupt the large clay shingles that adorned the roof.

"Well, what do you think my hands are tied with? Soggy bread?" Gorath said.

Aroon went silent as he carefully navigated the shingles to reach Gorath's bindings. A long silence ensued as he scrutinized the bindings with no movement at all.

"Aroon, what is going on?" Gorath asked.

"It's licorice. Your hands are tied with licorice," Aroon said, with a pinch of anger.

"What flavor?" Gorath asked.

"What does it matter?" Aroon said. "It's candy."

"Just untie me," Gorath said.

Despite his objections, Aroon carefully deconstructed the knot, and handed the purple length of licorice to Gorath. Suddenly, the wind seemed to pick up.

"Perfect. This can still work," Gorath said. He began to carefully balance along the shingles toward the weather vain. Everything seemed to progress without a hitch as Gorath began to tie the purple licorice to the large ornament.

"Do you expect me to put my life in the hands of a piece of candy?" Aroon asked.

"We don't have a lot of options right now," Gorath said. He could hear the scuffle between Corporal Stevens and the hooded men coming to close inside the tower as the sound dwindled, and without knowing who was winning, they had to take the risk.

The two grabbed a hold of the candy and prepared to rappel down when a strong wind caught them off guard and pushed them off the roof. For the first time ever, they were thinking the same thing. One word.

Brilliant.

As they started to fall, Gorath reached into his pocket and pulled out his *Handy Book of Spells to Use on the Go*. Quickly he thumbed through the pages and began to recite a short incantation. A moment later, the two men were sitting on top of the *Master Book of Magic*, safely inside the Candlestick.

"Wow, I did not see that coming," Aroon said.

EPISODE
17

No one was more startled that Gorath and Aroon had appeared on the *Master Book of Magic* more than the Head Monk's right-hand man, Mussashi. This was mostly because he was in the middle of studying the book.

"Gorath?!" Mussashi asked in astonishment. "How? Why? What?"

"Ah, Mussashi my good man, I must apologize for the entry. It was either this or..." Gorath paused a moment. "You know, I'm not really sure what the alternative was. Never mind that now, we will be going on our way, if you would please move."

"Yes?" Mussashi said in an asking tone. Overwhelmed at the situation, he took a few steps back.

Carefully, Aroon and Gorath dismounted the book and headed for the exit. Mussashi simply stood silent as they walked away. Everyone in the next room also had stopped and stared in confusion as the two snaked their way through the maze of desks and books.

Mussashi wished that the Head Monk himself would have been present to see the unheard of spectacle. However, with little else to do, he turned back to the book to study. After about thirty minutes of studying the logistical rules of a declaration of war, he turned the page to review the requirements to engage in battle when something odd happened. Right in the middle of the paragraph stating that armies could only attack or occupy territories that they were officially at war with, it suddenly started to talk about supply line agreements.

Stepping back from the book, Mussashi realized that something was terribly wrong. As he began to process what could have happened, he decided that there needed to be another set of eyes on this problem.

"Cary, come here for a moment," Mussashi said, summoning the closest monk.

"Yes, Master Mussashi?" Cary asked.

"Look at the page and tell me if you see anything wrong," Mussashi ordered.

On cue, Cary began to examine the book. Then, unexpectedly, he paused.

"Well, what do you see?" Mussashi asked.

"There is half a page missing. You can tell if you run your hand down the page," Cary said.

"That is what I was afraid of. I need you to track down Gorath, and see if you can locate the missing half a page and recover it," Mussashi said. "You cannot tell him you know about the page, so tell him that we have assigned you to aid him in his quest."

"Yes Sir," Cary said, and quickly exited the room.

—

Gorath let out a long sigh after what seemed to be a never ending lecture from Aroon about various topics, but the most prevalent one being how Gorath would be his demise.

"Okay, well that was a nice talk, I will look forward to our next one as usual," Gorath said in a very casual tone.

"Next time! *Next time!*" Aroon growled angrily. "There won't be a next time."

"I'm just curious, of everyone on the guard, why was it you and your team that came to rescue me?" Gorath asked.

"We did not know it was you, just that someone had been abducted," Aroon said.

"Very well then," Gorath replied, "I will see you when I see you."

Gorath began to walk away from the front door of the Candlestick, when Corporal Stevens walked up to Aroon.

"With all due respect, Sir," Stevens said, "but we knew it was Gorath being held in the tower all along."

Aroon slowly shook his head and ran his hands down his face. "Stevens, he nearly got us killed."

"Yeah, but from the sound of it, he saved both of you," Stevens replied.

"That he did, this time," Aroon admitted. "I don't know how many lives he has left, and I do not want to be around when he runs out."

Meanwhile, Gorath decided that he would put off thinking about what had just happened, and get on with the quest at hand. *After all, I am the leader of an expedition, and people are looking up to me*, Gorath thought to himself. He paused for a moment and then prepared to take a step into the armory to return to his companions.

"There you are, Gorath!" Thomas said as she and Drip exited the armory before Gorath could enter. "We are ready to head out. What have you been doing?"

"Um, it's a long story," Gorath said.

"I'd like to hear it," Drip said.

"Yeah, I don't think we have time for it," Thomas said.

"How far is our destination again?" Drip asked.

"That is beside the point," Thomas said. "Let's move out."

"Very well," Gorath said. "Which way?"

"Our orders have us leaving from the gate closest to our destination," Thomas said, looking at the parchment.

"The North Gate?" Gorath said in amazement. "That is truly extraordinary."

"What is the big deal with the North Gate?" Thomas asked.

"Perhaps Gorath is astonished because it has not been opened in three ages, and even then it was a tragedy waiting to happen," Boot said.

"Why was it a tragedy?" Drip asked.

"Don't worry about it, Drip," Thomas said. "Let's just move out."

The three made their way through the maze of streets and buildings, to finally arrive at the North Gate. Only a couple of people were waiting at the gate for their arrival.

"Ah, Orielia, how are you doing?" Gorath asked as they approached.

"I am doing well," Orielia replied. "And yourself?"

"I guess you can say that I've been hanging in there, and everything seems to be falling into place," Gorath said with a slight giggle. It was moments like these that Gorath never realized no one but him would get his inside jokes.

"Very good," Towe said with a hint of confusion and annoyance. "We have prepped your horses and packed your gear."

"Before you leave, I will cast a spell of protection," Orielia said.

Towe turned as if to protest the measure, but decided not to risk drawing any unnecessary attention to himself or raise any unnecessary concerns.

"*Orantooth, tramathine, protectos,*" Orielia said, then flung her fingers in an outward motion towards the three. A bright blue light danced from her fingertips, and for a moment, surrounded all three of them. Afterwards, Orielia's shoulders slumped and her physical appearance seemed diminished and tired.

An uncomfortable feeling came over Drip, and looking back at the Witch of Ormlu, something didn't feel right. Drip walked over to her.

"Orielia, are you alright?" Drip asked.

"Yes, thank you for your concern, Drip," Orielia replied in a weak voice.

Drip shrugged his shoulders at the response and moved to walk past her to go to the horses, when he tripped and fell towards the witch instead. Oddly enough, Drip never actually touched Orielia, but fell against something that felt like an invisible person. Then as if an unexpected spotlight had been turned on the otherwise invisible figure, Drip watched a ripple of movement run away from the group and out of sight. Almost instantly, Orielia's complexion returned to normal.

"What was that?" Thomas asked.

After a moment, Orielia looked angry, but it was clear that the anger was not focused on them.

"That was something you don't need to worry about," Orielia said. "Good luck on your quest."

"Yes, please proceed on your quest. You have already lost enough time," Towe said, ushering them towards the horses.

"Grendle!" Thomas said with a pleasantly surprised tone. "I was hoping they would set you up."

The horse promptly leaned her head down and nodded to Thomas in approval. Without any hesitation, Thomas mounted the former horse of the Dark Scouts. She glanced back to see Drip and Gorath ready to go on their horses as well.

As she turned to look forward, the great gate opened, tremendous amounts of dirt and dust falling from it as it did so. As the falling dirt mixed with the gentle breeze and an amazing noon day sun, it set up their exit to seem like a divine force had chosen them to embark on this quest. The three slowly left the city. Then just as Gorath's horse cleared the gate, the great door slammed shut with a very loud crashing sound. It was at that moment that Thomas realized why no one used the gate, as she watched two full battalions of dark and light units clashing just twenty yards in front of them, and several troops from both sides were now headed towards them.

"Not good," Gorath commented.

EPISODE
18

Thomas looked over at Gorath with irritation. It was obvious that the situation was not good. Unable to come up with a solution, she found herself doing the one thing that she never thought she would ever do. She looked to the imp.

Drip recognized that Thomas was looking to him for answers, so he shrugged his shoulders and decided to encourage his horse forward.

"Oh, this is going to be good," Boot added.

"Started, guarded, winded.... " Bean spouted.

Glancing back, Drip noticed the other two were actually following him.

"What are you doing?!" Boot demanded.

"Interesting, I thought you could read my mind," Drip said with a little smirk.

"Not always, apparently," Boot replied.

"Trust me, we are going to be just fine," Drip said loud enough for Gorath and Thomas to hear him.

Soldiers from both sides seemed to be approaching at breakneck speeds. It was only a moment later that Drip could make out the eye color of the first advancing soldier. It was at that moment that he elected to raise a small banner. The banner was adorned with half a gold crest of a lion and half a red python; both were clear symbols of the royal houses on each side. No one was permitted to carry such a banner without direct and personal permission of the Royal leaders themselves.

The advancing soldiers strained to halt their advance at the sight of the flag. Each respective side stopped within only a few feet of the three, offering up a sharp salute.

"I say, how long have you had that, might I ask?" Gorath asked.

"Yeah, I thought it would come in handy," Drip said, "so I snagged it from the royal armory."

"How did I miss that?" Boot asked.

"My thoughts exactly," Thomas said.

"Fortune favors the prepared," Drip said.

"Well said, Drip," Gorath said with a grin.

―

Watching the group's departure as he joined Towe at The North Gate, Aroon could hardly believe what he was seeing. Never before had he seen troops stop on a dime, or an imp brave enough to walk out into an oncoming charge.

"Well that was a bit dramatic, wasn't it?" Aroon said. The situation was enough to cause him, a battle hardened veteran, to nervously clench his fist and draw a bead of sweat.

"That was the point," Towe said.

"Pardon," Aroon said. The Master Monk's comment caught him off guard.

"This has never been done before," Towe said, "and we cannot expect that the typical would be good enough for this situation, don't you agree?"

"Yes," Aroon replied.

"Good, then I need you to take a contingent of the best soldiers available and follow them," Towe said. "You must not be seen, and you must ensure they are not harmed on their quest."

"Sir, I only have one concern about that order," Aroon said.

"And that would be?" Towe asked.

"Well, when they fight the dragon, I am not sure a contingent will be enough to protect them," Aroon said.

"Your concern is noted, and for now, my order stands, until you reach the dragon," Towe said. He glared at Aroon. "Will that suffice?"

"Yes, Sir," Aroon said.

"Let me remind you this is your one and possibly only chance to regain your rightful place with the elites," Towe said.

"Yes Sir, thank you, Sir," Aroon said.

"Dismissed," Towe commanded.

Aroon put his helmet on and walked back to his anxiously waiting friend nearby. He pulled a paper from his horse's saddle, and began to write on it.

"So, what did he have to say?" Corporal Stevens asked.

"It is as I have feared: we are to follow them," Aroon said. "Take this to the Candlestick garrison, and return with those listed."

"Very good, Sir," Stevens answered.

"And have them loaded to the teeth," Aroon said. "This is going to get messy."

Orielia decided that it was unfortunate she was unable to see them any further than The North Gate, but she knew something was not right. The feeling that had come over her was unnatural.

As she made her way back to the Candlestick, she began to ponder on her current state of mind. After all, 48 hours earlier she was positive that the air was part of a conspiracy to poison her and had attempted several times to defeat the evil air by holding her breath.

Her thoughts were abruptly interrupted when a monk nearly knocked her down as he ran past.

"Excuse you," she said. That's when she noticed the oddest thing about the monk that was now disappearing into the distance—long hair.

Huh, Orielia thought, then shook her head and began to start towards the tower again, when she saw something in a shop window she had missed before. There was a dark apparition clearly following her. A feeling of uncomfortable fear ran down her spine, and without warning, she took off running for the Candlestick. As she cleared the doors, she turned.

"Guards, close the doors," she ordered. The guards quickly shut the doors and braced for something to strike them, but nothing ever came.

"Ma'am, are you alright?" one of the guards asked.

"Yes, I suppose," she reluctantly replied. "You can open the doors again."

"Very good, ma'am," the guard said.

Orielia began to walk up the steps when the feeling came back to her.

"No sense in hiding any more, I know you are there," Orielia said.

"Oh really? Then call out my name," an airy voice whispered.

"I don't know your name, apparition," Orielia said in a strong tone. "I command you to show yourself!"

"Oh clever and misguided, you know my name and you will remember it soon," the voice whispered, "because I will be the one who kills the three, and you will be next, no matter what your devious sisters tell you."

"I don't think so," Orielia said with a grin. Then she turned and reached out and, for a moment, she could firmly take a hold of the shadow's shoulder. Then, with a shriek, the apparition vanished.

All three were pretty amazed at the progress they made riding north down the line that divided the Light and Dark. As they progressed, units stopped engaging each other and would offer the three a salute.

"How much longer before this won't work anymore?" Drip asked.

"We have a few days' ride north, and then we will run into the hill giants that pledge no allegiance to anyone," Gorath said.

"I am not looking forward to that," Thomas said. One of her brothers had died in combat with one of the hill giants. Though there were no details on exactly how he had died, her imagination filled in the gaps without any problems.

"I could get us to the hill giants right now, if you want," Gorath said.

"Hold up!" Thomas shouted. The command was loud enough to grab the attention of soldiers within a good half mile.

"What is wrong?" Gorath asked.

"You are telling me we have been riding hard this whole time, killing our horses and wearing ourselves out, and you have the power to move us a two days' distance in just a moment?!" Thomas shouted.

"If you put it that way, you would think I was trying to hide something," Gorath said, "Then again, if you put anything that way, you could really hurt someone's feelings."

"Yeah, I vote we move ahead by two days," Drip said.

"You have got to be kidding me!" Thomas replied to the two. She took a deep breath, and decided arguing was not the best way to spend their limited time. She nodded at Gorath, fully intending to give him an earful later. "Well, do your thing."

"I am sorry, I did not hear a request in that statement," Gorath said as he folded his arms.

"Gorath, can you please get us to just before the hill giants?" Drip asked.

"No, Thomas has to ask or I won't move us up," Gorath said, now glaring in Thomas's direction.

"Please move us," Thomas said, gritting her teeth. Apparently, Gorath was the oldest teenager she had ever dealt with.

"Good enough," Gorath said. He opened his bag and reached in to grab his yellow powder, but a confused look came across his face instead. He pulled out an odd looking leather glove, looked at it, and slid it back into the bag. This happened about ten more times, each time pulling out a random object, before he finally pulled out the bag of yellow powder.

"That was odd," Gorath said to himself. He then pulled out a pinch of the yellow powder and flipped it towards Drip, Thomas, and on himself.

Drip and Thomas watched as a horrified expression came over Gorath's face. Just as they were about to say something, they suddenly found themselves standing in front of a hill giant.

EPISODE 19

The three were frozen with fear as the hill giant glared down at them. Thomas could not believe that her hand was still on the hilt of her sword. Gorath was unmoving because he had reached into his bag in an attempt to pull out his quick book of spells, but instead found his hand in some sort of slime. Though Drip had worked around hill giants, he had never felt threatened by one before.

In one quick motion the hill giant raised his arm above his head. All three of them were certain they were about to be crushed. The hill giant opened his mouth, but instead of the expected loud, ground-shaking war cry, the hill giant just let out a yawn. Then he wandered off.

"Huh, of all the things, I have never witnessed that," Boot remarked.

"What do you make of that?" Thomas asked.

"I should have guessed; he was sleepwalking," Drip said.

"That was close enough," Gorath said as he began to wipe the slime from his hand onto his robe. He glanced into his bag trying to figure out how he could have guessed so wrong on the item placement.

"I think we should call it a day," Thomas said. "Where should we go, oh great leader?"

Gorath ignored the sarcasm-laden comment, and pulled out his trusty area map. Using his thumb he figured out that the closest shelter would be about a half of a mile into the Light Side. On the map, the outpost they were planning on seeking shelter was marked "Ari-Stran."

"We will be heading to Ari-Stran, half a mile that way," Gorath pointed towards the Light Side.

"Are you sure that is where you want to go?" Boot asked.

Gorath raised an eyebrow at the question, then answered sternly, "Absolutely."

"Very well," Boot replied. The three turned and headed towards the designated shelter.

"Out of curiosity, why did you ask that back there?" Gorath asked.

Thomas and Drip looked at Gorath suspiciously.

"To be honest, I thought that place had been destroyed a long time ago," Boot replied.

"If that is the case when we get there, we will use the ruins to make camp," Gorath said.

It was only a short time later the party caught a glimpse of their shelter after cresting a hill. To everyone's surprise, before them stood a large three-floor tower and stone-walled courtyard.

"Oh good, it's not in bad shape at all," Gorath said cheerfully. Then as if the structure decided to mock him openly, a small portion of the tower collapsed, and slid over the courtyard wall smashing two innocent cows standing in the wrong place at the wrong time.

"Yeah, I'm not staying in there," Thomas said.

"Um, I enjoy sleeping in dark holes in the ground, but I am not sure that I want to be here," Drip said.

"Oh come on. I mean look, let's at least stay for dinner, since it has been provided," Gorath said. His gut was instinctively telling him that he was making a terrible decision, but he was determined to be the leader of this quest no matter how doomed it was.

"Let me guess, 'let's have the imp dig out the cows'," Drip said in a mocking tone.

"I appreciate the offer, Drip, but I have this covered," Gorath said. "I just need my quick reference guide to building with magic."

Gorath's forehead wrinkled with a mixture of confusion and frustration, as he pulled out a long sword. Quickly he dropped the sword on the ground and reached into his bag and pulled out a leather glove.

"Where did I get all of this junk?" Gorath asked as he continued to search his bag.

"So *that* is what happened!" Drip said, looking at Thomas.

"Shame on you," Boot said.

"What?" Thomas asked.

"You took the items from the armory and stashed them in Gorath's bag," Drip said.

"Yes, but we had full permission to use items from the armory," Thomas said.

"I don't think that was what they meant," Drip said.

"That is how I heard it," Thomas replied.

"Why did you grab so much stuff?" Drip asked. We probably won't use most of it."

"I thought it would be better to have it and not need it, than to need it and not have it," Thomas replied.

Gorath, ignorant of the exchange between Thomas and Drip, had about twenty items on the ground in front of him at this point, and counting.

"Out of curiosity, Gorath, how can you carry so much stuff in that little bag?" Drip asked.

"Um, that is kind of tough to explain, but imagine the stuff inside is actually being sent to an alternate universe, and the opening is the portal, so you see, technically, I'm only carrying the portal around, which weighs nothing at all,," Gorath said.

"Is it really an alternate universe?" Drip asked.

"Well, no, it's complicated, and that was the best analogy I had," Gorath said.

"It is a magic bag of holding, it weighs a fraction of its contents, and the shape does not represent the items you put into it," Boot said.

"Oh, that's pretty awesome. How do I get a bag like that?" Drip asked.

"Right, a bag like this," Gorath said in an irritated tone. "This was hand-woven by the master monks, from the finest mix of materials, and on top of that you need a top-level monk to enchant the bag."

"Really? That is fascinating. How much does it cost?" Drip asked.

"Cost? Cost? Priceless. Only the top monks carry bags like this one," Gorath said. Then Gorath's expression changed from frustration to excitement.

"Have you found that book yet?" Thomas asked.

"As a matter of fact, I just did," Gorath answered.

"Great, let's get this stuff back into your bag and get moving," Thomas said.

"Why should I carry this junk around?" Gorath asked.

"Because it isn't junk," Thomas replied. "Boot, would you like to explain?"

"What you have there are at least thirty of the top known enchanted items, between the two kingdoms," Boot said. "I wouldn't be surprised if Arkanim's Wand of Wonder was in your possession."

"Are you kidding me?!" Gorath replied. "How did all of this get into my bag?"

"I sort of borrowed your bag after you passed out," Thomas said.

"That is outrageous! Wait, did you say Arkanim's Wand of Wonder?" Gorath said.

"It was definitely in the collection; it could be in there," Boot said.

"Okay, I am going to let you off with a warning, this time," Gorath said. He started to put the items on the ground back in the bag, one at a time, when he stopped suddenly. He reached down and pulled out a wand from the pile of what he had called 'junk.' Speechless, all Gorath could do for several minutes was swoon over the wand.

They all stared at it in wonder.

"Told you," Boot said, but they all ignored him.

"What is so special about the wand?" Thomas asked.

"It was created and wielded by the powerful wizard, Arkanim, several ages ago," Boot explained. "The power of the wand is not entirely defined, but it was rumored that it nearly wiped out the Dark Side. One day, just before a pinnacle battle, Arkanim disappeared. The wand was discovered later, but since then, no wizard has been powerful enough to wield it."

"You need to finish, Boot," Gorath interjected. "No wizard has been powerful enough to wield it *in battle*. However, for everyday use, it is simple enough to wield." Then, with a flick of his wrist, all the items on the ground stood up and jumped into the bag one at a time. While that was happening, he turned and raised the wand. The rubble from the building flew back up into the air and slid back into place. Unexpectedly, he accidently brought the two cows back to life.

"Yeah, Thomas, go grab us something for dinner while Drip and I set up our quarters," Gorath said. An odd confidence began to well up inside of him.

"What happened to the other wizards who tried to wield the wand?" Drip asked in a quite tone.

"The wand overwhelmed the wizard and absorbed them," Boot replied.

"Great," Drip said.

EPISODE
20

Drip looked around the run-down abandoned outpost, and honestly didn't think much of Ari-Stran. However, it seemed to have an eerie, familiar feeling to it. The outpost would have been unbearable to set up camp in, but thanks to Gorath and his newly acquired wand, everything was tolerable. With a flick of his wrist, Gorath was moving large sections of stone back into place, and clearing out things like stale water and massive plant growth.

"Did you want to create a door while you're at it?" Drip asked. He was half joking, but was hoping the crazy wizard would actually put a door up to keep out snooping people and creatures.

"Oh, ah, I almost forgot," Gorath said. He turned and waved his wand at the doorway, making a massive oak door appear.

"I hope it doesn't go to his head," Boot said quietly. "Literally."

"No kidding," Drip said.

The two made their way into the great room on the third floor. Drip was amazed to see a mixture of skeletons of light and dark soldiers, presumably killed in battle. With a little imagination, Drip could picture the battle that raged through the once great hall. Without realizing it, he had pulled out his pad of paper and began to write his thoughts.

"This won't do at all," Gorath said. He waved his wand to remove the dust and old skeletons, but accidentally brought the bones of the old soldiers to life. Gorath and Drip retreated back to the stairwell.

"You really need to get that under control," Boot said.

"You really need to put that wand away," Drip said.

"Oops," Gorath said, "I can fix this."

Gorath waved the wand again, and this time it restored the weapons from their ancient rusted state, to their prime condition. The skeletons examined the weapons and quickly picked them up.

"Wow, that fixed things," Drip said sarcastically.

"Ah, perhaps I should stop using the wand," Gorath said.

"You think?" Drip quickly added.

Then something odd happened. The skeletons lined up in a large formation. Then one skeleton in particular stepped forward, and saluted.

"The troops are at your command," the haunting voice of the skeleton said.

"Who, me?" Gorath asked. "What do I do?"

"Now is probably not a good time to ask that," Boot said. The skeleton army began to become restless at the exchange.

"Hey now, what's this?" Thomas asked, carrying up two rabbits.

"Genius here created a skeleton army, and they're looking for a commander," Drip said.

"Surprise," Gorath said.

Thomas scanned the skinless soldiers, and their tight formation, and felt a wave of sympathy for their situation. But, seeing as how they were magically animated with a singular purpose in mind, they did need a commander.

"Alright, let's stand at attention!" Thomas shouted.

"Who are these two, Sir?" the lead skeleton asked Gorath. Several skeletons began to raise their weapons and walk toward Thomas and Drip.

"They are my generals, and you will listen to them," Gorath said.

"That's right, now stand at attention!" Thomas shouted again. Instantly the skeletons stood upright, obeying her.

"Impressive," Drip said.

"Enough lying around here; get this place cleaned up! I don't want to see any dust in the hall! I want to see my face in all the plates! Get a fire started, and someone get us some food!" Thomas shouted. Without hesitation, the skeletons formed small groups and began to follow the orders provided by Thomas.

"I did not see that coming," Boot said.

"You're amazing," Drip said.

Thomas turned and looked back at the two. It was clear by the grin on her face that she was enjoying the situation even more than they were. Then she began to offer Gorath an angry glare.

"You!" Thomas said.

"Me?" Gorath asked.

"Put that wand away before you get us all killed," Thomas said. "There is no way I could have fought off that many skeletons."

"So what you are saying is save it for when we need it," Gorath said.

"Something like that," Thomas said. Irritated at the monk, she turned back to see what her new army was doing.

"You have to be kidding me," Aroon said. "The trail goes dead right here?"

Aroon looked back through the crazy terrain and battling armies, then looked forward in the direction of the dragon.

"Yes, Sir, I don't know how, but they just disappear," Corporal Stevens said.

"I guess we have to push on without tracks," Aroon said with his typical irritation.

Cary had been clever enough to sneak onto the guard's tracking party, and stay oblivious to the soldiers. However, this situation posed an issue. Cary knew they had to catch up to Gorath and his party, but while he knew they must have been transported forward, he didn't know how.

"Sir, they could have teleported forward," a soldier in the back said.

"And what can we do about that?" Aroon asked sharply. "Even if we attempted to follow the same way, we don't know where they've teleported to."

"Should we keep moving?" Corporal Stevens asked.

"Move out!" Aroon ordered.

Cary decided that it was time for drastic action, especially since Aroon was not open to the idea of teleporting. Cary removed a small pouch of yellow dust and quickly flicked it at the group. No one noticed the simple action until everyone found themselves standing before a hill giant. This time the hill giant was definitely not sleeping. Aroon was seriously confused, but had enough presence of mind to bolster his men.

"Attack!" Aroon shouted. He raised his sword and charged forward.

Drip was enjoying the view from the third floor of the tower. He let himself gaze off in the distance towards the Light Side. He had never seen so much color before. Though he was missing his hole in the ground, there was something that was very attractive about the Light Side. He glanced down at the skeleton guards patrolling the perimeter, and found comfort in their presence. Suddenly he noticed a large band of soldiers approaching the tower from the Light Side.

"I think we have a problem," Drip announced to the group.

"We sure do," Gorath said, looking at the cooking rabbit. "We don't have any spices."

"No, this is much more serious," Drip said. Quickly the other two came over to the window and looked out to see the advancing troops.

"Oh boy," Thomas said. "To arms!"

The three walked down the stairs bolstered by their garrison of skeleton troops. They walked out to meet the troops before they could reach the tower.

"Ho there!" the approaching commander shouted from about fifteen feet away.

"Ho yourself," Thomas said. "What do you want?"

"We are the fifth platoon of the second division of light troops, and we were moving to occupy the restored tower behind you," the commander said. "Who are you?"

"We are special envoys to Candlestick, and you cannot have the tower. It is occupied," Thomas said.

"I can see you have skeletons, and that would suggest you are Dark Side, but you do not appear to be Dark Side," the commander said.

"It is complicated, but either way you cannot have the tower," Thomas said.

"I do not understand. Special envoy or not, if that tower is Light Side, then we will occupy it, and if it is occupied by the Dark

Side, we are obligated to attack it," the commander replied. "So which is it?"

"Neither," Gorath interjected.

"There is no neither here," the commander said. He drew his sword.

"There is, as this tower and its occupied lands are neutral," Gorath said. "At least as long as we are here."

"This is foolishness, there is no neutral!" the commander shouted. "Attack!"

The Light Side platoon charged forward, and the skeletons prepared to meet their attackers, except the platoon never made it to the skeletons. Instead, about ten feet away they were all laid out, as if they had run straight into a wall.

"Mark my words," the commander said. "We will be back in greater numbers, and we will have that tower!"

EPISODE
21

The sun was just finishing its rise over the horizon when the three exited the tower. During the night, the skeletons had continued to work relentlessly to restore the tower to its full glory, but that was not the most interesting development. Along the furthest perimeter, one full battalion from the Light Side was attempting to attack the tower. However, the neutral tower and its ground seemed to be protected by the same rules that protected Ormlu.

"You're leaving, Sir?" the lead skeleton asked.

"Yes. Be well, and keep this place secure. We will be back," Gorath said. He walked over and mounted his horse, joining the other two, who were already set to move out.

"I hope we will be back," Drip mumbled.

Thomas nodded her head at the comment and gave the skeletons a sharp salute. The whole company of skeletons stopped and saluted in response.

"Alright, enough standing around. Back to work. We have to get this place into tip top shape!" the lead skeleton shouted.

Impressed by his drive, Thomas walked her horse over to Gorath and prompted him to lean in for a conversation.

"Do me a favor, grab a named weapon from the bag and give it to the lead skeleton," Thomas said.

"Why would I do that?" Gorath asked, looking down at the bag.

"Let's be straight here, he deserves it. Plus, he won't last ten minutes in a real fight without it," Thomas said. "Let's call it a promotion."

"I guess it really can't hurt," Gorath said. He reached into the bag and pulled out a small shield.

"Captain!" Thomas shouted.

The commanding skeleton turned and walked over to the three.

"Yes Sir?" the skeleton asked. Even though this was just a skeleton standing before them, he seemed to have more pride and enthusiasm in his motions than most of the living.

"What is your name?" Gorath asked.

"I am...I am...Thornguard," the skeleton said, seeming to pull the name from his previously forgotten memories.

"Very good. I hereby promote you to general of these forces and give to you this token of our gratitude for your service," Gorath said, handing the small shield down to the newly appointed general. "Don't let me down, General Thornguard."

The skeleton silently nodded, speechless at the act. The other skeletons standing in the area saluted their new general.

The three then turned and headed into the heart of hill giant country.

"You remember that wasn't yours to give away," Boot said. "Right?"

Exhausted, Aroon guided his horse to the top of a hill. He turned and counted his men. He shook his head at the result.

"How many did we lose?" Corporal Stevens asked.

"Two," Aroon replied. "That's not as bad as I thought it would be," Stevens said. "I never imagined that the troops would break and run so quickly."

"Yeah, well, I never thought I would be charging a hill giant all by myself," Aroon said as he glared back at Stevens.

"I was trying to rally the troops," Stevens replied.

"Right, well, anyway," Aroon said, "what do you make of this?" He turned to indicate two entire Light battalions attempting to attack an outpost ahead of them.

"I don't think I have ever seen anything like it before," Stevens replied.

"Hum," Aroon said, looking through a long spyglass. "It looks like a large contingent of skeletons has captured that outpost. Very odd. I don't know that I have ever seen skeletons capture anything this large before."

"Yeah, and look at that one," Stevens said. "The one ordering the others around."

"Interesting," Aroon said.

"Let me have the spyglass for a better look," Stevens requested.

Aroon sighed at the notion, but gave into his request. However, during the exchange, the spyglass was fumbled and dropped.

Cary saw the botched hand-off, and dismounted, seeing it as an opportunity to examine the situation. In one quick motion, Cary snatched up the spyglass and looked through it, clearly able to see the three leaving the north side of the outpost.

"You there! Please hand me the spyglass," Aroon said. He thought it was curious that he did not know the person standing before him. Suddenly the unknown soldier tossed the spyglass at him. Out of the corner of his eye, Aroon could swear he saw a glimpse of long brown hair, just before the person simply disappeared.

"Didn't see that coming," Stevens said.

"Yes, well it appears we had a spy in our midst," Aroon said.

"What, exactly, was that person spying on?" Stevens asked.

"Let's figure out the riddle before us before we take on another," Aroon said, but secretly began to try and figure out why there would be a spy amidst a party of troops sent on a mission to spy in the first place.

Aroon ordered his men to march down to the Light troops laying siege to the tower.

"Who is in command here?" Aroon asked, once they arrived amidst the troops at the bottom of the hill. He had dismounted and approached the soldiers on foot.

"That would be me," a short man answered.

"I am on special mission on behalf of the Candlestick, and I am looking for a party of three. A male monk, a female warrior, and a male imp," Aroon said.

"I have met your friends. They are, or were, in the outpost we are attempting to recapture. However, they have used very powerful magic and we have yet to gain access to the grounds," the Light commander said.

"Thank you for the information," Aroon said. He remounted his horse and headed back to his party.

"Sir, the rumor is that they left a short time before we got here," Corporal Stevens reported.

"Let's move out," Aroon said, heading away from the outpost. His men followed.

Just before the army was out of sight, the distinct sound of hill giants attacking filled the air. A quick glance back verified that the Light Side battalion was scattering for their lives.

―

The three found themselves to be fortunate thus far as they had not come across any hill giants. The time was being spent with Gorath taking inventory of his new temporary collection. Thomas was sharpening her enchanted sword, while Drip was using a dagger to carve simple designs into the smooth stones he had picked up from the outpost. Drip was excited to put his new sling to the test but had yet to have a chance to.

Suddenly a person appeared in the path in front of them. The origin of the rider was unmistakable, as the stranger was wearing gear only found in Ormlu.

"Who goes there?" Thomas asked. With no response, the three began to grow nervous.

"State your name and business," Gorath requested. Again silence filled the air.

"This is your last chance," Drip said. He armed his sling and prepared to attack.

With silence in the air, Drip pulled back the sling a little further and unintentionally released. The rock flew through the air and struck its target perfectly. However, the result was less than spectacular. The individual sat up straighter on their horse and removed their hood. *Her* hood.

"Who are you?" Gorath asked, recognizing that they were from the same monk order. However, he could not place her face.

"Gorath, I am Cary, and I am here to kill you."

EPISODE 22

Gorath was truly speechless. Though many had tried to kill him, none had put it so plainly. Of course he knew that it would be a great challenge going head to head with a monk from his order, though he was still astonished that she was a woman. That was the moment he remembered he had something that would give him a clear advantage.

"Bold, but foolish," Boot said first.

"Gorath, I wanted to let you know, I have your back," Drip said. Everyone turned and looked at the small imp for a moment.

"Okay, let's do this!" Thomas shouted.

"I'll take care of this," Gorath said. "Let's see what you have." He turned his nose up at the monk and folded his arms.

Then with super agile reflexes, Cary pointed a finger at him and launched a lightning bolt.

Gorath gave a puzzled look as he began to climb to his feet from where the unexpected lightning bolt had sent him. "No book reference, impressive," Gorath said. "But pretty weak if that is the best you've got."

Cary seemed visibly irritated at the result of the lightning bolt, as it would have killed anyone else. She then squatted and began to gather the magic in the air until it formed a massive sphere of electricity.

"Um, that looks problematic, you sure you don't need any help with this?" Thomas asked.

"Nope, I'm good," Gorath said.

"Good, I'm not sure I could do anything to help you out on this one anyway," Thomas said.

Gorath slid his right foot behind him to brace for the strike. A wind began to swirl around the two monks. It was the first time Thomas and Drip had noticed that Gorath's arms were incredibly muscular. It was a bit of a surprise, since the robes made him look like a twig of a man.

Cary launched the massive ball of electricity, now about four feet in diameter. Everyone watched in anticipation as the ball exploded on impact, causing a blinding light and forcing everyone to turn away. However, as the smoke cleared, Gorath was still standing and apparently unharmed as he casually brushed the dust off his robe.

"Whoa, that was pretty awesome," Drip said.

"Yeah. And impossible," Thomas said.

"Really, that is all you have in you?" Gorath asked. Then, uncharacteristically, he mocked the monk. "So weak."

"AAAAHHHHH!!!" Cary shouted, then executed a series of impressive martial arts moves, each causing a wave of energy to reach forward as an extension of her body. Gorath seemed to effortlessly avoid each attack.

"No way," Thomas said in disbelief.

"Just wait," Gorath remarked, while dodging the attacks. He then raised his arm and made a flicking motion. The simple move carried the smallest trace of energy that pierced the oncoming attack, until it reached Cary. It gently, almost barely touched her nose. Suddenly, Cary was violently thrown to the ground.

Gorath leaped forward exposing the wand that he had been wielding the entire time. He pointed the wand at Cary's tired body. In one motion, Gorath raised Cary into the air, and began to slash side to side. To everyone's astonishment and horror, Gorath's magic seemed to peel away a layer of Cary's body, like a snake shedding its skin. However, upon closer examination, Cary was just fine, but an apparition had now appeared about five feet behind her.

"How dare you use this monk to attack me," Gorath seethed. "You are revealed, you abhorrent creature!"

"I may have failed this time, but mark my words, I will see your demise!" the apparition's voice shrieked. Then, in dramatic fashion, the ghost seemed to explode.

Gorath walked over to Cary, whose lifeless body lay crumpled on the ground. He took note again of her long brown hair. There was a very specific rule in the monk order against having long hair—and about being a woman. He reached down and brushed his fingers against it. Then in one motion, a hand reached up and grabbed Gorath's throat.

"Wand or no wand, no one touches my hair," Cary said.

Gorath found it hard to breathe, let alone speak, but he managed to get one phrase out, "You can't hide that you're a woman! I've seen you!"

"Maybe. But if you tell anyone, I will end you! Do you understand?" Cary threatened. She slowly released her grip.

"Yes, yes..." Gorath answered, sputtering as he got his breath back. "How have you been able to get away with it?"

"Hum, not as smart as I thought you would be," Cary said. "About one third of the order is made up of women."

"Astonishing. I had no idea," Gorath said.

"Thank you for separating whatever that was from me," Cary said, although it sounded forced.

"Um...what are you doing here?" Thomas asked. "Did that spirit carry you out here just to try and kill Gorath?"

"Honestly, I don't remember," Cary said, and that was the truth.

"Well, you probably don't want to go the way we are going," Drip said.

"You're right, I don't think I do. Where are we, exactly?" Cary asked.

"We are in the heart of the hill giant territory," Drip replied.

"Wow, and all out of powder to get home," Cary said, looking inside a small leather pouch.

"Well, good luck then," Gorath said. He remounted his horse, and turned it to face north.

"Are you sure you will be okay alone?" Drip asked.

"She will be fine," Thomas said.

"Of course, given the circumstances, you *could* come with us," Gorath said with his head turned to the side.

Cary looked south and, right on cue, a massive series of thumping noises indicated hill giants were approaching. She quickly patted her pockets and realized that she did not have any of her quick reference guides.

"Very well, I accept," Cary said reluctantly.

"Perfect, you will ride with Thomas," Gorath said, and then made the clicking noise to tell his horse to trot.

Thomas's eyes were glaring at the back of Gorath's head, but not nearly as intense as Grendel was. Having to carry another person was no easy task. Regardless, the two irritated members of the party picked up Cary and began to follow behind Gorath.

"So what is it like being a woman in the monk order?" Boot asked.

"Oh my, enchanted boots on an imp! I did not see that coming," Cary said, "well it is interesting. I love the ability to wield magic and all."

"That was a very impressive display of magic back there," Drip said.

"Oh no, I'm not that powerful. That was mostly the...thing that was using my body as a coat. I can do some magic without a reference, but I mostly need a book," Cary said. "What is everyone's name?"

"I am Drip, that is Thomas, and of course Gorath over there," Drip said.

"Ahem," Boot said, sounding as if he was clearing his throat, if he'd had a throat.

"Of course, sorry. This is Boot and Bean," Drip said.

"How did you all end up together?" Cary asked.

"It was pretty random," Thomas said. "Strange things happen in the midst of battle."

"Ah," Cary replied.

"Okay, let's quiet down," Gorath ordered. "We will be in dragon territory very soon, and dragons have very sensitive hearing."

"She is dangerous," Orielia said, looking at the moving wall.

"Do you remember?" the first apparition asked.

"No," Orielia replied. "So familiar, though."

"It is time that we show her," the second apparition said.

"Yes, it is time," the first replied.

Everything on the wall stopped moving and a section of it cleared away. Four young girls and their father stood in the open space.

"Four sisters," the first apparition said. Then, unexpectedly the wall turned to black.

"NO, you will show her nothing," a deep voice said. "You will remember your place."

"So," Orielia said to the blackness. "It looks like you failed to kill the three."

"It is only a matter of time," the voice crackled. "I have foreseen it."

Orielia turned toward the window. "You should probably hurry then. The sky just turned red."

EPISODE 23

"Say that again?" Aroon asked. The massive wind storm caused a constant high-pitched hum, and he was having trouble hearing the disembodied voice.

"You heard me. You have forty-eight hours to kill the three," the voice shouted from the small rock.

To most people, it would look absurd for a military leader to be holding a small rock up to his ear, and shouting at it to speak up. However, the rock was a stone of communication and it was perfectly normal for this particular veteran leader.

"Very good, Sir," Aroon said, shocked at the orders and angry with himself for leading this expedition when he'd known from the beginning that something seemed off about it. It had only been an hour since they had caught sight of the three—well, four at the moment. However, the random windstorm was making everything difficult to see.

"What are our orders, Sir?" Stevens asked, with his massive hand blocking the wind from his face. The corporal had not noticed the five members of their party that were seeking shelter in his enormous shadow.

"We need to catch up to Gorath's party," Aroon said. He dropped the small stone into his pocket.

"Very good, Sir," Stevens said. "No way they've made it much farther than we have."

"No doubt," Aroon said.

Cary was proud of herself, as she had managed to cast a full windstorm from memory. However, she was disappointed at her lack of control of the force of nature, as the group found themselves caught in it as well. She decided to keep it to herself that she had been the one to conjure it. They had been fighting the storm for nearly eight hours, ever since she saw the other party approaching.

"Do you know where we are heading?" Drip asked.

"I hope we find our way out soon; the sand is collecting in unpleasant places," Boot said.

"Truly," Thomas added.

"Yes, it is this way," Gorath said. He did not want to say anything but he knew that this storm had been conjured, and to his knowledge there were only two people out this far with that ability.

"How long until sunset?" Drip asked. "We need to find shelter soon."

"We will keep moving for another hour or so, unless we find suitable shelter before then," Gorath announced.

"I think that is shelter up ahead!" Thomas shouted over the wind. She was pointing to a large dark area ahead of them.

"Alright, let's rest there," Gorath announced. As they approached the large mound that they took for a hill, they realized they would be able to keep out of the storm quite well.

"That is exactly what I said!" Aroon shouted.

"I don't understand; why would they want us to kill them?" Corporal Stevens asked.

"I don't know," Aroon replied.

"What are you planning on doing about it, Sir?" Stevens asked.

"I am hoping I don't have to worry about that," Aroon said.

"I don't understand," Aroon replied.

"We are no longer headed towards them, so the odds that we would run into them are slim," Aroon replied.

"Aroon, that's why you're the one in charge," Stevens replied with a big smile.

"Yeah, I would hate to have to kill them..." Aroon said, then looked up to realize he had walked right into the middle of a camp on the other side of a hill obscured by the storm.

"Aroon!" Gorath said in a very cheerful tone. "Stevens!"

Completely speechless, Aroon stood still in shock. Gorath quickly raced over and embraced him. Aroon was trying frantically to think of how to escape this situation and not have to obey his orders.

"What are you doing here?" Thomas asked. She noticed that Cary was staring closely at the new visitors.

"Gorath, it was good seeing you, but we must be off, we are patrolling the edge for wandering bandits," Aroon said, in a hurry to get as far away from the four as possible.

"If your journey has been half as tough as ours, then you need to rest. You should camp here with us tonight," Gorath said. "Strength in numbers and all."

"That sounds great," Stevens said. He gave a thumbs-up to a very confused Aroon.

"I don't think that is such a great idea," Aroon contributed.

"You're too late," Thomas said very unenthusiastically.

Aroon turned to see his party had dismounted and was already starting to assemble tents and digging in, all this despite the clear lack of an order to do so. After a moment, Aroon conceded the choice and began to mope his way over to a small fire where Cary sat.

"It is impressive that you are able to make a fire like this in the middle of a windstorm with no wood," Aroon observed.

Cary looked up with a grin, realizing that he had no idea she had smuggled her way into Gorath's small group after hiding in his ranks first. Doing so even while being possessed by a very clever spirit was a tricky thing, and she knew Aroon was the best of the best from the stories she had heard.

"This is a special tar from the St. Tomerick. The stuff burns forever with no source of fuel needed," Cary said.

Gorath couldn't help but overhear the statement made by Cary. He was genuinely impressed by her ingenuity, but something about her kept bugging him. Gorath couldn't shake the thought that he would like to spend more time with her, and even found himself a little irritated at the time she was now spending with Aroon.

"Whoa, I did not see that coming," Drip said.

"No kidding, but it makes sense. They *are* from the same order," Boot added.

It took an extra moment for Gorath to realize they were talking about him. He offered them a stiff glare and rolled his eyes.

"Please, like I would give in to a weakness like that," Gorath said. "Just a distraction."

He considered that and then realized he was again staring at her. Gorath promptly looked away, walked over to Thomas, and sat down on the ground next to her.

"Is everything okay?" Thomas asked.

"Fine, why?" Gorath asked.

"You seem a little, well flustered," Thomas added.

"I just have, well, let's say there is a person I know who is struggling with thinking about someone else, but it has never happened to him before," Gorath said.

"Has this been going on for very long?" Thomas asked.

"No, you know, don't worry about it," Gorath said. Then he mumbled to himself, "dumb feelings."

"Okay, this is interesting and all," Thomas said, "but you need to get yourself under control. After all, we're all counting on you."

"I need to go clear my head," Gorath said. He promptly got up again and walked away from the group into the windstorm.

Thomas stood up and walked over to the never-ending fire where most of the group had congregated. She had been suspicious of the group's intentions from the beginning, especially since no one, not even strapping soldiers, were dumb enough to stumble into dragon or hill giant territory.

"So who is it that you would hate to have to kill?" Thomas asked, obviously having overheard Aroon's words before he'd realized where he was.

Aroon felt the question like a knife at his rib cage. He resisted the chill that ran down his spine, and remained calm. His mixture of staunch and rigorous training, and his thirty combat missions kept him composed, more or less.

"Bandits," Aroon said. "I prefer capturing over killing."

"Have you captured bandits before?" Thomas asked. She noticed his clever counter, but knew something else was going on, and like a good chess match, she felt confident engaging him.

"Many," Aroon said.

"Really," Thomas said with a hint of sarcasm. "And to what places have you chased these bandits?"

Aroon knew that he needed to figure a way out of this conversation. "All over Wax, but that isn't important. I think we should call it a night."

"Sure, just one last question," Thomas said. "How many have you killed?"

"Only a few," Aroon said. Inside he was letting out a sigh of relief that the damage was contained. Then he heard Stevens chime in.

"Ah, Aroon is just being humble, he has killed no less than two hundred, and charged in head first, even when the odds were unbelievably against him," Stevens said proudly, right up until he caught Aroon glaring at him.

"Wow, I am surprised there are any bandits left in Wax at all," Thomas said. She was both pleased and irritated. She had managed to glean a piece of truth, but it left her with little to work with.

The two parties went to their respective sides of the camp and turned in for the night. Gorath had barely managed to make it back to the camp through the storm just before Cary wrapped the burning piece of tar and put it away. It was about that time when the windstorm died down.

Thomas vowed to keep one eye open throughout the night, but eventually fell asleep. That is until Boot cried out.

"Thomas!" Boot shouted.

Thomas's eyes opened just in time to watch her sword rise up to defend her from the powerful down-stroke of a massive axe. The loud clang woke everyone up. The axe rose again to reveal Corporal Stevens behind the attack.

"Wait!" Aroon shouted. "Stop!"

It was too late for the command to process, and again Stevens swung his powerful blade downward with even more strength. Gracefully, Thomas's sword deflected the axe, and it sunk deep into the ground. That's when everything changed, and a thunderous growl filled the air. The mound the parties had been seeking shelter behind suddenly came to life to expose an extraordinarily large eye.

"AAAHHHHH!" The dragon roared, causing the ground to tremble violently.

EPISODE 24

The party panicked in unison and, unsure of exactly what to do or what direction to run, everyone scattered, except for Gorath and Cary. Gorath stood completely calm and stared straight into the large eye of the dragon they had been sent to slay. Cary raised her hands, pointing them outwardly and focusing on an imaginary point in space. Time began to slow, until it stopped altogether. Only Cary and Gorath were unaffected

"What is this?" Gorath asked as he glanced around at the others, now statues.

"Despite what the order teaches, each of us has one or two very special abilities that could be classified as…rare," Cary said. "I have the ability to pause time, temporarily, and I can pull one other into my bubble."

"Why choose me?" Gorath asked. "Why not Aroon or Thomas?"

"We only have a few moments. We can run and escape the dragon," Cary said.

"No! Everyone else will die if we do," Gorath said.

"If we don't, we all die," Cary said.

"Listen to the girl. Run, I will be satisfied with these morsels," the dragon's voice filled the air. "For now at least."

"Time is catching up, you must decide!" Cary shouted. "Now!"

Gorath had made up his mind, and pulled Arkanim's wand from his robe. He could feel the power coursing through him, and it instantly gave him a boost of confidence and bravery. Every magic user who had used the wand previously described the feeling he was experiencing as "magic drunk." Tragically, this sensational came upon them right before they were absorbed by the wand's power.

As time inched closer to catching up, Gorath raised the wand and slowly turned until his back was to the dragon. In the blink of an eye, Gorath safely teleported the two parties outside the dragon's immediate sphere of influence. The ground continued to shake violently around Gorath, and that was about the time he realized the dragon was much larger than any previous guess—he was standing on top of its back! The dragon had to have been slumbering within a large crater, with most of its body concealed. Gorath could feel the dragon start to climb into the air and quickly cast a massive spell to create a harness of sorts to hold onto.

"Ha!" Argentauth, the dragon, shouted. "You're going to need more than that!"

"Let's see what you've got!" Gorath taunted. He could hear the words exit his mouth, but he was positive that it did not come from his brain. He glanced down at his right hand and could see the wand was glowing white, and that his hand seemed to reflect a light blue color.

The dragon lifted into the air, and Gorath felt everything slow again, though this time not from a spell. His adrenaline had kicked in, and the power of the wand was coursing through him. Gorath had been in what seemed like certain doom before; however, it did not take a genius to recognize the situation for what it was. He could feel the wand slowly absorbing him, and he was now riding on top of the largest dragon anyone had ever seen. Gorath knew this would be his last adventure.

The party watched helplessly as the dragon began to ascend rapidly, with a terrible screeching noise. Without thought, Thomas jumped onto Grendel and raced towards the dragon. Drip watched as everyone else stood with their mouths agape. He decided to get onto his horse and head after Thomas.

"What are you doing!?" Aroon shouted at those giving chase. "It's suicide!"

"Stay here if you want!" Cary replied, yelling over the dragon sounds. Then she disappeared behind a magic cloud of yellow powder.

Thomas could sense as the others approached behind her. She carefully studied the dragon's movements as it darted left and right, trying to shake Gorath off its back.

You can still turn back. Why risk anything for this guy? a voice in the back of her mind asked. Grendel glanced back occasionally, seeming to ask the same question.

"Because it's the right thing to do," Thomas said out loud.

"How do we attack it?" Drip shouted as he rode up beside her.

"I don't know yet," Thomas replied.

"I think I can make him get close to the ground," Cary added. She was now gliding over the ground next to the two horses.

"Do it!" Thomas shouted. She looked up just in time to see Gorath almost fall off the giant beast.

Gorath's heart nearly stopped as he barely regained his footing. He could feel his arms struggling to hold on to the reigns he had magically summoned, as well as his right hand gripping the wand that was slowly trying to absorb him. Gorath used the wand again to enhance the harness and reinforce his position by creating a saddle. Suddenly, his hand became transparent, as he stared in horror through it. Argentauth seemed to get angrier by the second.

"I like a challenge, but you are becoming a pain!" Argentauth shouted. Then the dragon climbed straight up for what seemed like forever. Suddenly, the dragon dove straight for the ground, while exhaling a long stream of fire. This caused the air around Gorath to heat up enough to cook an ox.

Gorath managed to use the wand to protect himself from the heat, creating a barrier around him, and then he threw a large lightning bolt at Argentauth's head. The bolt grazed the large dragon's ear. Even though it wasn't a direct hit, the strike delivered a vicious jolt, causing the dragon to nearly topple from the sky. As the dragon looped and twisted more aggressively than before, desperate to get his bearing, a series of large snowballs came up from the ground and struck the beast several times.

"Good job!" Thomas shouted to Cary.

"Don't celebrate yet," Cary said. She pointed to the dragon rapidly approaching. Sure enough, Argentauth was now flying mere feet from the ground.

"Can you shield us?" Thomas asked.

"Only enough for a single strike," Cary said. "What's the plan?"

"Drip and I will ride up under the dragon and see what damage we can cause," Thomas said. She looked back at the Imp. As she had seen him do a handful of times before, he was furiously scratching something out in his book.

"I think that is your cue," Boot said.

"Good to go," Drip said.

"You better be, I'm not eager to see if I am dragon-fire proof," Boot added.

Cary raised her arms just as the dragon reached them, and a long streak of fire raced over them. As promised, Cary had protected them from sure death, but then she collapsed under the strain of the intense spell.

Thomas and Drip raced along under the dragon. Thomas drew her sword and thrust it upward to catch the dragon's underbelly, but she was just a foot-and-a-half too short.

"Drip!" Thomas shouted.

Drip had already prepped to jump from his horse to Thomas's. He gave his enchanted armor a quick pat, and then he jumped. Drip barely made the crossing, but with no time for praise, he climbed onto Thomas's shoulders. He snatched up the heavy sword that he could barely lift, but the sword recognized the situation and darted upward in Drip's hands. It bounced off the heavy scales, until it hit a soft spot and pierced the dragon's flesh.

With a loud cry, Argentauth darted up. Thomas and Drip stopped to see what effect this had caused, realizing then that the dragon was turning to run them down. Thomas and Drip raced away as quickly as Grendel could carry them, but even the trusty horse was starting to show her wear. The dragon began to spew fire at them, and just as it seemed they would be engulfed, a huge axe in his path caused the dragon to veer off. Thomas and Drip were elated to see Aroon and his party had come to their senses.

"Do you give up yet?" Gorath asked.

"Never!" the dragon shouted.

Gorath had noticed a mildly active volcano in the area, and wondered if the dragon could take that kind of heat. The problem was how to get the dragon close enough to find out. He looked up to see a massive storm gathering above them. He knew his time was running short before he would be totally absorbed by the wand. He had to act quickly.

"Gorath," a ghostly figure said, appearing before him. "I am so sorry. I cannot save you, but I can help you."

"Orielia?" Gorath asked, squinting at the apparition.

A smile crossed the ghost's face. "Not quite."

Cary's body was telling her to sleep and recover, but she had to see how the battle was going. As she lifted her head, she felt a drop of rain hit her hand. Cary climbed to her knees. That is when a ghostly figure appeared to her.

"Cary," the apparition said. "I know you are tired, but you must do one last thing, and you must do it now!"

"What?" Cary asked with her tired voice.

"You need to aggravate the pending storm and build it up to the most powerful storm you can," the ghost said.

"I can't, I've got nothing for that," Cary said.

"You must if you are to defeat the dragon," the ghost said urgently.

Cary shook her head, but then raised her hands and focused her thoughts on a violent lightning storm, and after a moment, she released whatever magic she had left.

Gorath was amazed as the storm became incredibly brutal. Argentauth was far too large to avoid lightning strikes of the magnitude the storm was producing. With no other choice, the dragon began to race towards the edge of the storm directly at the volcano. As they were about to pass over the top of the burning mountain, Gorath closed his eyes. He could feel the wand absorbing more of him, and instinctively raised it up. He gathered the massive power of the electrical storm into the wand, and like a giant hammer, smashed it into the back of Argentauth's head.

Gorath opened his eyes to see the lava rising up, ready to embrace the two. He raised his hands to brace for impact, and knew there would be no escape. His hands were completely transparent now, and it was just a matter of seconds before the wand would take him completely. The thunderous impact collapsed the upper crust of the volcano in on itself, swallowing Argentauth and his passenger with it.

EPISODE 25

Thomas collapsed to her knees at the sight of the large explosion. She felt physically spent, and let her body fall to the ground. Thomas rolled to her back just in time to see the unnatural storm move out of the area. The bright sunlight of the early morning blinded her for a moment, and caused her to close her visor.

"Thomas, are you okay?" Drip asked.

Thomas could feel the imp nudge her leg in an attempt to gain a response. She managed a soft groan. Her muscles were crying out in familiar agony. Thomas's worn body had seen much longer and more physically draining battles, but there was something different about this one. She recognized that there had been a new kind of sensation.

"I am exhausted," Thomas said.

"It's not like we just defeated the largest dragon in the world," Drip said sarcastically. "Oh wait, we did."

"Technically, Gorath did the defeating," Boot said.

The phrase struck a chord with Drip, and he sat down next to Thomas. A sudden sadness came over Drip and Thomas at the same time.

"At least he was able to take the dragon down with him," Aroon said from behind them.

"Yeah," Drip and Thomas said at the same time.

Then, like a lightning bolt had struck Thomas, she jumped to her feet in one motion, with her sword drawn. The point was clearly aimed at Aroon.

"What's the deal with your guy attacking me in my sleep!?" Thomas shouted.

Aroon was so caught off guard, he fell back into Corporal Stevens. His mind raced to find an answer that would not mean his certain death.

"Yeah!" Aroon shouted. "What's the deal with the attack, Corporal Stevens?"

In one motion, Aroon spun around to face Stevens. He could feel Thomas' sword resting against the armor plating covering his back. He could tell this was going to be tough to sell, as Stevens looked at him in confusion.

"Answer me, why did you attack?" Aroon asked again.

"I don't know, Sir. I could see everything that was happening, but...couldn't control myself," Stevens reported, at least knowing to play along.

"That's no excuse, you are a trained professional," Aroon said with a very worried look. He glanced back for a moment and recognized that Thomas was not buying the redirect.

Thomas flicked her wrist and, in one quick motion, cut a portion of Aroon's hair. Everyone started to laugh as Aroon reached up just in time to hold a fist full of hair. He panicked for a moment and began to buff up Stevens' chest plate so he could see his reflection. Aroon turned in anger towards Thomas and, without hesitation, drew his sword and crossed blades with her.

"You sure you want to do this?" Thomas asked with a smile across her face.

"Oh yes! You are going down," Aroon said. He was relishing the thought of putting this little twerp in her place. It helped that he knew full well that she had exerted herself far more than he had in the skirmish with the dragon.

"Huh, that's odd, it looks like you might be balding," Thomas taunted.

Aroon reached back and touched the back of his head where a portion of his hair used to be. This caused him to focus his anger. In his first motion, he thrust the sword forward in an attempt to catch Thomas off guard. However, she countered with no problem.

Even with the enchanted sword and armor aiding her, she noted how quick and strong Aroon was. Thomas patiently waited for Aroon to make a mistake, but he never seemed to leave an opening for her to catch a break.

"Should someone tell him about the armor and sword?" Boot asked.

"I don't think so," Drip said. Then after a quick head count he realized they were missing more than Gorath. "Where is Cary?"

"Sleep, steep, strong..." Bean added.

Drip wandered away from the dueling pair in search of the newest member of their group. After a quick sweep, he found Cary, with no apparent signs of life, lying in a small hole in the ground.

"Cary?" Drip asked as he attempted to rouse her with a nudge of his foot. When there was no reaction, he kneeled down beside her. He lifted her hand and let it fall to the ground.

"Oh, this is not good," Boot said.

"Cary!" Drip shouted. He put his hand on her forehead, which felt damp and cold. He then rested his head on her chest to listen for her heart. Then Drip was startled and nearly jumped out of his skin when Cary let out the loudest snore he had ever heard. This included the likes of giants, orcs, and goblins.

"At lease she isn't dead," Boot said.

Drip made a terrific effort to move her closer to the group, but after just a few feet, he recognized that it was more than a one-imp job. He stood over the sleeping female who had saved all their lives, out of breath and at a loss.

Suddenly, a loud rumble permeated from the volcano, causing him to look up, startled from his thoughts. He squinted up at the top of the angry mountain, blinking and trying to convince himself he wasn't seeing what he was seeing.

Lava was now heading in their direction.

As fast as his feet could carry him, he raced back to the group, now amused as the two were still attempting to run each other through. Drip poked his head through the crowd just in time to see Thomas lean back out of the way of Aroon's sword and then lunge forward, missing her opponent by only an inch.

"Listen, you two have to stop this, we are in danger here and Cary needs help," Drip said with a sense of urgency.

"In just a moment, Drip," Thomas said as she took a full swing at Aroon. "I have him right where I want him."

"Ha!" Aroon shouted as he deflected the attack and offered a quick counter. "You won't last five more minutes."

Drip was frustrated at the group and quickly raced to the horses and began searching for anything that could help them. With little choice, he found himself looking over Gorath's stash. He looked into a small blue bag, and recognized that it was a bag of holding, smaller than the red one Gorath had carried with him to his demise. As Drip looked inside, a ghostly version of Gorath appeared before him.

"If you have opened this bag, then either you are a thief or I am dead, or both now that I think about it. Of course I could just be unresponsive…" the image of Gorath began to say. "Anyway, if something has gone terribly wrong, please state the nature of your emergency. If you are a thief, I don't really have anything all that valuable."

"Are you a ghost?" Drip asked.

"No, this is an emergency enchantment," Gorath's image said. "Now please state the nature of your emergency."

"Okay, well…you're dead," Drip began.

"Oh crap, I'm dead?" Gorath's image asked. "Did I have a good death?"

"I'd say. You killed a dragon," Drip replied.

"I'm not sure what to say," the image said.

"How do we escape the lava?" Drip asked.

"Lava? What lava?" Gorath's image asked.

"The lava from the volcano that is headed towards us," Drip said.

"Brilliant, now that is a challenge," the image said.

"And, how do we escape?" Drip asked.

"You have to do exactly what I tell you," Gorath's image said.

The combat had been so fast-paced and frantic for both Aroon and Thomas that the two had grown tired, and were now engaged in more of a verbal battle than a physical one. Then the ground shook violently, causing the group to all fall to the ground. It was only at that moment that everyone else noticed the lava rushing towards them.

Suddenly they were engulfed by a bright white light, then everything went dark. As daylight seemed to be slowly restored, they looked around to find themselves back at Ormlu. Thomas glanced around and saw Drip standing in front of everyone, and for a moment, she could swear Gorath was standing right behind him.

"How?" Thomas asked. Then she passed out.

EPISODE 26

Drip watched as the party lay unconscious. He too felt very drowsy but he was able to resist the temptation to sleep because of his concern for the slumbering group. One by one, he checked to make sure everyone was breathing and that they were set in comfortable positions. It was only a matter of time before the city guards were alerted to their presence.

"What is the meaning of this?" the first guard asked Drip.

"I am Drip, assistant to the High Standard of the Watch," Drip said, standing toe to toe with the guard. "And I order you to assist my efforts."

"High Standard of the what?" the guard asked. "Never heard of it, and I think you need to answer for this."

"I really don't have time," Drip said, waving his hand at the ignorant guard. "Let me know when your superior has arrived."

"Oye, I'll have you know I have the right to arrest you for that little comment," the guard said. He began to fumble for the pair of handcuffs on his belt.

Drip rolled his eyes at the show of power, and continued to check on the welfare of his people.

"I said you need to come with me," the guard announced.

"I don't think he is kidding around," Boot chimed in.

"I really don't care right now," Drip said. "I need to look after everyone."

"That's it, as required by The Book, I am stating my legal action, and under section 129 subsection 32, I hereby place you under arrest," the guard stated.

This was ironic because the guard had actually quoted the section and subsection referencing the exchange of prisoners between the light and dark. So as the guard reached over to restrain Drip, he was teleported back about five feet for technically being in the wrong. It was about that time a squad of city guards reached the scene.

"What is going on here?" the constable over the city watch squad asked.

"This imp is resisting arrest," the first guard reported.

"If I am resisting, then why am I standing here, and the guard is over there?" Drip asked.

"Interesting," the constable said.

"At any rate, maybe you know who I am," Drip said with a tired tone behind his voice.

"I'm afraid not." the constable said.

"Brilliant," Boot scoffed.

"I am the assistant to the High Standard of the Watch, appointed by the Light King and the Dark Lord," Drip said. That is when he began to feel light-headed and was forced to sit down.

"My apologies, Sir, what do you need us to help you with?" the constable asked.

"Take the soldiers to the Candlestick, take the female mage to the hospital, and take me and the warrior to the Master Field Inn," Drip said as sleep began to overtake him. He was exhausted from their ordeals, just like the others, and could no longer keep his eyes open.

"Yes, Sir," the constable said.

Orielia watched the moving wall again and again replay the entire battle with the dragon. She was having a hard time understanding all the events, especially why Corporal Stevens had attacked Thomas.

"What are you looking for?" the first apparition asked.

"Several things, like, why the unprovoked attack, why the interference from the spirit, and how this failed," Orielia said.

"It is time you knew," the second apparition said.

"Yes," the first apparition said. "It all started with a great wizard and his four daughters, in a chaotic world." The moving wall cleared again.

"The mother was taken by darkness," the second apparition said.

"The father vowed to protect his daughters at any cost, he studied and researched ways to increase his powers," the first apparition said. The wall mimicked the story with a series of painted images.

"There came a point when two of his daughters came down with an infection that he could not cure, and he feared their deaths," the second apparition said.

"He felt helpless as they lay on their death beds, and recognized what he needed to do," the first apparition said.

"So he sacrificed himself to save them?" Orielia asked.

"Yes," the second apparition said.

"What he did not know is that his sacrifice would be so powerful as to not only save his daughters, but it would preserve all four of them forever, immortal but not immune to fatal injury," the first apparition said. "They could be killed, but his magic was powerful enough to make that nearly impossible."

"You call me sister...but if I am one of the sisters from the story, as you are, then why do I only remember the past few years?" Orielia asked.

"Because, sister, I nearly killed you, like I did the other two, but you managed to escape," a different voice entered the conversation.

"You killed your own sisters? Why?" Orielia asked.

"It is simple, really; Father's powers were extended to protect all four of us, and it was only a matter of time before I realized that the fewer the sisters, the more magic would be available to me," the dark voice said.

"So this is nothing but a power play?" Orielia asked.

"So simple minded. Once you are gone and there is no threat to my power, then I will be able to do anything I want. I can create or destroy. There won't be a light or dark, there will only be my empire," the voice replied, "and I have already succeeded in killing one of your three champions."

Memories danced at the back of Orielia's mind. Memories of her once beloved sisters, and how one had turned on them all. "It is a blur, but I remember you now, Olpetrion, and our sisters, Ponopoli and Naomi."

"Very good," Olpetrion said. "But your memory won't be able to save you."

Thomas opened her eyes to see the ornate celling of her room at the Master Field Inn. She rubbed her aching forehead as she looked around, awkwardly climbing out of the bed still in her armor as she had done many, many times before.

The smell of breakfast permeated throughout the chamber and instantly caught her attention. With no prompting at all, she raced out the door and into the faulty elevator. As she exited, she found that she had the whole buffet to herself.

"Good to see you awake," Carter, the inn keeper said.

"How did I end up here?" Thomas asked as she skipped the traditional formalities, and began eating food right off the large table.

The action clearly irritated the inn keeper, but he held his thoughts on her manners. "You were brought here by the city watch, as per Master Drip's command."

"Ah, I love Drip, and I am loving these eggs," Thomas said. With her initial wave of hunger satisfied, she began to put food onto a plate.

"Yes, ma'am," Carter said.

"Where is the imp, and where is Gorath?" Thomas asked. "I need to ask him how he escaped the dragon."

"I am sorry, Gorath did not join you on your return," Carter said.

Thomas had known all along that it was impossible for the monk to escape the volcano, but something inside her kept telling her that she had seen him after it erupted.

A short time later Drip made it to the breakfast table.

"Drip!" Thomas exclaimed. She raced over to him and gave him a tight hug. She quickly looked around and released him, surprised and a little embarrassed by her own gush of emotion.

"It is good to see you too," Drip said. He was unsure how to feel in this circumstance as this was the first time anyone had hugged him to his recollection.

"What do you mean, they killed the dragon?!" Dark Lord Twiller exclaimed.

"I understand they lost the monk in the fight," Head Monk Towe reported.

"This is good news," King Ragmon said. "We need to send them out again, right away, to make sure the others share his fate before we do."

"What do you suggest?" Twiller asked with both joy and annoyance at his counterpart.

"I don't know. I thought the dragon would take them all out for sure," Ragmon said.

"Wait, I know just the thing," Twiller said with a smile.

EPISODE 27

The Dark Lord picked up a folder of papers, and quickly sorted through them, eventually pulling one out. He looked over the paper before sliding it onto the table before King Ragmon and Head Monk Towe. The two men scanned the document.

"I don't understand," Ragmon said. "What are we looking at here?"

The Dark Lord rolled his eyes and let out a quick sigh. Then he walked over to the table and pointed his finger at the bottom of the paper.

"You are looking at an official report outlining an area of the Dark Kingdom where everything has gone...well, dark," Twiller said. He watched as confusion crossed Ragmon's face. "No, it wasn't a Light Side attack. There have been two scouting parties sent to investigate. The first was never heard from again. The second party was made up of far more experienced troops, and no one has heard back from that group either."

"So why are we sending the soldier and imp there?" Ragmon asked.

"The area that has become unresponsive has increased in size, and will soon spill into the Light Side territory," Twiller said.

"Then we are agreed to send the group to the south this time," Towe said.

"Yes, they will go to the necromancer," Orielia said. No one had noticed that she had entered the room.

"Necromancer? That's nonsense, there hasn't been a true necro for over an age," Twiller said.

"But if it is true, then it will be perfect," Ragmon said.

Thomas and Drip had found themselves unexpectedly talking to each other quite a bit over breakfast. Then they were interrupted with a message from the Candlestick, as a scroll was handed to Thomas.

"Orders," Thomas said.

"How do you know?" Drip asked.

"As a professional soldier, I have learned the moment you relax is always when you get your orders," Thomas said. She opened the scroll to revile their orders as predicted. However something strange happened. A portion of the scroll appeared for just a moment and then disappeared.

"What does it say?" Drip asked.

"It promotes me to party leader, and it says we are to head for a southern area in the dark lands to investigate an issue," Thomas said.

"Sounds fun. To the armory?" Drip asked.

"I would be surprised if they let you back in there, after last time," Boot added.

"Yeah, that's probably not going to happen," Thomas said. "However, we need to make a couple of stops on the way out of town. Where is Cary?"

"She is in the hospital still," Drip said.

"Okay, let's go make a visit," Thomas said. "Right after one last omelet."

"You should probably leave before the parade starts," Carter said, standing at the ready in case they requested anything.

"True, let's head out," Drip said. He leapt up from the table and headed for the door.

Thomas was trying to process what was going on, but could not quite make sense of it. She shrugged and followed after Drip. As they exited the inn, she noticed a great deal of decoration adorning the streets.

"What parade is this?" Thomas asked.

"Oh, whichever one," Drip said, brushing off the question and starting to move at a quicker pace.

Thomas again was left to shrug, since there were no clear answers to be had. She continued to follow until she was stopped by a strange looking reflection of herself. That is when she realized that it wasn't a reflection, instead it was an artist's rendering of her.

"Drip, why is there a painting of me over here?" she asked. Then she turned the corner and all of her questions were answered. Large elaborate floats were lined up in a long line. One after another was clearly telling the story of their defeat of the dragon. Thomas caught up to Drip just as he was entering the hospital.

"Ah, Master Drip, good to see you again as always," the charge nurse said.

"Has there been any change?" Drip asked.

"Unfortunately not. Did you and your guest want to see the lady you brought in?" the nurse asked.

"Yes, thank you," Drip said. He began to head down his usual route to the VIP section of the hospital.

"Master Drip? A parade about our fight with the dragon?" Thomas asked. "Exactly how long have I been asleep?"

"You know, a little while," Drip said.

"That is one way to put it," Boot added.

"How long is a little while?" Thomas asked as they reached a large room.

"Oh, a month, or so," Drip said. He walked over to a large bed with two mages standing at the bedside.

"A month!?" Thomas exclaimed, then quickly quieted her tone as she realized where she was. Reverently she walked over to the bed where Drip was standing.

"It's funny, but other than the fact that she tried to kill Gorath, we barely even know her, yet I feel responsible for making sure she's okay," Drip said. He rested his hand on Cary's forehead.

"Did everyone sleep for a long time after we got back?" Thomas asked.

"No," a familiar voice said.

Thomas turned to see a ghostly version of Gorath. The shock nearly caused her to draw her sword.

"Are you a ghost? I saw you die," Thomas asked.

"No, he is not a ghost, he is an emergency curse, and much like Boot, he just randomly chimes in," Drip said.

"Not amused," Boot said.

"I don't understand," Thomas said. "An emergency curse?"

"Yeah, it took me a while to get my head wrapped around this," Drip said. "He is a curse on the small bag of holding I procured from Gorath's things."

"It is far more complicated than that, but that is the simple version," Gorath's image said.

"Is he very useful?" Thomas asked.

"About twenty-five percent of the time he has something good to say," Drip said with a grin.

"What about Cary? Will she be alright?" Thomas asked.

"We were hoping that she would wake up when you did," Gorath's image said. "However, since that is not the case, we hope she wakes up when the others wake."

"Where are the others?" Thomas asked. "Especially that brute who attacked me."

"They are being taken care of at the Candlestick," Drip answered.

"We are going to need to try and get some help, but I don't trust the guards loyal to the Candlestick," Thomas said.

"What were you thinking?" Drip asked.

"To be honest, I'm not positive," Thomas said.

"I think we should ask Orielia," Drip suggested.

"Ask Orielia what?" Orielia asked as she entered the room.

"That is kind of odd. We were just talking about looking for help, and we thought about asking you, and here you are," Drip said.

"No offense, but I think that is suspicious," Thomas said. She rested her right hand on the hilt of her sword

"I actually appreciate that," Orielia said, gesturing to Thomas' hand on her sword. "That is the kind of thinking that will keep you alive. However, I am here to see Cary."

"Thanks, I think," Thomas said, though she didn't release the grip on her sword just yet.

"Now what were you going to ask me?" Orielia asked.

"We need help, but we don't trust the guards with an allegiance to the Candlestick," Drip said. "Who would you recommend?"

"That is the right question," Orielia said. "Everyone knows that the enemy of your enemy is your friend, so I would start there."

"What does that mean?" Thomas asked.

"I apologize, my time is limited with Cary, and I wish to spend it alone," Orielia said.

"As you wish," Drip said.

As the two left the room, Orielia sat down on the side of the bed, and held Cary's hand in her own.

"I am so sorry that you are here," Orielia said. "It is a long story, but it is my fault you are in this mess. I had hoped that things would have ended differently with the dragon."

"Cary is still alive, just sleeping," Gorath's image said.

"I know, I was talking to *you*."

"But I am just an image of the actual person," Gorath's image replied.

"Still, I have to apologize," Orielia said. "You and Cary have paid such a heavy price. Tell the others what I said when Drip comes back to get you."

"What do you mean?" the image asked.

"They left you here to see what I would have to say," Orielia said with a smile. "Good for them."

"What did you mean when you said the enemy of their enemy?" the image asked. "Is the Candlestick the enemy? And if so, who is the Candlestick's enemy?"

"That is the right question," Orielia said.

EPISODE 28

Drip led Thomas out of the hospital and back out into the open streets. Drip closed his eyes for a moment and took in a deep breath before continuing on. There was something about the action that made Thomas pause and do the same.

"We need to get ready for this trip," Thomas said.

"Yes, but first we need to take a moment and gather our thoughts," Drip said. "Over at that little shop."

Thomas looked in the direction that Drip was pointing. The little shop was cute enough, and everything appeared well maintained, but nothing seemed special about it at all. She shrugged and followed the imp over to a small table just outside the shop.

"Okay, now what?" Thomas asked. She was impressed that Drip was taking command, and a bit amazed that she was actually going along with it.

"Who is the enemy of our enemy?" Drip asked openly.

"That would be easier if we knew who our enemy was," Thomas pointed out.

"Would the two champions like anything?" the waitress asked.

"Yes please, just a small cup of middle berry," Drip requested.

"And you?" the waitress asked Thomas.

"I will have what he is having," Thomas replied.

"Very good," the waitress said. "I just wanted to say it is a pleasure to serve amazing heroes like yourselves."

Thomas looked confused as the waitress offered a little bow and then scurried back into the shop. She could see through the glass as she pointed in their direction excitedly and let the other waitresses and patrons know who she had just talked to.

"This is...well..." Thomas began to say, staring at all the people looking at them in awe.

"Odd?" Boot added. "We know. A week ago there was an actual entourage, but Drip was able to convince them that it was better if they observed from a greater distance."

"Are there people following us right now?" Thomas asked, looking around.

"They have gotten better, but every once in a while they stick out like sore thumbs," Drip said.

"Hidden, driven, leading..." Bean added.

"Why are we just sitting here again?" Thomas asked.

"We are gathering our thoughts and trying to solve the riddle in front of us," Drip said.

The waitress quickly served their drinks and retreated back into the shop. Thomas and Drip sat back in their chairs thoughtfully, pondering the question. Suddenly, a loud band began marching down the street, followed by a dozen ornate floats depicting the dragon slaying. A large crowd followed the parade and the streets were instantly packed full of people.

"I don't remember some of the things on the float," Thomas said. "How do they know what happened?"

"The leaders watched it on the moving wall in the Candlestick," Drip said calmly. Then something shiny caught his eye on the far side of the street. A pair of hooded men stood unmoving in the crowd. The shade of the hoods cancelled their faces, but he was certain they were looking at them.

"Crazy. I would like to go see it," Thomas said. She could see that Drip was no longer paying attention to her. His eyes were fixed on something else altogether.

"Yeah," Drip said instinctually. He was looking for any sort of detail that would reveal who the two hooded figures were and what their intentions might be, but there was nothing obvious.

"Drip, what is it?" Thomas asked. She waved her hand in front of his face to get his attention.

Drip glanced at her. "Look at those two over there."

"Who?" Thomas asked, gazing hard to see if there was anyone who stuck out in the crowd.

"Of course, the enemy of our enemy!" Drip said. "We need to move; we have so very little time."

"To go where?" Thomas asked.

By that time Drip had grabbed her hand and was tugging at it with great effort. Thomas was surprised at the strength the little imp had, as she found herself pulled to her feet and moving at a quick pace.

"Drip?" Thomas asked again.

Drip still did not answer, but rushed back into the hospital. This time he did not offer the nurses any greetings and ran into Cary's room to retrieve the bag he had left. Then he began to race for the exit.

"Drip!" Thomas shouted in an attempt to resist his momentum.

"Drip?" Gorath's image said. "Hold still! I cannot keep up."

Gorath's image had a limited distance from the bag, and could only be within a fifteen foot radius of it. However, the biggest downfall was the fact that it took a moment for him to reappear. Several times, Drip raced right through Gorath's image. As Drip raced along with Thomas and bag in tow, he ducked under a small funeral procession, of which everyone was completely startled when Gorath's image appeared for a moment on top of the casket.

"Drip! Where are we going?" Thomas called after him.

"Hold on, we are almost there," Drip replied.

"Drip, slow down!" Boot shouted.

As they turned the corner, they ran into another parade celebrating the dragon's defeat. Regardless, Drip began to push his way through the crowd that was trying to express their gratitude and celebration for the group's deeds.

Then, finally, Thomas was able to give Drip a good yank and cause him to stop. The two stood for a moment to catch their breath.

"What are we doing?" Thomas asked.

Drip had not yet recovered from the run with an armored Thomas in tow. Instead he pointed up at the large sign that designated the guild headquarters of none other than the assassins.

"The enemy of our enemy…of course," Thomas said. "But who do we have assassinated?"

"No one. But imagine a lethal escort who can be trusted as long as we have the money and a contract," Boot said.

"Exactly," Drip said.

"I don't think this is the wisest thing to do," Gorath's image advised.

"Yeah, well, right now, only living people get a vote," Thomas said.

"Oh, now that was uncalled for," Gorath's image replied.

"Come on give him a break, he just barely died," Drip said. He knocked on the large ominous door before them.

"Thank you, Drip," Gorath's image said.

"Of course he did die over a month ago and is celebrated as a hero," Drip added. Gorath's image simply shook his head at the imp.

"If I were alive, then I would teach you not to say such things," Gorath's image said. Drip and Thomas started laughing. Then the large doors opened, and an old man stepped out, seeming less than amused to find the two laughing aloud.

"Is this some sort of prank?" the caretaker asked. "Because I don't find it funny. I mean what kind of sick person pranks the assassin's guild?"

The two promptly stopped as they recognized the situation they were in.

"No Sir, we are here to take out a contract," Thomas said.

"Is that so?" the caretaker asked. "And how do you intend to pay?"

"We have plenty of money," Drip said.

"An imp with plenty of money? Ha, on your way before I put a contract on you," the caretaker said as he pointed his boney finger at Drip.

"We are serious, Sir. Don't you know who we are?" Thomas asked.

"And who are you exactly?" the caretaker asked.

"We are the High Standard of the Watch," Thomas said with authority.

"Never heard of it, now on your way," the caretaker said. Then as he attempted to close the door, Drip cleverly slid Boot between the door and the jam.

"Ow!" Boot yelped.

"Who is at the door?" a voice from inside asked.

"Some hooligans who have it in mind to prank the assassin's guild. They call themselves the High Standards of the Watch," the caretaker said.

"Let them enter," the voice said.

"But Sir?" the caretaker replied.

"Let them enter, at their own risk," the voice said. The caretaker opened the door and ushered the party into the assassin's guild, shutting the main door behind them with a thunderous crack, and Thomas swallowed hard as she heard several locks latch.

EPISODE 29

"Welcome, Standards of the Watch," the voice carried through the halls.

From the angles in the room it was tough for the trio to pinpoint the exact location of the voice. Gorath's image took that chance to explore everything within his fifteen-foot radius in the room. However, the round entryway must have been just over fifteen feet in radius, as he kept disappearing and reappearing next to the bag again.

"Hello, your honor?" Thomas inquired, unsure of how to address the disembodied voice.

"I see you have brought a spirit in with you," the voice said with irritation. "I am not amused."

"No, Sir, he isn't a spirit, he is a curse," Drip said. "Sometimes in more than one way."

"Hey," Gorath's image said.

"Nevertheless, state why you have sought my audience," the voice echoed in the chamber.

"We need to take out a contract," Thomas said.

"Actually, two contracts," Drip added. The comment caught Thomas off guard.

"And how will you be paying for these contracts?" the voice asked. "Hopefully not with cursed gold."

The three paused for a moment trying to comprehend the last statement, creating an awkward silence. Then a hooded figure appeared out of the shadows behind the three, startling them. Gorath's image let out the loudest shriek.

"No one seems to get my humor," the cloaked figure said, sighing. "Follow me this way, please."

The three followed the tall figure down a side hallway and into an office, where he waved his hand and the doors slammed shut. The assassins' leader walked behind the large desk. Thomas glanced around the room and noticed that it seemed more like a library than an office, fit with ornate rugs, and a small fire in the fireplace. The leader turned to face the three with a large curved knife pointed towards them.

"Now to get down to business," he said, then stabbed the blade into the desk. The motion caused all three of them to again jump, and, on cue, Gorath's image was the loudest to shriek. Then the leader removed the hood to reveal a surprisingly short five-foot-six woman with bright red hair.

"You should see the looks on your faces," the deep male voice came out of the petite woman. "Oh, sorry."

The assassin leader removed a necklace with a small conch shell from around her neck and set it on the desk. Then she cleared her throat a few times, with a very noticeable octave change.

"Who are you?" Thomas asked.

"I am Nina, assistant to the Chief Assassin," she said. It was clear that she must be from an obscure province considering her strong, unique accent.

"Assistant to the Chief Assassin? So, like the second in charge?" Drip asked.

"No, I am a little further down the totem pole," Nina replied. "Oh, and by the way, the Thieves' Guild is ticked at you."

"Are you the one we see to take out contracts?" Thomas asked, ignoring the woman's last comment for the moment.

"Not exactly. Only the Chief Assassin can issue large contracts," Nina replied. "Don't get me wrong, if you want me to off someone's pet or send a message people would never forget, I am your man, or, well, woman, but I'm not authorized to draw up a contract."

"Okay so when do we see the Chief Assassin?" Drip asked.

"You don't. There is a power struggle going on right now, and there isn't exactly a Chief Assassin currently," Nina replied.

"What?!" Thomas asked. "I thought there were contingencies for things like this."

"Normally there are, but something odd is happening," Nina said. "Of course I am not at liberty to talk about that right now."

"Okay, so can you help us at all?" Thomas asked.

"For a price," Nina replied with a grin.

"We have money," Drip said. He tossed seven gold coins onto the table.

"That is impressive, it really is, and tempting, but I have something else in mind," Nina said.

"Like what?" Drip asked cautiously.

"I need you to complete one task. Get me two gold pieces," Nina said.

"Ha, just take two of the seven on the table," Thomas said.

"Not just any two gold pieces. You see, there is a meeting to decide the next Chief Assassin. One of the gold pieces I require is held by Ordinary Ormsby, who will be in attendance, and one by Anvil Adams. Retrieve them and bring them back to me," Nina said.

"Okay, let's say we agree to do this. How can you help us?" Thomas asked.

"I have only two contracts that were signed by the last chief. However, they are missing a few details that I can fill in to make them valid," Nina replied.

"Wait, did you say the Thieves' Guild is already mad at us, and now you want us to steal something—ah, two somethings," Drip interjected.

"Yeah, something about cleaning out the royal armory," Nina replied. "Anyway, to show that I mean fair business, I will complete one of the contracts now, and upon receipt of the gold, I will complete the second contract. However, if you fail to complete the task, I will use the second contract on you."

"You're not seriously considering agreeing to this? It isn't worth it," Boot argued.

"Why do you need the two coins?" Drip asked.

"I have my reasons," Nina said. "Now, do we have a deal?"

"Two coins, for two contracts?" Thomas asked.

"Straight up," Nina replied.

"Deal," Thomas said.

"Perfect, now let's fill out the first contract," Nina said.

"The first contract is for an assassin to accompany us on our next quest and back, duties are to defend and or attack targets designated by myself or Master Drip," Thomas said.

"Okay, just so you know, the first kill is free, then there is a silver charge per kill 'til the assassin hits five, then there is a five gold per kill fee after that," Nina said. "High-profile targets are ten gold no matter what kill it is. It's the standard escort contract."

"If we donate seven gold up front, can we get one of your top assassins?" Thomas asked.

"Have you done this before?" Nina asked.

"No," Thomas replied.

"Sure thing, we will assign you Kap Kaplan," Nina replied. "And for the second contract, what will that be when you return?"

"The second contract is to put a hit out on the top person trying to kill us," Drip said.

"Here at the Assassin's Guild, we like to be just a bit more specific," Nina replied.

"I cannot give you a specific target, because we do not know who it is, so the contract is for you to find out and eliminate the target," Drip said. Then before Nina could reply, he tossed a bag onto the table. "I believe that will cover the expenses to the guild to look into this matter."

"Okay, done. Contract to be issued upon delivery of said requested product," Nina replied.

"We will be departing the city soon. First, the meeting is being held *where* exactly again, and where can we find the two coins? And second, when do we meet our assassin for the quest?" Thomas asked.

Nina pulled down a map, and pointed at a small outpost on the Dark Side of the line, only five miles to the south.

"That is where the meeting is, and as for Kap, he will meet up with you when you leave the city. Trust me, you will know him when you see him," Nina said.

"Thank you for receiving us and not having us killed," Drip said.

"No problem. You know what they say, a paying customer is better than a dead customer who intended on paying you."

With that, the three exited the office and promptly left the building.

EPISODE 30

Orielia sat down next to Cary again, and held her hand. Something in the action seemed to calm her troubling thoughts. She looked out the window at the green lush garden, and watched a pair of blue birds playfully chase each other around a large cherry tree.

"What is troubling you, sister?" the first apparition, Ponopoli, asked. It was the first time Orielia had seen them outside of the Candlestick.

"I am slowly remembering things, but it isn't enough; we have already lost one of the three. I want to go with them, but something is holding me back," Orielia said.

"Olpetrion is too powerful for you. If you leave the protection of the city, she will defeat you," the second apparition, Naomi, said.

"There must be something I can do," Orielia said. "I can't stand just watching them go to their deaths."

"There is something," Ponopoli said.

"No, it is too risky," Naomi retorted.

"Help me do something," Orielia begged.

"One of us already has, and it has cost more than you know," Naomi said.

"What do you mean?" Orielia asked. "How?"

"I assisted at the battle of the dragon," Ponopoli said. "And the cost, though great, was worth it."

"What cost?" Orielia asked.

"She used a portion of her power, and it has weakened her. We are not permanently here; we stand here only as a residue of our former power, and once we use up what we have, we are lost from this world," Naomi said.

"I cannot ask you to put yourselves at risk, but I need to do something," Orielia said.

"The only reason Olpetrion is stronger than you, is because she has access to her full menu of abilities, where you are still just remembering who you are," Naomi said. "However, you have just as much power."

"So what can I do?" Orielia asked.

"You can use the wall, and as events unfold, you can slightly adjust things," Ponopoli said. "In your state, you would be able to move someone over a foot or two, just once or twice, possibly whisper something to an individual."

"Look, doing this is risky," Naomi said, "and Olpetrion could take that opportunity to attack you in the city. However, it could save someone, or alter the outcome of a fight."

"It's good enough for now. Thank you for everything," Orielia said.

The two apparitions vaporized into a fine mist, then disappeared.

Orielia turned back to the sleeping woman, and raised Cary's hand to her own forehead. For a moment, she could see through Cary's eyes during the fight, as she bravely flung ice at the dragon, and then eventually used all the magic she had in her to enhance the storm. Then she saw something that did not show up on the retelling on the wall: Olpetrion standing over Cary chanting something. Then like electricity, Orielia's body jolted for a moment. She dropped Cary's hand with a tear racing down her face, and started back to the Candlestick as quickly as possible.

Thomas and Drip walked over to the South Gate as they had been instructed. As before, Head Monk Towe was there to send them off, with their horses packed and ready to go.

"Again, we regret the loss of Gorath. It was tough on the whole order when he was lost to us, and we wish you best journey," Towe said.

"Thank you," Drip said. "Is Orielia going to be sending us off again as well?"

"Unfortunately, she will not," Towe said. He seemed to be in a hurry to usher them out of the city.

Unlike the Northern gates, when the Southern gates opened, there was no massive cloud of dust. Also on the pleasant side, both armies were not clashing just outside the doors, but they were instead pulled back off of the line, and standing in formation.

Thomas turned to Drip and said, "I wonder where this Kip guy is from the assassins' guild."

"It is Kap, and he is here with you already," a shaky voice said.

Drip and Thomas looked around for a moment, when finally they noticed Gorath's image trying to point at Drip's horse. Sure enough, they saw a small bump attached to the back of the horse.

Kap was a very small man, and he had the unique ability to fold himself up into a ball. He sat up straight on the horse to reveal his four-foot-two stature.

"Don't you have your own horse?" Drip asked.

"Sure do," Kap said. He pulled out a whistle and gave it a hard blow. No sound seemed to come from the effort, until a massive animal came sprinting seemingly out of nowhere. Kap dismounted Drip's horse with a graceful flip and landed flawlessly onto the animal that closely resembled a Great Dane.

"Kap at your service," he said with a bow. "I understand that I am to escort you on your quest."

"That is correct," Thomas said warily.

"Kind of flashy for an assassin," Boot said with his own suspicions.

"I do have a flair, but be assured, I am quite deadly," Kap said.

"Oh boy, this is going to be interesting," Drip said.

"I need to clarify that you understand the fees, correct?" Kap asked.

"We understand them very well," Thomas said.

"Good, now where to?" Kap asked.

"Just follow our lead, and don't get us killed," Thomas said. Then she gave Grendle a quick pat on the neck, and spurred her on into a full gallop.

Aroon opened his eyes, unsure as to where he was. He rubbed his throbbing head, and glanced around the simply furnished room.

"Take it easy," a soft voice said to him.

"The lava, the party," Aroon said in a panicked tone. "Where am I?"

"You're safe, everyone is safe, just relax," the voice said.

Aroon looked around the room again, but could not see anyone. Wondering if he had gone crazy, he climbed out of the bed, and found a bowl of water. He looked in the reflection and recognized that he had not shaved in a long time.

"How long?" he asked, hoping not to get a response.

"A month," the voice said. It was so close, he could swear the person it belonged to was standing right behind him. He quickly turned to confront whoever he was talking to, but in the process his sore muscles betrayed him and he fell to the ground, knocking the bowl of water with him. Instantly, a monk entered the room.

"Are you okay?" the monk asked.

"I am fine," Aroon said. "Out of curiosity, who was in here just before you?"

"No one, you haven't had an official visitor since you arrived," the monk said.

With the help of the monk, Aroon climbed back into bed as a wave of depression came over him, then anger. He grabbed ahold of the blanket and began to squeeze it.

"Are you sure you are okay?" the monk asked. "Is there anything I can get you?"

"No," Aroon answered shortly.

"Just in case you were wondering, the rest of your party is alright, they just haven't woken up yet," the monk said. After an awkward silence, the monk left the room.

"Are you still here?" Aroon asked after a few minutes had passed.

"Yes," the voice said.

"Who are you? And what do you want?" Aroon requested.

"Who I am is not important, just understand you have an essential role yet to fill," the voice said.

"I don't understand," Aroon said.

"You must train harder than you ever have before, and get your party ready for when you are called on by the Standards of the Watch," the voice said.

"Standards of the Watch? Are you mad?" Aroon asked. "Surely they have disbanded with Gorath's death."

"Not only have they not disbanded, they are stronger, but they will need you," the voice said. "You must not let them down like you did Gorath."

"Gorath," Aroon said quietly. "Who says I'm not happy that the fool monk isn't around anymore?"

"I never said he wasn't around anymore, just prepare yourself," the voice said.

"What?!" Aroon asked in confusion. "What did you mean by that?"

Silence filled the air, and then Aroon grabbed a small plate off the night stand and threw it across the room.

"Answer me!" he shouted.

In no time, the monk entered the room again.

"What is going on?" the monk asked.

"What kind of question is that?" Aroon shouted angrily. "There is work to be done!"

EPISODE 31

It was nightfall before the party was close enough to see the structure. Thomas stood in confusion as the building seemed too lit up to be a meeting of assassins. Something was off but she just couldn't put her finger on it.

"Okay, Drip you stay here with the horses, and dog-looking creature. Kap and I will head in on foot; if there is any kind of trouble, you come in and get us," Thomas said.

"A den of assassins? I'm good here," Drip said.

"That is the first smart thing you have done in a long time," Boot added.

"Don't worry about me, I will be out here just kicking rocks around," Drip replied. He was certain that if Boot had eyes, he would be glaring at him right now.

Thomas nodded, and then started to walk towards the structure. About that time Drip decided to be true to his word and gave a large rock a solid kick.

"Are you ready for this?" Kap asked.

"I am," Thomas said. "Let's keep it down until we get inside."

"Roger that," Kap replied.

The two skulked along until they reached the very edge of the guard's vision. Thomas was trying hard to think of a way they could make it past the guards.

"Tell you what," Thomas said, "I will distract them, and you knock them out."

"Sounds good," Kap said.

Thomas ran up to the guards with a frantic look on her face. "Please help me!" she cried out.

The two guards ran to her to investigate the perimeter breach. Just as they reached her, one of the guards fell to his knees and collapsed, quickly followed by the second. It was at that point, Thomas noticed the puddle of blood the two were now lying in.

"What was that?" Thomas asked. "I said knock them out, not kill them."

Kap shrugged at the comment and headed for the door. Thomas followed after with an occasional glance at the two bodies.

"Okay," Kap said. "I will sneak around back, count to twenty, and kick open the door, and while they are looking at you, I will see what I can do to thin out their numbers."

"No unnecessary kills," Thomas said. She could hardly believe that she cared if a bunch of assassins were killed or not. After all, she didn't know any of them, and they all probably deserved it in one way or another.

"Sure thing, boss," Kap said, and then he started walking around the building.

Slowly Thomas began to count as instructed. At twenty, she did as she was instructed and kicked open the door. However, as the door flew open, she noticed that there were only two men in the room. Thomas recognized that Kap was not making the dynamic entrance she had hoped for, and ducked back out of the room.

"Ah, now that wasn't very nice," Ordinary Ormsby said from inside. "Come back and play!"

"Tell you what, I'll take care of the girl, and you take care of Kap. He is bound to be out there too," Anvil Adams said in a gruff tone.

"Five gold says I get a kill before you," Ormsby said with a chuckle.

"You're on!" Adams said.

Thomas was listening for anything that might give away the position of the two very large assassins. Then, just as she thought she heard something, a large fist punched through the wall just two inches from her head. She let out a loud shriek and drew her sword.

Outside, Drip recognized Thomas's shriek coming from the building. He mounted his horse and began to race to her aid. A cold chill ran down his spine when he thought about the worst-case scenario.

"Now don't be like that!" Adams said. "Be a good girl and die."

Thomas had been in combat so many times before, but nothing like this. She watched the large man literally tear a beam from the house and wield it like a club. Thomas found out exactly why he was called Anvil Adams, as he swung the beam striking her in the side and throwing her five feet across the room. The reliable armor absorbed as much of the blow as it could before crumpling. After a moment, the armor repaired itself. Thomas had her doubts about surviving this attack as she could feel her bruised ribs hinder her from raising her sword quickly. Then she heard a thunderous crash and a loud scream that immediately faded.

"Ha, you owe me five gold!" Ormsby shouted.

Thomas could tell the statement made Adams angry as he let out a war cry and charged at her. She remembered her training and prepared herself for the strike. Adams seemed to be moving faster than last time and she was frantically looking for an opening, but nothing was presenting itself. She was able to jump back and avoid the powerful swing, but she was not prepared for how quickly he swung the beam back. Again the beam struck her side and threw her, this time a good ten feet. She knew that under normal circumstances anyone else would have been killed by the strike.

Her armor held out as long as it could, but the impact did not merely bruise her ribs this time. She knew that one or two had to be broken now. Thomas was focused on getting to her feet, but it was too late; Adams was standing over her with the beam held over his head ready to strike again.

Drip was just in time to see Thomas get thrown from the last strike. He sympathetically winced at the deep thud made when Thomas hit the ground. He spurred his horse as he watched the large man move into position to strike a killing blow. Drip had no time to think, and lunged off his horse at the assassin. He was able to grab ahold of the man's hair and pull back. With the beam over his head, Adams was off balance, and even more so with the imp pulling backwards. As the giant of a man was in the process of falling, Drip saw Kap jump off the roof and onto the beam that Adams was holding, and then in one motion, he jumped propelled himself from the beam and straight at Adams' chest.

For a moment, Drip was trapped under the dead assassin's head. It took several moments before he could free himself.

"You saved me," Thomas said to Kap. "He was about to kill me."

"That is what I do," Kap said.

Drip was crushed as he heard the dialogue between the two, but elected to keep his thoughts to himself.

"I heard you die inside," Thomas said.

"No, it was quite the opposite," Kap said.

Drip was finally clear of the dead man and walked over to Thomas.

"Drip, you should have seen it! Kap saved me," Thomas said excitedly. She winced from the pain as she tried to move.

"Also, I think you are looking for these," Kap said. He pulled two coins from Adams' pocket and tossed them to Thomas.

"I don't know what we would have done without you," Thomas said.

Carefully Kap and Drip helped Thomas mount her horse, and they began to head for the next town where they could send a messenger back to the assassin's guild. As they rode, Drip fell back just a little as Thomas seemed to have a sudden change of interest in Kap.

"You should tell her, you know," Gorath's image said. The image had figured out how to kind of hover along instead of appearing and disappearing.

"I don't know what you are talking about," Drip said.

"Look, I may just be an image, but I am not blind," Gorath's image said. "I saw everything."

"It's not important," Drip said. He found a little comfort as he scribbled down some of his thoughts on his pad of paper.

"Don't let this come between you," Gorath's image said. "I really think you had a thing going."

"I thought so too, but I was just fooling myself," Drip said. "In the end, I am just an imp. Kap may be only four-foot-two, but he is human."

"That's hogwash," Gorath's image said. "You want to know a secret?"

Drip was not excited about the direction of the conversation, and it seemed to be making him feel worse. "Sure."

"I came across a book that talked about the creation of the first imps, and there is a sound theory out there that imps were an attempt to magically recreate one of the top farmers from the Light Side, and the only reason you are not human, is that there was a word or two out of place, as simple as that," Gorath's image said.

"That sucks," Drip said. He found Gorath's revealed secret lacking.

"What I'm saying is I think there is a way to fix it and turn you human," Gorath's image said excitedly.

"You mean, you 'thought'," Drip said. It was clear the depression was beginning to take over.

"What?" Gorath's image asked.

"You mean, you 'thought', but you can't do anything about it now. You are dead," Drip said. "Just get back into the bag."

"Wow, that was not very nice, and I am not a genie; I don't just live in the bag, ironically. I'm not sure where I go when I'm not here," Gorath's image said.

"Would you prefer I leave the bag here, and curse you to live in the middle of nowhere?" Drip asked.

"You're bluffing," Gorath's image said.

Drip offered the image a very serious look, and began to untie the bag from his belt.

"Okay, okay, but you should still talk to her," Gorath's image said one last time before disappearing.

"In the end, I am just an imp," Drip said. He looked down at his book and traced his finger around a well-drawn picture he had created of Thomas. Drip shook his head and then closed the book and slid it into the magic bag.

EPISODE 32

Nina read over the message again, this time much slower to make sure she didn't miss anything. A chill ran down her spine when she realized that there really wasn't anything to mistake.

```
Nina,
Mission accomplished.
Waiting in town of Drueblat.
Standards of the High Watch
```

"Prepare the carriage, I must go to Drueblat immediately," Nina said.

"Very good, ma'am," the caretaker said as he pulled a rope on the wall. "May I add that this might be a trap?"

"I appreciate your concern, but this is worth the risk," Nina said. For a moment she held up a gold coin, studying it as if in deep thought.

"Would you like for me to escort you or would you prefer the usual driver?" the caretaker asked. He walked over to the door in preparation to open it.

"The usual should be just fine," Nina said. "It is about time someone with real wit had control over the Assassin's Guild."

"Yes, ma'am, good luck," the caretaker said. Right on cue he swung open the door just in time for the carriage to approach. As tradition dictated, Nina got a running start and dove into the open carriage as it passed.

Drip was in the process of rolling his eyes at yet another tale of how Kap had defeated evildoers. Something didn't sit right in Drip's mind; Kap seemed to have an awfully loose tongue for being an assassin. On the other hand, it was hard for him to disregard what he had seen and what had happened.

"Are you allowed to talk about your previous assassinations openly like this?" Drip added to the conversation. The comment drew glares from both Kap and Thomas.

"Normally I am bound by my oaths, but I must admit there is something about Thomas that compels me," Kap said. He glanced over at Thomas and gave her a shy smile.

"Plus, I want to hear more," Thomas said. She let out a soft giggle. The sound felt like a small dagger to Drip, and he slumped in his chair.

"Should we wait for Nina outside?" Boot asked.

"Broken, token, cart..." Bean added.

Drip cupped his hand around Bean. "I wish I understood what you were saying sometimes."

Then Drip slipped away as Thomas and Kap continued to talk, obviously unaware of what he was doing. He walked outside and sat down on a small bench. Drip retrieved his notepad and began to write.

"I don't know how much you listen to me, but you have to hear me right now," Boot said urgently. "Look towards the southern end of town, now."

"What is it?" Drip asked. He glanced down the street and couldn't help but notice the people and creatures running from the southern end of town.

"I don't know what that is all about, but it can't be good," Boot said.

"Agreed," Drip said. He closed up the notebook and ran back into the tavern.

"And that is how I single-handedly defeated the ten brothers of Granthum," Kap said.

"Wow, that is impressive," Thomas said.

"Hey, you both need to look at this!" Drip cried.

"Not right now," Kap said.

"No you need to look, now," Drip insisted.

"Listen, little man, not right now," Kap said.

"This is serious!" Drip cried again. This time his anger welled up enough for him to kick the table. This caused everyone in the inn to pause and stare at him. Ironically, the general pause let everyone hear the screaming people outside. Thomas stood up like she was about to reprimand Drip, but started to see people running past the window.

"What is that?" Thomas asked.

"What I have been trying to tell you," Drip said.

"Whoa, we better get out of here," Kap said.

"That is coming from the direction we are supposed to be headed," Drip added.

"No doubt. We better investigate this," Thomas said.

"Well, if you insist," Kap said.

"You mean if the contract insists," Boot added.

Thomas led them out into the street. Large groups of people were pushing past them, but there did not seem to be any actual evidence of what was chasing them.

"Gorath, can you get up high?" Drip said to the bag. That is when he noticed for the first time that Gorath's image was no longer around.

"You told him to go back into the bag," Boot said.

Drip opened the bag, and shouted, "Gorath come out! We need you!"

After a moment Drip offered a concerned look while he searched the bag. "I'm sorry, I did not mean to offend you. I was angry. We need you."

"I am glad you are panicking. I accept your apology, but you deserved that, you know," Gorath's image said as he manifested beside Drip.

Drip let out a sigh of relief. "Please. I need you to go up high and see what is chasing these people."

"No problem," Gorath's image said. Some people stopped for a moment as they watched the image rise up from the ground until he was floating in the air about fifteen feet. Then, gracefully, he floated down.

"I see what your problem is," Gorath's image said.

"And?" Thomas asked.

"There is an attack by the undead," Gorath's image replied.

"Brilliant, zombies," Drip said.

"How many?" Kap asked.

"One or two, I think, I did not get a good look. Maybe you can dispose of them?" Gorath's image suggested.

"It will be my pleasure," Kap said as he charged down the street against the stream of people.

"Brilliant, he is going to get himself killed," Drip said.

"Are you concerned?" Boot asked.

"Yeah, that we won't have an escort for the rest of this quest," Drip replied.

Drip found himself racing behind Thomas down the street after Kap. It seemed odd to both Drip and Thomas that so many people would be running from just one or two zombies. Then they figured out why the people seemed so afraid. It was only two zombies alright—zombie ogres. Kap was already actively attacking one of the two.

"I've got this one," Kap said. "You two get that one."

"Okay," Thomas said with a hesitation in her voice.

"Come on," Drip said, charging towards the second ogre.

"What are you doing?" Boot asked with a very panicked tone.

"Yeah, I don't know, but just go with me on this," Drip said.

"Like I have a choice," Boot added.

Drip wasn't prepared for the upgraded reflexes the undead status had given the normally clumsy ogre, and barely dodged a lightning-fast right hook. Drip used the trampled ground to slide past the ogre, and instinctively drew his slingshot and fired off one solid strike against the monster's head. This caused it to pause and think for a moment.

"Should that work?" Drip asked.

"It seems to have done something," Boot said.

While the ogre stood in a thoughtful stupor, Thomas drew her sword and finished it off. The large body fell to the ground.

"Good job, Drip," Thomas said.

The two turned to watch Kap in his struggle to take down his undead ogre. Drip watched in amusement as the very quick Kap had failed to take into calculation that the ogre was already dead, as he struck vital points over and over again. The points being vital only for living ogres of course.

"Are you just going to watch him?" Thomas asked.

"I don't want to intervene and miss his greatness at work," Drip said.

"Are you jealous of him?"

"What? Me? No way," Drip said.

Thomas took a moment to look at Drip suspiciously. "Just hit it with your slingshot," she said.

"Why don't you jump in and finish it off?" Drip asked.

"Really?" Thomas prompted. "You want me to risk my life in there?"

Drip paused and realized that at this point, no matter what he chose to do, he was going to lose. So he pulled back a stone and struck the remaining ogre in the head like the first. Right on cue, the ogre paused in a state of what seemed to be endless thought. Drip smiled as Kap continued his futile attacks, clearly not realizing that the ogre was disabled and was now an easy target. Thomas rolled her eyes, and finished off the second ogre with her sword.

"Good work," Kap said. "I almost had him."

"Sure," Drip said. "Now where is Nina?"

Nina looked out of the carriage window from on top of a small hill overlooking her destination. They had paused there mainly because there seemed to be a very large group of people running from the town.

"What are your orders?" the driver asked.

"Press on, this is too important," Nina said. She sat back in her seat and felt the carriage move quickly towards the town. Again she held up a single gold coin, and stared at it as she watched it glimmer in the light.

EPISODE
33

Thomas paused a moment after the short battle with the undead Ogres, and wondered what was going on with Drip. It didn't take long for her to figure out that Drip was jealous over the attention she was giving Kap.

But he can't seriously think that we would ever be more than friends, right? Thomas thought to herself. She turned to watch Drip and Kap sitting next to each other, barely speaking.

"There has to be peace between everyone if we are to survive this thing," Thomas said aloud. She stood up and walked over to the two.

"Listen, I think we need to talk," she said. Instantly she noticed the two perk up and their dispositions change.

"Yes?" they both ask near simultaneously.

"Yeah, you see there isn't any easy way to put this," Thomas said.

"Actually there is," Boot said. Everyone paused for a moment to recover from the sarcastic remark.

"You see, I like both of you, but to be honest, neither of you have a chance of being the man I want to marry," Thomas said directly. She paused a moment to see how well the news was sinking in, but was confused at the fact that neither of them seemed phased by the information.

"Yeah, well, we have a professional relationship, and that is all," Kap said.

"Exactly," Drip said. "I thought we were just friends."

"Okay...?" Thomas said mostly to herself. She had never had anyone swoon over her, and this was after all her first experience rejecting pursuers. It seemed odd, but then again the whole thing seemed somewhat silly to Thomas. Maybe she was just making a big deal over nothing.

Suddenly, their attention was refocused at a carriage that was coming down the road. They looked around and it was clear that no one was left in the small town. As the carriage approached, it seemed to be coming in way too fast, jerking and jarring all over the road. Just as it seemed that it would crash right into them, it stopped with unexpected accuracy. No one was surprised to see Nina emerge.

"A deal is a deal, please give me the two coins I have requested," Nina said.

Thomas stepped forward and reached into her pouch to retrieve the two coins but found them missing. She gave a brief look of panic as she started recalling her steps.

"You do have the coins, right?" Nina asked. Her patience was not subtly melting away; it seemed to disappear like an avalanche.

"Of course," Thomas replied.

"You don't actually have the third one on you right now?" Kap asked with disbelief.

"What?" Nina asked.

"The coin, you have the third coin on you right now, don't you?" Kap asked.

Thomas watched as Nina instinctively drew her two short swords. This caused Drip to arm his slingshot, Kap to draw his short sword and wrist blade, and Thomas to pull her sword.

"What is this betrayal?" Nina asked, as she took a step backwards.

"She is here to kill us!" Kap shouted.

"I'm confused," Drip said. He was aiming at Nina, but looking suspiciously over at Kap.

"She drew on us first," Thomas said, backing up Kap.

"Okay, let's just talk this through," Nina said. "Do you or don't you have the two coins you agreed to get?"

"We took them from the two as promised, and I put them right in this secured pouch, but they are gone," Thomas said.

"This is a trick, she just wants to know where the coins are, so she can kill us," Kap said.

"Why would she do that?" Drip asked.

"Whoever has possession of the three coins after the death of an assassins guild chief is the next in line, no questions asked," Kap said.

"You have no honor, Kap. You used them to get the two coins for yourself, and now you want to use them again to get the third," Nina accused.

"Oh, like you weren't using them to get the two coins as well," Kap said. Then he realized he had said too much.

"I am giving them the contracts in exchange for the coins," Nina said, "What is it that you are giving them?"

"My presence," Kap said. At this point he knew that both Thomas and Drip were now aiming their weapons at him.

Without another word, Kap used his sword to knock back Nina's, and then used his wrist blade to knock back Thomas's sword in a similar manner. Then, in quick motion, he twisted his body to push off the wheel of the carriage in a lunging attack. Nina was swift enough to step back and put her sword between the two of them. As their blades met, Kap reached over with his wrist blade and caught the edge of Nina's shoulder. This caused her to jump back in pain. Kap pushed his relentless attack against Nina and prepared for another lunge. This time Thomas stood between the two of them and moved to swing her sword against Kap, but her damaged ribs caused her to miss her mark.

Seeing his attack rebuffed, Kap changed up his tactics and swung in a high arch to keep Thomas's arms up, springing forward and catching her square in the right side with his wrist blade.

Thomas realized as the sharp pain shot through her body that the wrist blade must be enchanted. She crumpled to her side as Kap withdrew the blade. She had been cut before, and even had an arrow pass through her body, but her armor had always pulled her though. This time was different, as she could tell the wound was deep.

Kap wheeled around and lunged for Drip, since he noticed that Nina was not in position to attack him. Drip struck Kap in the forehead with a smooth stone from his sling. He was disappointed as Kap continued his advance. Drip managed to avoid the two attacks Kap directed at him, but he cursed his slingshot as he managed to arm it again and get off a quick shot only to be forced to dodge a swing of Kap's sword. Again, his stone struck Kap perfectly in the forehead but did little to slow his advance. Kap raised his short sword in an attempt to get the imp to raise his hands, when something picked him up and threw him.

"Caretaker!" Nina exclaimed. "You shouldn't be outside the city!"

"You want me to go back?" asked the tall, hooded figure that had tossed Kap aside.

"No! He has the two other coins," Nina said. She quickly examined the wound on her shoulder.

"Ha, you got lucky, I was just getting warmed up," Kap said as he recovered and began to run towards the Caretaker. Kap let out a primal scream then hopped on his right foot to cause the

Caretaker to shift positions. As the Caretaker was unbalanced for just a moment, Kap stabbed the new foe with both his short sword and his wrist blade. Kap soon began to recognize that something was wrong, however, when he looked up to face the Caretaker, and only saw red glowing eyes.

"I hope you enjoyed that, because I think I speak for everyone else when I say," the Caretaker said, "just die."

The caretaker let his hood slip off to reveal a skeleton head looking down at Kap. As Kap attempted to retrieve his weapons, the skeleton put his dead hands on the short sword and ripped it from Kap.

"How?" Kap asked.

"Enough of this," the Caretaker said, then in one motion, he used Kap's sword against him and the battle was over.

"So...are you actually Death?" Drip asked cautiously, after an eerie silence had befallen them all.

"I am *a* Death, I am not *the* Death," the Caretaker said. "Or at least I hope not, because I am doing a very poor job if I am."

Drip walked over to Kap's body and quickly searched it over, discovering the two gold coins as suspected. He slowly walked them over to Nina and dropped them into her hand.

"Incredible," Nina remarked.

"What's that?" Drip asked.

"You are a rare oddity," Nina said. "I know of no imp who would get two strikes in on a top assassin, let alone take one on in the first place."

"It was all luck I suppose," Drip said. He ran over to Thomas then, whose eyes seemed to indicate she was tired.

"Drip," Thomas said, "any girl would be lucky to have you."

Then Thomas's eyes closed as she fell into a deep sleep.

The Caretaker walked over and kneeled down next to her. "Good news," the skeletal figure said.

"What's that?" Drip asked.

"It isn't her time," the Caretaker replied. Then he took his two bony hands and held them over her, and suddenly Thomas shot up coughing. The Caretaker repeated the process with Nina.

"Well, we have to honor our contract," Nina said as she swung her arm around to test the magic repair.

"What do you mean?" Thomas asked.

"I will accompany you on your quest," Nina said.

EPISODE 34

"Are you allowed to do accompany us?" Thomas asked. She stood examining the new Chief of the Assassins Guild.

"As it turns out, I can do pretty much whatever I want now," Nina said. "Plus it has been a long time since I have been out in the field. It might be fun."

"Ma'am, I do not recommend this course of action," the Caretaker said in his deep voice.

"I know, and I understand your apprehension, but I must do this one last contract before I settle in," Nina said. "Plus no one else knows that I am the chief other than you, so the other assassins won't be coming after me."

"Very good, ma'am," the Caretaker said. "And what are your instructions for me?"

"Return to the city, and await my return or my summons," Nina said.

"As you wish," the Caretaker said. Then he climbed in the carriage that had carried Nina there.

"So what is the quest?" Nina asked.

"This is going to be good. I love watching this part," Boot said.

"We are going to investigate a disturbance on the Dark Side of the land," Drip explained.

"Yup, from the fight we had just before you got here, it looks like we are dealing with a full blown necromancer," Thomas added.

"A necromancer?" Nina asked. "You're kidding? There hasn't been one in a few ages at least."

"Well we are sure to find out," Drip said.

"Fair enough, I suppose," Nina said. "Which way?"

"That way." Thomas pointed straight towards the pitch black area in the dark lands.

Since Kap's dog-like mount appeared to have run off with the loss of its master and Nina's previous ride had been the carriage, the Chief of the Assassins Guild was forced to join Drip on the back of his horse.

As the party moved out, no one noticed that they were missing something important—Gorath's image was no longer with them.

—

"Where am I?" Gorath's image asked.

"You are back at the Candlestick," Orielia said.

"How did I get here?" the image replied.

"Ironically, you chose to come."

"How can I choose to do anything? I am just an emergency curse, an image."

"There are a few things you need to think about," Orielia said. "First, there is no such thing as an emergency curse."

"That is not true! I created it, didn't I?" Gorath's image asked himself.

"Second, you have been making decisions ever since you revealed yourself," Orielia said.

"But...how....?" Gorath's image asked. It was clear that he was thoroughly confused.

"Third, if you are not an emergency curse, then what are you?" Orielia asked.

Gorath's image held his hand up and took a close look at it. It was at that moment that he realized that one of his hands was completely see-through. Then he glanced over at the moving wall and watched the image of the dragon plummet into the volcano.

"I remember the wind racing past my face as I fell with the dragon," Gorath said. "I am dead. I am a ghost."

"Gorath, no matter what you are, you need to recognize that you are here for most likely a very short time," Orielia said.

"This is so odd. I don't understand what might be keeping me here," Gorath stated.

"Only you know why you are here, and I strongly suggest you figure it out," Orielia said.

"I should get back to Drip and Thomas," Gorath said.

"I don't know if that is possible, but know this: I will do everything in my power to keep them safe," Orielia said. Then Gorath disappeared from the room. This was followed by a single solitary clap meant to mock Orielia's promise.

"How do you expect to protect them when you couldn't protect him?" Olpetrion said.

"I will not let you win, I cannot let you win," Orielia said defiantly.

"Oh, how little you understand," Olpetrion said. "Look at the gathering clouds. They seem to have a red tint to them. Soon, another will perish."

Thomas carried a blank stare as she looked off into the distance. Grendel was keeping pace with the others in the party, but Thomas merely stared ahead, trying to process everything that had happened since they left the city.

How could I have started to fall for an assassin? Thomas thought to herself. *How dumb can I be?*

She shook her head as if to throw off the thoughts. Instinctually, she reached down and ran her hand along Grendel's long neck.

"That's it, I won't let my personal feelings interfere with my decisions until all of this questing nonsense is done," Thomas thought aloud. She nodded her head.

"Look at that!" Drip called out.

"I see it," Nina replied. "I don't think we can go around it."

"What?" Thomas asked as she escaped her distracting thoughts.

"Undead," Drip replied. "Looks like goblins."

"Brilliant, undead goblins," Thomas replied. "If we charge them with the horses, we might be able to take a bunch of them out before we have to fight."

"I don't think we have a choice," Nina replied.

"It is hard to count them with so little light," Drip said. He was used to seeing in a low level of light, but the eerily red cloud cover was making it even darker than usual for that time of day.

"I will take lead on this one," Thomas said. Grendel had always welcomed a good fight, but seemed irritated this time, mostly because she could not see the ground very well.

"Alright, lead on," Nina said.

With that, Thomas brought Grendel into a full charge. She drew her sword and held it tight in her right hand. The undead seemed to know that something was about to happen as they began to grow restless where they were milling about. Thomas raised her sword slightly, ready to strike as she approached the first line of them, when unexpectedly, she and Grendel found themselves falling. Instead of hitting flat ground, however, they were heading down a gentle slope, then sliding to a slow stop. Thomas looked back to see Drip and Nina in the exact same position.

"Is everyone alright?" Thomas asked. She righted herself in the saddle and began to inspect Grendel.

"I think," Drip said.

"Yes," Nina replied.

"That was pretty crazy," Thomas commented.

"Let's not do that again," Drip replied.

"Agreed," Thomas said. "It looks like we slid into some sort of sinkhole. But there seems to be a tunnel exit there." She pointed to what looked like an exit out of cave, despite the open sky above the slope.

"Hold on a second," Nina said. She raised her right hand and read a small piece of paper that promptly disintegrated when she was finished. Then a small blue orb appeared just above her hand.

"Assassins are magic users?" Thomas asked.

"No, well technically, we can cast one-time spells," Nina said. Then she raised her right hand to light the area around the party.

"Nice," Drip said, looking back at her in the saddle behind him. "I don't suppose you have something that will repel the undead?"

Nina chuckled, "I wish."

"Let's go out this way," Thomas said. The three dismounted and began walking the horses towards the tunnel exit, since there didn't seem to be a way back up the slope.

"We don't know what is out there, so we need to be as quiet as possible moving forward," Nina said.

"Sounds good," Drip replied. It was at this point that he noticed the lack of sarcastic comments from Gorath or Boot.

"You okay, Boot?" Drip asked.

"Fine, just trying not to get anyone killed," Boot replied.

"Gorath, where are you?" Drip asked as he shook the bag of holding. There was no reply.

"Maybe he is pouting again," Boot added.

"That is possible," Drip replied.

Then the three found themselves at the tunnel exit, overlooking a small valley.

"I can't see much," Thomas said. Then as if right on cue, a lightning bolt raced across the sky above, lighting up the valley for just a moment. It revealed that the entire valley was crawling with undead.

EPISODE 35

"The plan?" Thomas asked as she focused on the pitch black valley in front of her. Even at her best, Thomas knew there was no way she would be able to fight her way through all of those undead. She noticed a small light that sat at the far end of the valley.

"What is that?" Nina asked, pointing at the light.

"My guess, that is where we need to go," Drip said.

"So Nina, what would you suggest we do to get over there?" Thomas asked.

"Yeah, we wouldn't be able to sneak past them, and a straight on fight would get us maybe halfway at best," Nina said. "I have nothing."

"I hate to say it, but it would be nice to have Gorath right now," Drip said.

"What are you talking about? Where is Gorath's image?" Thomas asked.

"Not sure," Drip said.

"It is possible that Drip made him a little upset," Boot said.

"Okay, well what assets do we have?" Thomas asked.

"Let's see…a fighter, an assassin, an imp, some enchanted items, and a couple of horses," Nina said.

"Now that I think of it, we do have a few options," Drip said. "Option one…"

Nina could feel the wind on her face as she spurred Grendel on. She let out a few war cries, throwing small glass balls that exploded into flame. Without fail, the undead were attracted to the excitement and began to pursue, until Grendel stumbled over some rocks that she was unable to see in the darkness. Drip and Thomas watched as the undead overtook the two in moments.

"We are not doing that," Nina said, "I choose life."

"What else do you have?" Thomas asked, curious after Drip's first suggestion.

"Well," Drip said. "Option two…."

Thomas lunged forward attacking the undead by swinging her sword wildly side to side. Nina started to throw glass balls that exploded into brilliant flames. Drip carefully weeded his way through the undead, who were now all charging at Thomas and Nina. As he broke through the undead ranks, he turned to see the horde surround Thomas and Nina like swarming ants.

"I don't like that one either," Nina said.

"I agree, that is no good," Thomas said, shaking the image loose from her head.

"Okay," Drip said. "Option three…"

"Wait, I have one," Nina said with a grin on her face.

Drip was helpless as Nina and Thomas picked him up and threw him down into the pit of undead. He furiously tossed glass ball after glass ball, flinching at each explosion they caused.

"Come on now, that isn't even a real idea," Drip said.

" I didn't think you'd like an idea where *you* perish to the undead," Nina commented.

"Calm down, I have something," Thomas said. "No questions. We are doing *this* one."

—

An undead orc stood motionless, unsure of what to do. Like his peers, he felt it necessary to occasionally groan, and it was at that very moment that he decided his life was pretty disappointing and this was definitely the lowest moment of it.

Then he squinted as something ran into his leg. He looked down in preparation to attack, when a muffled voice said, "Sorry, excuse me."

Unable to identify if the thing that had just apologized was living or not, the orc prepared to get angry and chase it, but it was already gone. He took a moment to look, but soon forgot what he was looking for and began to ponder on how disappointing his life was, and that this was clearly the lowest moment of it...

"This is both the most brilliant, and the most idiotic thing I've ever done," Nina said, holding onto a piece of fabric.

"Shhhh," Thomas said, holding onto a larger piece of the fabric as she attempted to lead. "Just focus on what direction we are headed."

"Which way are we going?" Drip asked, trying to hold on to what fabric he could grip.

"We need to head straight," Thomas said as she nodded her head in a random direction. The three could feel that they had run into something again, and quickly adjusted.

"Sorry, excuse me," Boot said.

"Cut that out, you are going to get us captured," Thomas chided.

A tall, thin man exited one of the three large tents set up in a small clearing. He looked out at the undead walking around to see if there was any sign of disturbance. Then something odd happened. A small bag standing only a foot tall hopped into the clearing near him. He examined it as it seemed to have several feet attached to it. He reached down and grabbed ahold of it and gave it a sharp tug. The man jumped back as two women and an imp fell out the bottom.

"I know you!" the man shouted.

"Tekan!?" Drip exclaimed. "Oh crap!"

"You know him?" Thomas asked.

"Not good," Drip said.

"Attack!" Tekan shouted.

Suddenly, three ninja-like figures entered the area from the shadows. Thomas pulled out her sword, and Nina carefully hid two small pouches in the palms of her hands.

"How do you know this guy?" Thomas asked.

"Long story. He works for a former employer of mine," Drip said, as he armed his slingshot.

"Huh?" Thomas asked.

There was no chance for Drip to reply as the three ninjas attacked. Facing the first ninja, Thomas found her sword met with a counter at every move. Nina threw down one set of pouches at the feet of the second ninja. The bright flash gave her a moment to attack, but despite the advantage, she found her hit was blocked. Drip fired out three stones in rapid succession at the third ninja, but each stone missed its target.

"What is this?" Nina asked.

"It is your worst nightmare, and you will lose," Tekan said with a laugh.

As the fighting continued on, the three remained perfectly matched against their respective ninja, each unable to strike a fatal blow. After another minute of stalemate, fatigue began to set in.

"We need to try something different," Thomas said.

Without thinking, Drip armed his sling, but instead of aiming for his assailant, he caught Thomas's opponent in the head. This caused just enough pause for Thomas to clear her ninja and quickly strike at Drips'. It only took a moment for the three to gang up and clear out the last one. Then they turned towards Tekan.

"Tekan, I would never have thought *you'd* dabble in the undead," Drip said. "You will end this now."

Tekan began to back up, knowing he was beaten, but tripped and fell onto his back. The three stood over him with their weapons at the ready. Then, unexpectedly, Tekan broke out into a loud laugh.

"What is so funny?" Thomas asked.

"You think I'm the necromancer?" Tekan replied.

"What do you mean? Of course you are," Nina said.

"Drip, you should have just died when you had the chance," Tekan said. "Because this is going to be painful."

"I don't understand," Drip said in confusion.

Then a loud rumble shook the ground behind them.

"You fools are dead," a deep voice said.

The startled three turned to look at the newest combatant. Drip and Thomas were shocked as they saw none other than Dragin, the subpar wizard.

"Dragin? No way. *You* are behind this? You're only subpar at best," Drip said.

"I dealt with you once before, and I can deal with you again," Thomas added.

"Things have changed since we last faced each other," Dragin said. He lifted his right hand, causing huge sections of the land of Wax to rise into the air.

"We've seen this trick," Drip said. He dodged a large piece of Wax as it flew at him.

"You're right, time to show you what a full necromancer can do," Dragin said. Then he raised his left hand, and ten undead humans rose up out of the ground, and one large troll.

"Got ya!" Tekan said as he grabbed Nina's ankle. Without a chance to act, Nina's foot was pulled out from under her and she fell hard to the ground.

Drip fired off one stone from his slingshot and hit Tekan in the head. With no warning, Tekan's face changed from pure confidence to pure terror. He stood up and ran as fast as he could in the opposite direction. Thomas took a step back as Dragin raised another batch of undead to face them. Nina grudgingly got up from the ground.

"This is not good," Drip said. He fired off a clean shot at Dragin. Just before it reached the wizard, however, it stopped in midair. Dragin reached out and snatched the stone from the air, and then tossed it to the side.

"Oh boy," Thomas said.

EPISODE 36

Thomas struck down two of the undead that were charging her. She watched as they began to spread out, giving the three some space.

"I don't like this," Thomas said. "We could sure use some help right now."

"No doubt," Drip said. "I think Nina is out of the fight."

"Oh, I don't think so," Dragin said with a chuckle. He raised his hand and directed two quick fireballs at Nina.

Thomas instinctually reached out and cut the fireball in half. As always, she was surprised that it worked. However, she missed the second fireball. Drip had very little time to react, and without something to block the fireball, he threw himself onto Nina, causing her to fall over and into safety.

"Sorry about this," Drip said. He could see that Nina could only move her eyes. Drip was trying to figure out what she was trying to say, when he noticed a line on the ground that appeared to form a circle around the camp. The undead were becoming excited and were approaching fast, but seemed unable to cross over into the circle. That was when he noticed that Nina was just outside of it.

Drip pulled Nina's frozen body back inside the circle, and then turned to rejoin the fight. Thomas was engaged in combat with two undead wearing the elite seal of the Dark Scouts.

"Drip, jump in any time," Thomas said. She adjusted her swing in midflight to strike one of the undead standing off to the side.

Drip armed his slingshot and let one of the stones fly. It glided past Thomas's head, striking another undead standing off to the side. This caused a dumb stupor to come over the undead and he wandered off.

"Watch your aim!" Thomas shouted. "I don't want to end up a frightened vegetable."

"I'm trying," Drip said as he loosed another stone, striking another undead and causing it to wander off.

"You are getting pretty good with that," Boot added.

"Watch, defend, learn..." Bean said.

"Right," Drip said in reply.

Thomas blocked a quick attack by the elite undead, then dodged another. Deep down inside, she knew that she could not keep this up indefinitely.

"Thomas, you need to run outside the circle, then run back in!" Drip shouted.

"What?" Thomas asked.

"Trust me!" Drip shouted.

Thomas glanced over at the edge of the circle to see several undead plastered against an invisible wall. She recognized how crazy Drip's plan was, but she trusted the imp. With her thoughts screaming for her to stop, she ran towards the edge of the circle, waving her sword in front of her, hoping to clear just enough space to exit and then return. As she crossed the line, all of the recently summoned undead followed her. As she raced back in, the undead that had pursued her were now trapped on the outside of the bubble.

"Good thinking," Thomas said.

"Watch out!" Drip shouted.

However, it was too late, for two fireballs and an arrow were streaking towards Thomas. She raised her sword preparing for impact, but the first fireball was already too close to stop. As the fireball struck Thomas, it threw her back a couple of feet even as the armor absorbed the damage, but it seemed to leave a scar in the trusty metal. She managed to cut the second fireball in half, but the arrow snuck through.

Thomas winced as the arrow pierced the armor and also penetrated her side. However, one of the greatest advantages to having enchanted armor was that it tended to take care of you. It pulled the arrow through and out the other side, quickly healing her wound. Unlike the bruised and broken ribs she had suffered previously, the armor seemed built to help clean up wounds like this, but when she took a step forward, she knew something was wrong. A terrible pain doubled her over and forced her to drop to her knees.

"I had heard about your enchanted armor," Dragin said. "And I was curious to know if it could heal a strong poison."

"Poison," she whispered to herself. The pain was agonizing, but it wasn't the first time she had felt pain of this magnitude. Once she had been thrown into a large fire pit by her peers. She had thought of them as friends until that event. The humiliation had been nearly as excruciating as the physical pain.

"Thomas, hold still! I have something," Drip said. He frantically searched the bag of holding and emerged with a small blue bottle. He looked over at her and realized that Dragin had summoned more minions, and with the advancing army, he would not be able to reach her.

Drip armed his sling shot and began to fire, confusing several undead and causing them to wander off harmlessly, while the remaining seemed to get angrier. As they charged at him, Drip resorted to jumping out of the circle of protection and then back in. As they had with Thomas, the zombies followed after the imp.

Suddenly, the pool of undead were not only ogres, but consisted of almost everything imaginable, from trolls, orcs, goblins, humans, and even a massive cave troll.

"How much longer do you think you can do this?" Boot asked. It was odd, but it seemed as though Boot was actually out of breath.

"I don't know, but it looks like Dragin is getting tired of summoning undead," Drip replied.

Thomas's vision darkened, and for the first time she wondered what was waiting for her in the afterlife. From everything she had seen, she knew that there was most definitely something after death. She put her hands up to her face and slid the face plate of her helmet up so she could see.

"Something is wrong," she mumbled to herself. "You're poisoned, of course something is wrong…and now you're talking to yourself."

The pain was starting to fade a little, and though she had fought back the tears during the worst of it, she could feel them streaming down her face. She turned to see Drip desperately risking his life for her.

"Why?" she managed to ask out loud.

"Remarkable, isn't he?" a voice whispered into her ear.

"Why does he not run and escape?" Thomas asked.

"Drip would never leave a friend behind, it isn't in him," the voice replied.

"I am going to die here, aren't I?" Thomas asked.

"That is up to you," the voice whispered. "When you get the antidote, you can stay still, recover and live, or you can choose to die."

"What kind of choice is that?" Thomas asked.

This time there was no reply.

Drip's lungs felt like they were on fire from the pace he was trying to maintain.

"You can't keep this up," Boot said. "I don't think you can save her."

"Try, buy, cry…" Bean added.

"I have to try," Drip said.

A fresh batch of undead appeared, but something seemed wrong with the group. Instead of the killer instinct with direction, they seemed distracted, as if they had no idea what they were supposed to do. Drip took the opportunity to run over to Thomas.

"She doesn't look good," Boot said.

Drip opened the bottle and put it to Thomas's mouth. His heart began to race with fear as he noticed that her eyes seemed to be yellowed and staring off at nothing. He was relieved when she coughed.

Thomas could barely control her muscles but managed to look up at Drip and raise her hand to touch his face. That is when a fireball raced past Drip's head.

"Die already!" Dragin shouted.

"I have had enough of you," Drip said with an angry look on his face. Then he dove out of the way of another fireball. Drip flipped and jumped back and forth, dodging everything that was thrown at him. He began to advance towards Dragin, which made Dragin even more angry and intense.

Then Drip watched helplessly as a fireball caught him in midair. The leather armor took the brunt of the damage and it threw him back beyond where Thomas was laying.

"Dodge THIS!" Dragin shouted. Then he gathered every ounce of magic in him and formed the largest fireball he had ever created, and launched it at Drip.

Drip was still recovering from the first impact when he looked up to see the massive fireball leave Dragin's hands.

Thomas could feel the strength returning to her limbs, and watched as the massive fireball traveled straight towards Drip. "Funny," she said as she got to her feet. "There was only ever one option."

Thomas flung herself into the fireball, and everything seemed to move in very slow motion. Then something odd happened. Pictures and memories of events that had never happened flooded her mind. The memories were of another life, what would have happened if she had been born on the Light Side, where she had belonged all along.

Drip could only watch in horror as the fireball engulfed Thomas and then exploded. It sent out massive shock waves that threw Drip about twenty-five yards back. The explosion reached up into the sky and tore a hole in the clouds, letting direct sunlight reach the ground for the first time in that place in ages. Drip managed to stand up for only a moment to see the massive crater where the impact had been, and saw pieces of armor strewn about. Then he saw Thomas's sword stabbed into the ground right in the center of the crater.

He fell to his knees as his legs seemed unable to sustain his weight. Off in the distance, he could see Dragin impaled on a wooden pole that had been thrown through the air from the explosion. After all that, his death had happened so quickly. Confident that Dragin was done for, Drip closed his eyes and passed out.

EPISODE 37

Drip opened his eyes to the blinding light of the sun. He slowly sat up, feeling the massive headache left by the concussion he had suffered from the explosion. After checking for wounds, and thankfully finding none, he stood up.

Instinctually he shouted, "Thomas?"

That is when he realized two things: Thomas would not be responding to his query, and second, he was having a hard time hearing. He could hear a couple of muffled sounds, as he stumbled over to the large crater. He knelt down next to the partly melted, twisted and torn breastplate that had been protecting Thomas. Next to it, the large sword was buried halfway into the ground, but seemed unharmed. He reached down and wrapped his small hands around the hilt and attempted to pull it out of the ground. Then he felt someone's hand touch his shoulder. Just like an electrical shock, his reflexes suddenly jolted his body. He turned to face his potential assailant, when he realized he was looking at Chief Assassin Nina.

"Whoa, easy there," Nina said. "Friend."

"What?" Drip asked. Then he looked down and realized that not only had he managed to pull the sword from the ground, he was wielding it ready for combat. "Oh, sorry."

Drip lowered the sword, and shook his head realizing that his headache was gone and his hearing had been restored.

"That was an impressive move," Nina said. "I am so sorry for your loss. Thomas was extraordinary."

"Yes she was," Drip said.

"At least this is over," Nina said.

Then right on cue, Dragin let out a long dramatic cough, followed by a painful groan.

"Not just yet," Drip said. He began to walk toward where Dragin was weakly standing on the defensive, still alive, when he realized the sword was actually very heavy, forcing him to drag it behind him.

"How…did you…survive?" Dragin asked slowly.

"That doesn't matter," Drip said with an angry tone. He reached over and grabbed Dragin's collar, forcing the wizard to look at him. "Why did you do this? *How* did you do this?"

"I despise you, imp," Dragin said weakly. "And you have lost. You are surrounded by my army."

"Forget your army, why did you do this?" Drip asked again.

"I did...all of this to kill *you*," Dragin said. "She said you would come to me…and you did."

"What was that? Who is this 'she'?" Drip asked. His anger began to escalate, and his grip on the sword tightened.

"It doesn't… matter…you are done for. I grant my closest minion power over my army, so they might destroy you," Dragin said with a smile crossing his face. Then he waved his hands and a light blue orb appeared over his damaged body. It seemed to just hang in the air, and then it shot up about five feet, then unexpectedly, the blue orb came back down towards the dying necromancer.

"Ha, it looks like you have no more minions left," Drip said. Instead of the orb being reabsorbed into Dragin, it hit Drip.

"No!" Dragin said. "It can't be."

Drip wanted more answers from Dragin, but before he could ask him anything else, the wizard closed his eyes and passed on.

"That was unexpected," Boot said.

"No kidding," Nina said. "Does this mean you can control the undead?"

"I don't know," Drip said. "I didn't feel much when the orb hit me, but I suppose it is worth a try."

Cautiously Drip walked over to where the horde of undead was waiting. He raised the sword and focused his thoughts on the phrase, "Make a path." However, nothing seemed to happen. Then, out of the blue, the oddest thing happened.

"What is he doing?" a man's voice asked.

"I don't know, I think he needs to use the outhouse," another man's voice said.

"No, I am trying to get the zombies to make a path for me and my friend to walk down," Drip said.

"Wow, really? Why didn't you say that to begin with?" the first man asked. "Form up!" he shouted, and suddenly, the zombies formed up in two lines, creating a foot path for Drip and Nina to walk down.

"Huh, what do you know? The zombies can talk," Drip said, realizing that the voices must have come from the undead ranks. "Look Nina, they *will* listen to me."

Nina looked over at Drip with a confused expression. She had just witnessed a series of moaning and grunting between Drip and a couple of the undead creatures and was not amused that Drip had turned and was now grunting and moaning at her.

"Yeah," Nina managed to say. "I'm not sure what you are doing, but that is a little creepy."

It was Drip's turn to be confused. He turned back and looked at the undead, and realized that they didn't appear to be all that undead.

"Nina?" Drip asked.

This time Nina understood Drip, "What was that grunting and moaning all about?"

"It is fantastic, I can talk with the undead and they will do what I ask," Drip replied.

"Great," Nina said with a hint of sarcasm. "Well, you need to figure out how to get rid of them so they don't turn anyone else."

"Good point," Drip said. He turned back to the undead and began to concentrate again. "I need you all to do me a favor."

"Yeah?" all of the undead asked together. Of course it sounded like a chorus of grunts to Nina.

"I need you all to bury yourselves until I come back and get you," Drip said.

All of the undead shrugged at the request, but immediately started to bury themselves. Drip was proud of himself for thinking of the solution. Then he turned back to Nina and walked over to her.

"What do you know, the quest has been completed," Nina said with a deceiving smirk on her face.

"Yes, but with a very high cost," Drip said, looking down at the sword he was carrying.

"Speaking of which, we need to settle up," Nina said.

"What do you mean?" Drip asked. "We paid you what you requested. What more is there?"

"No assassin ever wants to be in the position I am in, let alone the Chief Assassin," Nina said. "I don't know if there is an easy way to say this."

"Do you have feelings for Drip?" Boot asked. The question seemed to startle Drip and Nina.

"No," Nina said incredulously. This both embarrassed Drip and irritated him in the same moment.

"What is it then?" Drip asked.

"I...I...owe *you*, okay? Are you happy now? I said it," Nina said with her nosed turned up and her arms folded.

"For what?" Drip asked.

"After I was paralyzed, you saved me," Nina said, still holding her stance.

"Technically, you owe Drip several times over, with him single-handedly drawing away so many of the undead, and all," Boot added. "Just saying."

The argument Boot had presented clearly irritated Nina, and she let out a deep breath. This seemed to calm her down a little. Eventually, she pulled two silver pieces out and carved something into each one, then tossed them both to Drip.

"There, I owe you twice, and nothing more," Nina said. "Each one is more valuable than all the king's gold, so don't lose them."

"Wow," Drip said with genuine surprise. "I will keep them safe."

"Now with this contract completed, I must bid you farewell," Nina said. She pulled a cloak from her bag and wrapped it around her. As Nina walked away she seemed to get shorter, until just five feet away, the cloak lay on the ground with nothing but dirt underneath.

"Now that is an exit," Boot said.

Drip kicked a very large rock in response, causing Boot to shout in pain. "That was for asking if she was falling for me," Drip said before Boot had a chance to ask about the assault. In return, Boot said nothing.

Drip slowly walked over to the twisted metal that once was Thomas's armor, again, and ran his fingers across it.

"I will miss you my friend," Drip said. Then he headed for the horses. By that time, the undead were all nearly buried. With no sheath to put the sword away, Drip found himself dragging the long blade behind him.

"You know you can always put that into the bag of holding, so you don't have to drag it around," Boot added.

"Sad, mad, had…" Bean added.

"Bean has it right, Boot. I need to do this," Drip said. "Even if it doesn't bring her back."

Drip could feel the muscles in his arm as they throbbed in pain from the unusual tasking, but despite this fact, he continued on. Finally, he reached the cave where the horses were hidden. However, to Drip's frustration, the horses were all gone.

"Oh boy," Boot said.

"Yup, it looks like it will be a long walk back to Ormlu," Drip replied. He lowered his head and started to head back to the main city as a light rain began.

EPISODE
38

Drip could feel the sun beating down on him as he slowly moved towards Ormlu. He was tired, hungry, and thirsty, but would not let himself rest until he was inside the city. He was just barely on the edge of the Light Side. Troops from both sides had heard about his legendary defeat of the dragon, and simply watched him as he walked past.

"Drip, we made it," Boot said in an exhausted voice. "You are going to live!"

All that Drip could manage was a confused, "Huh?"

"We are within sight of the city!" Boot said cheerfully.

"Hope, end, cope…" Bean added.

"How long has it been?" Drip asked.

"You don't remember?" Boot asked. "How much do you remember?"

"The horses weren't where they were supposed to be, and I started walking, and here we are," Drip said. "What did I miss?"

"Well, I guess there really isn't too much you missed, other than four days and nights of constant walking," Boot added.

"Huh…" Drip said. "Well, I am glad that we made it."

That is when Drip noticed the large groups of Light and Dark standing in awe of the passing imp. No one was saluting, but there was a lot of whispering and mumbling. Regardless of what was being said, Drip had a feeling it was all bad.

"Open the...!" Drip started to shout up to the gatekeeper, but it was already starting to open at his approach.

"Brilliant, finally an appropriate entrance," Boot said.

Drip walked into the city with everyone lining the streets inside as well, but this time instead of celebration, everyone was standing in a mourning kind of silence.

"What is going on?" Drip asked.

"We are so sorry for your loss. At least the necro got what was coming to him," a woman said. She then handed Drip a yellow flower.

"Apparently, news travels fast," Boot said.

"Apparently," Drip replied in a daze.

Everything seemed like a blur as Drip carried himself through the streets back to the Master Field Inn. He walked past an outraged and horrified Carter, who was helpless as Thomas' sword etched a fine line dragging behind Drip. As he exited the elevator, he walked over and entered Thomas's old room instead of his own. He climbed up onto the plush bed and rested the sword next to him.

Drip reached over and gently placed his hand on the hilt. "Goodnight, Thomas," he whispered.

"Drip, you should get something to eat," Boot said.

"I just got comfortable. I will get something in the morning," Drip replied.

"Drip, you have been asleep for eighteen hours," Boot said. "It's morning."

Drip lifted his head off the satin pillow and glanced around the room. He located a small tray of food sitting on a table near the bed. He carefully slid over to the tray and ate a few items, then drank a cup of water. With that, Drip felt satisfied and settled back into bed.

"Drip, how long do you intend to do this?" Boot asked.

"I am just tired, okay?" Drip said with an uncharacteristically irritated tone. "Just leave me alone."

"This won't bring Thomas back," Boot said. He realized that it was a mistake to offer that thought the moment he said it. Drip balled up his fist in rage and frustration and let out an angry shout.

"If you say one more thing, I will cut my foot off and drop you down the deepest well I can find!" Drip bellowed.

"Above, worried, love..." Bean added.

Drip responded by pulling the pillow over his head and falling back asleep.

"Sir," Carter said, "I apologize for my conduct, but it has been a week since I have seen you outside your room."

"Is there a policy about it?" Drip asked, with a tired and irritated tone to his voice.

"No, but you have a request from the Witch of Ormlu to join her in the Candlestick," Carter said.

"Fine," Drip said. He climbed out of the bed and headed downstairs with the large sword in tow.

"Please don't drag that through the lobby," Carter pled with the imp.

Drip offered him an irritated glance, but attempted to comply with the request anyway. He couldn't explain it, but everything seemed to bug him.

As Drip exited the Master Field Inn, he rested the sword on the ground again, and paused at the view. A brief memory flashed before him of Thomas and Gorath as they ran out of the Inn headed for the armory. In that moment, Drip felt like a part of his heart was breaking.

"Keep it together," Drip whispered to himself. He decided to take a quick detour to the royal armory, but as he approached, the guard was not ready to welcome him in.

"Halt!" the guard said in a firm voice.

"I have been given permission to enter by the King and the Dark Lord," Drip said firmly.

The guard stood firm in his position, determined to deny Drip entry.

"You know who I am?" Drip asked.

"Yes, and that is why I cannot let you in," the guard said.

"I have slayed a dragon and a necromancer. Do you think you can stop me from entering?" Drip asked.

"Please, I am only trying to do my job," the guard replied.

"How about this? What if you and some of your friends escort me into the armory to ensure nothing goes missing," Drip said.

"Okay, but please don't try anything weird," the guard said. After summoning two other guards, the four entered the armory. Drip knew exactly where to go without any assistance. This time, when they entered the vault with the pedestals, there were only a handful of items gathered together.

"What is he doing here?!" the Master of Arms demanded.

"Relax, I am only here to trade out a piece," Drip said.

"Yes, well unless you are here to give up all the missing items, then I am afraid we cannot help you," the Master of Arms said.

"About that, I am just curious, but does your policy override those dictated by the King and Dark Lord?" Drip asked.

"No, but you can't just walk in here and bully us out of our last few items," he responded.

"Calm down," Drip said. "I am looking to see if you have something I can use."

"Very well, one item, and you trade for something you already have," the Master of Arms replied.

Drip walked between the last set of enchanted relics, unsure of what he was looking for. He rubbed his head. He could feel everyone in the room watching him.

"Okay, Boot, I am sorry about what I said before. I need your help," Drip said.

"I understand why you said what you did," Boot replied. "We only want to help you."

"I appreciate it," Drip said. "Now I need something to help me with this sword. Any ideas?"

"Yes, ironically. Over on pedestal seventy-six, there is an item marked as the Sash of Jorgen," Boot said. "But that is not a sash at all, it is a sheath, and that is what you want."

"That is absurd! Of course it's a sash! Do you not think I can tell the difference?" the Master of Arms asked.

"No offense intended, but I want to trade my slingshot for the 'sash'," Drip said. He made air quotes when saying sash to emphasize his point. The Master of Arms agreed and quickly snatched up the slingshot.

Drip picked up the sheath and quickly wrapped it around his body. Sure enough, it did not look or feel like a sheath.

"See, I told you," the Master of Arms said.

"Drip, don't listen to him, just take the sword and slide it over your shoulder onto your back," Boot said.

Drip did as he was told and carefully slid the sword over his shoulder. Then, as if a harness had grabbed hold of the sword, it gracefully locked into place on Drip's back.

"Nice," Drip said in response.

"Just wait, it gets better," Boot said.

Right on cue, the sheath transformed to match Drip's armor and created extra straps to keep the sword upright, just behind his head, creating a perfect balancing point.

"That will do," Drip said, satisfied that he had found exactly what he needed.

EPISODE
39

It was much easier for Drip to walk about when he wasn't dragging a sword everywhere. He found himself striding with a little bit of confidence now. People recognized him and they would stop him and ask him questions like…

"Were you afraid of the dragon?" and "How did you know how to fight the undead like that?"

Even with a slight spring in his step, a sword on his back, and tremendous popularity, something was missing. Drip stopped just before entering the Candlestick and glanced to his left and right. He found that he was most definitely longing for his two companions, even if they hadn't been together for very long. He could hear quick snippets of conversations they had exchanged in his head.

"Wait, I'm the leader of this party?" Gorath asked.

"Technically," Thomas said.

Drip shook his head as he entered the Candlestick. Everyone he passed acknowledged him with a proper greeting. Before his adventures, he had been widely ignored and dismissed like a servant.

After ascending two different magic lifts, he exited at the base of the large winding staircase with the moving wall off to the side.

"Don't look," Boot whispered.

"Horror, pain, drain..." Bean added.

Despite the warnings, he turned to watch the battle unfold against the necromancer. As he watched, images of the combat flooded his mind. He took a deep breath and braced himself as he watched Thomas intercept the massive fireball.

"I know how painful this is," Orielia said, standing beside the wall. "But you must find the strength to carry on."

"Why?" Drip asked. "Why did they die?"

"The question is bigger than you know, as are your quests," Orielia said. She lowered her head and walked over to the staircase railing.

Drip replied with a confused and frustrated expression. "Look, I don't even know why I am here. It wasn't that long ago that my life was simple. Why was I picked for this?"

"I don't know for sure why you were chosen, but if I had to guess, I would say it's because you are extraordinary," Orielia said. "I know that there is no one else who can complete this other than you."

"Can you tell me why I should keep doing quests?" Drip asked.

"There is no way to sugar coat this," Orielia replied. "You have to keep doing these quests, because the world depends on you."

"What? What does that mean?" Drip said with a spark of irritation.

"It will be easier if I showed you," Orielia said. She waved her hand at the wall causing the moving characters to shift and create an open space. Orielia waved again, and a picture of Ormlu appeared, along with a map of the light and dark kingdoms. As she moved her hands, a large purple figure appeared and slowly consumed the light and dark until they were no more.

"This new threat to the world will consume everything and enslave everyone, and now there is only one person who can stop it," Orielia said. "I am truly sorry, but all the burden sits with you."

"With no help?" Drip asked.

Orielia smiled as if she knew something she could not say... not yet. "The only help I can give is this. Trust no one," Orielia replied. "Many will offer companionship, but the corruption is too widespread. You must do it alone."

"How many more quests?" Drip asked.

"One more quest and after that, one choice to make," Orielia said. She could see that Drip's heart was heavy. "No one can force you to go, and I would not blame you if you walked away."

"What is the next quest? Can I know before I decide?" Drip asked.

"Yes," Orielia said. "The head monk is in the large conference room over there."

"Thank you, for everything," Drip said. He slowly walked into the conference room. Boot and Bean were uncharacteristically silent, and without their constant chattering, the quiet seemed to engulf Drip. He had never known such lonely quiet before.

"Ah. Drip," Head Monk Towe said. "It is good to see you alive and well."

"Thank you. Unfortunately, Thomas did not make it," Drip said sadly.

"I know, that was a terrible blow to our cause," Towe said. "Are you here to find out what your next quest is?"

"Yes," Drip quickly replied.

"To be honest, there isn't one. We have decided not to send the High Standard of the Watch on any more quests," Towe said.

"I am confused. I was under the impression there was a quest," Drip replied. He could feel Boot holding his tongue.

"There is a labor issue with the mountain men of the Sevari, and they have stopped sending needed supplies," Towe said.

"We need someone to go up there and broker a deal with them to resolve their issues, and get things moving again."

"That is all, just a labor issue?" Drip asked. "No demons, dragons, necromancers, or wizards?"

"None that I am aware of," Towe said. "But you don't need to worry yourself with this mater, I am sure we can find someone else."

"That won't be necessary. I can do it," Drip said. "Send the instructions to the Master Field Inn. I will leave in the morning."

"As you wish," Towe said.

"Also, I am going to need new supplies and a horse," Drip said.

"I will make all the arrangements," Towe said.

Drip exited the room in the hopes of running into Orielia again. He was disappointed when he could not immediately find her. Drip thought it was interesting that the image Orielia had shown him was still on the wall. This time, however, he noticed a small gray triangle that stood out in the sea of purple.

"Look, guys, I need you more than ever before, and I know you don't want to say anything that will make me upset," Drip said, "but I am lost without you."

"Ironically, this might not be the right place to talk," Boot finally chimed in.

"Secret, hidden, deceived..." Bean said.

"No worries, it is time to go see our friend in the hospital," Drip replied. He truly wondered how Cary was doing, and hoped she might be awake and willing to join him on his quest.

After the long walk to the hospital, he found her still sleeping peacefully.

"Any change?" Drip asked the nurse in the room.

"None," the nurse replied. Then the tall woman started to walk out of the room. Something about the nurse seemed to bother

Drip, and if it weren't for her deep ice blue eyes, short blonde hair, and her very unique green necklace, he would have ignored his feelings.

"Wait," Drip said, following her out the door. "Do I know you?"

"Perhaps you have seen me around the hospital," the nurse replied.

"Have you been to Drueblat recently?" Drip asked. As he spoke the words, he noticed that the nurse kept turning her face away from him.

"No, I'm sorry. I have things to do, if you don't mind," the nurse said.

"I do mind, actually," Drip said with loud authority. "Charge nurse!"

As Drip had hoped, the charge nurse came running down the hall. Drip knew he could not restrain the nurse in question all by himself, but he could limit her escape options.

"Drip, what is going on?" the charge nurse asked.

"Do you know this nurse?"

The charge nurse scrutinized the tall woman before replying. "I have no idea who this is. She is not one of my nurses."

The suspicious woman just stood there, frozen. Drip wondered if she was too scared to move, or if she was carefully plotting her escape route.

"Call the guards," Drip commanded.

As the charge nurse ran back down the hall, Drip moved to block the impersonator. This time, the nurse turned and looked directly in his eyes. Her gaze was cold and full of rage.

"Go on your quest or don't. It doesn't matter. But know this. I have been successful at killing your companions, and you are next. You have no idea what you are up against."

"Who are you?" Drip asked in anger and confusion.

"I am the rightful heir to these lands, and I will not be denied," the suspect said. "Not by anyone! Especially a lowly little imp!"

Just as the charge nurse returned with several guards, the suspect changed into a thin wisp of smoke and vanished. A large tray that she was carrying crashed to the ground.

"Whoa, did you see that?" the charge nurse asked.

"Our time is short. Tell me, what was she carrying?" Drip asked. The charge nurse rushed forward and dabbed her pinky in the substance on the floor.

"It is wristleweed," the charge nurse said. "Poison!"

EPISODE
40

Drip wasted no time at the discovery of the poison and ran back into Cary's room. All noise seemed muffled to him, but he could definitely hear the sounds of people running and shouting different things as they entered behind him. He could tell that Cary's sleeping body was struggling to breathe.

"I have seen this before," Boot said. "I am sorry to say, from my experience, she will be lucky to survive this."

Within moments, a dozen people were surrounding the bed, and Drip found himself being crowded out. He knew that the images of the two doctors instructing mages on how to contort Cary's body would haunt him later. A nurse ushered Drip back towards the entrance of the room.

"I think it would be best if you wait in the front office," the nurse suggested.

He slowly walked down the hall, people running back and forth. Everyone was pushing past him and seemed to be moving a hundred miles per hour. Finally he reached the front office and sat down.

"Why is this happening?" Drip asked.

"Drip, this isn't your fault," Boot said. "Bad things happen to people all the time."

"Rain, shine, good…" Bean said.

"I know, but after losing Thomas and Gorath, I needed some good news," Drip said. His hands were now rubbing his face.

"I have some good news for you," Orielia said.

Drip glanced up to find the oracle standing beside him, and then resumed his face rubbing. "What good news do you bring?"

"Cary will live, and will most likely make a good recovery," Orielia said.

"Oh good," Drip said. He let out a very loud sigh of relief.

"I know you were hoping that she would be able to go with you, but this one you will have to do on your own," Orielia said, then she offered a little grin. "Besides Boot and Bean of course." She offered Drip an uncharacteristic nudge, causing him to let out a much needed smile.

"I just wish the other two were here," Drip said softly. "But I will get this quest done."

"Just be careful out there," Orielia said. "I want to see you come back alive."

"That's the plan," Drip replied.

"I will watch over Cary. Good luck on your quest," Orielia said. "Oh, and a word of advice, not everything is as it seems out there."

"Thanks…I think."

―

"Why won't you let us help him?" Aroon asked.

"You are helping him," Orielia said. "You need to recover your strength and recruit more soldiers to your cause."

"How many are you thinking we need?" Aroon asked.

"Think about this: all the light armies and all the dark armies versus Drip," Orielia said. "How many do you think you might need?"

"Are you kidding?" Corporal Stevens asked.

"No, I am not kidding. Soon the whole world will be against Drip."

"Alright, we are going to need a lot more guys," Aroon said. "Where is the rally point again?"

"The southern field of Chanazog de Felzi," Orielia said. A sense of prophetic irony swept over her after saying the phrase. Few knew how to read or speak ancient Gogamen, mostly because they had all died out two ages ago. However, it was fortunate for Orielia that she understood what the name of the field really meant, and it translated loosely as 'Field of the Fallen Champions'.

"You heard the lady! Get your friends together. We need to make this happen," Aroon ordered.

"Will do. I won't let you down," Corporal Stevens said.

―

Drip entered the small elevator at the inn and braced himself against the wall. He recalled the brief moment he had shared with Thomas, and gazed at the wall as he replayed the exchange in his mind.

"Drip?" Boot asked. The comment startled Drip back into the moment. The elevator doors had opened and were patiently waiting for Drip to exit.

"Oh, yes, what was I doing?" Drip asked, stepping off the elevator.

"Breakfast," Boot replied.

"Right," Drip said. He walked over to the table he had sat at last, when Carter promptly greeted him.

"Good morning, Sir," Carter said.

"Morning, Carter. I don't suppose you would like to join me for breakfast?" Drip asked.

Carter looked shocked, but eventually said, "I appreciate the offer, but I am good."

Gracefully, Carter then placed a small scroll on the table next to the plate of food in front of Drip and quickly walked away. Drip looked at the scroll and chose to ignore it, choosing instead to concentrate on his food.

"You already know what the scroll says, why not take a look?" Boot asked after Drip had eaten most of his breakfast.

"Look, hook, mistook...." Bean added.

Drip let out a sigh, then picked up the scroll. Slowly he opened it and scanned its contents. Drip noticed something written on the bottom of the page that seemed to disappear just as quickly as his eyes could chase the scrollwork. He wasn't able to read it, but dismissed the words as unimportant.

"So what does it say?" Carter asked, returning to remove the plate in front of Drip.

"Oh, well, it promoted me to leader of the High Standard of the Watch, and tasked me to resolve a labor issue in the Sevari mountains," Drip said as he climbed to his feet.

"Huh, the Sevari mountains. There is no place in the whole of Wax like those mountains; the views are breathtaking," Carter said.

"Have you been there before?" Drip asked.

"When I was young and foolish, I traveled there with friends," Carter said, and the expression on his face revealed that it was not a pleasant experience. "Even the most beautiful places can be treacherous."

"What happened?" Drip asked. A growing concern began to build in his stomach.

"It was so very long ago, but I will never forget," Carter said now gazing off into nowhere. "Greed comes with a price, and I was fortunate to escape when I did."

"That doesn't sound good," Boot said.

"Warning, storming, swarming..." Bean said.

"Listen, I am sure things have changed, but just in case... take this," Carter said. He produced a small stuffed rabbit's foot. "This may save your life."

"Is it enchanted?" Drip asked.

Carter let out a little laugh at the question, "No, my friend, but if you ever have need of it, you will think it was."

"Thank you, I will bring this back to you," Drip said.

"Yes, I would very much like for you to return, but the rabbit's foot isn't as important," Carter said. "Now enough of this rambling, is there anything else I can do for you?"

"No. As always, thank you for everything you do," Drip said. He slid the rabbit's foot into his pocket, and stood, deciding to make one more stop before heading off to begin his next quest.

He found himself admiring the city and streets a little more than he had before. A wave of nostalgia raced over him as he turned the corner to see the Assassins Guild. Drip walked over and gave the door a quick knock.

"Master Drip, you must learn how to knock properly one of these days," the Caretaker said. "What brings you to our corner?"

"I was hoping to talk with Nina for just a moment," Drip said.

"Oh, you would like to talk to the Chief Assassin?" the Caretaker asked.

"Yes, please," Drip replied.

"Very well, a moment has been allocated for you. Please proceed."

The Caretaker stepped to one side, revealing a very dressed up Nina standing in the entryway. Drip quickly walked in to talk to her.

"Drip, good to see you made it back," Nina said.

"Yes, but I don't have much time. I am headed up to the Sevari mountains for my next quest, and—" Drip started to say but was interrupted.

"Sorry Drip, I have duties to attend to, and my assassins are all currently out under contract," Nina said.

"Oh, no that wasn't what I was going to ask," Drip said. "I wanted to see how things were progressing on the other contract."

"Ah, yes, the other contract," Nina said. "We are still looking into it."

"I ran into the person who is trying to kill me. You see, there was an incident at the hospital," Drip said.

"We will look into it. I have my best person on it," Nina said.

Then she set herself in a running pose, and after a moment, the front door opened. Nina ran as fast as she could towards the door and dove into a moving carriage. Drip could faintly make out one last phrase from Nina.

"Good luck, and don't die!"

EPISODE
41

Drip exited the Assassins Guild cautiously under the watchful eye of the Caretaker. Ormlu or no, Drip had decided that he was not going to take any chances messing with Death, or with one of the deaths.

"So should we head off then?" Boot asked.

"Let's get this over with," Drip replied.

"Travel, quest, unravel…" Bean added.

Drip headed for the East gate leading out into the Light Side. He noticed something was off about the normally super busy city. It seemed nearly deserted.

"Where is everyone?" Drip asked.

"Most perplexing, I've never seen it so slow before," Boot said.

Drip stopped a goblin passing by and asked, "Where is everyone?"

"I don't know, how should I know? I don't really care," the goblin grumbled.

"Probably not the best candidate," Boot said.

"Nice," Drip replied sarcastically. "Who would you ask?"

"How about the soldiers over there?" Boot said. Sure enough just about ten feet away, two soldiers were standing at a street light.

"Excuse me, where is everyone?" Drip asked.

"Not sure, it is the oddest thing," the soldier responded. "It is like huge groups of people up and left the city."

"Alright...thanks," Drip said and headed towards the East gate.

"It's even worse that the people still left in the city have no idea why everyone else left," Boot said.

"Look at that. Most of the shops are even closed," Drip said.

"An exodus this large has to have a trace," Boot remarked.

The trend seemed to keep up as Drip approached the edge of the city. As expected, Head Monk Towe was waiting for him with a new horse and supplies.

"Ah, Master Drip," Towe said. "I am glad to see you well."

"Sure," Drip said. He had felt the luster of adventure dissipate with each departure of the city. "Do you have a map of my destination?"

"Yes, everything is prepared for you on your horse," Towe said.

"Perfect," Drip said with a faint smile. "Is there any chance you know why so many people have left the city?"

"I do, actually," Towe replied. "There have been rumors going around that large amounts of gold have turned up in a couple different provinces."

"Do you think there is really gold out there?" Drip asked.

"Highly doubtful, it is a fool's errand at best," Towe said.

"Greed seems to be the downfall of so many," Drip replied. He walked over and carefully mounted his horse.

"Safe passage on your trip," Towe said.

"Oh yes, one last question," Drip said.

"What can it possibly be?" Towe asked with a hint of irritation.

"What is my horse's name?"

"Strong Wind," Towe said quickly.

"Thanks." Drip turned Strong Wind and trotted out of the east city gates.

As they left the city behind, even the area just outside the gates seemed abandoned.

"Was it me, or did the head monk seem angry?" Boot asked.

"I noticed that too, I decided not to press my luck," Drip replied.

"Sir, would you be so kind as to help me," an old man asked on the side of the road.

Drip pulled his horse up short, surprised to be stopped so soon. "What is the problem, Sir?" he asked.

"All my help has left me, and took my horses. I have no way of getting the seed for my crop back to my farm," the old man said.

"I am afraid, Sir, that this horse is not strong enough to pull your cart," Drip replied.

"Then my family and I are ruined."

"I am truly sorry, Sir, but we are on an important quest," Boot replied.

"Wait, I think I have a solution for this," Drip said with a grin.

"What?" Boot asked.

"We just need another dimension," Drip said.

"Say again?" Boot sputtered.

With that, Drip dismounted his horse, and walked around the large cart of seed. The old man eyed him suspiciously.

"Alright, let's see what we can do," Drip said. He quickly removed his small bag of holding, and opened it as wide as it would go.

"Oh boy, I don't think this is going to work," Boot said.

"Don't be a pessimist," Drip replied. He had already managed to slide two smaller bags of seed into the bag of holding.

Eventually, Drip and the old man had methodically loaded each and every five-pound-bag of seed into the bag of holding. Finally, Drip held the bag up as if he had conquered a demon.

"How much does that weigh now?" Boot asked. He could tell that Drip was physically straining to manipulate the bag.

"A few pounds more than before," Drip replied.

"I appreciate this," the old man said.

"No problem. Now where to?" Drip asked.

"The village of Asoka in the foothills to the east," the old man said.

"Perfect," Drip replied. Drip and the old man both mounted Strong Wind together. "Let's go."

"Where did they *really* go?" Orielia asked.

"We don't know," Naomi said with a ghostly whisper.

"What can she be up to?" Ponopoli asked.

"Personally I think she is arming the peasants to use in her great battle," Orielia said.

"What about Drip?" Naomi asked. "Will he make it through this quest?"

"That is the right question," Orielia replied. "To be honest, I never thought he would be the last one of the three."

"Do not underestimate the imp," Ponopoli said. "His heart and character are strong."

"I don't doubt that, but is it strong enough to risk the whole of the world on?" Orielia questioned. "Even I cannot see what happens next."

"We think the head monk and both leaders are coordinating with Olpetrion," Ponopoli said.

"We have given the gray army as much help as we can, but without Drip, all is lost," Naomi added.

"I know, sister. I just can't help but feel like something else is happening," Orielia said. She reached out and touched the moving wall, and instantly she could see Drip's progress towards the mountains of Sevari.

"Of everything we know, I can't say I recall an imp ever facing a werewolf," Naomi said.

"Of everything we know," Orielia said, "there has never been an imp like Drip."

Cary watched as the dragon passed over her. Her powers strained to the limits with the protective shell she had created to guard Thomas, Drip, and herself from the deadly flames. As she collapsed to the ground from exhaustion, she saw a blurry figure approach her.

"Cary, this isn't really happening," Gorath said. "You're dreaming."

"What do you mean?" Cary managed to ask between heavy breaths.

"I don't have much time, but you need to know this. You have been reliving this over and over, locked in the nightmare," Gorath said.

"Did we win?" Cary asked.

"Yes," Gorath said with a smile. "All because of you."

"Really? You know, I always wanted to be on one of your legendary quests, ever since I studied you in the order."

"This was by far my greatest quest," Gorath said as he looked up to see the dragon racing through the sky.

"I look forward to our next quest," Cary said.

"Me too," Gorath said with a small tear welling up in his eye. He reached out and brushed her cheek.

"What is it?" Cary asked.

"If only we had met sooner," Gorath said in a sad tone.

"We did, you big jerk. I worked right next to you every day for years," Cary said with a little laugh.

"As it turns out, sometimes it takes an epic quest to fight a dragon in a faraway land to find out a missing piece to your life was right next to you the whole time," Gorath said with a smile, but his face suddenly fell. "Oh no, I have to go."

"What do I need to do?" Cary asked.

"Wake up, and prepare yourself to cast more magic than you could possibly imagine," Gorath said as he started to fade.

"What? Why?" Cary asked.

"There will be a great battle, and I am so sorry to put this on you, but you alone will determine the fate of the battle."

"Don't go!" Cary shouted.

"You might not remember right away, but you have to wake up!" Gorath yelled. "Wake UP!"

Cary opened her eyes and sat straight up to find herself in a hospital. A couple of nurses quickly ran over to her.

"It's okay," a nurse said. "Do you know where you are?"

"Dragon!" Cary shouted.

EPISODE
42

Drip had slouched in his saddle as they were nearing ten hours of riding. The old man had drifted off to sleep several times, drooling on Drip's back on occasion.

"There it is," the old man said as he pointed towards a small farm.

This perked Drip up, eager to get rid of his extra passenger and get going with his quest. He brought the horse to a quick trot to end the trip just a little quicker.

"I didn't ask; where are you off to after this?" the old man said.

"I'm headed up to the Sevari Mountains to settle a labor dispute."

"What?! Do you know what is up there? Do they know you are coming?"

"Whoa, calm down there. It's just a little labor dispute, and I am not sure if they have been notified or not," Drip said. "What is the big deal anyway?"

"Look, I don't want any trouble, just let me off here," the old man said.

"That's crazy, we are almost to your house."

"This is good, just give me a few of the bags of seed and get out of here!" the old man shouted. He forcefully dismounted the horse. Without warning, he fidgeted with the bag of holding until it came open. Four bags of seed fell out.

"Why are you doing this?" Drip asked.

"I don't want to die just yet," the old man said. "Now just get out of here!"

Drip stared intently at the man in confusion. Unable to read anything but a mixture of fear and anger, he secured the bag of holding, turned the horse, and headed away from the farm.

"You know you have a special way with people," Boot said.

"Don't listen to him," Bean said.

The comment from Bean caused Drip to stop the horse and look down at the small enchanted bean. "Did you just say a full sentence?" Drip asked.

"Watch, listen, rain..." Bean said.

"Okay, there are a lot of weird things going on," Boot commented.

"So you heard it too?" Drip asked.

"I think so," Boot said.

"Well according to the map we have a two-day ride ahead of us."

Drip came up short as a large tree suddenly fell in the road about a hundred yards ahead of him.

"Huh, what do you make of that?" Boot asked.

"Nothing. Trees fall all the time," Drip replied. Then, just as sudden as the first, a second tree fell right behind them. This caused Drip to scan the tree line, as there seemed to be something wrestling behind some of them. Drip reached up behind his head with his right hand and grabbed the hilt of the sword. Then a large deer and doe raced out of the forest past them.

"Okay, let's get out of here," Boot said.

"No kidding," Drip replied. He nudged the horse, speeding her up to a quick trot.

"Do you ever get the sense that something is watching you?" Boot asked.

"Yes," Bean said.

Cary closed her eyes for a moment and could see the dragon's eye as if she were standing in front of it. She quickly opened her eyes again, unable to sleep as the doctor had recommended. She climbed out of bed, barely able to stand with her weak legs. She walked over to the window, bracing her hands on the ledge. Cary watched the fireflies dance around the tree. Then, as one firefly began to approach her, her breath began to quicken. She knew it was just a firefly, but she felt compelled to raise her hands in a defensive posture.

"Calm down, just breathe and focus," Gorath's voice whispered in her ear.

She quickly turned, almost falling to the ground to find no one standing behind her. Cary sat down on the ground and rubbed her head trying to make sure she was sane.

"Get up and try again," Gorath's voice whispered once more.

Confused at the instruction, Cary stood up and looked out the window again. She was unsure why, but she found herself focusing on a small tree in the garden. As she raised her hands, this time she did not form a defensive posture, but gestured as if she were holding a wand.

A gust of energy flowed through Cary and out through her fingertips. She had felt magic before, but only once had she felt this kind of magic, when she had enhanced the storm. She watched as the tree grew with explosive force upward towards the sky. The floor shook around her as the roots of the tree rapidly expanded and the trunk grew wider. Then she fell to the floor, strained from the magic use.

"Good, very good," Gorath's voice whispered.

Cary looked around to see a nurse running into the room. Confused as to where Gorath's voice was coming from, she let the nurse put her back into bed.

"That was impressive, but not very useful," Olpetrion said.

"What?" Cary asked.

"I didn't say anything, ma'am," the nurse replied. It was apparent that the nurse was unable to see or hear the other person standing in the room.

"It's nothing, leave me be," Cary said as she instead acknowledged the transparent person in the room.

"Yes ma'am," the nurse said. She slowly exited.

"Smart, but don't you think it is odd that she didn't notice or even care about the tree outside?" Olpetrion asked.

"Who are you? And what do you want?" Cary demanded.

"I am a simple servant, only looking out for what is best in this world, a protector of this city," Olpetrion said. She offered a couple of elegant hand gestures to emphasize her point. Then she approached the bed.

"And what do you want?" Cary asked again.

"I want to save your life," Olpetrion replied. "The witch of Ormlu is out to put you in harm's way, and would see your demise, just like Gorath. When the time comes, run and you will be safe."

"When?" Cary asked.

"You will know," Olpetrion said.

"Know what?" Orielia asked, appearing in the doorway. "Go on. Know what, my dark sister?"

"Dark? Why do you greet me with such a hostile tone?" Olpetrion asked. "I only have love for you."

"You are a sad, twisted thing, and you must leave," Orielia said. She walked slowly into the room and raised her hand. A light blue glowing light began to gather around Olpetrion.

"You are hurting me, my sister," Olpetrion said in a whiny tone. "Cary, save me."

"Stop!" Cary said. "Stop this!"

"What lies has she told you?" Orielia asked.

"I have told no lies, every word is the truth," Olpetrion replied.

Cary raised her hands and paused time. The two women stood motionless, staring right at the bed. Confused by the rhetoric, Cary opted to try and escape. Her sore, weak legs slowly carried her out of the room. She couldn't help but notice that the nurses in the hall were also frozen, and as she exited the hospital, even people on the street stood still in time. She looked at her hands in confusion, as she had never cast a time bubble of this magnitude or for this extended duration. Cary then slipped into the night.

When time finally resumed, Orielia and Olpetrion found themselves staring at an empty bed. They also noticed the lighting was all wrong for the time of day they had started their conversation in.

"How long?" Olpetrion asked.

Orielia raised her hand, showing a picture of the solar system Wax resided in and watched it rotate for a moment.

"Two days," Orielia said. She glared at her evil sibling. "When this is over, I promise, I will end you."

"Not if I end you first, and your precious imp," Olpetrion said. Then in a small wisp of smoke, she disappeared.

"Huh. The whole city missed two days. Good for Cary," Orielia said. "I wonder if anyone else noticed."

"It happened, just like the *Master Book of Magic* predicted," Mussashi said, staring blankly out the window. Behind him the room was filled full of monks.

"What does this mean?" one of the monks asked.

"The order must prepare for war," Mussashi said with no emotion.

"What side do we fight for?" another monk asked.

"It isn't about what side we fight for, it is about what side we will be fighting against," Head Monk Towe said.

"No offense, Sir, but what does that mean?"

"It means we are to go to war against the gray," Towe announced.

"You are wise, but I am afraid there is no gray army," Mussashi replied.

"Yes, I am wise," Towe said. "Look to the moving wall and you will see. There is a gray army. And we must crush it."

EPISODE
43

Drip stood up from his makeshift bed and stretched. The sound of his leather armor crackling brought him comfort as he had grown used to it. Most of all, he had grown used to the extra dexterity the enchantment on the armor was granting him. As he started his usual routine of popping his neck, fingers, and toes, he recognized that there was a light soft smell in the breeze.

"You know, you don't have to sleep in the armor," Boot said.

"Yes," Bean added.

Even though it had happened nearly a dozen times in the last two days, Drip was caught off guard at Bean's atypical response. He rubbed it between his finger and thumb, which caused Bean to slightly vibrate with approval.

"Are you ready to say anything else yet?" Drip asked Bean. However, as Bean had responded every time he had asked this, there was no reply.

"Bean will open up when Bean is ready to," Boot replied. "Even I went through a silent phase for a while."

"Ah, man, and I ended up with you on a speaking phase," Drip said sarcastically. The light smell in the air had started to grow a little stronger, and though he could still not identify it, his stomach was growling.

"Now that wasn't very nice," Boot replied.

"According to the map we are still a few hours away from the village of Sturg, where the heart of the labor dispute is taking place, but I can swear I smell something familiar," Drip said.

"It's probably a hunter," Boot said.

"We should announce ourselves so they know we are friendly," Drip said.

"I don't think that is such a great idea." Boot realized he had missed his opportunity to sway Drip from acting on his last thought, when he noticed Drip had already managed to pack up the camp and load it onto the horse. "But what do I know, I'm just an enchanted item with ages of experience…"

"Quiet," Drip replied. Instinctually he found himself walking softly on foot instead of mounting Swift Wind. Drip carefully wrapped the reigns around a branch. "I thought you were going to announce yourself? This seems more like sneaking," Boot said quietly.

"Something is wrong," Drip replied. He could now clearly see a small campfire with some sort of food cooking on a spit. However, there was no one around.

"We shouldn't be here," Boot said. "Turn around and get out of here."

"Look out!" Bean shouted.

Drip instinctively dove to the left. What he had not seen was a large claw reach out and nearly take his head off. He caught sight of his attacker and quickly dove to the left again, as the large creature was right on top of him nearly instantly.

"It's a werewolf; of course it's a werewolf," Boot said.

Drip didn't have time to respond to the comment as he found himself dodging lightning-fast attacks. One attack barely raked across the back of his armor and struck his bag of holding. Drip's survival instincts were now working overtime to find an escape. He backed up against a medium-sized tree, but was forced to duck almost immediately. He ran for his horse as the werewolf's claws had cut the tree down and it was falling between them. Drip was able to mount his horse, but the werewolf's attacks were relentless. This time it caught a part of Drip's left leg.

Drip leaped back down from the horse, but the bag of holding caught on the saddle. With a quick yank, Drip untied the bag of holding and dove for the ground. He turned, expecting the werewolf to be right on top of him again, but instead it was struggling as something had gotten in its eyes.

Drip climbed to his feet and assessed that his leg was in no shape to flee.

"Where are you?" the werewolf growled. "No matter. I will find you and tear you to shreds!"

"I will stand and fight you honorably," Drip said. He pulled on a strap, allowing the sword to tilt to the right just enough for him to get both hands on the hilt. The enchanted sheath released the sword. Drip held it in front of him, as ready as he could be for combat with a werewolf about ten times his size.

The werewolf paused for a moment and began to sniff the air. Then he began to slowly head towards the imp. As he passed a couple of smaller trees, he reached out and cut them down with ease, in an effort to intimidate the imp.

"I warn you, I have slayed a dragon and a necromancer. You do not stand a chance," Drip said. He tested his leg again by resting a little more weight on it. It was throbbing in pain, but was operable.

"I know who you are, assassin, and I will stop you," the werewolf responded.

Drip could feel the sword begin to take over, swaying with each of the creature's steps. Then in the blink of an eye, the werewolf raced around behind Drip, and reached out to strike him down, but his attack was thwarted when Bean shouted at the very moment the werewolf made his move.

"Dive!"

Drip dove to the ground and turned with sword pointed at the werewolf. The large creature was content being on the offensive and, with little exertion, charged over to the imp. However, with his vision impaired, he miscalculated the placement of the sword, and it struck his right arm. The werewolf jumped back in pain and surprise. Drip instinctively threw the sword at the recovering creature. The sword knew exactly what to do and clipped the back of the werewolf's knee as it passed.

Drip realized that he was completely defenseless since he had thrown his only weapon. However the werewolf had fallen to the ground. Drip stood up and walked over to the beast. He reached out and touched the side of the creature's head with his pointer finger.

"I told you: dragon, necromancer," Drip said, nearly out of breath. "You are lucky I don't feel like adding 'werewolf' to that list. Now withdraw and I will spare you, or I can end you right here and now."

"Impossible," the werewolf quietly mumbled. "Finish me off!"

"My compassion is bigger than your pride," Drip said. He walked away from the creature to retrieve his sword when the werewolf let out a tremendous roar, and whimpered as it hopped off.

"So, good news and bad news," Boot said.

"Oh yeah, what is the bad news?" Drip asked, as he sat down on the ground to assess his leg.

"The horse is gone," Boot said. "Swift Wind took off during the battle."

"And the good news?"

"You survived and defeated a werewolf."

"Ha, that is good news, I suppose," Drip replied.

"Really, would you prefer to be dead? You are aware that the odds were against you on this one?"

"The odds always seem against me, in case you hadn't noticed," Drip replied absently, almost to himself.

Boot didn't respond.

"How much do you want to bet, that won't be the last werewolf we see on this trip?" Drip asked.

"Given our luck, a hoard of werewolves might be exactly what we are walking into," Boot said.

"My thoughts exactly."

Cary was both tremendously disappointed and extremely proud that she had managed to create a bubble to freeze time in Ormlu. There was no doubt in her mind that the Book should have stopped her from completing the spell. And besides, with the city frozen, she was unable to seek out any of her friends. Unlike before, she had failed to pull anyone into the bubble with her.

"Brilliant," Cary said. She looked down at the sickly horse she had found wandering around just outside the city. It looked like it was on the verge of death. "I don't suppose you could go a little faster?"

She was being driven back to the sight of the epic dragon battle by the haunting images that seemed to replay every time she fell asleep. Something kept calling to her to go back. Regardless, she somehow knew that her time was running out.

"Stay strong, Cary, and we will get through this," she said to herself. She chuckled at the sound of her own voice, but her laughter faded when she once again heard Gorath's voice instead.

"Stay strong," he whispered.

EPISODE 44

Drip limped into the village, only barely registering the fact that it wasn't much to look at, especially after the intense battle he had endured. However, he was feeling the weight of Bean, who had started to grow heavy and was pulling down on his neck.

"The hill I shared with a hundred imps underground is more impressive than this," Drip said.

"I count five houses and two main buildings," Boot added.

Drip managed to get to the first house and knock on the door. "Hello?" Drip asked the air. "Is anyone home?"

"No," Bean said.

"Bean, are you going psychic on me?" Drip asked.

"I find Bean's progress fascinating," Boot said.

"No kidding," Drip replied. "Finally, someone else to have real conversations with."

"Very funny," Boot said. "At any rate, you should probably clean yourself up."

Drip looked himself over, and recognized that maybe he needed to make himself a little more presentable. He ran his fingers through his hair, and straightened up his armor. He was disappointed at the amount of apparent werewolf blood that now adorned his leather chest plate.

Drip walked over to the largest building and knocked on the door. He was surprised when the door swung open, but there was no one in sight. He walked into the building.

"I think they need a few more trophies," Boot observed. "There are at least three dozen types of animals represented here."

Drip began to examine one of the animal head trophies when it slipped off the wall. He managed to keep the large antlers from hitting the floor.

"Good save," Boot said.

Drip let out a sigh of relief before he gently set it on the floor. However, when he made the move to stand back up, Bean had grown to more than triple in size.

"Holy cow, Bean, what have you been eating?" Drip asked as he struggled to stand up.

"Are you okay?" Boot asked.

"I don't know what is happening," Drip said as he used one hand to keep himself off the floor, and the other to check out Bean. It was clear that Bean was continuing to grow. Drip was concerned about the events, especially since Bean was not responding to his questions.

"This might be a problem," Boot said. "A really big problem."

Without warning, the leather strap that held Bean snapped under the increasing weight. Drip stood back as Bean continued to grow, until it looked like a full-sized cocoon.

Drip was startled when a hand grabbed a hold of his left arm.

"What have you done?!" the owner of the hand asked.

Drip looked up at the intimidating man. He felt even smaller than usual against the six-foot-five stranger, who had the kind of broad shoulders and muscles only a woodsman could develop.

The man's dark brown eyes seemed to challenge Drip's very existence. With no effort, the strong man tossed Drip backwards toward the entrance, where two people now stood.

"Who are you? What is going on?" a woman asked, grabbing a hold of Drip and dragging him outside.

"I'm the High Standard of the Watch," Drip said as he watched his own feet drag along the ground.

"The what?" the woman asked.

"High Standard of the Watch. I am from Ormlu, and I am here to negotiate a labor dispute," Drip said. At that moment the woman let him go. He fell flat on his back, almost knocking the wind out of him. He could now see about six people standing over him.

"Kala, you need to see this," the intimidating man said, poking his head out the door.

"What is it, Drel?" Kala, the old woman, asked.

"It is unlike anything I have ever seen before," Drel replied. I need water and fresh blankets."

"You stay right there, we are not done with you yet," Kala said to Drip with a sharp look.

A chill ran down Drip's spine, and he recognized that, despite winning a fight against a werewolf, he might not make it past this quest. He watched as everyone scattered to gather the requested resources.

"This might be a good time to escape," Boot said.

"Really?" Drip said sarcastically. He had just climbed to his feet when Drel emerged from the building.

"You!" Drel said.

Instinctively, Drip's fight-or-flight kicked in, and he decided flight sounded pretty good. He started to back pedal, and then he turned, breaking out into a full sprint. He could clearly hear the sounds of pine tree branches breaking against his pursuer.

"You'll not get away that easy!" Drel shouted.

Drip could tell the man was only one step behind him. A couple of times he could swear Drel's hand was only inches from him. Drip looked left and right for an escape route.

"Over there," Boot said.

"Yes," Drip said, as he could see blue sky indicating a clearing. As he broke into the opening, a sense of horror crossed over him as he realized it was a cliff, and there was no time to stop. Drip could feel his feet slide out from under him and over the cliff. Then as everything seemed doomed, a large hand grabbed his arm and pulled him back.

"Wow, you were so dead," Boot said.

Drip looked up at the large man, who wasn't even out of breath.

"Are you going to come back to the village, or should I throw you over?" Drel asked.

"I'll come back," Drip said in a defeated tone.

Drip walked ahead of the large man, and even though he had no idea where the village was, he knew he was headed in the right direction as he could see the trail of natural destruction that had been caused by the chase.

"Sorry about running, I was just afraid you were going to kill me," Drip said.

"Who says we aren't?" Drel asked.

Drip was very concerned at this point as he was unable to read the expression on the man's face. Then, as they came into view of the town, he remembered that Bean was inside the large building.

"Now I want some answers," Drel said. "Who are you and what are you doing here?"

"As I tried to explain, I am the High Standard of the Watch, and I have been sent here from Ormlu to resolve a labor dispute," Drip said.

"Ha!" Drel laughed. "A labor dispute, that is a good one."

"What do you mean?" Drip asked.

"We don't have any labor disputes," Drel said. "It sounds like you are an assassin."

"You think he is an assassin?" Boot asked. "Now that is funny."

Drip instantly wanted to take offense to the comments, but recognized that this might not be the best moment to get into an argument.

"I am no assassin," Drip said.

"Drel!" Kala shouted. The old woman was now standing next to a young woman who seemed very out of place for this environment. The woman stood barely six inches taller than Drip, and her blue eyes and blonde hair seemed to gleam.

"Drip?" the woman asked.

Drip's eyes went wide and he began looking around for someone else named Drip. However, the woman ran over to him and wrapped her arms around him.

"Oh Drip, I am free at last, and it is all because of you," the woman said in a soft cheerful tone.

"Bean!?" Drip exclaimed.

"Yes," she softly answered.

Now it was Drip's turn to pass out.

EPISODE 45

Everything seemed to be moving in slow motion to Drip. He knew exactly where he was and what was going to happen next, or at least what was supposed to happen next. Drip looked up to see the large dragon with Gorath on top. He reached out to touch Thomas or at least get her to look back at him, but she was just out of his reach.

"Thomas!" Drip shouted. The effort seemed futile as it was clear she could not hear him. He could feel his heart breaking all over again as Thomas outpaced him, and was unreachable. He was powerless, and this brought on taunts people had thrown at him over the years.

"Weak," "Pathetic," "Worthless," "Useless," "Nothing," the voices in his head echoed. That was about the time he heard something odd.

"Drip, come back to me, I won't lose you now!" a female voice faintly shouted.

"What?" Drip asked as he looked around the dreamscape battleground.

"Drip, come back!" The female voice seemed closer and clearer.

Drip looked around as quick as the slow motion would let him, but as he looked forward again, Thomas was standing in front of him.

"Drip!" the female voice said. Thomas's mouth moved, but he knew it wasn't her voice. Then he was forced to look away as the fireball that had taken Thomas down blinded him a second time.

Suddenly, his eyes shot open and he found himself lying on the ground with the sun shining down on him. Slowly he sat up and began to look around, recalling the current situation in its entirety.

"How long have I been out?" Drip asked.

"A few hours," Bean said—the young woman version of Bean with lovely blonde hair and blue eyes. Drip still wasn't used to that.

"A few hours? And you couldn't at least move me in out of the sun?" he asked, as he jumped to his feet.

"They wouldn't let me," Bean replied. She nodded her head in the direction of a trio of irritated looking people.

"I see," Drip said.

"High Standard of the Watch, eh?" Drel asked. "More like High Snore of the Watch." The three people began to laugh at the comment. Drip noticed that even Bean snickered a little.

"Did I snore?" Drip asked.

"Just a tad," Bean said.

"A tad?" Boot chimed in. "It sounded like a landslide."

"Let me get this straight. *You* are Bean?" Drip asked. Bean quickly nodded at the question. "What happened?"

"A woman named Eleanor Straight cursed me so she could marry my love, Prince Timothy Ragmon," Bean explained. "Apparently the only thing that could break the spell was werewolf blood."

"Whoa, what?" Drip asked. "You were slated to marry the king? What is your real name?"

"My name is Elizabeth Mary Louise Alisa Templeton," Bean said. "But my close friends call me Bean."

"Why did they call you Bean?" Drip asked.

Then a large thump interrupted the conversation. Drip looked over to see Drel's face red with anger.

"Enough of this," Drel said. "Who sent you, assassin?"

"Why does everyone keep calling me assassin?" Drip asked. "I'm not an assassin, I am an emissary."

"First of all, an imp has never been seen in these parts. Second, your armor was clearly made for an assassin, and from the way you were moving when I was chasing you through the forest, I would say enchanted with extra dexterity."

"Who was your father, girl?" Kala asked. It was clear that Bean was being examined with suspicion as well.

"My father was Captain Johnathan Templeton," Bean announced.

Instantly, everyone within earshot gasped. It was tough for Drip to figure out if it was terror, offense, or shock.

"How long have you been cursed?" Kala followed up.

"It has been ten years now," Bean replied.

"Our deepest apologies, we did not know," Drel said, suddenly reverent instead of indignant. "Why would you travel with such as this?"

"Drip is the kindest imp you will ever find, and he has sacrificed so much to be here," Bean said.

"I don't know if we can trust him," Drel said.

"He saved my life twice," Bean insisted.

"Yes, but he is covered in blood," Kala said. "He has killed someone on this mountain."

"No, he spared his life. He only wounded in defense," Bean said. "He had no choice."

"Unfortunately, we must find Finn. His pride is probably pretty beat up," Drel said. Two men from the group headed back down the trail Drip had come from.

"The werewolf who attacked me is one of you? You are all like him?" Drip asked. His limbs went cold at the thought.

"Do you have a problem with that?" Drel said, then he let out a deep growl.

"No, no problem," Drip said quickly. "I just need to solve the labor issue and then be on my way."

"I told you there is no labor issue," Drel said.

"Then why have we been sent here?" Bean asked.

"Ever since the tragic death of Captain Johnathan Templeton, King Ragmon has sent his army up here to make sure we keep our quotas," Drel said.

"That is until they went too far," Kala added.

"How?" Drip asked.

"They wanted to teach us a lesson for missing a quota and they cornered our leader and attacked him," Drel said. "He was only trying to defend himself, but the army unit did not stand a chance."

"However, the sight of so much blood and carnage drove him into a frenzy, and he has since killed two of our kind, and wounded three others," Kala said.

"At this rate, there won't be anyone to fill the king's precious quota," Drel said.

"So, if we take care of your frenzied leader, you will start working again?" Drip asked.

"Drip, the king's tyranny of these people cannot go unchecked," Bean said. "My family has watched over these mountains for ten generations."

"We can talk to the king about this, but for now, if we take care of your leader, you will resume work?" Drip asked.

"We will, but there is only one problem," Drel said. "There is no way you will take down William by yourself."

"To my credit, I was able to defend myself against one of your kind," Drip said.

"That is not a victory I would brag about around here," Drel said.

Right on cue, the two men were escorting a wounded teenage boy, barely thirteen years old.

"Finn is the youngest and weakest member of the clan. You would be up against a hundred times more strength, and significantly larger size." Drel said.

For a moment, Drip considered his options very carefully. Then he said, "I know you think I'm crazy, but I will take care of him."

"Hey, your death, man," Drel said. Then he started to walk away from the conversation.

"A word of caution," Kala said. "You will die, that is certain, but it will be a slow, painful death. William likes to horribly mangle his victims before he lets them die."

"Very nice," Drip said as he walked over to her. "How big could he possibly be?"

"Big," Kala said nonchalantly, but her meaning was not lost of Drip.

At that exact moment, a deep rumble shook the ground around them for a few seconds.

"What was that?" Drip asked.

"William," Kala said. "Good luck."

"That was a tremendous fight," Naomi said.

"Yes, but that was against the youngest and weakest of them," Ponopoli said.

"Drip will survive this, but always at great cost," Orielia added.

"Maybe we can help him," Naomi said.
"No, everything has already taken a toll on you," Ponopoli said.
"We have already helped," Orielia broke in.
"How?" Naomi asked.
"Spoilers."

EPISODE 46

Without hesitation, Drip took off running into the woods in the direction he thought the rumble had come from. Everyone else stood taken aback at the action.

"I didn't see that coming," Drel said.

"You don't know Drip," Bean said. She followed after Drip into the woods.

"So what is the plan? Tell me you have a plan right?" Boot asked Drip as they ran.

"Haven't you noticed yet?" Drip said as he paused a moment to get his bearings.

"Noticed what?" Boot asked.

"My leg is healed," Drip said. His pause was rewarded with the very clear sound of a large tree crashing to the ground. Drip raced off.

"How did that happen?" Boot asked. "And how does that justify you running off after a werewolf without a plan?"

"Look, we were able to fight off one werewolf, this one can't be that much different."

"I think you missed the part where they said this one was bigger and stronger?" Boot replied. "By the way, what are your thoughts on Bean turning out to be a gorgeous woman?"

"It won't be long before she takes off," Drip said. "It doesn't matter anyway."

Drip stopped at the tree that had fallen. He nodded his head as he realized that the tree had only one set of claw marks, and that the trunk had a three foot diameter.

"Okay, maybe this was a mistake," Drip said as he compared his hand against the claw marks.

"Well, it's too late to change your mind," Boot said.

"What do you mean?"

A deep growl shook the ground. Drip turned to see a massive dark grey werewolf. As advertised, he was much larger and obviously stronger than the young Finn.

"Run?" Boot suggested.

"Yeah right," Drip said, sure that running would just speed up his execution.

"Why are you here?" the werewolf, William, asked gruffly. It was clear he was positioning to attack.

"I am here to stop you from preventing the villagers from working," Drip said. He pulled the sheath strap, shifting his sword to the side so he could draw it.

"And how do you suppose you are going to do that when you are dead?" Without warning, the werewolf charged Drip.

Drip had just enough time to duck the huge claws, and then jump to avoid the second pair. He felt better with his sword between him and the werewolf as he quickly drew it.

"Drip, jump left!" Bean's voice shouted behind him. "I mean right!" But Drip was already in mid-jump to the left and didn't hear her correction. He caught the force of William's large paw and found himself tumbling through the air and in pain, his least favorite combination short of death.

"Bean... Why?" Drip managed to ask after he hit the ground.

"Sorry! Get up!" Bean shouted. "No wait—duck!"

"Jump!" Boot said.

Confused, Drip did neither and again got struck, this time by William's head. Drip somersaulted through the foliage.

"No more directions!" Drip shouted in desperation. He had already taken two more hits than he thought he would have survived, but did not want to gamble on a third.

"Where is he?" Drip asked. He looked around for a moment, then dove into a hollow log. It only took a moment before two sets of huge claws pierced the side of the log like paper. Instead of cutting the log to shreds, William picked it up over his head and threw it. Drip felt weightless for a moment as the fall seemed to take forever. Then everything went black.

Cary wearily opened her eyes and looked around. It was clear that she was traveling down the light and dark divide, but surprisingly, no one was fighting.

"That is odd, there is no one in sight," Cary thought to herself. "There aren't even any sounds of battle."

At this point, it seemed like the horse knew to keep traveling north towards the Dragon's former home. As she looked around again, she could see someone heading towards her on a horse. She squinted her eyes to try and focus on the approaching person. As she got closer, Cary could swear she recognized the other rider, but couldn't place the face. She rubbed her eyes, and realized that it could be a mirage. Cary leaned down to grab the small pouch of water, and took a few sips. Then she looked around again to find the other person no longer in her field of view. She was starting to question her sanity, and hoped it had been a mirage after all.

"Wow, remind me to drink just a little more water," Cary said and gave the severely dehydrated and weary horse a pat on the neck. She shook her head to try and clear her thoughts, but as she thought about it more, Cary wondered if it hadn't been a mirage, but an omen. She looked around to see if she could make out the figure anywhere, but it had indeed vanished.

"Something is wrong," Cary said to herself, "I'm sure of it."

Once again, Drip opened his eyes to the sight of the sun, and the same three people standing over him. He slowly sat up and looked around.

"I have to say, that was pretty much the dumbest thing I have ever seen," Drel said.

"And brave," Bean said, while running her hand over his head in comfort.

"So, I just survived a fight with William?" Drip asked.

"I don't know if I would call that a fight. You got batted around by William like a rag doll," Drel said.

"Yes, but he lived," Kala said. "He might be what we need."

"What do you mean?" Drip asked. He stood up slowly and dusted himself off, assessing his injuries.

"It's nothing, there is no way *you* are what we need," Drel said.

"But if he could stay alive long enough, we can make it work," Kala insisted.

"So, I'm still lost here," Drip piped up louder.

"They have a plan they have tried a few times, but have yet to pull off," Bean said. "You see, if someone can wear William out enough, the rest of the werewolves could hold him down, while they administer an antidote."

"How could you know that?" Drel asked her.

"Sometimes I can hear people's thoughts," Bean replied.

Wow, Drip thought to himself. *I better watch what I think.*

Bean shot him a curious look.

"He is not the one," Drel said again.

"And who is? You?" Kala challenged. "Can I remind you of what happened the first few times we tried this plan?"

"Don't test me," Drel said. "Of course I remember what happened, I was there!"

"I don't know if I am the one you are looking for," Drip interrupted.

"If Drip will not do it, then I will," Bean said. "I volunteer to fight William."

"You? You won't last two seconds," Drel said.

"What are you doing?" Drip asked Bean. "Are you crazy?"

"You know this quest must be completed, and I have a duty to the people on this mountain, as my family has done for generations," Bean said.

"I cannot let you do this," Drip said.

"I don't see another option," Boot put in.

Drip took a deep breath before responding. "Fine, I will do this, but only after a good night's sleep."

"That or we can go after him right now," Bean said, looking into the forest.

"That is not going to happen," Drip said. "I barely escaped the last fight with my life."

"Then rest here and I'll be the one to distract him," Bean said. She gave him a quick pat on the back, before walking toward the forest.

"You're crazy!" Drip cried. "What is your problem?"

"You're my problem! You're fine! You've been resting the last few hours, which might I add, the werewolf has also. Waiting any longer will only make him stronger."

"Are you trying to kill me?" Drip asked.

"No, let's just say, I know what I'm doing," Bean said.

"I'm doomed," Drip muttered to himself.

"Trust me," Bean whispered.

With that, Drip started off into the woods with Bean in tow. Though they could not see the other werewolves, Drip could hear them following. He cautiously looked around as he approached the sight of the last battle. A clear path led to a nearby waterfall.

"If that is his camp, it is pretty close to the village," Drip said. As he closed in on the waterfall, he could see a distinct cave behind it.

"Okay, now to get his attention," Bean said.

"Sure, just go back to the village, I don't want you to get hurt out here."

"Like it or not, I am here with you."

"Get out of here, now!" Drip hissed with irritation, keeping his voice low so as not to alert William to their presence. "That is an order."

"You're going to need my help," Bean said calmly.

"Like I needed Thomas's help?" Drip asked. "No more sacrifices. Get out of here."

"Don't underestimate me, Drip. We can beat this werewolf together," Bean replied.

"Look, go back to your noble life, and leave me alone," Drip said. "Why are you even following me? Just go home."

"Why are you being like this?" Bean asked.

"Just get out of here. Go back to the people you care about."

Drip gave Bean a light shove to get his point across, and then headed for the mouth of the cave.

"I am with the people I care about," Bean said after Drip was well out of range. "If only you knew how much I love you."

EPISODE
47

Drip could feel the cold breeze from the wind blowing through the waterfall. He let his sword cut through the air in front of him. Small droplets of water sprinkled across his face. One quick sniff and he could tell that this was most defiantly the werewolf's den. Drip was counting on the loud noise from the water smashing against the rocks to cover his footsteps.

Careful, Drip thought to himself. About fifteen feet into the cave, he realized that his vision was having a hard time adapting to the odd lighting. Then he tripped on a piece of chest armor that had been torn in half. The loud clang the armor made as it skid across the floor was unmistakable, even with the rushing water.

"I have to give you credit for persistence," William growled. The rough voice echoed, just a little, as the water now acted as a buffer.

"I am here to give you an option, you can stop the attacks now and return to the village peacefully," Drip said. His eyes frantically searched the darkness for a clue as to where the creature was.

"Or what?" the werewolf asked.

"Or I make you," Drip said.

Instantly, William broke out into a thunderous laugh. For that brief moment, Drip got a glimpse of where William was as the meager light glinted of what he assumed to be drops of water from the waterfall.

"Now I will end you," William said.

Drip readied himself for the attack, now that he knew what direction it would most likely come from. However, he realized that this would be a losing effort with so little time to properly identify an attack. With no hesitation, Drip raced forward, catching William off guard. Drip instinctively jumped where he imagined the werewolf's leg would be and then reached out with the sword, nicking the beast with his blade.

The laughter quickly turned to anger and William howled with rage. Drip could hear and feel the werewolf turning to attack him, so he quickly pushed off a nearby wall and turned to head towards the exit.

"You're going to pay for that little stunt," William said. He reached over to lash out at Drip, but raked his claws across the rock wall. Instantly, William let out a loud roar.

Drip knew that it would only be a moment before the large creature would be upon him again. He sprinted as fast as he could towards the waterfall.

"Left!" Boot shouted. He jumped to the left. Drip did not need to look back to know the massive creature had missed him by only inches, as William had smashed his hands into the rock once again. It was at that moment that the fifteen feet Drip had ventured inside the cave seemed to turn into a hundred.

"This is going to be close!" Drip shouted as he dove out through the torrent of water.

As his hands broke the surface, he quickly sheathed his sword, and started swimming as hard as he could. As he had hoped, the werewolf was so stirred up, he had jumped into the water after him. Drip used the current and swam as close to the bottom as he could. Occasionally he would quickly look around to see William still heading straight for him. As Drip pulled his small body through the water, he found himself being thankful for his second job, recovering failed experiments at the bottom of a small lake.

His body started to remind him that he was running out of air. Drip pushed off from the bottom of the riverbed and held his breath until his lips cleared the water.

"Get out of the water, get out now!" Drip shouted at himself. He was just barely able to drag his water-soaked body out of the river and onto a large rock. He lifted his head to see an area covered with medium-sized trees. Drip managed to get his body upright and started a sloppy jog in that direction.

"See! I told you he could do it!," Bean said to the pack of werewolves who had joined her. "You must attack now!"

"No, he is not tired enough yet," Drel said in an ominous tone.

"Are you really going to pass up probably the only opportunity to contain William?" Bean asked. For a moment, she thought she was unable to read their thoughts, but then realized they honestly did not know if they were going to attack or not.

Bean felt helpless as she watched Drip head into a group of trees. Then, unexpectedly, William threw a large boulder at the imp. With near pinpoint accuracy, the boulder appeared to land directly on him.

"NO!" Bean shouted and then ran towards the battle. She could see William approaching the impact site. Bean reached down and picked up a small, smooth stone and threw it with all of her might. The rock struck William square in the head; however, it didn't seem to faze the creature. With little effort, the giant werewolf pushed the boulder aside. Bean fell to her knees as

William raised up his hands in a loud roar and smashed his fists into the ground.

Bean couldn't watch the devastating and relentless attack. She buried her tear-filled eyes into her hands and collapsed to her knees. She imagined she could still hear Drip's voice arguing with Boot.

"There are just as many dangerous creatures that could be in these tunnels," Boot said.

"And what was your idea, stand there and get pummeled?" Drip replied.

The conversation confused Bean as she did not recall ever hearing it before. She began to focus her mind on the werewolf to see if she could read his thoughts.

I can still smell them, must smash them, William was thinking.

Bean quickly straightened and peered over a log to see what the werewolf was doing.

Dig, smash, dig smash" William repeated in his mind.

Bean watched as the werewolf frantically dug into the dirt, then smashing into the ground again. She let a smile cross her face for a moment as she realized that she had been listening to Drip's and Boot's current conversation, just with her mind—they were still alive!

Her body still ached somewhat from the transformation from literal bean to figurative Bean, but she knew she had to do something. She looked back into the forest to see how far the other werewolves were, but she could not see them, nor could she read their thoughts.

She scanned the forest to see a small archery target set up on the other side of William. Though she didn't see any arrows in the target, she knew there had to be one or two lying in the grass around it.

Meanwhile, Drip was now starting to become concerned at their situation. With the werewolf smashing the tunnel behind him, he knew they would eventually run into whatever had created the tunnel, and it would most likely not be pleased they were there.

"So, what's the plan?" Boot asked.

"Keep moving," Drip said.

"It's a good thing this werewolf isn't very smart."

"What do you mean?" Drip asked.

"If he had any wits, he would simply smash the section of tunnel ahead of us, and trap us in a small area."

Suddenly, William stopped digging and smashing. Both Boot and Drip were confused at first. Then as Drip moved a little further along the tunnel, they heard William leap into the air above them to land hard on the ground ahead of them. He smashed a section in front of them just as Boot had mentioned, trapping them in the tunnel.

"Not so stupid now!" William shouted.

"How was I supposed to know he could hear us?" Boot asked.

"Oh, I should cut you off right here and now," Drip muttered. He pointed his sword at the enchanted boot.

Then in one motion, William pulled Drip from the ground like a giant carrot. Drip couldn't help but let out a scream in pain as his arms were crushed under the pressure of the giant werewolf's strength.

"Any last words, assassin imp?" William asked.

"I'm not... an... assassin," Drip managed to get out.

"Not exactly what I thought you would say," William said, increasing the pressure on Drip, intending to crush him to death.

Suddenly, a huge snake emerged from the ground, and bit William in his furry leg. The werewolf let out a loud scream and released Drip. Barely able to breathe, Drip drifted in and out of consciousness.

Not far away, Bean was proud of herself for recovering two arrows in relatively decent shape, but was disappointed a bow hadn't magically appeared. Then something really odd happened: she heard a female voice calling out to her.

"Over here!" the voice shouted. Bean paused for a moment and looked around, the only things moving nearby was William now fighting with a large snake.

"Hello?" Bean asked in curiosity.

"Yes, you, get over here!" the female voice shouted. "Behind the large tree to your right."

Bean walked over to the tree and looked around, to find a bow hanging in the tree just above her. She reached up and picked it out of the branches.

"Ah, yes. Finally, I get to be used by a proper archer," the bow said.

Bean grinned at her luck in finding not just any bow but an enchanted one at that. "Let's do this," she said.

"Not so fast, I think we need proper introductions," the bow interrupted.

"I am Bean. And you are?" Bean asked.

"I am Gwendolyn of Iron Vale," the bow said. "My previous owner called me Gwen."

"Good to meet you, Gwen. Can we take care of the large creature now?" Bean asked. "Time is really of the essence."

"Right, right," Gwen said. "Just promise me one thing."

"What's that?" Bean asked. She looked up to see that William was now done with the large snake and was headed over to finish off Drip.

"Promise me that we will travel together," Gwen said. "Forever."

"Sure, whatever you want," Bean said, eager to save Drip before it was too late.

"Wonderful. Let's take that beast down," Gwen said.

Bean drew the first arrow and carefully aimed at the back of the werewolf's leg.

EPISODE 48

Drip could feel his body lift up into the air, and then fall back to the ground. The sounds of growling were muffled, and he could sense Boot trying frantically to try and tell him something. Everything seemed calm for a moment and he attempted to get to his feet. That is when he realized that his left arm was not responding, and his right arm was in severe pain. Drip resolved to roll onto his side to see what was happening. His eyes went wide as he saw Bean standing alone in front of the massive and seemingly docile werewolf William.

"Drip?" Bean asked. Her voice sounded distant.

"I…you…how?" Drip managed to ask. He rolled his eyes to look around as he seemed unable to move his head.

"It's a long story," Bean said. "Just know you are safe now."

"Where are we?" Drip asked.

"We're back at the village. We're set to leave in the morning. You should get more rest."

Drip did not argue with the diagnosis, and let his eyes close. However, he was disappointed that he did not find darkness or peaceful sleep. Instead, he found himself hovering over a battlefield. Drip could clearly see himself standing defiant against what looked like the light and dark armies. He could see the dead surrounding his likeness and a handful of others. The odds seemed insurmountable, and then the light and dark armies began to charge with their massive forces. Before they collided, he woke up with a start.

"Finally, you're awake again," Bean said.

"So…we won?" Drip asked, slowly sitting up.

"Did we ever. You missed quite a show," Boot said.

"Really?" Drip asked.

"Boot's exaggerating. What he meant to say is that you managed to tire out the werewolf," Bean said.

"Then the quest is complete?" Drip asked.

"A deal is a deal," Drel said from nearby. Other villagers were gathered as well, including a human looking William, who seemed content to remain in the background. "We will resume production, and we are forever in your debt."

"I have never seen bravery like that before," Kala added.

Drip blushed and let out a cheesy grin. "Well, it was all in a day's work."

Then, in a very abrupt motion, Kala backhanded Drip, catching him off guard. His body went limp and he collapsed back onto the bed. Still in shock, he ran his hand over his face.

"Not you, idiot," Kala followed up. "I was talking to her, you lazy bum."

"Whaaaat?" Drip asked, trying to comprehend the situation.

"It was nothing. Drip did all the hard work," Bean said as she placed a wet cloth across Drip's face.

"Whatever," Drel said. "We all know what we saw."

"Someone tell me what everyone is talking about," Drip demanded.

"Later," Bean mouthed to him.

"You would know more if you hadn't slept through the whole thing," Kala retorted.

"Well, we must be on our way. Is the wagon ready?" Bean asked.

"Yes, ma'am," one of the other villagers answered.

"Are you sure you have to leave?" Kala asked with genuine remorse. "Maybe we can just put the imp on the cart and send it away."

"I appreciate the offer, but we have to go. There are much larger things that need to be done," Bean replied.

"We understand," Drel said. "The winds are so strange these days, they whisper of a madness infecting the world, joining light and dark against a common foe."

"The winds are right, I have seen the madness first hand. Be safe," Bean told them.

"You too," said Kala. "Travel safe."

Drip felt kind of nauseous and extremely confused at the whole exchange. He was pretty sure he had fought the werewolf in the cave, through the water, and into the forest. However, it only took a moment for him to remember that he had also been caught by William and partially crushed.

He lifted his two hands and was able to move them without any complications. Then, without warning, Drel picked Drip up from the bed, carried him outside, and unceremoniously tossed him into the back of an open wagon.

"Thanks?" Drip said. He was unsure at this point how Drel would take any comment, but he was somewhat thankful for the lift.

"Yeah, whatever," Drel said.

Bean climbed up into the driver's seat and took the reins. She promptly got the wagon moving with a quick, "Heya."

As they departed from the village, Drip lifted his head and looked up at Bean. Something was different than the last time he had seen her.

"So, come on, tell me what happened. And why does the village seem to hate me?" Drip asked.

"They don't hate you, they just think that you are...how to put this...not much of a man," Bean said. "But I know better what happened."

"Regardless, she totally saved your butt!" came a female voice Drip had never heard before. He looked around, but only saw a simple bow in the cart with them.

"Not to deny that part, but Drip did a vast majority of the fighting," Boot said.

"What is that?" Drip asked, pointing to the bow.

"Her name is Gwen. Did you think you were the only one who could carry an enchanted item?" Bean said with a teasing smile.

"More like a cursed item," Boot quickly added.

"Takes one to know one," Gwen replied.

"Okay, let's start with the part where the werewolf was fighting with the large snake," Drip said.

"I'm driving here, why don't you two fill him in," Bean said.

"There she was, standing in front of the large werewolf, ready to take him head on," Boot began.

"Come on, you left out the best part," Gwen broke in. "Before that, Bean found me hanging in a tree, and she quickly drew an arrow and let it fly against the werewolf, striking it right on target."

"If 'on target' you mean, flesh wound on his ankle," Boot added mockingly.

"It happened to be on target; there was a stipulation that we bring him back alive," Gwen said. "Once she had wounded the creature with the first arrow, she drew a second and let it fly, striking him on the wrist."

"If you haven't figured it out yet, Gwen is unable to kill, or as it turns out, even seriously wound," Boot said.

"That really isn't important right now," Gwen interrupted once more. "Anyway, Bean charged the creature to stop him from killing the both of you."

"You forgot to mention that she had to charge the werewolf, because you refused to fire a third arrow," Boot said.

Gwen ignored him. "This is the best part. Bean got up in his face and demanded that he surrender or she would have to put him down."

"Again, you left out the fact that you were trash talking the creature the entire time, making him extremely angry," Boot injected.

"That's not important."

"Not important? That's what caused William to start swinging," Boot said.

"Which is what needed to happen," Gwen replied. "However, with her ability to read William's mind, she was able to dodge every attack he came at her with."

"It should be noted that the werewolf's attacks were dramatically slower, because of all the fighting and swimming you made him do," Boot said to Drip.

"Slower or not, it was an impressive sight. Once he was tired out, the other werewolves jumped in and were able to pin him down and get him the medicine he needed," Gwen said.

"Wait a minute, if that is it, why do the villagers hate me so?" Drip asked.

"We suspect it is because of the limited extend of the fight. They pretty much only saw you hiding in a hole and then getting caught. I think they think Bean defeated William with pretty much no help from you," Boot said.

Drip held back a groan. "Brilliant."

―

"You have got to be kidding me! An imp gets into three fights with werewolves and lives through all three!?" Dark lord Twiller asked in anger.

"Patience, your highness, two of the three are dead, and without them you are all but assured to defeat the imp, for as the vision said, with each one you kill, you get an extra year," Head Monk Towe reminded him.

"What should we do from here?" King Ragmon asked.

"Prepare your armies. Drip's army will be untrained rabble, and you will crush him with little to no effort," Towe said.

"If we are going to crush them, why are we committing the whole of our armies for this?" Twiller asked.

"Because it is far better to have them and not need them, than to need them and not have them," Towe said. "Trust me, this will all be over soon."

Drip finally felt comfortable sitting up and climbed into the wagon seat next to Bean, as Gwen and Boot seemed to ramble on for a majority of the day. Before they knew it, the sun was starting to set.

"Bean, I think we should stop for the night and set up camp," Drip said.

"I agree," Bean replied.

The two climbed down from the wagon, and as they were unloading the supplies, their hands touched. They both let their eyes lock for a moment, which seemed to last an eternity.

EPISODE 49

Cary looked up at the massive volcano where Gorath had plunged to his death. She looked around and could clearly see that the volcano was now dormant. She reached down and rested her hand on the cold magma. Then she looked back at her horse just as the creature ironically collapsed, giving up the ghost to old age.

"Perfect, now what?" Cary asked as she threw her hands up into the air. She walked over to the dead horse and began to strip off the supplies. Carefully, she glanced around until she found a flat spot to set up her tent.

—

Drip looked up at the tall spire also known as the Candlestick and noticed that there were only a few lights on. He looked at the great walls of the city and noticed that there was no movement at all.

"That is so odd," Drip said.

"Where is everyone?" Bean asked.

"The city seemed to be clearing out when we were leaving," Boot reminded them.

"Wow, I haven't seen the city in such a long time," Gwen said. "Hum, it looks exactly how I remember, except there were people in it last time."

"Well, let's report in. This was my last quest, so I'm not sure what's supposed to happen next," Drip said.

As the wind moved through the empty streets, Drip swore that he could hear whispering. The party looked around nervously as even the shadows seemed to be watching their every move. As they approached the Candlestick, the Master of Arms from the Royal Armory emerged to greet them.

"Not much of a welcoming committee," Gwen said.

"I would be lying if I said this was the worst welcome I'd ever received," Drip said with a chuckle.

"Hey, the city watch was just doing their job," Boot added.

"Ignorantly, might I add," Bean said.

"Ah, Drip, the High Standard of the Watch, I had my doubts that you would show up, but they said you would be here at this very moment," the Master of Arms said.

"Who said?" Drip asked.

"That really doesn't matter at this point," the Master of Arms replied. "I am to let you know that your army is waiting for you in the field, and as soon as you signal that you're ready, the battle will begin."

"Army? What army?" Drip asked in confusion.

"Don't ask me, this was the message I was instructed to relay to you. Now, if you would excuse me, I must be on my way."

"To where? Where is everyone?" Drip asked.

"You're kidding, right? Son, I would wish you luck if it weren't my job to kill you," the Master of Arms said plainly. Then he mounted a horse and rode off.

"I'm going to be honest, I did not see that coming," Boot said.

"Oh boy," Bean added. "This is not good."

"What is it?" Drip asked.

"I was able to read some of his thoughts, and he was very serious about what he said about killing you."

"Well, let's head over to the inn and get settled," Drip said, pointing in the direction he was talking about, when he realized two things. First, Bean was in fact telepathic, and second, she had been there before—in her human form.

As they turned the corner, Drip noticed that the lights seemed to be on at the White Knight Tower, the Light Side newspaper.

"Hold on, we need to stop here," he said.

"Oh boy, not the paper," Boot said.

"With no one in town, he actually has a real shot at fulfilling his dream," Bean added.

Drip jumped down from the cart, straightened himself up, and started to walk into the hub of news and communication for the Light Side.

"Of course, with no one around, there would be no one to read his work," Bean said.

The large door creaked open before Drip as he entered the newspaper headquarters. He had dreamed of that exact moment hundreds of times. He was disappointed that the various printing mechanisms were sitting still. Only a single teenage boy sat behind the counter, flipping through a book marked "Advanced Combat."

"We are closed. You're going to have to come back after they kill the imp," the boy said without looking up from his book.

"I wanted to see if you were perhaps…hiring," Drip asked. He was angry with himself for letting his voice sound nervous.

"Nope," the boy said, once again without looking up. "Later. Kill imp."

"Would the imp's name happen to be Drip?" Boot asked.

"That is his nickname, or so I hear. It's actually some super long ridiculous thing," the boy said, turning the page of his book.

"I don't suppose you would be accepting any independent writings?" Drip asked.

The boy simply shook his head this time. Then he held up his hands as if to mimic a move from the combat book.

"How about a writing from Drip the imp himself?" Boot asked.

With that, the boy finally looked over at Drip. His eyes went wide and he nearly fell off the chair he was sitting on. "Are you Drip?" the boy asked.

"Yes," Drip replied.

"*The* Drip?"

"The one and only."

"I can vouch for that," Boot added.

"I...um...well, the editor you see...never mind, what do you have?" the boy asked.

"Well, most of it is made up of things I just scribbled down, but..." Drip started.

"Ah, I'm sorry, I almost forgot, I need you to sign something for me," the boy said. Then he retreated into a back room.

"Can you trust this boy with your work?" Boot asked.

"I don't know that I have a choice," Drip replied. "This may be my only chance to get something published, especially if I'm expected in a battle to the death."

The boy reentered the room with a loud crash and papers flying out behind him as he closed the door to the back room. "This is the standard royalties and release forms," the boy said. "I just need you to sign where the three X's are."

"Sure," Drip said, then took the pen and quickly signed the paper.

"Now, what would you like to submit for consideration?"

"I have my book of stories and poems. I would like to see if any of them will work."

"Certainly, just leave them with me, and come back in the morning to recover your items."

As Drip reached for the book, both his stories and poems fell to the floor along with his scratch journal.

"Drip?" Bean shouted from outside. "Are you almost done in there?"

Drip let out a little chuckle and then slid the book onto the counter. As he left the building, something about the Bean sitting in the moonlight caused him to pause for a moment.

"Well, are we going?" Bean asked.

"Yes, of course," Drip said. He quickly climbed back onto the cart. "I just hope someone is still manning the inn."

After a couple of minutes, they turned the corner to see the welcome sight of the Master Field Inn. As usual, every light that could be lit was. Quickly, they dismounted the wagon. Just before they were to enter, Drip stopped.

"I just remembered there may be a problem," Drip said.

"Like what?" Bean asked.

"To stay at the Master Field Inn, you need to be royalty or have a letter from royalty. I don't know if we qualify anymore."

"Okay, let's see what happens," Bean said.

"Ladies first," Drip offered, and held the door open for her. He cringed in anticipation of the *Master Book of Magic* recognizing they weren't allowed—or at least that Bean wasn't since she hadn't been part of the original Watch—and hoped Bean wasn't suddenly transported back outside the building.

"Are you coming in?" Bean asked.

Drip cautiously entered the Master Field Inn, relieved that Bean was still standing next to him.

"Wow, this is a nice place," Gwen said from where the bow was now strapped to Bean's back.

"Really, 'nice' is the best you could come up with?" Boot asked.

"I'm just saying," Gwen replied.

"As usual, welcome," Carter said, appearing in the entryway. "It is so good to see you again, Elizabeth. The Templeton's are always welcome."

"Thank you, Carter," Bean said.

"After all, it is not every day we get a princess and an emperor."

EPISODE 50

Drip quickly looked around and noticed that there wasn't anyone else there. It was too quiet.

"Wait, what did you say?" Drip asked with a very concerned look on his face. He had forgotten that Bean had been slated to marry the Light Side King at one time.

"Master Emperor Imp, you jest. I was however very surprised when I found out that you were the Emperor of the Gray Territories," Carter replied.

"When was that announcement made?" Boot asked.

"And by who?" Drip quickly followed up.

"Well, it was just before you arrived at the city last time. We were told not to make a big deal out of it, I should say; the word came down in a joint statement from the Light King, Dark Lord, and the Head Monk," Carter reported.

"So, why is the city empty?" Bean asked.

"I am afraid that everyone has been enlisted in the army, and they are going to go fight against your army," Carter said.

"There it is again," Drip said in frustration. "I don't have an army, let alone territories."

"I kind of saw this coming, after the discussion with the Master of Arms," Boot said.

"Where is the gray army?" Bean asked.

"I am not sure on that, I think south somewhere," Carter replied. "Please, you look exhausted. Why don't you come in and rest and we can talk in the morning."

"I think that sounds great," Drip said.

"That sounds horrible, we need to be off to battle," Gwen said.

"Easy," Bean said. "It appears there will be plenty of time for that later."

"Indeed," Boot said. "Rest would be prudent."

"Very good, I think we will retire for the night," Drip decided.

"Excellent, I will meet you on the sixth floor," Carter promptly replied.

"Sixth floor? I thought our rooms were on the fifth floor?" Drip asked.

"You are correct in that you were previously on the fifth floor," Carter said. "Given the circumstances and present company, we have moved you to the sixth."

"If you insist," Bean replied.

The two began to walk towards the broken lift, when a sound caught their attention.

"Ah," Carter said. "The sixth floor lift is on the other side, and I am happy to report that it is working."

Drip and Bean followed the direction from Carter, and entered the larger, well-lit lift. As Drip was about to ask how to get the lift to go up, the door shut and the lift started moving. As the lift passed the second floor it shuddered a little causing Drip to fall against Bean. Quickly Drip jumped back and straightened himself.

"Really?" Bean asked. "I thought we were beyond that."

"I'm just…tired," Drip retorted.

"Look, I understand things take time, and I will always be here for you," Bean replied. "By the way, I can read your thoughts, remember?"

"Brilliant," Drip said.

"By any chance, can you read *my* thoughts?" Boot asked.

"No," Bean said.

"Interesting," Boot replied.

It was at that moment the elevator dinged. When the doors slid open, Drip and Bean gasped as they exited. They walked forward onto the walkway and into a massive rooftop garden. As they turned the corner, Carter was waiting for them. Torchlight adorned the walkways, giving a warm glow to the amazing area in front of them.

"These quarters are reserved for the Kings, Emperors, and designated royalty of Wax," Carter said.

"This is amazing," Bean said. The remarkable view of the stars caught her gaze.

Drip was used to the dense brown dirt of the Dark Side, and had been amused at the green trees of the forest on the Sevari Mountains, but the deep green and amazing colors of the different plants in the garden caused him to stand speechless.

"So, this isn't the first time, but it never gets old to point out that Drip has nothing to say," Boot said.

"What a view," Gwen commented.

"I am embarrassed to say that despite the state of the city being so empty, we are full and only have one room available," Carter said. "I have prepared the joint royal suite."

"That will be fine," Bean said.

"Excellent," Carter quickly answered.

"Oh, okay," Boot responded.

"Ah, what?" Drip asked. He looked over at Bean with a confused look on his face.

"Like I said, it will be fine," Bean confirmed.

"Right this way," Carter said. That is when everyone noticed that there were several small buildings on the roof. The two followed behind.

"What is going on?" Drip asked.

"We all get to stay in the only room left in the inn," Boot said. "All cozy-like."

"Oh boy," Drip said.

Then Carter raised his keys and began to open the door to the smallest building on the roof. It looked no more than a three-foot by three-foot storage closet.

"We are staying in that?" Drip asked.

"This is the best room in the place," Carter said.

Then he opened the door to reveal a massive room. As they entered, Bean let out a squeak as she ran through the large entryway into the great room adorned with couches, fireplaces, bookcases, and expensive art. Before Drip and Carter could make it inside, Bean had already looked through everything.

"So will this be okay?" Carter asked.

"Yes. A million times, yes," Bean said.

"That good, eh?" Drip asked.

"Walk-in closets, massive bathroom, and a huge bedroom. This place is perfect," Bean said with a massive smile on her face.

"It is sort of bigger than I expected on the inside," Drip said. He looked around and felt out of place in such a fancy room.

"Excellent, now I must take my leave, and prepare the meal for everyone staying on the roof," Carter said.

"Who is everyone?" Boot asked.

"Why, that would be King Ragmon, and his officers, and Dark Lord Twiller, and his officers," Carter said.

"I am confused. I thought they were in the field getting ready to go to war," Drip said.

"Ah yes, one of the perks of being a resident of the roof are the portals," Carter replied, "You see, on the far side of the roof, there are three portals. Any one will take you to your command tent in the field, and once you are in your command tent, there will be a portal that only you and your officers can enter. However, given that we are at capacity, we are unable to offer quarters to your officers."

"Sounds good. I am curious, of course," Drip said.

"Curious of what, Sir?" Carter asked.

"Curious of who my officers are," Drip replied.

"I apologize, I don't have that information," Carter said.

"Don't worry about it. We appreciate everything," Bean told him.

"Very good," Carter said before promptly exiting the room.

"Brilliant, I am going to go get cleaned up before dinner," Bean said.

"Sounds good," Drip said. He accepted Gwen when Bean handed the bow over, then walked to the large weapons rack that was built into the wall, and carefully hung the bow up.

"Wow, this is so nice compared to the tree limb," Gwen said.

"I imagine that anything would be better than that," Boot remarked.

Gently, Drip released the strap that held the blade on his back upright, and pulled it out to set it on the stand next to the bow. Then he sat down in one of the large chairs and put his feet up on the table in front of him.

"Don't get too comfortable now," Boot said.

"No worries. It is nice to get a rest after that last fight," Drip said. He closed his eyes, planning to just rest them for a few seconds, but immediately drifted into a deep sleep.

EPISODE
51

A strong cold wind brushed hard against Drip's face. His eyes shot open, and quickly he jumped to his feet, realizing that he was in the middle of a field. With no visible land marks in sight, Drip felt completely lost and confused.

"Drip, you must lead your army into battle," an airy voice said.

"Like I keep telling people, I don't have an army," Drip answered the omnipotent voice.

"Regardless of what you think, they wait for you even now," the voice replied.

"Why? Why must I go to war?"

"It is time you knew," the voice said. "It started with a very powerful wizard who lived before ages were counted." As the voice continued, Drip found himself watching events play out by wax figures in front of him. "The wizard had four daughters, Olpetrion, Ponopoli, Naomi, and Orielia, who he loved more than anything in the whole of Wax. One day, his very young daughters came down with an illness, the same that had taken the wizard's wife."

Drip felt emotions emulating the play run though him as the shapes continued to act out the story being told. As such, a deep sadness overcame him.

"As he had done with his wife, he tried everything to break the illness, but nothing worked. And as the girls grew weaker and weaker, his heart was breaking. Then he found a moment of clarity deep in his sorrow. The wizard would sacrifice everything he had, including himself to protect his daughters. He created the *Master Book of Magic* and in the process he paid a tremendous sacrifice. However, the book would give his daughters great powers and eternal life as long as it existed. The magic in the book recognized the unnatural event, and cursed the wizard to only ever be able to watch his daughters, but never communicate with them. The book created the city of Ormlu, and organized the world as you know it."

"What happened to the daughters afterward?" Drip asked.

"The daughters lived through ages, and though the book granted eternal life, it did not grant eternal youth. As they grew old, one of the sisters began to plot and scheme, suspecting that if she removed her sisters, then she would have the power to give herself eternal youth."

"Let me guess. Olpetrion was the plotting sister," Drip said from instinct.

"No, it was Orielia, and when she had trapped her sister Naomi—"

"Orielia?!" Drip remarked in disbelief. "Orielia, the Witch of Ormlu? *She* was the evil one?"

"Yes, but when she moved in for the kill, she found that she could not hurt her sister," the voice replied. "However, the event set off a chain reaction. The eldest sister, Olpetrion, would come to the same conclusion after learning about the attempted assassination. She killed Naomi in the northern fields of Wax, Ponopoli in the southern fields, saving Orielia for last. However, Orielia wouldn't leave Ormlu, and as long as she remained under the protection of the city, she could not be harmed. Olpetrion figured out how to poison her last living sister, but her plan backfired when Orielia went missing."

"And Gorath found her in a small town on the Dark Side," Drip said.

"Yes, and when she became the Witch of Ormlu, ensuring that she would not leave the city, Orielia then exploited a loophole that had been written in the *Master Book of Magic* that even her father didn't know about. If Olpetrion wins, then the whole of Wax will be shrouded in darkness and suffering forever, because her intentions are evil, but if I win," Orielia revealed herself as the voice, "then it will destroy the *Master Book of Magic* and release us from the spell. The world will be thrown into chaos without the Book, but for the first time there will be hope."

"But there is no way I can help you and win against all the light and dark armies," Drip said.

"It is worse than that," Orielia said. Then Drip found himself looking at a massive army that stretched as far as he could see. "All the light and dark people, not just the armies."

"We don't stand a chance," Drip said. "If they are all against us, then who is for us?"

"My sisters and I have been helping you as much as we could, and your army is more powerful than you know," Orielia said. Then she pointed behind him.

Drip turned to see a large force of humans, skeletons, undead, and a small contingent of orcs, goblins, and a single troll. They were from all of his quests.

"Whoa," Drip said.

Without warning, Drip woke up from his deep sleep. He glanced around and realized he was still in his room in the inn. He found a note on the table next to him.

Drip,
Couldn't wake you up, went out to eat dinner.
-Bean

Drip rose to his feet with a sense of purpose. Without hesitation, he grabbed his sword and placed it back in its sheath, then picked up Gwen the bow. He walked out the front door to be promptly greeted by Carter.

"It's good to see you will be joining the others for dinner," Carter said.

"Thank you, Carter, but you didn't need to wait for me up here. I was going to come downstairs," Drip said.

"I apologize for not communicating this earlier. Dinner for those on this level is up here," Carter said. "This way, please."

He followed Carter and could hear people laughing and talking. They turned the corner to find a massive rectangle of tables with a great feast set out. Everyone stopped talking as he approached the table.

"Drip!" Bean said as she stood up. She was wearing an emerald dress, with her hair done up. Drip had a hard time identifying her. To his horror, several guys were sitting around her in close proximity.

"I propose a toast, to the emperor imp, and his short reign," Dark Lord Twiller said as he raised his cup.

"Here, here," several of the men cheered.

Drip realized who he would be dining with, and suddenly didn't want to be there anymore. "I think I have lost my appetite. Bean, are you coming?"

"Drip, I will meet up with you after dinner," Bean replied.

The words felt like a knife into his barely mending heart. A chill ran down his spine, and he could feel his fists clench and his teeth grind a little.

"Sure," Drip said in an angry tone. Then he proceeded to walk past the feast and head towards the portal. It wasn't difficult for him to hear the mocking comments that followed.

I knew this would happen, Drip thought to himself.

"I don't know that it is what you think it is," Boot added.

"It doesn't matter," Drip said. Then he entered the gray portal.

Instantly he found himself standing inside a large command tent with a table in the middle of the room and a sand sculpture of the battlefield on it. Off to the side, a table with several maps lay scattered across it. Then, a familiar voice startled him.

"Aroon?" Drip asked.

"What took you so long?" Aroon asked. "We have been trying to prep the troops."

"It is good to see you," Drip said.

"Yeah, well, if this war starts in the next twenty-four hours it won't matter," Aroon replied.

"Give me the breakdown. Where are we on things?" Drip asked.

"We have a massive ten-thousand-man zombie division, a select fifteen-hundred-member skeleton battalion, three platoons of humans—mind you, the humans aren't your ordinary group, they are all from the Elite Eagles from the Light Side—and I would say twenty-five goblins, fifteen orcs, and a very big troll," Aroon said. "And that is the good news."

"Okay, what is the bad news?" Drip asked.

"We are outnumbered at the moment, at least one hundred to one, and we have no Cavalry. If they charge with their Cavalry they will chew right through us."

"How comfortable are you at leading?" Drip asked, as he looked over the map of the terrain.

"I am fine leading; that is, leading the Elite Eagles. I've never commanded anything larger than that."

"Brilliant," Drip said. "Would you like to?"

"Look, no disrespect, but I will work hard and take care of my crew, but I am no general. And we are sunk without one."

"We may have to call in a few favors to help us."

"A few favors?" Aroon chuckled. "We need a few thousand favors—no, make that a few hundred thousand."

"I have the next best thing," Drip said as he removed a coin from his pocket.

"What's that?" Aroon asked.

"Oh, just a favor someone owes me," Drip said.

The two were startled as the portal from the Master Field Inn activated, and after a moment of bright light, Bean stood with a very pleased look on her face.

"Oh boy," Boot said.

EPISODE
52

"Who's that?" Aroon asked.

"Drip, we need to talk," Bean said as she walked over to him.

"This is Bean, please give me a moment alone," Drip said.

Aroon walked backwards out of the tent, nearly tripping over his own feet as he gawked at the girl. Despite a successful exit from the tent, Aroon could be heard knocking over a weapons rack.

"Look, Bean, you don't have to explain. You came from that society, and I understand if you want to go back," Drip said. He shifted his eyes to look at the map table.

"Drip, the most wonderful thing has happened," Bean said with excitement in her voice.

"Oh come on, do you have to tout your escapades?" Drip asked in a defeated voice.

"It's not like that, I went to school with the bulk of King Ragmon's officers, and the reason I wanted to stay back at dinner was to convince most of them to not attack."

"What? Wait, what did you promise them?" Drip asked. "Are you getting married?"

"To be honest, I hope to get married, actually," Bean said.

Drip walked over to a chair and slumped, "Has someone asked yet, then?"

"No, but I hope he does sooner than later," Bean replied.

"Wow, Drip. Have you been listening to anything she has been saying?" Boot asked.

"Of course, she is planning on marrying one of those royal brats," Drip replied.

"More like a royal pain," Bean chuckled. Boot added his little laugh to the comment, and shortly after, Gwen joined in.

The trio of laughing friends simply served to frustrate Drip. His eyes grew wide and his nostrils began to flare. "Then why don't you go to this royal pain!"

"Is that a command to marry the royal pain I'm after?" Bean asked.

"Yes, I command you to go marry your royal pain," Drip said with a bitter tone.

"Very well then, as you command. I have just one question," Bean said.

"What is that?" Drip asked.

"Should we have our ceremony before or after the battle?" Bean asked.

"Why should I care?" Drip asked suspiciously.

"Well, because you are the royal pain I am marrying as per your command."

Drip stood speechless and embarrassed at his temperament. He simply pointed at Bean and then himself.

"You mean, you and I?" Drip asked weakly.

"Yes," Bean replied.

"Well, this was a surprising turn of events," Boot said, though not without a touch of sarcasm.

"Oh, I've never been a part of a wedding, well at least I don't think I have been," Gwen said. "I may have been a part of an attack on a wedding, does that count?"

"Technically, yes," Boot said.

"When do we have the wedding?" Drip repeated, unsure of the answer himself.

"We will have the wedding after you win the war, my love," Bean said. Suddenly Drip was filled with newfound energy as Bean wrapped her arms around him and kissed him. Surprisingly, Drip found himself kissing her back. His head was swimming as they let go of each other, and it took him a few seconds to recover. When he did, he looked down at the map. He was determined to get this war over with and get to his wedding.

"Aroon!" Drip shouted.

Aroon instantly appeared in the command tent next to the table. It was obvious that he was stilly checking out Bean.

"Aroon, I would appreciate it if you would please stop ogling my fiancée," Drip said. "Plus, I cannot have one of my generals distracted right now."

"Yes, Sir," Aroon answered. "Fiancée? Really?" Then, as if a light had turned on in Aroon's head, "General?"

"Yes, yes, and yes," Drip said. "Anything else? Or can we get started?"

"No, Sir. Let's get started," Aroon said.

"Great. Let's go over our five biggest issues," Drip said.

"First things first, I like to tout my skills, but we still need another general," Aroon said. "I am proficient in special forces combat, direct hand-to-hand combat, and I would be great a reinforcement specialist, but that isn't enough to win a war." "Okay, what else do we need?" Drip asked.

"Someone who can help us counteract the enemy cavalry. They would be able to flank us and smash us to bits," Aroon said.

"Yeah, that is a big problem. What else?" Drip asked.

"Manpower, the lack of proper catapults, and ammunition round out the top five things we're still missing," Aroon said.

Both Drip and Aroon felt the impact of the last three like a band aid being ripped off.

"I am at a loss for manpower and another general," Drip said, "but I do have something in mind that could deal with the cavalry, the enemy catapults, and possibly the ammunition shortage. It's a long shot, but…"

"Sir, what do you have in mind?" Aroon asked.

"I will have to call in some favors. However, as I said, it's a long shot."

"Well, whatever the battle plan, we need to appoint captains and brief them," Aroon said.

"Very good," Drip said. He looked back to see that Bean was flipping through a catalogue with Orielia standing next to her.

"Oh, I love that one," Bean said quietly to Orielia.

"So do I," Orielia replied.

"Wedding planning in the middle of a war. I've never heard of such a thing," Aroon said.

Drip shrugged. "I think this war will have a lot of firsts."

"Your highness, I have an urgent message for you from our outlying edge of the army," a messenger said as he bowed before King Ragmon.

"If it is about people seeing Bean, I already know. She has become a thorn in my side," the king said as he looked out at his army. "These cowards are talking about not attacking at all."

"No Sir, this is something different," the messenger said.

"Then please, do tell," Ragmon said.

"Yes Sir. Some of the men have reported seeing...a ghost, Sir."

"What was that?" Ragmon asked.

"It is best if you read the note yourself, Sir," the messenger replied. He extended his hand with a letter sealed by the outlying area commander.

The king quickly opened the letter and read over the contents a couple of times. "It can't be, there must be some mistake!"

―

The undead troops on the front line were in their typical chaotic milling formation, where they kind of wandered around inside a set area. One zombie looked up to find a large horse's snout in his face.

"Let me pass, it is urgent." A large hood obscured the stranger's face.

Typically, this would cause the zombies to rile up, but just the opposite happened. They parted to make a path directly to the command tent. The zombies were confused for a moment, then they continued their aimless milling.

The stranger passed through the remaining defense with little effort, and quickly dismounted at the entrance of the command tent, entering without hesitation.

"If we move the undead ogre, he could hold the far left flank by himself for some time," Aroon said. Then his thought was interrupted by the new person in the tent.

Drip instinctively unlatched the sword on his back to prepare for combat. Bean raced over to him.

"Is that any way to treat a friend?" the stranger asked, as she pulled back her hood.

"Thomas?!" Drip exclaimed.

EPISODE
53

"The one and only," Thomas said with a large smile across her face.

"We thought you were dead, what happened?!" Drip asked. He couldn't help but notice the long flowing red dress she wore, and the black hooded jacket, which was very out of place on Thomas.

"Do you mind if I sit down first? You were not easy to track down," Thomas said. She looked around the tent to see where she could sit.

"Yes, please," Aroon offered as he pulled a chair forward for her.

As Thomas sat down, she stretched, still not used to being outside the protective shell that she had lived in for what had seemed like years. Then Thomas noticed the very pretty young woman attached to Drip.

"When the fireball struck, everything began to move in slow motion," Thomas said, "and I watched my life flash before my eyes, but it was odd, it wasn't the life that I know now, but it was my life as if I had grown up on the Light Side."

"That is different," Boot said.

"I don't understand. How did you live through that?" Bean asked.

"I'm sorry, your name is? And how do you know Drip?" Thomas asked. She felt shocked as she couldn't help some jealousy bleed through her question.

"My apologies. It is me, Bean. I used to be trapped in a bean around Drip's neck," Bean said. "You were saying?"

"Oh." She blinked a moment, processing the idea of Drip's bean now being a beautiful young woman, but pushed those thoughts aside for now. "Anyway, the armor absorbed most of the explosion, and then I felt a hand push me, and the next thing I knew, I was standing in the middle of the field where we had fought the dragon. I was fortunate that as I began to walk back to Ormlu, I came across a stranger who offered me clothes and a horse, albeit the worst looking horse I've ever seen."

"Why did it take you so long to find me?" Drip asked.

"By the time I made it back to Ormlu, most everyone had left, and no one seemed to know where you were for sure, and recommended that I come all the way out here to this camp to find you."

"I will be forever grateful for what you did, and am relieved that you are alive," Drip said. "I am sure you would like to have this back." He pulled the sword from its sheath and offered it to Thomas.

Thomas took it and ran her hand down the blade, then presented Drip with a confused look. "You have been using the sword?" she asked. As far as she could remember, the sword would only work for her family.

"Yes, it has been incredibly helpful," Drip said.

Thomas's hand rested on the hilt of the sword, but then she pulled her hand back. "Nicknamed by the Elven in the First Age as 'Everlasting Edge', and 'Feared Messenger' by the dwarves in the Second Age, the sword was said to be handed down father to son through the ages, protecting those worthy enough to wield it. It seems it has chosen you now."

"I don't know what to say," Drip replied. "I am honored."

Thomas watched as Drip slid the sword into its sheath on his back once more. She looked around the room and couldn't help but notice how attached Bean was to Drip, and how Aroon was gawking at her.

"Hey, what's your deal?" Thomas asked Aroon.

"Ah, nothing, it's just that I never pictured you in a dress, that's all," he replied. "Do you plan on fighting in that?"

Even in her weakened state, Thomas found the strength to grab a short flag pole and in one motion jumped up out of the chair she'd been in and jabbed it at Aroon like a staff.

Aroon watched as the end of the pole just barely missed his face, and found himself dodging another half dozen attacks with only one thing on his mind. *She is amazing.*

Thomas found herself out of breath resting on the pole, with a still-gawking Aroon standing about five feet away.

"Aroon, ceiling," Bean said.

Confused at the statement, Aroon looked up at the ceiling of the tent. This gave Thomas just enough of a window to smash Aroon in the gut with the pole. The surprising strike caused Aroon to double over, where his head discovered the bottom of Thomas's shoe. The kick caused him to fall to the ground.

Thomas looked over at Bean just in time to catch a wink.

"Bean is it?" Thomas asked, and was quickly answered with a nod. "I think we are going to be good friends."

"Me too," Bean said.

"Okay, with that over with, I need to ask Thomas, do you think you would be up to the task of being General of the Army?" Drip said.

"Certainty of death?" Thomas asked.

"Yes."

"Small chance of success?"

"Very small."

"Well, what are we waiting for? Let's take a look," Thomas replied. "Aroon, are you going to join us over here?"

"Cheater," Aroon said under his breath as he made his way over to the table.

"Here are some of the challenges we are facing," Drip began.

"There is no way that report is true," Ragmon said, looking over the note again. "Right?"

"It doesn't matter, look at the size of the combined army," Head Monk Towe said.

"It does matter. This is one more piece closer to the prophecy coming true and to our deaths," Dark Lord Twiller said.

"What capacity would they use Thomas in?" Ragmon asked.

"According to her commanders, she is adept in strategy, and she is very familiar with the dark army strategy. She could be a commander, but I don't think she is capable of any more than that," Twiller said.

"It is certain that Aroon, former commander of the elites, is one of their commanding generals as well," Ragmon said. "But he is passionate and clumsy in large formations."

"Regardless, with both Light and Dark cavalry charging their flanks, with arrows raining down upon them, it won't matter one bit who is in command of what," Head Monk Towe said.

"I don't see how we can lose this battle," Dark Lord Twiller added.

"I don't like it," said King Ragmon. "My gut is telling me that there are unseen moving pieces that are setting against us."

"So I meant to ask, what is the deal with your ex-girlfriend fighting for the imp?" Twiller asked.

"I am not sure, to be honest. She dropped off the face of Wax, and then all of the sudden, she is here," Ragmon said. "There are rumors of dark magic involved."

"Do you still have feelings for her?" Twiller asked.

"I don't know—I mean, of course not, I am married," Ragmon said hastily.

"Let's keep things focused here," interrupted Towe. "Soon it will be time to attack."

Thomas sat back and stared at the ceiling. Her mind was racing with possibilities and suggestions. Every scenario she ran through her head, she found herself being squashed by heavy cavalry and catapults.

"Even if your plans work, I don't see how we will be able to escape the horses and the large artillery," Thomas finally said.

"Leave those two pieces to me. I have a solution," Drip said with a grin on his face. "Let's just say, they will be a nonfactor in this battle."

"Wait, what?" Thomas asked. "How on Wax are you going to accomplish that?"

"We may be small," Drip said, "but they are going to learn quickly that we are not going down easy."

EPISODE 54

Drip rubbed his forehead as he looked over the battlefield map again. It had already been twelve hours of planning and debate, and everyone was desperate for a break. Drip looked over the three scrolls on the table in front of him with dispatches that could just help them win.

"I don't like it, this is a bad plan," Aroon said finally as he looked out the front door. "I don't think we can trust them."

"It is definitely risky," Thomas said from across the room. "But bold. It just might work."

"I don't see another way, do you?" Drip asked.

"I am with you," Bean said as she rested her hands on Drip's shoulders.

Drip lowered his head and smiled at the action. Never before could he remember such a simple act relieving so much stress.

"Everyone knows their assignment then," Drip said as he stood up. "We don't have much time. Good luck to you all."

"We will need it," Aroon said, picking up his scroll, and then walked through the portal back to Ormlu.

"I trust you, my love," Bean said, as she picked up her scroll and entered the portal.

"Drip, I will always have your back," Thomas said, grabbing the last scroll and disappearing after the others

"Alight, Orielia, please summon the other leaders," Drip said.

"Of course, my lord," Orielia said with a smile.

"Wait," Drip quickly added.

"Yes?"

"We are going to survive this, right?"

"You have given us the greatest chance of that," Orielia said. "It is a good plan."

"Thank you for everything," Drip replied.

"It is I who should be thanking you," Orielia said. She smiled at Drip, and then entered the portal.

Drip stood up and prepared himself to receive the Light King, Dark Lord, and the Head Monk. He pulled a cord that summoned a few skeleton assistants.

"We live to serve thee," the skeleton hissed.

"Are you ready to receive our guests?" Drip asked.

"Yes," the skeleton replied.

"Very good, then, look lively. They will be upon us shortly," Drip said.

The skeletons noisily exited the tent, their bones clanking together as they moved. Drip stepped forward and cleared his throat to ready their reception. Right on cue, the portal flashed. However, instead of any of the leaders, Olpetrion stood before him.

"Olpetrion, this is an unexpected visit, I am so glad that you stopped by," Drip said. He walked over to the meeting area where he sat in the largest chair.

"Drip, I will have you know that you will be—" Olpetrion began to say.

"Crushed? Or destroyed?" Drip finished her sentence.

"Obliterated."

"Of course, how stupid of me, we will of course be obliterated," Drip said.

"I have to admit, you are remarkably calm for someone about to die," Olpetrion said.

"Yes, well your visit has brought me comfort," Drip said.

"How so?"

"If you were so confident that you are going to win, then you wouldn't be here," Drip said. "There is a little sliver of doubt in your mind, and that sliver will be your undoing. After all, you weren't able to defeat Orielia last time, and you won't win today."

"Don't be so smug, I came here to extinguish any little bit of hope you have. Every one of your friends is being followed and will be unable to complete their tasks."

"Of course," Drip said. "Now, if you would please excuse me, I have a summit to conduct shortly."

"It is only a matter of time before your demise," Olpetrion said in an irritated tone.

"That goes without saying, and with that, I have to ask you to leave with a little less reverence, if you please," Drip said.

Olpetrion quickly turned in a huff and walked into the portal. As the bright light subsided, Head Monk Towe appeared, along with the two other leaders.

"Welcome, your highnesses, thank you for entertaining my request for a summit," Drip said with a smile.

"As I understand it, we didn't have a choice, thanks to the *Master Book of Magic*," Twiller said, clearly irritated with Drip.

"What would you like to discuss?" Ragmon asked.

"Let's talk plainly. My army is outnumbered, and I would like to talk about our options," Drip said.

"Surrender?" Head Monk Towe asked.

"Please have a seat," Drip said as he held his hand out toward the chair on his right.

"Other direction," Boot said quietly. Drip quickly changed direction with his hands.

"I don't think we will be accepting your surrender," Head Monk Towe said quickly. "So we will be on our way."

As the Head Monk turned to reenter the portal, an invisible force prevented him from accessing it. The force pushed him back and caused him to land on his butt.

"I must apologize for that," Drip said.

Boot snickered.

Towe jumped to his feet and raced over to the imp. "Are you holding us hostage?"

"No, Sir, I would never do such a thing," Drip said.

"Then what is this?" Twiller asked.

"As per the written traditions of the Gray Empire, a peace summit must be for no less than twelve hours, or until everyone agrees on a few options for peace," Drip said.

"Very well, we have considered a few options for peace and will be returning to our armies now," Ragmon said.

"Once again, I apologize. The options must be identical between the assembled leaders," Drip said. "So, please, let's have a seat."

"I don't see how we have a choice," Towe said. "I thought you were a stand-up leader, but this is disgraceful."

Twiller caught a good glance at the edge of the battlefield table, and quickly moved to sit in the assigned area as to have a good view of the plans that were laid out. Reluctantly, both King Ragmon and Head Monk Towe joined the Dark Lord.

"Thank you. Now, let's begin," Drip said. "Oh wait, where are my manners? I will summon the traditional refreshments."

"I think I am speaking for all of us when I say, we are fine," Towe said.

"I would like some refreshments," Twiller said eagerly.

"Perfect," Drip said. Then he walked over to the rope and pulled on it to summon the skeletons. As they entered the tent, he walked over to talk to them.

"What are you doing?" Ragmon hissed at Twiller. "The faster we finish this, the faster this whole thing will be over."

"Yes, let's get this over with," Towe agreed.

"No, if we can buy some time, we will learn their defenses, and the end battle will be even shorter," Twiller said in a whisper as he pointed towards the battle plans.

"What does it matter? We will crush them anyway," Towe said.

"I am with Twiller, the more of my people who live through this, the better," Ragmon said.

"Brilliant, here is the first course," Drip said, returning to his reluctant guests. The skeletons brought in trays of food and set them on a long table.

"First course? How many are we talking about?" Towe asked.

"Why," Drip said, "all ten of course."

EPISODE
55

"Okay, let's make this happen. We will only have one shot," Thomas said.

"Right, this isn't going to be easy," Aroon said. "But probably fun."

Bean simply nodded as she looked out the entrance of the Master Field Inn. She could clearly see six men waiting outside for them, and held up her hand to indicate as many.

"Go," Thomas said.

—

Mussashi felt out of place waiting to stalk members of the Gray Empire. He glanced longingly back at the tower where he had spent the bulk of his life. His attention was drawn to movement as three figures ran from the entrance of the Master Field Inn.

"Let's move," he said just above a whisper. He followed the other monks as they chased after the three shadows. Mussashi was impressed at how quick the three ducked in and out of alleyways. Then, as he turned a corner, a wooden sign struck him in the head, and everything went black.

Mussashi opened his eyes and found his hands bound behind his back. A confused look crossed his face as he discovered Aroon standing over him.

"You? But why?" Mussashi asked. "How is this even possible in Ormlu? Shouldn't the *Master Book of Magic* have prevented this?"

"It is important that you reevaluate what the monks are doing," Aroon said, ignoring his questions.

"What are you talking about? The *Master Book of Magic* dictates our actions,"

"Think about it. The Book dictates that the monks must be neutral. How is it that a neutral party must go to war?" Aroon asked.

"There is an exception in Section 128, subsection 12, paragraph 2, when armies of East and West lands are engaged in the defense of the land by the same enemy, then the monk's duty is to align with the powers. This was created during the great war against the elves in the South and the dwarves in the North," Mussashi answered.

"Just a thought, but the gray armies are made up from the East and West lands, and we aren't attacking," Aroon replied as he started walking away. "We are defending."

"What do you expect me to do? I am tied up here in Ormlu," Mussashi said.

"You have ten hours, and you're tied up with licorice. I am pretty sure you can escape," Aroon said as he turned the corner.

To Mussashi's surprise, he was able to pull his hands apart with a little extra effort. He stared with disbelief at the two broken strands of black licorice.

―

Thomas felt the adrenalin course through her veins as she slipped the two monks that had been chasing after her. She looked around to find the Assassin's Guild right around the corner. However, there were four of the city police standing guard at the front door. Thomas noticed a small window slightly ajar on the second floor of the building, halfway between her and the policemen at the front.

Are you actually going to break into the assassin's guild? she asked herself. *That tends to be a bad idea, you know.*

Thomas shook her head and then took off, deciding to ignore her inner voice. Instantly, the guards saw her and raced towards her.

They are too fast! she thought, then shook it off. *Nah, you got this.*

As Thomas closed in on the wall, she gracefully jumped, her feet landing on the solid surface, and pushed off. She found herself right on target as she fell towards one of the guards.

On cue, the *Master Book of Magic* moved her three feet backwards to protect the guard she would have wounded within city walls, and landed her safely inside the Assassin's Guild in a crouched position. The guards could be heard shouting to each other and racing away, not realizing that Thomas had been transported inside the Guild. Before she could celebrate, however, she reached up to her belt and found the message she had been carrying was gone.

"Brilliant but stupid," Nina said as six of her top assassins stood in a semi-circle around Thomas.

Then without a word, Nina found herself catching a pair of silver coins that were flung at her. She looked down and instantly recognized them.

"Who are you?" Nina asked with genuine surprise.

"I have a message for you from Drip," Thomas said as she slowly stood up with her hands raised.

"Thomas?" Nina questioned. "I had heard rumors of your return."

"It is time to turn in the two favors you owe Drip," Thomas said.

"We are not a standing army; I will not commit my assassins to his war."

"No, this is much more suited for your skills," Thomas said with a large smile on her face. She leaned forward and whispered into Nina's ear, "Poison and sabotage elements within the enemy army."

Instantly Nina stiffened, and a very serious look crossed her face. Then Nina balled up her fist. "That is insane, and I would be remiss if I accepted those tasks."

"Then you would be turning your back on your debt," Thomas said.

"You don't have to remind me. However, we cannot. Security will be too tight."

"Actually we have made arrangements that I think will please you," Thomas said.

Nina rubbed her chin for a moment, before responding. "Very well, give me a list of targets, but if I feel security is too tight, we will have to withdraw."

"Understood," Thomas said with a grin.

―

Unexpectedly, Bean felt her feet struggle to keep ahead of the two monks that were chasing close after. Time seemed to slow as she lost her footing and fell to the ground.

"I give up!" Bean announced.

"What is your destination?" one of the two monks asked.

"I was headed to the gate to send a message," Bean said as she looked at the ground.

"What message?" the other monk asked.

With an ashamed look on her face she handed the scroll over to the two men. Quickly they took the paper and ran away. Bean stood back up and dusted herself off.

I gave it to them too easy, she thought to herself. *I should have put up more of a fight.*

After a few minutes of walking, the gate she was looking for loomed ahead. However, instead of walking directly to it, she veered to the left, heading instead for the archaic signal tower. She took the small magic lift to the top of the tower, where she was greeted by an old man.

"Oh good, I was hoping you would be here," Bean said.

"Yes, ma'am, forty years of dedication," the old man said. "What can I do for you?"

"I need you to send a message to the Sevari Mountains," Bean said.

"No problem, just write it down on the paper on the table, and I will get you squared away," the old man said. "Give me a minute to wake up the network."

"Wake up the network?" Bean asked.

"Yes, of course, it takes at least a dozen of us to get a message through to the Sevari Mountains," the old man said, as he pulled down some levers on the wall.

"How long will it take to get a message up there?"

"Depends on how long the message is. Probably half a day for a full page."

"Brilliant," Bean said. "Well let's get started."

"So you see, gentlemen, if we surrender, I don't think it is unreasonable for appropriate parties to be sent to the corresponding alignment," Drip said.

"Sure, sounds fine, whatever," Ragmon said. "How many more items are on your list?"

"For our surrender, only a dozen more items. How many points would you like to review under the terms of surrender for *your* troops?" Drip asked.

"*Our* troops?" Twiller said. "You have to be kidding me, we would never surrender to you."

"I can understand your position. Should I put you down for unconditional then?" Drip asked.

"Whatever, this is ridiculous," Twiller said.

"It won't be so ridiculous if you surrender," Drip said.

"Okay, we agree to your points if you surrender. Just release us from this summit," Towe said.

"Are you sure you want to concede the rest of the surrender points? There are a few zingers in here," Drip said. Then the skeletons entered with the seventh course of the meal, and took away the mostly untouched sixth course. The men were too out of sorts to eat.

"Yes, yes, that is fine, release us," Ragmon said.

"Very well, I just need your signatures on the corresponding copies, verifying that you agree to the terms," Drip said.

The three men quickly raced over to sign the document.

"You will die painfully," Twiller said as he signed.

"Very good, I am going to wish you the best of luck," Drip said. "Shame, we still have two hours left."

"It has been ten hours too many already," Ragmon said as he signed.

Without hesitation, the three men dashed through the portal back to the Master Field Inn, where they found their commanders standing by.

"Report," Ragmon said.

"We managed to intercept two of the three messages the gray army attempted to send out, and we have made preparations to counteract their plans," the Light Commander said.

"We have as well," the Dark Commander reported.

"Why are the monks not here to report?" Towe asked.

"Sir, they seem to have disappeared," the Light Commander said.

"No matter," said Ragmon, "give the word. We attack at dawn."

EPISODE 56

Cary opened her eyes to the ground rumbling violently. Quickly she raced out of her tent to find large fiery boulders rolling down from the top of the volcano towards her camp in the twilight. She could see that there was no escape from her certain demise.

You can do this, she said to herself.

Then she raised her hands and concentrated. As Cary had hoped, her magic unleashed a large time bubble in front of her. As the first bolder was set to strike her, it suddenly crumbled into lava, then cooled in place. A smile crossed her face as the remaining boulders also turned into lava then cooled as they had been rapidly aged by the magic.

Satisfied that the danger was over, Cary willed the magic to stop, but found that she could not pull her hands away.

Something is wrong! Stop! she thought to herself.

Her hands failed to respond despite her command. Cary watched as the volcano would erupt then cool, over and over, as if on repeat. She began to panic as the magic drained from her, worried that this might be the end after all.

Drip collapsed back into his chair, and began to rub his forehead with his right hand. At the moment, he could feel the weight of Wax on his shoulders. Then a bright flash indicated the return of Thomas, Bean, and Aroon.

"How did we do?" Drip asked.

"It could have gone better. They got two of the three messages," Thomas said.

"Which ones?" Drip quickly asked as he climbed to his feet.

"The assassins and the werewolves," Bean said.

"This is going to be fun. I was hoping for all three, but two will have to do," Drip said. "They will most likely attack at dawn. We have work to do."

"We can only hope everyone got their job done right," Bean said cautiously.

"Thomas, go get armored up and get the troops ready," Drip said.

"Very good. I wish everyone luck. We have a slim chance of surviving this, but we have a chance," Thomas said. Quickly she turned and exited the command tent.

"Aroon, prep the Special Forces, but remember to hold them back until we have containment on their archers," Drip said.

"This is going to sound really odd, but I wish Gorath were here," Aroon said. "Let's give them one they will remember forever."

"I am with you on that one," Drip said. Then Aroon left the command tent.

"Where do you want me, my love?" Bean asked.

"Right here next to me," Drip said "A lot of people are going to die in a few hours, and none of it is necessary."

"The world has gone mad, but I think everything will be as it is supposed to be in the end," Bean replied.

"I hope it will be a good ending," Drip said as he grabbed ahold of Bean's hand.

Then the portal flashed again to indicate someone had entered the tent. Drip turned to see Orielia walking over to them.

"Is everything okay?" Bean asked.

"Oh, maybe and maybe not," Orielia said. "They may come before dawn."

"What makes you say that?" Drip asked.

"Call it a hunch," Orielia said as she handed Drip a small booklet.

Drip looked down at the book, which was labeled clearly on the cover: *Odd Drip the Imp: The Story of an Extraordinary Imp in an Oppressive Empire*. It only took him a second to recognize his own writings inside the book.

"I don't see how this will affect anything," Drip said.

Orielia looked doubtful. "Hope is a powerful thing."

"These orders are pretty aggressive and over reaching," Twiller said. He began to draw on a piece of paper.

"It's because of their inferior leadership," Ragmon said. "The imp has no idea what he is doing."

"Still, I think something is wrong," Twiller said, looking at the scrolls open on the table. "The assassins attacking the leadership and the food supply makes sense but we have double their guards. Surely it would be a death trap for anyone, even a trained assassin."

"Wasting the werewolves on the reserves is just dumb," Ragmon added.

"We should keep our guard up and look for anything suspicious," Twiller said.

"Commanders, get some rest, but triple the guards on your own tents and food supplies," Ragmon ordered.

"Very good," the Light and Dark commanders said before they departed.

"Have you found your monks yet?" Twiller asked the panicky-looking head monk.

"No, and no one seems to know where they went," Towe said. "They have no reason to abandon their posts."

"Thankfully I think we have more than enough to deal with the opposing army," Ragmon added. "What are you drawing, Twiller?"

"I memorized the gray army's plan of attack during the summit."

Towe let out a little chuckle. "You are already going to crush them. I am surprised you would put forth the effort."

"If it is all the same, I would prefer to have something left of my men after this fight," Twiller said. "We have a real war to start, remember?"

"Prudent action," Ragmon commented.

"Sir, we have a problem," a dark scout reported.

"What is it now? Wait, does this have to do with the orcs again?" Twiller asked.

"No, Sir, it is the imps," the scout said. Then he handed the Dark Lord a small booklet.

Twiller glanced at it as recognition spread across his face. He threw the book down in anger. "What is the impact of this?"

"Sir, we have lost about one-third of our imp work force," the scout said.

"What!?" Twiller shouted. "Have you threatened to kill them?"

"Of course, Sir," the scout responded.

"Have you killed some as an example?" Twiller asked.

"Of course, Sir," the scout again replied.

"How did this get into our camp? Is this contained?" Twiller asked as he began to rub his forehead.

"We aren't quite sure how it ended up in our camp, but there seem to be copies of it everywhere. We are estimating that by dawn we will have lost half of our workforce, and by end of day tomorrow…two-thirds," the scout offered the estimate hesitantly.

"Have the mages create new imps, isolated from the corrupt ones," Twiller said.

"Sir, that will take the mages out of combat for the day."

Twiller raised his hand and magically pulled the scout over to him, then he raised him into the air and shouted, "Do as I command!"

"Yes, Sir," the scout said. Then Twiller released him, letting him fall to the ground with a thud.

"What does that mean for your forces?" Towe asked.

"Oh, just the core of our logistics, ammo, food, water, removing wounded from the field, and what not," Twiller said with a deceptively calm voice.

"Then what are our choices?" Towe asked.

"We have no choice, we have to attack now before our logistics are all gone," Twiller said.

"Sounds like a personal problem to me," Ragmon said with a chuckle.

"Last time I checked, half your army doesn't want to have anything to do with this," Twiller said with a very irritated tone.

"I am going to be personally leading my troops into battle! Where are you going to be?" Ragmon snapped as he matched the dark lord's temperament.

"Calm yourselves, we need to attack the gray army now, not each other!" Towe said.

"It would sure be nice if the monks could join us on this attack," Twiller said snidely.

Recognizing the dire situation for what it was, Ragmon turned and shouted for the guards. "Wake the commanders! We attack immediately!"

EPISODE 57

"Archers, prepare to fire!" King Ragmon ordered.

"Archers!" a voice was heard in the background, spreading the order.

Ragmon mounted his horse, as did Twiller, but they knew something was wrong when their horses elected to sit and then lie down on their sides.

"What magic is this?" Ragmon asked. He looked left down his half of the army to see all the horses in his cavalry acting the same way as his own.

"This is no magic, they have been poisoned," Twiller said instantly.

"Call the healers up! We need to get this resolved immediately," Ragmon shouted.

"Of course, this is the work of the assassins," Towe said.

"If so, then it will take a lot of time per horse," Twiller said. "Time we don't have."

"With all due respect, Sir, can we fire now?!" the commander over the archers asked.

Ragmon and Twiller looked over to see the soldiers struggling to hold the arrows in the firing position.

"Fire away!" Ragmon shouted.

On cue, the first volley of arrows raced forward toward the front lines of the gray army. Of every hundred archers there was one designated range finder with his arrow lit on fire to light the way, so it was easy to see that the majority of arrows did indeed strike their intended targets.

"We have to reform the lines to strike on foot," Twiller said.

"Very well, make your preparations. I will keep my word and lead my men into battle," Ragmon shouted. He looked up to see lightning streak across the sky, as rain began to slowly pelt the armies.

"Fire the catapults!" Towe shouted.

"Yes, fire the catapults!" Ragmon repeated. He looked back twenty yards to watch in horror as one by one the catapults released, but instead of stopping at the height of the catapult to launch their load, each one continued on, smashing the arm into the ground, effectively destroying every one.

"AAAHHH!" Ragmon shouted. He picked up a large rock and threw it in the general direction of the gray army.

"We can get out in front of this. Lead your men into battle," Towe said.

"Yes!" Ragmon shouted. "Flag bearer, on me!"

"I am glad you were able to adjust your battle plans. So far, everything is starting to fall into place," Thomas reported to Drip.

"Brilliant. Let's pull in the skeletons and prepare for their attack," Drip ordered. "If we act quickly, we can cause their first lines some real headaches. Get the zombies to turn them back."

"Yes, Sir," Thomas said. "I'm on it!"

"Aroon, we are going to need your men to get on the bows first," Drip said.

"Yes Sir. Where would you like for us to focus?" Aroon asked.

"Hit them hard on the dark army, we are going to need a lot of help on that side."

Thomas enjoyed riding up to her command position at the center of the line. Something seemed to be missing, however, as she patted her horse on the neck.

Grendle, I hope you are safe wherever you are, she thought to herself.

"Captain Red, bring the skeletons in and get set for archers," she shouted into the darkness.

After a moment, she could see the long line of skeleton warriors come within torch light. They looked like giant porcupines with arrows stuck through most, and others carried stacks of arrows.

"General, it looks like the plan worked," the red skeleton hissed.

"Did you lose anyone out there, Captain?" Thomas asked.

"Only a handful," Red replied.

"Very good, Red. By the time you get set up to fire, they will be in range, so you may fire when ready," Thomas ordered.

"It will be done," Red answered. Then he turned and let out a low hissing noise, to which a series of crackles and hisses replied.

"Messenger, send word back to General Aroon to douse the torches, and let the emperor know that Phase One has worked," Thomas said. She looked up at the sky.

We are only going to get one shot at this before the dawn.

"Yes, ma'am," the messenger replied.

A faint groan let her know that the zombies were ready for the next phase.

"Emperor Drip, General Thomas has reported that Phase One has worked, and has ordered General Aroon to douse the torches," the messenger reported to Drip.

"This will work, your plan is brilliant," Bean said.

"The next phase is the most important," Drip said. "The assassins took down the catapults, but the horses are the real challenge."

"I don't care for your sense of doubt," Nina said from behind Drip. "Don't turn around, I was never here."

"Thank you for everything," Drip said.

"Don't thank me, and never mention it again. This one was off the books," Nina said. "I wish you luck. Now, unfortunately, I have to sit the rest of this fight out."

"Where are you going to be seated?" Bean asked, but by the time she turned, Nina was nowhere to be seen. "That was unexpected."

"Speaking of unexpected, let's hope the first lines run into our trap before twilight," Drip said, "or this will be a short war."

King Ragmon's personal guards were on foot with him, as well as his flag-bearer next to him. He felt concerned at his lack of a point of reference as the enemy had doused the flames on their torches. Regardless, confidence coursed through his veins.

"Sir, is it wise to press so hard in the dark?" one of his guards asked.

"We have numbers. We will cause them to route after five minutes of fighting," Ragmon said. What he was really thinking was, *We killed off at least one of the twerps, and that means I still have months before I can be killed, according to the witch.*

Then a high pitched whistle flew past Ragmon's head, followed by dozens more. Instantly, he recognized the sound of his own arrows being fired at him.

"Charge!" Ragmon shouted at the top of his lungs. He knew that if he could get his men under the arrow range, it would reduce the number of dead and wounded. What he wasn't counting on was the fact that the skeletons firing the arrows were both cursed and blessed with infa-vision, which allowed them to see in the dark just fine, and that they were not aiming for the first line of attack.

As they raced forward, Ragmon could feel something grab his feet and then let go. He swung his sword at the ground a few times, but it never felt like he was making contact with anything. For a moment, he felt a little disoriented, but was determined to press the attack.

"Lay into them, take no prisoners!" King Ragmon shouted. The men gave a fierce war cry, then the sounds of swords clashing began.

Dark Lord Twiller had used a powerful spell to be able to see in the dark, and watched in horror as the engagement began. Unlike Ragmon, he was far off the front line, and was unable to warn anyone about what was happening.

"Get up there and straighten them out!" Twiller shouted to his closest commander.

"Yes, Sir," the commander responded "And how should I do that in the dark?"

"Have the mages shoot fireballs into the air to give light!" Twiller shouted.

"But, Sir…" the commander began.

"What?!" Twiller asked in a rage, grabbing the commander and pulling him close.

"The mages, Sir. They are tied up creating new imps," the commander reminded him.

Twiller reeled back with frustration. "Then order the men to push through."

"Yes, Sir!" the commander replied, then rushed off.

The Dark Lord swallowed hard as he watched his troops fighting fiercely against each other in the confusion.

Cary felt exhausted and finally, the magic let her collapse to the ground. A massive wall of cold magma stood before her. She fell to her back as her vision began to go dark. As her eyes closed, she felt someone pick her up.

EPISODE 58

Thomas watched in satisfaction as twilight illuminated the sky, revealing the two massive armies battling with themselves. She rode over to the skeleton commander to see where they were on ammo.

"Red, how many volleys do we have left?" Thomas asked.

"Sssseven," Red said with an eerie hiss.

"Very good. Brace for contact as soon as you have fired five more," Thomas ordered.

"Yesss...Ssssir," Red replied.

Despite the early success, Thomas knew that the day was far from over when she watched the massive army before her start to reorganize and prepare a proper charge.

"Messenger!" Thomas shouted. Within moments, a rider approached.

"Yes, ma'am," the messenger asked.

"Send word to Emperor Drip that I would like to charge the right flank," Thomas said. "Then pass word on to General Aroon that I think he should hold back as long as possible."

"Yes, ma'am."

"Form lines! Commander, get the men back into lines!" Ragmon shouted. "Line up on me!"

Ragmon grabbed the flag from the standard bearer and raised it high in the air. Then he began to move toward the Gray lines. He looked left and right to find that he was about ten steps ahead of everyone, but his army was following him forward in the right direction.

"Forward!" he shouted. As he pressed forward, he was surprised to see the Gray Army charging at him, and at the front, heading straight for him, was none other than Thomas.

"Where are those archers?!" Ragmon asked. Despite the request from the king, no one had an answer for him.

Dark Lord Twiller was happy to see his men finally advancing in the right direction, led ironically by King Ragmon. He raised his hand to call up one of his commanders.

"It looks like they are charging on the light flank, let's concentrate arrows on that side," Twiller said.

"Very good, Sir," the commander said then scurried off.

I'm not seeing the troll. He should be on the edge of the dark flank, but I am not seeing half of their undead army either. What sort of madness is this? Twiller asked himself.

"Dark Lord, we have a problem!" the commander he had sent off moments ago reported.

"Yes?" Twiller asked. "What is it now?"

"The archers are under attack!" the commander answered.

"What?! By who?" Twiller asked as he spun around.

"The werewolves!" the commander shouted in a panic.

Twiller could only watch in horror, again, as his archers were forced to flee, or be killed by a large group of unchecked werewolves.

"How did we not see them coming!? Where are the reserves?" Twiller asked. "It's not important, just get some units tasked to take care of them!"

"Yes, Sir!" the commander reported as he again scurried off.

They might be clever, but we still have them on numbers. Ragmon just needs to break through the first line, Twiller thought.

—

Thomas directed her path to collide with King Ragmon. She was filled with a sense of irony that everyone she had known on the Dark Side would have loved a chance to take a shot at the Light King, and now they were all fighting together.

Even at the quick pace her army was charging, she was able to dismount her horse.

You're ready for this, she reassured herself. In the back of her mind, she was worried as this was the first time she would be in battle without her enchanted armor and sword.

Thomas noticed that Ragmon had at least four of his elite guards hovering around him. Now, just fifteen feet from contact, she executed her first moves.

"Now!" Thomas shouted. At the command, the first two lines of undead slipped into the ground effortlessly, and two rows of skeletons with arrows at the ready let loose. Thomas felt the arrows scream past her and smash into the oncoming soldiers.

Instead of attacking Ragmon, she sidestepped to the left and surprised one of his elite guards with a deadly blow. Then she spun to the left to attack another of the elite guards. In the meantime Ragmon had taken two swings at Thomas, but she kept just out of reach. With no good position left, she engaged Ragmon directly. The sound of another group of arrows smashing into the light army could be heard.

"You will die here!" Ragmon said with confidence. He tossed the flag back to the bearer, and drew a second sword.

Thomas felt a little intimidated as Ragmon's large frame towered over her. She swung high as she prepared to block with her other arm. As their swords clashed, his second sword hit her shield, the strength of it tossing her back. Then he took two quick steps towards her and swung his swords in a scissor motion. It took everything for Thomas to defend against it.

King Ragmon let a smile cross his face as he easily deflected another attack from Thomas. "This is it? This is all you have to offer?" Ragmon asked mockingly.

"I don't want to kill you, but I will if you don't yield!" Thomas shouted. It was clear that she was winded.

"Ha, you don't have the skill or strength to kill me," Ragmon taunted.

"Don't underestimate me!" Thomas yelled in irritation.

Ragmon then attacked with a full swing of his dominant hand. The strike nearly caused her to fall to the ground. Thomas knew that she had to strike back quickly and stabbed forward, barely catching his left elbow. Despite the protective armor, Ragmon let out an audible grunt.

He then lashed out with faster strikes filled with rage. Thomas managed to weather each one as they came in, waiting for him to leave another opening. When he did, she reached forward with her sword and managed to clip his left armpit. This time, the strike caused him to reel back in pain. As he did so, she advanced and caught him off guard with a backhand across his face. Thomas could see that he was stunned, and before he could recover, she gathered her strength and ran the king through.

"But, how?" Ragmon asked with a week breath "The prophecy said I had more time."

Thomas was confused at the rambling, but before she could ask him anything, his soldiers were pulling him back. This action caused the entire Light Side line to retreat.

Drip gave an auditory celebration as he watched Thomas's victory from the command area, but couldn't help but notice that the line on that side had taken quite a hit from the engagement.

"Messenger, tell Aroon to spring the trap," Drip said.
"Yes, Sir."

Twiller took a step back and sat down on a nearby chair with a horrified look on his face. He put his hand to his forehead.

"Sir, we have found the undead troll," a commander reported.
"Where?" Twiller asked as he quickly climbed to his feet.
"There," the commander pointed, "between the second and third lines."

Twiller watched as the troll was effortlessly demolishing their lines. He looked to the left to see the Light Side lines in retreat.

"We need to stop this now!" Twiller shouted. "Is my horse ready?"

"Yes, Sir, and so are your personal guards," the commander said.

"Brilliant, let's do this."

EPISODE 59

Aroon let a smile cross his face for a moment as he watched his elite soldiers respond perfectly to each instruction and movement. He held his hand up to signal his second squad to shift to the left to respond to a veteran unit of orcs that was about to make contact with the line. He glanced right to see Thomas regrouping her troops as the Light Side fell into retreat.

One good thrust and we can get this side turned back as well, Aroon thought. He could see the undead troll about fifty yards ahead of him, smashing large sections of the Dark Side lines.

"Right Green Platoon, on me, we are making a push!" Aroon shouted. His instincts told him that if he pushed towards the troll, then he could flank the lines and get the Dark Army turned around.

Aroon moved through the ranks until he arrived at the front line. He began to frantically hack and slash his way forward. A surge of energy ran through him as he recognized that his plan was going to work. Now just twenty-five feet from the troll, he could hear someone shouting for him.

"Sir!" a messenger shouted.

"What?! Can't you see we are about to turn the tide on this side?" Aroon shouted back.

"Emperor Drip wanted you to know that the Dark Lord is heading right for you," the messenger said. "He is ordering you to pull back."

"Form up, we need to pull back to the line!" Aroon shouted without hesitation. Deep down he wanted to keep pushing, but knew that Drip was in charge.

"General! Look!" one of his men called as he pointed frantically towards the dark lines.

Aroon turned to see the undead troll topple backwards to his demise. He could see four horses pushing towards them. Aroon raised his shield just in time to deflect a sword's downswing.

Dark Lord Twiller quickly dismounted and began to attack Aroon fiercely with his long sword. Everyone around him stood back and created a circle for the two to resolve the fight.

Aroon dashed forward while stabbing his sword at Twiller, and then quickly jumping back to avoid the counterattack. His heart was racing as Twiller's strikes were lightning fast and he hit harder than anything Aroon had felt before. He finally saw an opening, but when he swung his sword to take advantage of it, Twiller simply disappeared.

Aroon looked around the circle frantically, then swung his sword in the hopes of getting a lucky strike. That was when Twiller's blade struck Aroon from behind through the right side of his armor. The pain gave Aroon a moment of adrenalin and with the sword stuck in place, he wheeled around and caught Twiller off guard. His sword cut Twiller's arm and face.

Instantly the two were pulled back by their respective armies. Aroon felt like he was flying when he looked up to find Corporal Stevens carrying him as he raced back towards the command tent. For a moment, the Dark Army retreated.

"He is hurt. What can we do?" Stevens asked once he'd arrived with Aroon back at the tent.

"I will work with him, take him inside," Orielia said. "Bean, I might need your help."

"Anything," Bean replied.

"Messenger, call for General Thomas to reform the whole line and bring it in tighter, and let her know that Aroon is down," Drip said.

Aroon let out a loud grunt as Stevens laid him on the table inside the tent.

"Stevens," Aroon said.

"Yes, boss," Stevens replied.

"You did well, now I need you to lead the Elite Eagles," Aroon said weakly.

"I'm not a thinker like you, I don't know that I can."

"You will do fine. Now get out there, and get the men ready."

"Yes, boss. I just want you to know," Stevens said, "if you need anything, I will be right outside."

"Aroon, we need to get the sword out of your back," Orielia said.

"Tell Drip I am sorry. I had Twiller…" Aroon muttered.

"Drip is proud of you. Just hang in there," Bean said.

Just outside the tent, Drip looked at the map laid out before him with magical blocks representing the units under his command. He rubbed his forehead as he knew that it would be brute force now, and he had no answer for that.

"Drip, the units are forming up now. What are we looking at?" Thomas asked as she rushed over, having regrouped her soldiers back at camp.

"Not good. We lost a lot in that first attack, but we only saw the surface of the Light and Dark armies. Let's have the undead bury themselves two deep along our front lines, and have them pull down the first two lines of the next wave, then advance the skeletons to shock the third line. By the time we have all the undead engaged, the Light and Dark armies will be on the verge of overrunning our lines. We will need to start falling back at that point and condensing on the command tent, so let's make these points here, Alpha, Delta, and Zeta."

"I will make the preparations," Thomas calmly replied. "How is Aroon?"

"It didn't look good. Orielia and Bean are working on him now."

Twiller pushed his two commanders back in anger as he watched the last of his first attack still scuttling back.

"You fools! I had him, and we didn't need to retreat!" Twiller shouted.

"Sir, we wanted to make sure you were safe," one commander replied.

Twiller responded by picking up the commander with one arm and throwing him back ten feet. "They are a speck on this world! Order our entire army to charge, including the cooks, and send a messenger over to the Light Army to charge. We must eradicate them now!"

"Yes, Sir!" the other commander replied.

Twiller smiled as the attack horn sounded and the core of his army began moving towards the Gray.

"Drip, here they come!" Thomas shouted.

"Holy Wax!" Drip said. This time it did not look like waves charging at him, but instead an endless cloud, as the bulk of the Dark and Light armies were moving.

"Thomas, take the right flank. Stevens will take the left, and I will take the center," Drip said as he pulled the leather tie that released his sword. He reached back and pulled it out.

"Yes, Sir," Thomas said, as she raced off to the right flank.

"Yes, Sir," Stevens echoed as he began running back to the left.

Drip raced forward towards the front line just as the armies were set to collide. As expected, the first two lines were pulled under by the undead, and the skeletons raced forward to create confusion. This time he knew, however, that there was no stopping the charge. He pushed himself into the fray with his enchanted sword. His small stature caused most to overlook him until it was too late.

"Fall back to Alpha!" Drip shouted.

The order caused the line to close in on the command tent. Tragically, by the time they reached Alpha, it was already time to fall back to Delta.

"Delta!" he shouted. He kept holding onto the sword as it danced back and forth, striking down enemies like butter.

Again, as soon as they fell back to Delta, it was time to fall back to their final position, the battle was now moving too fast for Drip to do anything more than choose the final spot where they would be defeated.

"Zeta!" Drip shouted.

This time he could see Thomas and Stevens with little effort. Just as it seemed that they would be completely overwhelmed, a massive wave of energy knocked everyone down, Light, Dark, and Gray.

As everyone started to climb back to their feet, Drip looked over to a large group of monks now standing next to his command tent.

—

"What is that?" Twiller asked.
"Halftime," Towe said. "Only the monks can call halftime."

EPISODE 60

Drip walked over to the monks, happy to see them. He could see the Dark and Light army scuttling back to their respective commands. Drip waved for Thomas and Stevens to join him.

"We are humbled by your presence, Master Monk," Drip said with a slight bow.

"Emperor Drip, it is an honor," Mussashi replied.

"Tell me, what will be your role in this?" Drip asked.

"I regret to inform you that as the official mediators of these lands, we will be remaining neutral," Mussashi answered. "We will have little more influence over this fight than the action we have taken to call the official halftime of the grand battle."

"I don't suppose 'neutral' would include healing troops or anything of that nature?" Thomas asked.

Mussashi let out a light chuckle, then replied, "Unfortunately not, as we must reciprocate any action taken here and do the same for the other side."

"I appreciate your honesty and this opportunity for a moments rest before the resolution of this conflict," Drip said.

"It is truly remarkable. I have never encountered an imp with such an ability to think or communicate," Mussashi mentioned.

"I am fortunate to have the skills that I do," Drip replied.

"Truly," Mussashi said. "We must take our leave now."

"Thank you again. Please remember us in the history of this world," Drip said.

"There is one more thing you should know," Mussashi said, "according to the *Master Book of Magic*, you will have two choices that will affect the outcome of this fight, the right way and the wrong way. Choose carefully." Then the monks vanished.

"That was kind of disappointing," Thomas said.

"I am just happy they are not fighting against us," Drip said. "Get a count on the troops, and reform here at the front of the command tent."

"Yes, Sir," Thomas and Stevens said at the same time.

Drip walked into the tent to a painful sight. The bloody sword lay on the ground near where Aroon was lying, bandaged up. There was a large amount of blood around the table.

"Is he going to make it?" Drip asked.

"Possibly," Orielia said. "We have done everything we can for him."

"Unfortunately, it might not matter in an hour," Drip said.

"Is it that bad?" Bean asked.

"Worse than anything you can imagine," Boot chimed in.

"You have been silent lately," Drip said.

"It is tough to prepare oneself for the demise of a good friend," Boot said.

"Be more optimistic," Drip replied. "I believe we all will have a say in how this fight ends."

"Drip, we have a troop count for you," Thomas called as she entered the tent.

"Whoa, that was way too quick," Boot said.

"How many do we have left?" Drip asked.

"Fifty, if we count Bean and Orielia," Thomas said.

"Have them set up outside the tent and then meet me back here," Drip said weakly.

Thomas nodded and left.

"Drip, we must consider surrendering," Bean said pleadingly.

"They won't let us surrender, there is no quarter in this conflict," Drip said. "This is my fault. I have killed us all."

"No, Drip, Olpetrion has been working towards this the entire time. There was no escaping this conclusion," Orielia said.

"It was you who saved Thomas during the fight with the necromancer," Drip said.

"I can do that for one person, but no more than that," Orielia said. "What are you thinking?"

"I am ordering you to send Bean to the Light Side of the army that has yet to engage."

"Wait! What?" Bean asked.

"Are you sure?" Orielia asked.

"You can't be serious?" Bean called out.

"Bean, it will keep you safe," Drip said, then turned back to Orielia. "Do it."

"As you wish. It will take me a moment," Orielia replied.

"Drip, I don't want to be with anyone else but you. I would follow you anywhere," Bean said with tears in her eyes. "I love you."

"I love you, but you can have a future. I have to let you go so you can live," Drip said.

"If you survive, we are going to have a serious conversation about this," Bean said. She could see light gathering around Orielia's hands.

Drip couldn't stand to watch as the bright flash filled the room for a moment and then Bean was gone.

Thomas and Stevens came running into the tent at the commotion.

"What happened? Are you okay?" Thomas asked.

"Where is Bean?" Stevens asked.

"Safe," Drip said as he sat down in his chair.

"I'm sorry, Drip, but we have bigger problems," Thomas said. "Halftime is over."

"Brilliant," Drip said. He followed his two generals out of the command tent. Right on cue, he could see the armies marching toward them at a comfortable pace. The enemy stretched for as far as he could see.

Twiller isn't taking any chances. He will send everything he has this time, Drip thought to himself.

He walked to the front of his tiny army to address them. "We are all that is left. We are it, and they won't accept our surrender. Fifty of us against hundreds of thousands."

"Maybe more," Boot added.

"Yes, well, let us end this with dignity and honor," Drip said. "I intend on charging them, and I hope you will join me."

Large drops of rain began to pelt the battlefield, with lightning streaking across the sky. Drip drew his sword and turned towards the overwhelming army marching at them.

"Don't think you can leave me out of this," Aroon said weakly. It was easy to see that he was favoring his side where he was wounded.

"Rest up, Aroon. You are in no condition to charge," Thomas said.

"My place is on the battlefield with you. Let's make them remember this," Aroon said.

"Let's," Drip agreed.

"You have to be kidding me," Twiller said in disbelief. "They are charging us?"

"It appears to be so, Sir," a commander replied. "This rain will slow them down a little, though."

Twiller watched from his horse just a hundred yards back from the front of the line. He smiled with satisfaction that the end was near.

"Dark Lord, look!" a commander shouted as he pointed north.

Twiller turned, and his expression became one of horror. "It can't be!"

A deep rumble could be heard, and both sides stopped advancing as the ground began to shake.

EPISODE 61

"What is that?!" Aroon shouted to Drip.

Drip stopped running and looked at the sky, offering a worried look. "You know exactly what that is! It's the dragon! Argentauth!"

"How?" Thomas asked.

"I don't know, but he probably isn't happy that he ended up in a volcano," Drip said. "Fall back to the command tent!"

"You don't have to tell me twice!" Aroon shouted.

Drip turned his head just in time to see a massive wave of fire streak down from the sky and engulf a group of enemy soldiers.

"Run faster!" Drip shouted.

—

"Have our archers and catapults aim for the dragon!" Twiller shouted.

"Sir, we don't have any archers or catapults! They have been destroyed, remember?" a commander reported to Twiller.

"Aaahhh!" Twiller shouted in frustration.

Just as he was about to personally do away with the commander, he noticed the stream of fire heading towards them. Twiller shielded himself with his magical cloak just in time to protect himself from the dragon's attack. He turned to reprimand the commander, but found that he was standing alone in a massive path of singed grass and burnt earth.

"Retreat!" Twiller shouted as he watched the rest of his army getting carved up by the dragon.

"Watch out, it's coming right for us on this pass!" Thomas shouted.

Drip could hear the fear in her voice, and feel the strong wind generated by the dragon's powerful wings. He turned towards the dragon so he could confront the creature face to face. Any moment, he expected to be engulfed in flames.

"We thought you might need some help!" Gorath yelled from atop the dragon. "Sorry we didn't make it sooner!"

"Gorath?" Drip sputtered. "But, how?"

"It's a long story. Let's get this cleaned up and we can talk afterwards," Gorath said. The dragon lowered his head carefully and let Gorath and Cary off.

"I am going to go cause some more problems for the other armies," Argentauth rumbled.

"Sounds brilliant, just don't attack the part of the Light Army that is sitting back!" Drip called.

"I understand," Argentauth replied, then quickly climbed into the sky.

"Like I said, it's a long story how I survived and how we got here, but I promise to explain," Gorath said as he dumped out the magic bag of holding with the borrowed enchanted items from the Ormlu armory. "Now, grab whatever would be most useful to you."

"Is this really happening?" Aroon asked as he picked up an enchanted sword. "I'm not just hallucinating, right?"

"This is very real," Cary said as she patted him on the arm.

"Unbelievable," Thomas said, as she put an enchanted helmet on her head.

"What are we worried about? The dragon will finish them off," Drip chimed in.

"I don't think it will be that easy," Orielia said as she pointed towards a massive lightning bolt streak up into the sky from the enemy camp.

"What do you think you are doing?" Olpetrion asked.

"We are retreating. This wasn't part of the deal," Twiller replied.

"Hold on, let me talk some sense into him," Towe pleaded.

"You'd better hurry, I have no patience for this!" Olpetrion replied. Then she raised her hand and shot off another lightning bolt at the dragon.

"The dragon has been hit with lightning and lava before, and lived! Your bolts won't stop its attack," Twiller said. "And your threat of death is no greater than the dragon's."

"You have no idea what you are doing," Olpetrion said ominously. She launched another bolt, and this time, it struck the dragon in the side.

Twiller watched in disbelief as the giant creature screamed in pain and then gracefully fell to the ground.

"My men are scattered, it will take time to reorganize," Twiller said.

"No need." Olpetrion raised her hand and stopped the closest thousand troops in their tracks, then quickly put them back in formation with her magic. "Now screw your courage to the sticking place, and finish this," she ordered.

"Argentauth!" Gorath shouted in pain.

As the dragon plummeted to the ground, he was able to guide his landing to end up close to Gorath. Without hesitation, Gorath raced over to the wounded beast.

"Gorath, my friend, I am afraid this is the end," Argentauth said.

"No it can't be. Maybe the wand can heal you," Gorath said tearfully.

"The damage is too much, and I don't want you to see me like this. I must travel to the North, back to my resting place."

"You won't make it," Gorath said.

"Maybe not, but I must try. Farewell, my friend," the great creature said. Then without another word, the dragon painfully lifted off and turned north.

"The dragon was your friend?" Aroon asked. "The same one that tried to kill us?"

"Well, when you spend hundreds of years with only one other being, you eventually become friends with them," Gorath said.

"Hundreds of years?" Thomas asked.

"Yes. When I plummeted into the volcano with Argentauth, the wand was in the process of absorbing me, but it quickly realized that it could either have me and perish, or save itself, and us with it," Gorath said. "Sealed in a bubble in a sort of sleep, the powerful magic in the wand let us communicate. Then Cary was able to speed up time until the volcano spit us out. As it turns out, it took hundreds of years."

"I did not see that coming," Boot said.

"You know what I *do* see coming?" Thomas said "The thousands of troops heading for us."

"Prepare yourselves for combat!" Drip shouted. The group watched and waited as the troops began to bear down on them.

"Steady yourselves," Thomas said. "Remember, we have enchanted weapons."

Suddenly, Orielia stepped forward. "The stench of magic is in the air, and it's not mine," she said. She popped her knuckles and pointed her right hand at the incoming army. A small lightning burst raced out of her palm and struck the oncoming troops, but somehow, they seemed unfazed.

"Ha, you are weaker than I could ever imagine!" Olpetrion shouted to her from amongst the troops.

"Just wait for it," Orielia whispered to Drip, but he and Thomas had already raced forward and attacked the first wave.

Oddly, they didn't seem to be putting up a fight, but it wasn't by choice. Hard as they tried, the enemy soldiers could not draw their weapons.

"Magnetized. Child's play," Olpetrion said with a smirk. "Two can play at that game."

Olpetrion clapped her hands, and as she pulled them apart, the enemy troops all slid out of the way, leaving a direct path between the two sisters.

"Okay, let's do this," Orielia said. Then she conjured up a massive snowball and threw it at Olpetrion, who used a massive fireball spell to counter.

"Did you ever figure out how I defeated our sisters?" Olpetrion asked.

"You will not take me easily so easily," Orielia shouted as she threw a lightning bolt.

"It is all about misdirection," Olpetrion said with a laugh as she let the lightning bolt strike her. However, when she began to fall to the ground, it was not Olpetrion at all, but a regular soldier she had disguised with a hologram of herself.

Orielia quickly spin around just in time for her sister to stab her in the chest with a large knife. Everyone gasped in horror as Orielia collapsed, gasping for air. Without Orielia's magic binding the weapons of the dark soldiers, they now drew their weapons and began to engage in combat.

"And now it is time for you to die!" Twiller shouted.

EPISODE 62

Instantly, Drip's army dwindled from fifty to twenty, despite the enchanted advantage, and Gorath conjuring up massive boulders and fireballs with his powerful wand.

"We need to get to their leaders!" Drip shouted over the chaos.

"I got this!" Gorath shouted. He waved the wand and was able to pick up Head Monk Towe and pull him over to Aroon.

"Everyone stop, or I kill the monk—I mean Head Monk!" Aroon said. This action caused everyone to pause their combat.

Olpetrion stepped forward with an amused look on her face. "It really doesn't matter. He has outlived his usefulness."

Then Olpetrion raised her hand and everyone seemed to suddenly fall over, causing the Head Monk to fall against Aroon. Aroon was both panicked and confused as he pulled his sword from Towe's back.

"I'll show you!" Gorath screamed, pointing the wand at Olpetrion. A massive continuous bolt of electricity shot out towards her, but Olpetrion raise her left hand and started to produce her own stream of electricity.

"You need a wand? How cute. You're a joke, you puny mortal," she said.

Gorath realized he was in trouble as Olpetrion's electricity made a steady advance. He closed his eyes and began to channel what little magic he had into the wand. Despite his efforts, however, Gorath found himself thrown backwards with burns on his hands and no sign of the wand.

"Twiller, finish them off!" Olpetrion cried.

"Gladly," Twiller said nervously as he looked down at Towe's lifeless body.

"Not so fast!" Bean shouted.

Everyone turned to see Bean and the intact remainder of the Light Army. She carried a makeshift banner for the Gray Army in one hand.

"Bean?" Drip asked, still recovering from being thrown back.

"Twiller, if your army takes one more step, we will wipe you out," Bean said.

"Okay, now I am seriously annoyed!" Olpetrion shouted. "I am done playing around!"

Olpetrion raised her hands to the sky and began to harness the lighting from the clouds above, releasing a perpetual chain of lightning. Soldiers began to fall by the dozens.

Cary looked up to see three spirits hovering over her. She raised her hand as they came closer. She closed her eyes for a moment as they whispered into her ear, and then vanished.

Bean dove to the ground to avoid the massive chain lighting that streaked past her. She looked up to see people running and scattering to avoid death. Then, she noticed three ghosts standing over her. Bean could barely make out what they were saying before they vanished.

Drip managed to get to his feet with his sword in front of him, but found himself surrounded by three apparitions.

"Drip, we are with you. You need to charge now," Orielia whispered.

Drip was desperate and didn't hesitate to charge towards Olpetrion, his sword before him in the hopes of catching her off guard.

Olpetrion turned and aimed her lightning towards Drip. However, the sword managed to absorb the shock before Drip was forced to drop it, now void of any magic. He was defenseless.

"This wasn't a very good plan," Boot said. "I blame you if I melt."

"Not now!" Drip shouted.

"Now you die, imp," Olpetrion said with a hiss.

However, as she raised her hand, an arrow caught her wrist and she fired off a stray bolt that headed right for Gorath. Cary managed to knock Gorath back in time so that the bolt struck the bottom of his boot, bouncing off of it harmlessly and dislodging the torn page of the *Master Book of Magic* that had been stuck there since before Gorath had left the city to fight the dragon.

"Right on target!" Gwen, Bean's enchanted bow, shouted.

"Really, I was aiming for her head," Bean said in frustration.

"You know how I feel about death," Gwen retorted.

Olpetrion didn't bother trying to deflect the bolt of lightning that now headed back toward her, as something of her own power shouldn't be able to harm her, but something was different when it struck her. She found herself mortally wounded and collapsed to the ground, dead.

While the armies remained in disarray, a brilliant flash came from seemingly nowhere, and a massive wave of energy threw everyone off their feet.

Thomas gave a shocked look as the wave had thrown Twiller at her, and he was now fumbling with his weapon to stab her. In a knee jerk reaction, she quickly grabbed her dagger and stabbed him in the chest.

"Brilliant, the prophecy fulfilled," Twiller whispered as he fell backwards.

Another massive wave of energy pushed everyone back to the ground, but this time it also cleared the rain clouds from the sky.

Drip and company walked over to Olpetrion's body, which was lying not far from Orielia's. Aroon unceremoniously nudged her body with his foot. This action drew glares from the others.

"What? I wanted to make sure," Aroon said.

Another brilliant flash engulfed them for a moment, and before them, within the light, stood a man and three women.

"The wizard," Drip said reverently.

"The what?" Bean asked.

"It's the wizard who created the *Master Book of Magic*," Drip said.

"Very good, Drip," the familiar looking man said. "You have done well, and have far exceeded anything I could have hoped for."

"Do I know you?" Drip asked.

"We have met before, but that is not important. I have come to get my last daughter," the wizard replied. Then he reached out his hand to Olpetrion's lifeless body. A spirit hand reached out and grabbed the wizard's hand, and the spirit of Olpetrion arose.

"What happens now?" Thomas asked.

"Now, the future of this world is in your hands," the wizard said. "Ormlu is no more, and the *Master Book of Magic* has been done away with, thanks to all of you."

The wizard raised his hand and an image appeared of the city, empty with all of its occupants having left or been part of the battle, crumbling into the ground. Then he waved his hand and made the image fade.

"Good luck with the world. You are going to need it," the wizard said as he began to walk away, his daughters turning and following him. For a moment, Orielia stayed behind.

"The book forced certain people to unite, which caused nothing but conflict," Orielia said. "But now, anyone can unite. These people need real leadership. They will look to all of you now, Good luck." She smiled and then turned to join her family.

The five began to disappear into the bright light that had brought them.

"Oh, sorry about the whole trying to kill you thing!" Olpetrion shouted just before disappearing.

"Brilliant," Gorath said. "What do we do now?"

Fourteen years later

Drip walked onto the balcony of the modest castle and looked out at the surrounding lands. After a moment, Bean joined him, placing her hand over his shoulder, and pulling him near.

"It's time for them to blow out the candles," Bean whispered.

Drip let out a smile and turned back toward the room. "Where *are* the spoiled kids?"

The room full of children began to clamor in excitement as Drip and Bean entered.

"Here we are now, a present for Christine and twelve candles; a present for Austin, and thirteen candles; and finally, Tom and Ringo, eleven candles each," Drip said. He nodded to the parents standing next to each of the children, and each child took a turn blowing out their candles and ripping open presents.

"How are things with the mountain kingdom?" Drip asked Thomas and Aroon.

"Everything is great, you should come up this year for the fall festival," Thomas replied.

"We have discovered a most delightful new recipe that Christine just loves. You must come out and try it," Aroon added.

"No doubt," Bean said.

"How are the ambassadors doing?" Drip turned to Gorath and Cary.

"We have agreed on a new treaty with the Elves, but we must get back to the Dwarves soon on their proposal," Gorath said. "Tom enjoyed spending time with the Elves."

Cary took Gorath's hand in hers. "And we are hoping that Ringo will have a similar experience with the Dwarves."

"We're so pleased to have you all here," Bean said. "It is nice for Austin to spend time with the other children. It won't be long before they are all running the world."

"Father? Is this sword a gift too?" Christine asked Aroon.

"What sword?" Aroon replied.

"This one," Christine said as she held it up. Just then, a massive wind gathered and a loud clang sounded. Everyone was suddenly looking at Christine with fully intact armor and the sword Thomas had once carried.

"What?" the group asked near simultaneously.

"This can't be good," Boot said, as he noticed that he was now on Austin's foot.

"Where am I?" Gwen asked aloud, as she found herself around Ringo's shoulders.

"Brilliant," Drip said. "Just brilliant."

THE END

THE END

About the Author

JARED QUAN

Jared's childhood was split between Phoenix, AZ, and Snowflake, AZ. Jared's sense of writing and adventure was established with the help of his fourth grade teacher. She introduced him to authors like C.S. Lewis and J.R.R. Tolkien. This was combined with the stories of his grandfather as a Seabee with the U.S. Navy during World War II, and the stories of roles the Quan (Guan) family played in the romancing of the three kingdoms in China (184 AD – 280 AD). He possesses a great deal of love for history and war. Jared achieved a milestone with his book Ezekiel's Gun getting published in 2010, an adventure/spy novel. He has hopes to have several more books published in the future. He would like to travel the world and see places like China, Europe, and South Korea.

The World's Premiere Episodic Literary Network

BigWorldNetwork.com is a new form of entertainment, with written and audio eSeries episodes, updated weekly.

Like television...in book form.

Visit us at
www.bigworldnetwork.com

www.facebook.com/bigworldnetwork

www.twitter.com/BigWorldNetwork

Made in the USA
Middletown, DE
10 April 2023